Praise for Jack Cady

"An exceptional writer."

—Joyce Carol Oates

"[Jack Cady is] a lasting voice in modern American literature."

—Atlanta Constitution

"Jack Cady's knack for golden sentences is an alchemy any other writer has to admire."

—Ivan Doig

"Jack Cady is above all, a writer of great, unmistakable integrity and profound feeling. He never fakes it or coasts, and behind every one of his sentences is an emotional freight that bends it both outward, toward the reader, and inward, back to the source."

—Peter Straub

"A writer whose words reverberate with human insight."
—*Publishers Weekly*

"His structural control and the laconic richness of his style establish Cady in the front ranks of contemporary writers."
—*Library Journal*

"When Cady settles into yarn-spinning, his stories have the humor and comfortable mastery of Faulkner or Steinbeck."
—National Review

THE CADY COLLECTION

NOVELS

The Hauntings of Hood Canal
Inagehi
The Jonah Watch
McDowell's Ghost
The Man Who Could Make Things Vanish
The Off Season
Singleton
Street

Dark Dreaming [with Carol Orlock, as Pat Franklin]
Embrace of the Wolf [with Carol Orlock, as Pat Franklin]

OTHER WRITINGS

Phantoms
Fathoms
Ephemera
The American Writer

Phantoms

Phantoms

Collected Writings, Volume 1

Jack Cady

Underland Press

Copyright © 2015 the Estate of Jack Cady

Original publication information about the respective stories is located on page 289-290.

This is U017, and it has an ISBN of 978-1-63023-004-3.

This book was printed in the United States of America, and it is published by Underland Press, an imprint of Resurrection House (Puyallup, WA).

like a specter risen from distant waves . . .

Cover Design by Jennifer Tough
Book Design by Aaron Leis
Collection Editorial Direction by Mark Teppo

First Underland Press edition: February 2015.

www.resurrectionhouse.com

Contents

Introduction

Patrick Swenson

You've got to listen.

I certainly did. But more on that later.

I met Jack in the late 1980s when I took his creative writing class at Pacific Lutheran University; he taught there from 1985 until his retirement in 1998. I'm not a hundred percent sure about the timing, but I also (by quite a happy accident) took a correspondence writing course from Carol Orlock, his wife, at the University of Washington. For a number of years after taking Jack's class, I'd spot him at various author events. He was always delighted to see me, and as ever, treated me with the utmost respect. I'm not sure I've ever met a more kind and generous person in my life. He had the most infectious smile; he always looked like a man who seemed to know the secrets of the universe, and he was just waiting for you to ask about them.

In 1995, I began publishing *Talebones* magazine, which featured stories of science fiction and dark fantasy. It was a semi-prozine, paying just one cent a word, but it was well respected and gained a following. I also ran a popular interview series every issue, conducted in wonderful fashion by the late Ken Rand. On my suggestion, Ken interviewed Jack Cady, and the interview appeared in *Talebones* #12 in the summer of 1998.

Five years passed. Out of the blue, in early 2003, Jack sent me a story, "The Parable of Satan's Adversary." I was taken aback (in a good way), and read it with trembling hands. Oh, it was lovely fun. I published it as the lead story in *Talebones* #27, Winter 2003. It was to be the very last story he submitted to a fiction magazine market. Jack passed away from cancer in early 2004.

(Gordon Van Gelder, editor and owner of *The Magazine of Fantasy and Science Fiction*, published Jack's "The Twenty Pound Canary" the same year, but if I'm not mistaken, Gordon bought it much earlier than the story I bought for *Talebones*. And in 2004, *The Magazine of Fantasy and Science Fiction* published "Fog," a story found on Jack's desk after his death.)

In 2006, I published an anthology of Ken Rand's *Talebones* interviews called *Human Visions*, which included Jack's interview, and in 2010 I reprinted "The Parable of Satan's Adversary" in the anthology *The Best of Talebones*. The anthology was dedicated to both Jack and Ken, two writers published in the magazine who were now lost to me and the world.

But let me back up to that summer class at PLU. What I recall from the beginning was that Jack came in to the classroom in the early days of the course, feeling more than a little depressed, and explained that his dog Rufus had recently passed away. Some weeks later, however, he got himself a new pup, Molly, and the dog would be there at his heels every day when he came in to teach. He loved that dog, as he had loved the one before it. In this collection you'll find the wonderful "Miss Molly's Manners," a book of etiquette for dogs, dictated by a dog—Miss Molly Manners—and you'll see how important dogs were to him.

What I remember most about what Jack taught is that the things required of a writer are all in relation to *what ought to be eternal* in this universe, regardless of cost or consequence. Writing is a painful experience. It *should* be. Writers shouldn't suppress emotion. He'd sit us down and ask us to write a dramatic monologue where an *eternal ought to be* rose up. First person, of course, because we needed to get *intimate*. What does the character feel most? What does this person love?

These are some of the things you find in every Jack Cady story. He had an uncanny ability to understand the needs of the fundamental human being and transfer that to characters at the absolute base level. A character has essential needs, and Jack got in there and showed how the character expressed them.

Some of the way I write now is in response to his belief that the writer should be a witness. A character might be horrible, but there is always a justification, a complete respect. You watch. You *listen*.

There is a wonderful sense of place in Jack's work. He believed setting was even more important than character, because a character needed a place to *be*. Many of the stories in this collection are populated by ghosts and the people they interact with, and even ghosts have somewhere to *be*.

> The ghost of a ghost must surely be a walking memory.
> I felt the many memories of darkness surrounding this
> hospital, this century, the lives and deaths that skip or
> trample or stumble across time; and darkness stood
> before me like a slab of slate.
>
> (from "Kilroy Was Here.")

He gave respect to his settings, because he believed it was the only way for characters to come alive. He often quoted Joseph Conrad, who was famous for saying his task as a writer was to make readers *see*. If they could see, then readers could do the rest.

Jack taught poetry, and not surprisingly, his prose *reads* like poetry. He believed in economy and specificity. In class we wrote thirty word love poems and we weren't allowed to use the word *love*. We wrote thirty word religious poems and we weren't allowed to use the word *God*. He told us to go back to the poets of the seventeeth century, and the nineteenth century, and read poetry for the sound of it. Read it aloud for the "music" in it. Any good writer of fiction, he said, will have to go back to poetry. In "Poetry Makes Nothing Happen," at the end of this collection, he writes: "Poetry is the voice of love, of fury, of understanding. It does not preach. It does not pass laws, or throw anyone in jail. Poetry does not make anyone do anything."

In fact, Jack is famous for teaching the idea of using iambic pentameter in fiction as a powerful tool because *no one knows you have it*. At a high point in a scene, he would often end the paragraph in iambic pentameter to slam it home.

Look at this passage from "Kilroy Was Here" to see not only the poetry of his work, but the power of his description and narrative *voice*:

> "Outside, in darkness, a storm rose on Shakespearian wings. Black feathers of storm rode gusts tumultuous as passion. Darkness surrounded, clasped; a coffin of wind and rain in which a man becomes breathless and shroud-wrapped."

Or this passage from "The Ghosts of Dive Bomber Hill:"

> "And it is on such nights that visions, apparitions, and ghosts appear. Giant moths flicker pure white as they drift high above the road, and an occasional night-flyer, dark and invisible, splats against the windshield. Headlights bore into the mist, and if a man is not a fool he slows. But, he doesn't slow much, because half of what he sees probably isn't there."

When you read passages like that you realize you're not alone. You're with somebody. You're with the narrative voice. Jack Cady always found the right voice. "You don't choose voice," he said to us at PLU, "it chooses you and comes from the material." He understood the importance of the reader. He told us not to fall so in love with the characters that we forgot the *reader*, who needs to fall in to the same respect.

The same respect he had for readers he also had for young writers; he believed in them not just because he was a teacher, but because our society needed a new direction. He believed we were a society very much in search of a way to get along, and he believed in the importance of the new American writer to set things straight.

Jack Cady is one of our best American writers. He wrote, and he *listened*. His voice came early, and when it did, it carried him through, story after story. I envy those of you reading him for the first time. Prepare to feel his respect for you as you settle in with his narrative voice.

Just listen.

Phantoms

Dear Friends

Being a letter to the I.R.S. wherein the author explicates his non-compliance with certain Federal tax regulations and details a number of Inalienable Rights

[*This piece was originally published as a Copperhead chapbook for the* American Bicentennial 1776-1976.

Special thanks to Centrum Foundation, Port Townsend, WA, where Copperhead is press-in-residence.]

March 27, 1975
Port Townsend, Washington
District Director of Internal Revenue
Seattle, Washington

DEAR FRIENDS:

Since we are about to become legal opponents I write to you something of myself and my beliefs in the hope that there may be understanding between us. I am resigned that there may never be agreement. Our rules conflict, but that does not mean that we cannot care for and respect the condition in which we find each other. Yours is a large agency of government. I want you to know that my quarrel is with the agency, not with anyone employed by the agency. What I must say in this letter about illegalities is directed to the agency and to our government. It is not directed to any single person or group of persons. That is one reason why I start with personal description and personal matters. I want you

3

to know that I am not a statistic and that I do not consider any of you as nebulous, government enemies.

These were strange, windy days this winter. On the Washington Peninsula the rain held off through Christmas, the light on most days washed blue with touches of gold and red when I went downtown for morning coffee at a local cafe. When 1975 appeared it seemed that the wind picked up. The new year did not bring that much snow or rain, but the wail of the wind was like a continuing complaint. I reflected that it was not so much an ill wind, as a wind that complained of illness.

The wind kicks the high tide over the docks by the cafe. The water rolls in the channel, tumbling like a flow of gray, luminescent glass. By the door of the cafe is a newspaper rack. Before entering I always glance at the headlines and then try to think of something else. Sometimes I can succeed. It is a trick that a man picks up if he lives long enough.

The fact is that I really do not want to know what is happening in the rest of the world. What I really want is to live here in Port Townsend, work outside in all of our various weather, and watch the seasonal return of the water birds. Still, there is an exact appeal carried in those newspapers. They name people and events and places. The people are important. I think that most of them are not very different from myself. I enter the cafe knowing that if there is a loose paper about I'll surely read it.

Slurping coffee. Morning smoke. Turning pages, and feeling the presence around me of those of my neighbors who also start the day in this manner. Sometimes there is a tourist group. It is quiet and seems almost like a religious gathering although we drink coffee instead of breaking bread. I read the paper, reflect that for forty-three years I have loved my country, and also reflect that for forty-three years my country has been training me to go to prison. That is a difficult thing to accept and it is lonely. I turn the pages and realize how much of what I read is not news.

It is not news that there are insecure men in high places. It is not news that the business of armies is to kill. It is not news that large corporations regularly engage in criminal activities.

What is news is that conversations between military, government and industry are becoming more intelligible. As this happens decisions that affect us here in Port Townsend and which also affect citizens all over the world are made with no regard to anyone as human being or citizen. Our President speaks of future war while our young sons are getting older. In the cafe cynical remarks are sometimes made saying that once more the nation will be called on to make the world safe for Standard Oil. I hear those remarks and wonder if the speaker realizes that a new dictatorship is forming.

After reading as much as I can bear, I finish my coffee and leave. The truck I drive is old. It smells of loam and tree cuttings, of fertilizer and newly cut grass. The thing chugs up hills because the compression of the old engine is shot. It is a truck with good steering, good brakes, and little else. Even so, it is in better condition than our government.

My day's work may be grades or trees or plant beds. I'll be working with leaves and flowers, with soil and irrigation. I think that since I quit being a teacher this is another good and honest way to make a living. I drive down the road, past the new billboard that reminds our local kids that when eligible they must register for the draft, and first I am angry and then I am sad. The people of this town have no international enemies. These people did not appoint a government to make enemies for them. My neighbors are peaceable people and murder or violence around here is quite remarkable. We get along, and for the most part I think we like each other. Hatred is not in our streets, and hatred for people in like towns across the world is not in our hearts. That is one of the good reasons why I do not want to leave this place for the scurryings of a government that continually insists on my loyalty while negotiating destruction.

It seemed necessary to tell you this before our first confrontation which will be the examination of my 1973 tax return. I expect the examination is prompted by my refusal last year to pay half of my income tax. I will refuse to pay half of the tax again this year, although because of withholding your agency already has most of the money. I refuse to pay half of the tax on various grounds, some of which are moral, some of which are legal. The refusal is prompted by the expenditure by our government of over fifty percent of tax monies on the maintenance and purchase and use of armies and weapons. Through its agency, Internal Revenue

Service, the United States government seeks my complicity in the violation of twenty centuries of moral teaching. The government is in further violation of various international treaties and agreements, and is, in fact, engaged in crimes against peace and crimes against humanity.

These are serious charges and I make them not with indignation but with a great deal of personal pain. This is my beloved country. I have studied its history, its songs; and I have taught its beliefs and ideals. I think I have understood the real determination of freedom and respect that hundreds of thousands of its people have worked so hard to gain for others as well as for themselves. I know something about its religions, its painting and philosophy, its architecture and its politics. It is terrible to have to make those charges, because I know what its people have dreamed and believe I know that the dreams of equality and truth are still valid and alive. This affair of the tax is a trap. Either I believe in the United States of America as bastion of the free spirit, or I quit believing and simply pay my taxes. I am grieved to say that these are the charges, and I am even more grieved to say that the charges are so simply proved as to be prima facia:

The first charge is moral. The nation claims to be a Christian nation. Its code is, "One nation under God," and it proclaims that "In God we trust." I have observed that this is not true.

The Christian and Hebraic injunction, "Thou shalt not kill," is specific. It does not carry exemptions. The U.S. record in Korea (when I was a conscientious objector) and the later record of Vietnam demonstrates that the United States will kill at convenience. It will kill combatants and non-combatants alike. It will do so under the banner of maintaining a free world or to make people free, usually from the clutches of communism. In doing so, and without consulting the peoples involved, it will use bombs, gasses, explosives and napalm to destroy children. This is the record, and the record continues to be endorsed by the U.S. weaponry in Vietnam and Cambodia. No morality can attach to such action no matter what plea is given that U.S. political theory is more sacrosanct than other political theories. I do not see that the much inflated communist bear is less moral than demonstrated U.S. action in killing children. To answer that our nation must be immoral because other nations are immoral is to align us exactly on the same level of violence and degradation that the U.S. pretends to deplore.

In addition, it is increasingly clear that economics and not the threat of communism is the force that keeps our military so well supplied. The irony of the imprint, "In God we trust," is on our coins; but now, even our coins are watered with base metal between slivers of silver. It has only marginally to do with my objection, but I will point out that our current economic ills derive from incredible overspending which certainly aids and abets communist governments. If there is competition with those governments then it is clear the U.S. will eventually lose. It will not lose through military engagements but through moral and economic bankruptcy. When a free people fears to depend on their moral strength and turn instead to weapons stockpiling then it is certain that expensive and very inadequate insurance is being purchased.

In writing that is usually reprinted as "An Essay on Slavery," Thomas Jefferson pointed out that the enslavement of human beings degraded not only those enslaved, but degraded the masters. His moral observation was exact. He pointed out that when one person is placed about another in such a relationship the dehumanization and brutalization was as strong for the master as for the slave. He wrote, "I tremble for my country when I reflect that God is just." Approximately two hundred years later moral issues of the same import are before us. The first one is simply stated. The U.S. is still dealing in a kind of slavery by its dealings and support involving enslaving governments.

The second issue is internal. The U.S. is supporting destruction of national wealth to maintain not only an artificial way of life, but to maintain a false economy through useless and destructive weaponry and war. As I comprehend it, the issue is exactly this: The U.S., given its then unique economic and philosophic attitudes, could not fail in its beginnings to become a great nation. It could not fail because its natural resources literally did seem inexhaustible.

We know better now. The resources are exhaustible and many of them are nearly exhausted. Last year, doing research, I came to a realization of just how desperate the circumstances already are. The nation is clearly running out of petroleum, cropland and water. More cropland and water will be destroyed because of the extraction and processing of coal. I can demonstrate all this, although it is not necessary at the time. I will say that one great issue of the next ten years is the issue of water. Meanwhile, in order to support an artificial economy the nation continues to plow millions of tons of coal, steel, precious metals and hundreds of thousands of acre-feet of water into machines of destruction. The U.S. spends its real wealth in resources demonstrating to the world that it is too weak to depend on its moral strength.

We paid for slavery with the self-destruction that was the Civil War. I fear that we will pay as greatly for our current self-destruction. Already there is trouble among us. Once, Americans were concerned with living. Now many of our people seem only concerned with not dying.

The rest of the points of my objection are legal. They are:

In requiring that I pay taxes for the support of war, planning for war, offensive weapons and the maintenance of a standing armed force sufficient to engage combat on a worldwide scale, the U.S. government through its agent I.R.S. is in violation of the First Amendment to the Constitution which guarantees my religious freedom. I am a member of the Port Townsend meeting for worship of the Society of Friends, Quaker. The Quaker belief and effective detachment from war dates from the beginnings of the society in the middle 1660s. The precedent of refusal to pay war taxes in America dates from 1755 when John Woolman, John Churchman and Anthony Benezet refused to pay for the French and Indian wars. Nonviolence and refusal to pay or endorse either side in a combat dates in U.S. history from the revolution when Quakers who refused to kill were stoned or beaten under the brand of Tory. I claim my devout belief in God and the injunction that we may not kill as sufficient reason to refuse this tax. I would expect that opposition to this view would also have to overcome three hundred years of Quaker nonviolence, and two hundred years of U.S. acceptance of Quaker attitudes that insist on nonviolence.

The second point of objection is that the U.S. is in violation both historically and presently of the Geneva Accords. The accords are specific and so are the violations. They involve not only the control and killing of civilians, but the importation of weapons into a country and the manipulation of populations including the fifty percent of population that are now refugees in Cambodia.

The third point is that in asking taxes, the U.S.A. through its agent I.R.S. seeks my complicity in crimes against peace and crimes against humanity as defined by the Nuremberg Principles. These principles hold that a citizen of a nation is guilty of crimes committed by his nation if he acquiesces to those crimes when, in fact, a moral choice is open to him. A moral choice is open to me, and to endorse U.S. actions in perpetrating crimes against humanity is to announce in terms of the Nuremberg Principles that I am co-author of those crimes. I would detail such crimes, but they are numerous and can be detailed later as necessary. They have to do with destruction of non-combatants, destruction of villages, introduction of illegal weapons; in fact, they read like the newspapers.

The fourth point is that the U.S. is in violation of the Hague Conventions on several points including the use of poison gasses. (Also a violation of the Nuremberg Principles.) The current argument of "first use" is no more than political flummery. A nation that historically proved it will use atomic weapons may assume no legal validity by saying that it will not use gas until some other nation uses gas. I am sorry to say that the argument very much resembles the statement by a homicidal maniac that he will not kill again; this in spite of the fact that his psychological condition seems to have deteriorated.

In proof of the above point, the Pentagon request for fiscal year '75 is for $107 million for research and development of biological warfare. The military is currently defying a Congressional ban on the production of a specific nerve gas known as GB, and another known as VX. Either cause instantaneous death on contact with the skin. I think you can understand why many people would not want their taxes to be paying for this sort of thing.

The fifth point is that the U.S.A. is in violation of the United Nations Charter, Article 1, sections 2, 3 and 4.

The sixth point is that the U.S. in stockpiling weapons, planning for war, and maintaining a large military force is in violation of our basic law and international law deriving in this nation from

English law. It is a long accepted principle taught in law schools all over the country, and supported by the courts when it becomes an issue. The law derives originally from the writing of Thomas Hobbes. It states that the duty of the citizen to the state ceases when the state fails to protect, and actually threatens the life of the citizen. At this point, the citizen has not only the right but the obligation to resist.

In requiring that I pay taxes to support a war industry and armed forces capable of contending on a worldwide scale, the U.S. Government is threatening both my moral and physical existence. I am not being protected because the U.S. builds atomic weapons, B-1 bombers, atomic submarines, poison gas, lasers, rocketry, napalm and all of the other expensive paraphernalia of war. These do not protect me. They invoke the suspicion and fear of other nations and they provoke among other nations the building and stockpiling of similar weapons. Despite the assurance of manufacturers that these weapons are to make us strong and free, it is easy to see that they make us weak and vulnerable. They endanger the life of every U.S. citizen. I do not wish to be redundant, but weapons get used. The U.S., by record, has used atomics, poison gas, napalm, indiscriminate bombing against civilian targets and fielded armies against women and children. The nation has proved that it will use its weapons. I see no reason why any other nation on earth should trust a U.S. promise of non-use. This threatens my life. My nation no longer qualifies as protector. I owe no allegiance to tax rules designed ultimately to destroy me and those whom I love. In fact, under our law, I have the obligation to refuse.

My final, legal objection is that the U.S. now gives every indication that it is, in fact, not a nation of laws but a nation of men and corporations. This, despite the resignation from office of Richard Nixon and Spiro Agnew. I charge that the freedom of the citizen is largely illusory, and that the payment of taxes, the keeping of tax records, the invasion of privacy by I.R.S. and other agencies of government, the making of rules by agencies (rules that have the force and effect of law but which are not to be challenged in courts), the maintenance of records or files on the political, religious, economic and moral statements and actions of the individual, the power to levy fines and license by agency rule, and the presumption by government that the citizen is guilty of any agency charge and must therefore bear the burden of proof of his innocence; all of these show that the citizen of the U.S. is no longer free.

I have two main intentions in this tax refusal. The first is quite clear. I do not intend to pay for the destruction of other human beings, nor endorse by word or deed the crimes of the United States. The second intent is a little more nebulous but it is just as strong. It is strong because I love my country.

In this refusal I intend that the United States will display by its actions whether a citizen, raised to believe in U.S. principles of freedom, equality, protection under the laws; raised in fact, under statements like, "With a proper regard for the opinions of mankind," can indeed trust and believe in the way he has been raised. Either the Constitution is sound or it is not. The U.S. will either honor its national and international commitments or it will not. The courts will either face the issues or the courts will duck them.

Having loved this country for forty-three years it is now time for the country to either prove worthy of my regard and dedication, or it is time for it to show that what I've been taught (and what I have taught hundreds of others in American literature and American studies classes) is indeed a fraud. If the rules of I.R.S. are bigger than the Constitution, the U.N. Charter, the Nuremberg Principles and the Christian teaching of two thousand years then I believe it is time that the U.S. acknowledge this. At least the citizen would not be damaged, as I may have been, by illusions of truth, equality and freedom. I hope, in fact, that this nation may prove worthy of its beginnings as it approaches its two hundredth year. I hope that men like Jefferson, Woolman, Franklin and Penn were not wrong, and that their support of laws and ethical principles was not misplaced. I hope that it proves true that these principles are greater than the opportunistic violences wrought under the excuse of various crisis.

Please schedule my appointment at any convenient time, since I am no longer on jury duty. While I have more than adequate records I will appear without those records. As you probably know, the maintenance of records and the requirement that I show the records are in clear violation of the Fifth Amendment to the Constitution. Also I believe you may be in violation of your own regulations although I am unsure of this particular point. The letter I received also asked for information on my '72 return. As I understand it, your regulations allow you to see only one return. Then, if errors become evident, you may request others; although you may not go beyond the Statute of Limitations unless fraud is indicated. Will you please clarify this by letter? I assure you that you will not be able, no matter how many obscure rules, to find indication of fraud. However, I have been told by one I.R.S. employee that the rules are interpretable in such a way that he could find something wrong with my tax return, no matter when filed or by whom. This, and my past experience in calling I.R.S. and getting contradictory verbal opinions from two or even three I.R.S. employees makes me believe that both the agency and myself will be in a much stronger position if I come with a tape recorder and accompanied by a witness.

Thank you for your attention to this long letter. I hope that we can treat humanely with each other, dealing in terms of respect and kindness and that a great deal of understanding and learning may pass between us. Perhaps even our country will derive some small benefit, since finally, it is the condition and stance of this nation that I take to be in question.

[Editor's Note: When Carol Orlock, Jack's widow, sent us a number of Jack's stories and essays, "Dear Friends" was accompanied by the following note.

As a Quaker during the Vietnam War, Cady was among a number of "tax resisters" who withheld a percentage of their income taxes to protest expenditures for the war. This money was put in trust to be paid after the war ended.

As I understand it, the IRS took the tax resisters to federal court for nonpayment.

I first learned the story of what happened at that hearing many years later. On March 20, 2004, which would have been Cady's 72nd birthday, many of his friends and colleagues gathered to celebrate his life. One friend, Terry Mielke, had been present at the tax hearing.

According to Mielke, the hearing was held at the U.S. Federal Courthouse in Seattle. In the courtroom the tax resisters were seated in the area separated by a rail and gate from the front where attorneys and judges sat. The resisters were called upon one at a time to explain themselves. When Cady's name was called he stood and read aloud "Dear Friends, A Letter to the IRS."

As he finished, the courtroom erupted with applause. Then the judge stood and, still in his robes, descended from the bench, walked across the front area to the rail, came through the gate, walked up to Cady and shook his hand.

He returned to the bench and, as expected, his judgment required the resisters to pay all back taxes, plus penalties and interest.

—*Carol Orlock]*

The Parable of Satan's Adversary

IT'S SUPPOSED TO WORK THIS WAY:

Imp-Apprentices cruise the street at the lowest and most uninteresting level. They collect soul-remnants of pimps, pickpockets, and other city sweepings. After an Imp-Apprentice bags a thousand such, It is promoted to Imp Third Class.

Third Class deals with slightly more advanced levels of scumsuckers, i.e. drug dealers and Hell's Angels. By the time an Imp has progressed to First Class, It gets to handle the true toe-jam of humanity: presidents of great nations, and television evangelists. When a First Class Imp bags a big one—say, for example, a plank owner in the The Moral Morality, It is promoted to Demon.

Demons, of course, are the main handlers in the Hot Place. The Demon Third Class, if pushy and ambitious, gets to start His career barbecuing small fry used car salesmen, that sort of thing. He gradually moves up to stoking fires beneath CEOs of corporations and, of course, members of The Senate. That's the way it's supposed to work. Sooner or later, though, every business runs into labor trouble.

That is why The Devil (Old Nick or Nickie to his friends, if He had any) sat head in hands with his bottom firmly pressed against a lump of glowing anthracite.

Coal prices were up, don't even think of oil. He hadn't found a reputable pitchfork supplier in two centuries. Immorality had turned seedy, and standards had deteriorated to the point where even rock stars were going to Heaven. Now the Imps (goaded into it, He suspected, by the Demons) were talking Labor Union and Strike.

All around Him, Hell was just plain going to . . . but, that makes no sense. Think of it this way: things were not working out. The Devil (Nickie to his friends, if He had any) knew it was time to take a break . . . maybe start a war somewhere, or put new life into the white slave trade . . . something . . . and then He bethought himself of Westwind Retirement Apartments.

He told himself He had been saving those souls back for just such an occasion; prime sinners held in reserve for times when a fella needs a little cheer. Then He shuddered, actually, shivered, like before a chill breeze. Still, a guy had to take a chance.

The Devil (Nickie, etc) took the form of a slight, but distinguished-looking man: a college administrator, perhaps, or a mid-level executive, or maybe a high-level social worker. He smoothed his black hair, adjusted his eyes from red to greenish yellow, brushed a little flaming dandruff off the sleeves of his business suit. He strode forth on polished shoes. His collecting bag for souls lay hidden in an attaché case.

Westwind Retirement Apartments stands defiantly beside a manmade lake (only a little rancid), where ducks cohabit with joyful abandon. Pine trees surround the lake, while young poplars stand on each side of a road leading to the front of the building. Westwind looks for all the world like a rundown Junior High School untimely ripped from a seedy part of town.

It has charms, though, because it attracts clients of a type who regard it as homey, and who The Devil considers bait. Nickie parked his limo, strode through the front doors, and changed into vapor. He drifted along hallways, sniffing around, and hopeful. He took up residence in the dayroom by hiding in a clock. From that clock He could watch those souls who he considered rightly his, and they were bitching, as usual . . .

Whoever designed the hallway of Westwind Retirement Apartments . . . "home of shuffleboard, old broads, and bald duffers," according to Deke, who is a bald duffer, himself . . . whoever designed that hallway showed the sensitivity of rock, probably dolomite.

"... because," as Miss Victoria-Elizabeth Simpson often claims in a ladylike voice that contrasts with her words, "every step you take down that hallway is one more tick, one more nick, on your gravestone. Thank God I'll not die a virigin."

And 'tick' that hallway does. A polished floor of yellow oak leads between walls painted lunatic-asylum green. At the end of the hall, swinging doors to the dayroom stand beneath an antique clock doubtless bought ... "stolen, most likely," according to Deke ... from some now defunct telegraph office.

In the dread halls of Westwind Retirement, that clock ticks, ticks, ticks so inexorably that even those without hearing aids feel their last days passing on its indifferent meter.

They are, and take pride in the fact, a scruffy crew with bodies in roughly the shape of auto wrecks. Their minds and experience, though, are matters no one young and beautiful wants to mess with. "Worse," brags Deke, "than messing with Texas."

For example, Miss Victoria-Elizabeth Simpson is a Southern lady who wears pastel gowns, enjoys riots, and has caused several. From the tip-top of her head to the bottom of her chin (what with face lifts) she remains gorgeous, though, as she admits, "the rest has gone south, back to ma' dear old Georgia." Miss Victoria-Elizabeth stands 5'3" and looks back on a career as a television personality in days before Barbara Walters even had her first interview (which interview, as Miss Victoria-Elizabeth explains, occurred at age 7, when Babs interviewed a cat: "... made poor kitty blush ... it stayed stoned on catnip for a month.")

Deke sports a large tummy encased in checked pants, and clasped by red suspenders of the type used by pool hustlers—which Deke is. The gang also includes Janice Marie Jobravovich (Chicago cop), Maxie Stern (Reno bartender), Ms. Joyce Ann Summerfield (Fresno 5th grade teacher), and Winchester Morris (pawnbroker). It also includes a saintly creature (a goody-two-shoes) named Dear-Gwendolyn who (though opinions vary) is most likely a girl (or anyway, female).

The gang lounged in the dayroom as television broadcast crud, and as Miss Victoria-Elizabeth sneered during commercials. Dear-Gwendolyn, in gown pink and diaphanous, fretted over fates of soap opera characters. Deke stood at the pool table, hitched up his checkered pants, snapped his suspenders, and studied a complex shot. "Remind me," he said to no one in particular, "to tell about the time I cleaned Minnesota Fats in a night of nine ball. Only time anyone ever heard Fats whimper . . . brought tears to the Fat Man's eyes."

"Tell that B.S. one more time . . ." Maxie felt in his back pocket for the sap that wasn't there.

"If anyone reminds him to tell that again," Janice-Marie murmured, "what happens won't be a misdemeanor." Janice-Marie is largish, muscular, and still wears her cop pants. If she took it to mind, she could work Deke up so he looked like a pothole in Chicago streets.

Beyond the window sunlight dimmed. Ducks rose from the lake, shed a few feathers, circled, dropped back down to the lake. Ducks paddling. Ducks jumping back into the air. Duck confusion, lots of it, a stiff breeze beginning to bend pine trees, and storm clouds rolling in. The click of Deke's pool balls sounded hollow, like tiny echoes coming from some bad place; mausoleum, perhaps.

"Hush, now," Victoria-Elizabeth whispered, although it was not necessary. Folks all had their flappers shut. Expectation filled the dayroom. The ticking of the clock grew louder, but it slowed.

"He's back," Winchester-the-pawnbroker murmured. "Party time." Winchester still dresses slick, like a college administrator, or a midlevel executive, or a high-level social worker. He wears polished and pointy shoes. His remaining hair is dyed black, and lies against his head like thickish paint. He spoke to the clock. "What are-ya? Chicken crap? Cold cuts? Or just confused?"

Nickie stepped from the clock. He smelled only a little of sulphur. He and Winchester regarded each other like two pooches sniffing.

"You," Nickie hissed at Winchester. "You won't set no high standards, but you'll do."

"You," Winchester told Nickie, "don't know what trouble is." Winchester turned to Maxie-the-bartender. "How soon do we bounce this guy?"

"Give it a minute." Maxie pulled on his left ear lobe, rubbed his nose, and for all the world looked like a man about to snap a bar rag. "It beats watching television," he told Winchester. "I mean, this guy don't come up around all that often." Maxie is the slender, wiry type—fast with a bar rag.

Deke set up a three ball combination and stroked the object ball into the right corner pocket. He snapped a red suspender. He looked Nickie. "Better a has-been than a never-was."

"Not kind," Dear-Gwendolyn whispered. "That was simply not kind." Dear-Gwendolyn seemed torn between defending Nickie and following the tortured life of a soap opera character (who even at that moment, threatened to divorce his third wife whilst in the presence of his first and second). Dear-Gwendolyn's diaphanous skirts rustled.

It was then that Victoria-Elizabeth stepped forward, accompanied by fifth-grade teacher, Ms. Joyce-Ann Summerfield. Nickie found himself with a TV anchor on one side, and a K-12 teacher on the other. If between them the two had not seen everything, they'd seen most.

Joyce-Ann waved Nickie toward a seat. She waved Deke back to his pool table, and she turned away from Winchester and Maxie. In a voice that had intimidated legions of eleven-year-old boys, she told Nickie, "Sit, and stay sittin'. Don't move an inch." To Victoria-Elizabeth, she said, "Do it."

The interview that followed fell into a conventional pattern: Part I, Early Years (Young Rebellion and The Fall From Heaven); Part II, Professional Development (Construction of the Seven Stages of Hell); Part III, Sexual Proclivities (Unmentionable); and Part IV, Future Plans. By the time Victoria-Elizabeth got Nickie to Future Plans, Deke chuckled, Joyce-Ann tsked, and Dear-Gwendolyn twisted her hankie because of sexual proclivities. Nickie wept.

He sat, a rather frail figure in what had become a frayed business suit. He shivered, although warm air gushed from heating vents.

"Maybe things went too well for too long," he whispered between sniffles. "I came to depend on promoting standard stuff, the oldies and goodies: murder, rapine, corrupt priests, torture. Historically, there's a lot of promise in humanity."

"The good old days," murmured Maxie.

"I suffered a downturn," Nickie sniffled. "I didn't keep up with all the changes going on . . . but who would ever thought of stuff like Stallone flicks and chemical weapons?"

"Is that a problem?" Victoria-Elizabeth managed to look puzzled, although she already knew the answer.

"Folks used to fear me," Nickie sobbed. "I used to haunt their dreams. They smeared gargoyles all over everything. They hung horseshoes over their doorways. They actually feared my trolls, although a troll is so damn dumb that . . . and they wore garlic and smelled like Purgatory. And when it came to orneriness, which was mostly, they looked to me for guidance."

"And now . . . ?" Dramatic pause from Victoria-Elizabeth. Her voice sounded soft, almost cuddly.

"They do it all by themselves." Nickie mourned. "And they do it better. I blame technology. I sort of blame myself. I mean, look around you for Hell's sake. Even you people aren't afraid."

"I been handling the human race for 80 years," Maxie grumbled. "Nothin' Hell can show me is more'n a walk in the park."

"Welcome," Winchester sneered, "to Westwind Retirement Apartments."

The sum of it is that Nickie took up a vacation residence in the clock. For a while he traveled back to Hell most days, and reported on the power struggle that developed in his absence. Demons barbecued apostate Imps, and legions of renegade Imps tramped across burning plains and around molten pits, ignoring the customers while tearing the place to shreds.

"There comes a time to rack your cue," Deke finally advised Nickie.

Nickie took the advice. He retired to the clock in Westwind Retirement Apartments, a clock that ticks everyone's remaining seconds. Of course, sometimes Nickie slows the clock.

And perhaps He has His regrets, since most folks do. And perhaps even now He enjoys lusts (after all, Dear-Gwendolyn has peculiar charms), and perhaps He grows a bit creaky in the joints because the clock is not all that comfy. Plus, like everything else at Westwind, He occasionally gets sick of hearing that story about how Deke once took Minnesota Fats to the cleaners, and made the Fat Man cry.

Our Ground and Every
Fragrant Tree Is Shaded

ON MOST DAYS WE THOUGHT OF HIM AS RELIABLE, IF WE TROUBLED to think of him at all as we walked the streets of this small coastal town. Our northwest harbor lies mostly wrapped with rain. Wind swirls the hallmark-mist of Pacific beaches lying north of California. The reliable James would appear walking toward you from the mist, like a specter risen from distant waves and on its course toward the haunting of a maritime museum, or a moored ship, or to blow wraith-like above rain-filled and empty streets. There seemed always something moist about him. He gave the impression of being soaked, as though a sheen of water silvered the sidewalks on which he strode. He would only, in fact, be on his way to work at a general store where the main preoccupations dealt with groceries.

And groceries being what they are, and James being who he was—which is to say, reserved and distant—we townspeople could scarcely have realized how that moist man might herald eternal sorrow. We do not exactly blame the reliable James for our troubles; and we will certainly not blame ourselves, but blame looks for somewhere to alight. We can say that trouble centers around the store, and the center of that store expresses the 19th century. The store rises Victorian and fanciful and filled with whispering shadows.

Today the place seems only an ornate notion from long ago, but in 1870 its customers delighted in cathedral stained-glass windows through which occasional northwest sun painted sacks of feed with roseate glow, or bluely and greenly illuminated racks of corn brooms, new harness, axes, flour barrels; the hodge-podge of items either useful or ornamental on which Victorian lives depended.

And, if there is a curse on this town—and if we are doomed in some peculiar way—(because we recognize that to be human is to be doomed, but not necessarily in ways peculiar) doom began when Able Andrewes came to these parts in the late 1860s. Guns of the Civil War stood stilled. Frontier spread before settlers. Tall ships swam in our harbor surrounded by a babel of languages: Italian, Chinese, Japanese, English, German, Norwegian, Swedish and French. Andrewes traced his ancestry to English gentry; thus acted as a very proper type of gentlemanly adventurer—a bearer of the white man's burden—and he existed comfortably among Oriental faces, Mediterranean faces, Blacks, Indians, Hawaiians, and Samoans.

His Trading Post, as he chose to style it, became the largest building north of San Francisco. It rose four stories, with peaked Victorian roof and fanciful gables. Although structurally a warehouse, ten cathedral windows offered the impression of a church. The trading post stood more certainly, and certainly more handsomely, than any of the town's several churches.

The main floor displayed foodstuffs in kegs, barrels, loaves, bundles, and boxes. Spices and teas perfumed the store, while gas lamps provided light. Stained glass windows portrayed frontier trades: Indians bartering skins of sea otter, Chinese working lime, and, in this town, master builders erecting Victorian mansions.

In the basement rested what was then a modern miracle, a pulley-operated elevator capable of lifting a ton. The elevator carried new wood-burning cookstoves, pumps, bollards, ship fittings, bull tongue plows, wrought iron railings to surround widows' walks; heavy merchandise: ships' anchors to carriage axles. Andrewes made claim that his Trading Post carried at least one of every item manufactured.

The second floor displayed hardware, rifles, steel traps for gathering pelts. The third carried furniture: Victorian love seats, armoires, beds with richly carved roses, dressers, commodes, pier mirrors, hatstands in walnut and oak. On the fourth floor Andrewes established living quarters.

There are still folk in this town who remember Andrewes as an old, old man greeting dawn above the eastern range of mountains. By then, any consequences of Andrewes's actions lived among us. None of us can say that he engaged in criminal acts, but all of us know that he lived comfortably among those who did. He financed ships that carried bond slaves as well as goods. He discounted large orders of merchandise to men who dealt in marginally legal business, or in business that was neither moral or legal. People who remember Andrewes picture him standing on his fourth floor balcony, and he is clothed in proper Victorian attire. His hands reach toward the mountains, beckoning in the dawn, or, as some grumblers complain, calling for morning light to dispel his self-inflicted darkness.

By then and honorably, he was long married, siring sons Edward and Charles. And, by then, he was more wraith than man. The fine English figure became diminutive over years. Late one night he visited his sons in their rooms, spoke to his sons kindly, then departed. His physician suggested that Andrewes wafted away on winds because he weighed less than his clothes. Andrewes disappeared in 1935.

His sons, Edward and Charles, continued to mind the store and these two would, through the years, come to depend on their reliable employee James.

=

This is a Victorian tale, Gentle Reader, and I am thus allowed to take you by the arm as we stroll past echoes of horror. Although I tell the tale as if "we," the people of the town are speaking, it's obvious a single person pens these words. I introduce myself as Baruch, a modern scribbler of records. During those times when I do not scribble, I make my living selling old books from a storefront on Ocean Street. Local opinion holds me as surly, aging, irascible, crusty—in short, a curmudgeon—and I foster the illusion.

But, Gentle Reader, since we are unlikely ever to meet, I need not be curmudgeonly with you. In fact, I beg your indulgence.

For a long time no one knew or cared where James spent his sleeping hours. If asked, we might suspicion that he never left the store. After all, did he not always range from cellar to fourth floor of that mammoth enterprise? Did he not continually move, nearly ghostlike, between bundles of fresh asparagus and cans of pie mix? The man and the store intermingled. Only recently did we towns-people begin to fear. Inquiry brought discovery. James walks as a symbol of fear more dreadful than any of us have, heretofore, owned the courage to imagine.

James, we now understand, steps nightly from his round of groceries, walks the short distance to the harbor; is then swallowed by the tides, only to be spit ashore half an hour before the store opens. James sleeps, or walks, or God-knows-what beneath those waves. He in no manner resembles the living dead, is not a zombie. Such creatures walk the realms of the fantastic. About that reliable employee James, there is nothing fantastic.

=

We turn now, you and I, to a burden weighing heavy in this tale. That burden is the entire Victorian period, and Victorian dreams that toil and churn and thrust from the past; the calamities and the curse.

They saw themselves, those olden Englishmen, as bearers of the lamp of progress. They, like Able Andrewes, set forth as mission-aries to dark races, bringing Bibles and rifles and machines. They acted, sometimes unwisely, and did not understand the effects of their actions. Nations fell before them. In their grandest hours they bowed to the highest forms of duty, for "duty" intertwined them like strands of rope. The proper Victorian feared failure to his duty more than he feared dying.

They also spoke of purity, were sternly fascinated with sex, and romantically fascinated with death. They dreamed of progress as they fashioned the Industrial Revolution. It takes no scribbler of antiquities to note Victorian styles still alive within us. Are we not bound by duty, ofttimes obscene? Do we not bore the world with eternal tut-tuts and quacks concerning sex? Have we not turned technology into a hotly forged divinity? Are not most places close to them in spirit? Do we not now pilfer souls, whereas Victorians boldly stole them? Which brings us back to the reliable James.

=

Once the facts became known, our mayor, who administers the town after business hours, visited the store and asked James, "Whatever in the bird-brained world was he doing?"; which in this small town is the best we can manage in the way of diplomacy. James replied, but not distantly, that he "paid attention to his own business." He added that he was "minding the store."

The store has changed little during the 20th century, and to the store I went on behest of the mayor, for I am the town historian. James stood beneath soft light through stained glass. Fresh cabbages lay boxed at his feet. He made check marks on a packing list. His employers worked elsewhere: Edward handling receipts and deposits, Charles, who in his age is still sprightly, attending the cash register. Fatigue lined James's face, but his erect posture denied tiredness that drove bone deep. Groceries encircled him. In the cellar, beneath our feet, ranged drill presses and parts for modern tractors. Above us the store held sofas and china; screws, turnbuckles, manila rope and fishing gear.

"The mayor is a proud though foolish man," I told James. "He is also vexed."

"The mayor runs a feed lot," James replied in a soft voice. "He fattens stock. Nothing foolish about it for as long as folks need beef." Always before, James carried a Victorian reserve. Now his voice held quiet compassion. Thin brown hair lay sideways across his skull in vague attempt to cloak a bald spot. Large hands with stubby nails carried calluses from years of stocking merchandise. Brown eyes were guileless as a child's, though somehow moist. In any dry goods store he would be directed to ready-made shirts and pants marked "medium."

His reply slowed me for a moment. Although I'm in trade, I've never regarded my bookstore as a holy habitation. James spoke in Victorian terms. To him, the mayor's feed lot justified the mayor's ambitions. Victorians truly believed that commerce worked a missionary influence, and England was a great mercantile nation.

"Even were the mayor an angel," I replied, "you beg the question. You are presently the only subject of conversation. Our ladies suggest iniquities, our loafers make uncomfortable jokes, and our banker fears for business. You will soon be the subject of sermons."

"Business picked up last month." James folded invoices and looked across racks of foodstuff like a father regarding a favorite child.

"Because you are notorious."

"'Afflicted' is a better word. I could tell you more, but there's enough sorrow in the world, so I'll not add to it. Let us please allow 'afflicted' to be the last word." His was an anguished and weary spirit in a fatigued body, but only a sharp eye could uncover his distress. Victorians never blinked before a downturn in fortune. He lighted in me a spark of compassion.

"I am not as harsh as my reputation would have me," I told him. "It is not ungentlemanly to accept assistance."

It was he who viewed me with compassion, looking beyond me finally to our quiet streets. "There's enough trouble for everyone," he whispered. "I should say no more."

Momentary terror walked across my soul. I stood among cabbages burnished with light through stained glass windows. Only the banality of the store shone true, for all else seemed filled with threat. The terror passed. My mind changed from fear to hideous and alien knowledge that said I grow old in an alien country. I age in a shameless nation of strange language, which has no respect for old men.

"I do not understand," I told James in parting, "but fear that I will." I stepped from the store and into our streets.

Was James a modern Jonah—swallowed by the tides then belched ashore—and was not Jonah's sin the sin of Pride? I walked toward the harbor, walking by congeries of houses and huts. Victorian mansions glowered in company with rusting house trailers. A few split levels nested beside two-story frames; yet Victorian houses dominated. Before the turn of the century this town lay awash in wealth. Its fortunes saw decline when the first transcontinental railroad drove to tidewater at a different port. These great houses rose from trade; but trade not always luminous. Irish serving girls earned fifty cents a week, plus stingy room and board. Chinese bond slaves cooked lime and died in thousands. Indian and Malay prostitutes fell ravaged before sailors and disease. Fortunes flowered from that infamous poppy, opium.

I felt the press of antique darkness. Andrewes's spirit still touches here. Too many people died badly in these parts. Some townsfolk claim to hear spectral voices in the wind, or distant weeping at the beginning of each new day. Dirges moan beyond the cause of simple avarice. In the name of progress young boys died from shanghai to merchant ships. Indian children saw their parents lynched. When smugglers avoided apprehension by authorities, they bound illegal immigrants in chain and dropped them screaming overboard; while in these great houses sounded tinkling notes from harpsichords, sounded the assured voices of wealthy men, the lyrical voices of their ladies.

At the harbor water moved like restless spirits. We live precariously beside this sea. Darkness rises from all horizons, but it is dark waters that beckon us. Every year a boat or two is drowned. Many, many hulks of sailing ships, coal burning ships, and modern steamers moulder beneath these waters.

What must James see beneath the waves? Skeletons, no doubt, skeletons representing failed hopes. He must see fortunes in cargo, even cargo once destined for Andrewes's store. Perhaps he wanders beneath crystal chandeliers waving in water above dance floors of ships' salons. Our remaining piers stand above great darkness, and the pull of the sea draws that irrational part of our minds to self-destruction.

=

"It's Able Andrewes," Mamie Worthy told me when I encountered her at our Carnegie library. "You young ones have no notion of the weight of things." Mamie is as old as Edward and Charles, which is to say she is eighty; twenty years older than I. She takes her last name more seriously than she ought. In her case, duty asks inquiry into all of town life. She can trace the lineage of every cat and dog, can predict births occurring fewer than nine months after marriage, and knows when a preacher stumbles in prayer, and why.

Mamie's is not the voice of mirth, the voice of gladness. At the same time she is honest.

"I do not like you," she told me, "but that's not news. The news is why I do not like you. You are a lonely man who protects himself with loneliness. The rest of the town just thinks you're a snot."

"Yet, I like you," I replied with all truthfulness. "With the length of your nose from prying I should not, but there it is. Able Andrewes disappeared three years after I was born and two years after James saw life. By then Edward was twenty, and Charles nineteen. How can Able Andrewes have aught to do with us?"

Brightness faded briefly from her eyes. Her black dress, clean and pressed and ankle length, seemed more alive than she. Sadness overcame her face. "I do not give a holy hoot what people do," she told me. "If you think there's a contradiction I'll remind you that you are a grown man who digs at the past like a dog after small bones. You figure it out."

"I like you," I told her, "not because you offer pleasure or charm, but because until now you have always been honest."

"You chose to remain in this town," she said in a voice a little larger than a whisper. "Why?"

"It has always been my home." My response was not sufficient, but I had never pondered the question.

"No dream took you away. Your answer will be found in the realm of Able Andrewes's dreams. I'll say no more." She turned from me. Her black skirts whispered like the tears of widowhood.

Victorian secrecy caused loneliness, and I returned to Victorian streets. Mamie is acute, though I resented her comments. I reminded myself that a man with books is never lonely. Because a man chooses not to marry, or sit at the local cafe and talk crops or business spells nothing. And, all men age in a strange land because styles change and youth is ignorant. The landscape of memory becomes more real than modern landscape.

Mamie seemed inhibited. I sought one who is not. Our town drunk in no manner resembles the humorous Irishman so beloved by storytellers. He is Swede Andersen, a tall and broad man in his day, who in other days fisted sail. Vessels with auxiliary sail coasted these shores into the 1930s.

"Mamie takes things personal," he told me, "but it isn't Able Andrewes, it's the store. Come to think of it, it's both." His diminished frame anchored the corner stool of our only tavern. Beyond windows, gray light walked the horizon. It wrapped around a fishing vessel swimming moderately heavy seas. Swede's hands swell large around a beer glass, his knuckles dislodged in old accidents and fights. The rest of him seems no more than a cameo.

"How inebriated are you?"

"As well as can be expected," he told me, "but suds don't make me talk. I'd tell you anyway." Eyes of thin blue, decorated with lines of red, watched the fishing vessel. "Damn fools," he said about the fishermen, but his voice was filled with longing for the sea. "This business of getting old sure makes a fella think."

"I have all afternoon," I told him, "and the will to listen."

"So James pokes around under the harbor, and it's a wonder most of us ain't with him for the stroll. We're part of the store. You think I drink for fun?" Swede watched a young couple with a small child as they passed along the boardwalk. "Kids figure the world got made an hour before they were born," Swede said about the couple. "James sure thought that way."

Swede's tale meandered, but gradually told of waste and sorrow. It centered on a daily round of innocuous tasks and perceptions. At eighteen James left for college and found no joy. He returned claiming study as impractical. The reliable James took a job at Andrewes's store. He became reserved and distant.

"So he made a punk's decision at eighteen," Swede said, "and never looked back. He became the world's leading expert on that store, every nook and cranny and item in stock. To this day he can still find button hooks that ain't been used since World War I."

"Which does not explain his actions."

"It likely does," Swede told me, "if you think about the Andrewes store and Andrewes. You probably figure that store stays alive because of the town, and you figure wrong. The store is what holds all the power here. The town stays alive because of the store."

For a moment it seemed I owned someone else's memory, or someone else owned mine. Once, long ago, I wished to really study history, and really write it. Now I only record the events of a Victorian town gone stale.

"We all stayed too long," Swede said, "we stayed too long. Check with Mad Willie for the rest of it. He's the only sane man in town."

"And you are not?"

"I'm part of the store," Swede said, and said it sadly. "So are you, but Willie, nope." Swede returned to drink and silence as I departed.

Unlike most village idiots, Willie is not easily found. I walked, knowing a day or two might pass before we met. One generally discovers Mad Willie in search for mushrooms and roots and herbs, or conversing with cattle in a near valley. His Indian and Filipino forebears combine in his sturdy frame. He strolls costumed in ragtag clothing from charity bins of churches. Animals delight in his presence, and children follow him until called away by fearful parents.

=

Gentle Reader, some Victorians were honest men and true, as, sometimes, are we. I must not debase a hundred years of toil without exceptions. And, when the rapacious 19th century gave way to the 20th, only the century changed. Victorian minds and values did not disappear because of dates on a calendar. Notions of "progress" continued. Nineteenth century trading posts would be replaced by a beatitude of goods in 20th century shopping malls.

And we, like they, write history every day while horror walks. We plant gardens as ghettos rise in flame. We tsk over dry cleaning bills while statesmen name themselves honorable men. This augers ill. Able Andrewes, gentleman, did not intentionally join in corruption, but corruption reaches forth and implicates. Victorians killed hundreds of thousands, while Andrewes's trade built this town. Victorian houses, once gorgeous, line our streets. We live in them, preserve them, and our century kills millions.

=

I stood before dawn outside Andrewes's store. James would soon arrive, and through the early streets our people passed: Paul Stenkey trudging toward the post office where he will sort and curse colorful flyers advertising goods, Madge Plummer to the weekly paper where she will report quibbles from city hall, and Jason Preston, young developer who is always three dollars short and two days late. I thought of long nights of correspondence at my store. Much of my income derives from rare books sold by mail to collectors.

Lights flared from the store as the Andrewes boys prepared for the business day. The store towered in darkness, and stained glass windows seemed to leap toward the mist. The windows rose like candles, or like colorful lamps of Victorian pride. Red and purple and blue mixed with oranges, yellows, greens, and browns. Here and there a spark of crystal twinkled, and here and there other glass shone black as polished ebony. Figures in stained glass—fishermen and loggers, carpenters and peat miners, draftsmen and bartenders—seemed to move because of the mist, slowly counting days of endless toil. Far away a church bell tolled.

"Willie heard you calling," a voice said behind me. I turned to find Mad Willie dressed as a harlequin; faded yellow pants, red shirt, green cap. Willie may be mad, but he is well read, having mooched my cast-off books for years. His broad, olive-colored face shone with enthusiasm. He carried bunches of wild carrots and wild celery.

"I didn't call."

"You did," he said, "or else it's magic. But, just think of cows, just think of them. Cows don't miss much. Some are even Methodist." He perfervidly began to explain bovine doctrines.

"We have a mystery unlikely solved by cows," I told him.

"Unlikely solved by anyone else," he told me, "plus some are Presbyterian." He watched through dark mist as a milk truck pulled up before the store. The driver stepped slowly down, as if in dispraise of cows. "Miraculous," Willie breathed. "You put in grass, and out comes milk and cheese and ice cream." His delight sounded as large as his wonder.

"Something dark stalks this town," I said. "James has become peculiar in his way. His reserve is gone and he speaks most kindly. Swede drinks but doesn't care for it. Mamie is indifferent to events, and yet she pries. No one claims to fully understand. If someone does understand, that someone isn't talking."

"James does his eternal job," Willie said seriously. "You do yours. Able Andrewes does his, and maybe some of what happens is wonderful." For a moment the man seemed sane. His lips lost their silly smile, and his broad forehead furrowed with concentrated thought.

"There's wonderment to it," I said with grim voice, "but other words occur. Horror and death, for two."

"Celery," said Willie, and not unhappily. "*Apium graveolens.* In the wild state it is as rank as me, but with broader leaves. It is indigenous to marshy places near the sea. With breeding and blanching celery turns tame. Three varieties are cultivated, green, white, and red. Green is best, but James is white. Very little of the red shows up around here."

"You must be feigning madness," I told him, "while playing court jester spinning riddles." It is impossible to dislike Willie, but also impossible not to become impatient with him.

"James is a master of inventory," Willie said with dignity. "Do not speak of sanity and riddles in the same breath. Your sanity disappeared when you stopped riddling. When questions cease, people buy someone else's dream."

"As James bought Andrewes's dream?"

"And Andrewes, no doubt, bought an even older dream," Willie murmured, sounding his sadness. "Steam power was first used in 1698 by Englishmen, the same year Daniel Defoe suggested better roads and insane asylums." Willie looked toward cathedral windows still illuminated by electricity, more than by the first thin light of dawn. "*Borrow* all good dreams," he whispered, "but in the name of holy spirits don't *buy* them. When you buy, you may own something good, but you also own whatever evil those dreams spawned."

"James is not without honor," I said, feeling somehow that I defended myself more than I defended James.

"James is in the thrall of the store," Willie said. "He changes because he has nothing left to lose. And, the store is in the thrall of an elder dream." He cocked his head as if hearing distant voices in the mist. "They sometimes wail at sunrise," he trilled. "Sad spirits call from shallow graves where progress placed them. Oh, this town once produced evil, evil, evil, yes it did."

"But Andrewes only bought and sold—"

"And Andrewes wished to honorably work, and honorably raise children, and honorably grow old, and honorably die. But when a man begins to slide it seems like all creation gets greased up for the occasion. Andrewes became implicated. The store became greater than he. The store became the dream." Willie pointed to cathedral windows aglow with Victorian ideals, and with work of Victorian hands. His face wrenched with a silly smile, but his voice sounded low, bereaved, whispering horror. "And there he sits, there he sits, he sits . . . Andrewes." Willie choked, and pointed to a small space high on one window, a window overlooking the harbor. "See how slowly he works because he is old," Willie said bemused, though still muttering as if through pain. "He is old, old, old, and yet he will never die because his sentence is not death, but dying." Willie continued to point. "Dying, but never dead for as long as dreams that put him there exist."

Like cattle, we do not look up, yet walk beneath the stars. I turned to those windows I have passed for six decades, seeing but not seeing; turned toward glass which held the small, black-suited figure of Able Andrewes, his soul become one with his windows. Andrewes, disappearing, but forever present. The dark figure hunched before an account book. A quill pen moved with glacial slowness, yet moved. About him other figures moved, but glacially.

It is the mist, I told myself, only mist, and knew I lied. Did Mamie know of this, did Swede? How many knew, yet feared to give their knowledge voice? Did James know? And Charles and Edward, working each day beside this grim eternity?

And yes, James knew, but with charity of newly discovered kindness kept quiet.

"Andrewes tends the store," Willie said, "and so does James. The wild carrot, *Daucus carota*, a member of the family Umbelliferae . . ."

I turned from Willie, knowing that I would soon be shaking; knowing also, because I am old, that this horror must soon pass into a greater horror. Andrewes's quill pen moved, although one must concentrate to see it, for the life of the windows breathes slowly; ancient vapors; Victorian men and ladies caught in near stasis between half-known dreams.

And, yes, James knew. I thought of my own daily round, and the rounds of others in this town while understanding James; that master of inventory.

Who walked, I had no doubt, within the holds of sunken ships, and beside skeletons that once knew dreams. James, a creature of the store, inventorying drowned cargo destined for the store. James, a creature stepping always in behalf of the store, stepping more slowly each year; but always stepping. That genius of inventory.

And yes, I knew that all of us are creatures of the store. We bought Andrewes's dream. The store could not have gained such power otherwise. Now a violent circle closes with quiet violence. When the store became the dream, it made the dream immortal. We are trapped. The future becomes a dirge, belling through heat of day and frost of night above the bones of our fathers.

I might have been a prophet instead of a scribbler, or a true historian rather than a recorder of facts. I might not have been lonely. And, my fellow townsmen, what might they have been? No matter. In a way I am not lonely, for all of my townsmen are encased like Andrewes in his stained glass—trapped with less grace than a bee embalmed in amber, for the bee is dead—while we are only, and eternally—dying. Mamie will eternally gossip. Swede will eternally drink. I will eternally sell old dreams as the newspaper prints old news. Able Andrewes, green grocer, will keep accounts. I turned toward the harbor.

The reliable James appeared, walking toward me through mist to become my comrade as we plod through time. From somewhere in the mist Willie hummed a hymn to morning. James stopped before me.

"It isn't so bad," he said quietly. "But it does go on and on." His moist eyes dulled beyond horror, could no longer see horror. For a moment he trembled, thus still knew some emotion. "People do need things," he said, and visibly controlled his trembling, "but I suppose we should warn the children." Then he tasted the futility of his statement. "They wouldn't listen," he said vaguely, and moved toward the store.

I felt not fear, but anger, and the need to strike. It was a loathsome need. No man of honor, no gentleman, could answer this blow with cruelty. When there is nothing left to lose, one must at least answer as James does, with kindness.

Thin sunlight cut the mist, and stained glass windows dulled before me, Gentle Reader; dulled before me like slow movement through slow aeons. There was aught to say except give thanks—thanks—that—at least—you are spared: for surely you are wise, and do not buy other people's dreams. Surely you, unlike we, are not tending the store; are not, because of the store, enthroned by time forever, or, because of the store, forever perishing.

Ride the Thunder

A LOT OF PEOPLE WHO CLAIM NOT TO BELIEVE IN GHOSTS WILL NOT drive 150 above Mount Vernon. They are wrong. There is nothing there. Nothing with eyes gleaming from the roadside, or flickering as it smoothly glides not quite discernible along the fencerows. I know. I pull it now, although the Lexington route is better with the new sections of interstate. I do it because it feels good to know that the going-to-hell old road that carried so many billion tons of trucking is once more clean. The macabre presence that surrounded the road is gone, perhaps fleeing back into smoky valleys in some lost part of the Blue Ridge where haunted fires are said to gleam in great tribal circles and the forest is so thick that no man can make his way through.

Whatever, the road is clean. It can fall into respectable decay under the wheels of farmers bumbling along at 35 in their '53 Chevies.

Or have you driven Kentucky? Have you driven that land that was known as a dark and bloody ground? Because, otherwise you will not know about the mystery that sometimes surrounds those hills, where a mist edges the distant mountain ridges like a memory.

And, you will not know about Joe Indian who used to ride those hills like a curse, booming down out of Indiana or Southern Illinois and bound to Knoxville in an old B-61 that was only running because it was a Mack.

You would see the rig first on 150 around Vincennes in Indiana. Or below Louisville on 64, crying its stuttering wail into the wind and lightning of a river valley storm as it ran under the darkness of electricity-charged air. A picture of desolation riding a road between battered fields, the exhaust shooting coal into the fluttering white load that looked like windswept rags. Joe hauled turkeys. Always turkeys and always white ones. When he was downgrade he rode them at seventy plus. Uphill he rode them at whatever speed the Mack would fetch.

That part was all right. Anyone who has pulled poultry will tell you that you have to ride them. They are packed so tight. You always lose a few. The job is to keep an airstream moving through the cages so they will not suffocate.

But the rest of what Joe Indian did was wrong. He was worse than trash. Men can get used to trash, but Joe bothered guys you would swear could not be bothered by anything in the world. Guys who had seen everything. Twenty years on the road, maybe. Twenty years of seeing people broken by stupidness. Crazy people, torn-up people, drunks. But Joe Indian even bothered guys who had seen all of that. One of the reasons might be that he never drank or did much. He never cared about anything. He just blew heavy black exhaust into load after load of white turkeys.

The rest of what he did was worse. He hated the load. Not the way any man might want to swear over some particular load. No. He hated every one of those turkeys on every load. Hated it personally the way one man might hate another man. He treated the load in a way that showed how much he despised the easy death that was coming to most of those turkeys—the quick needle thrust up the beak into the brain the way poultry is killed commercially. Fast. Painless. The night I saw him close was only a week before the trouble started.

He came into a stop in Harrodsburg. I was out of Tennessee loaded with a special order of upholstered furniture to way and gone up in Michigan and wondering how the factory had ever caught that order. The boss looked sad when I left. That made me feel better. If I had to fight tourists all the way up to the lake instead of my usual Cincinnati run, at least he had to stay behind and build sick furniture. When I came into the stop, I noticed a North Carolina job, one of those straight thirty or thirty-five footers with the attic. He was out of Hickory. Maybe one of the reasons I stopped was because there would be someone there who had about the same kind of trouble. He turned out to be a dark-haired and serious man, one who was very quiet. He had a load of couches on that were made to sell but never, never to use. We compared junk for a while, then looked through the window to see Joe Indian pull in with a truck that looked like a disease.

The Mack sounded bad, but from the appearance of the load it must have found seventy on the downgrades. The load looked terrible at close hand. Joe had cages that were homemade, built from siding of coal company houses when the mines closed down. They had horizontal slats instead of the vertical dowel rod. All you could say of them was that they were sturdy, because you can see the kind of trouble that sort of cage would cause. A bird would shift a little, get a wing tip through the slat and the air stream would do the rest. The Mack came in with between seventy-five and a hundred broken wings fluttering along the sides of the crates. I figured that Joe must own the birds. No one was going to ship like that. When the rig stopped, the wings dropped like dead banners. It was hard to take.

"I know him," the driver who was sitting with me said.

"I know of him," I told the guy, "but nothing good."

"There isn't any, anymore," he said quietly and turned from the window. His face seemed tense. He shifted his chair so that he could see both the door and the restaurant counter. "My cousin," he told me.

I was surprised. The conversation kind of ran out of gas. We did not say anything because we seemed waiting for something. It did not happen.

All that happened was that Joe came in looking like his name.

"Is he really Indian?" I asked.

"Half," his cousin said. "The best half if there is any." Then he stopped talking and I watched Joe. He was dressed like anybody else and needed a haircut. His nose had been broken at one time. His knuckles were enlarged and beat-up. He was tall and rough looking, but there was nothing that you could pin down as unusual in a tough guy except that he wore a hunting knife sheathed and hung on his belt. The bottom of the sheath rode in his back pocket. The hilt was horn. The knife pushed away from his body when he sat at the counter.

He was quiet. The waitress must have known him from before. She just sat coffee in front of him and moved away. If Joe saw the driver beside me he gave no indication. Instead he sat rigid, tensed like a man being chased by something. He looked all set to hit, or yell, or kill if anyone had been stupid enough to slap him on the back and say hello. The restaurant was too quiet. I put a dime in the juke and pressed something just for the noise. Outside came the sound of another rig pulling in. Joe Indian finished his coffee, gulping it. Then he started out and stopped before us. He stared down at the guy beside me.

"Why?" the man said. Joe said nothing. "Because a man may come with thunder does not mean that he can ride the thunder," the driver told him. It made no sense. "A man is the thunder," Joe said. His voice sounded like the knife looked. He paused for a moment then went out. His rig did not pull away for nearly ten minutes. About the time it was in the roadway another driver came in angry and half-scared. He headed for the counter. We waved him over. He came, glad for some attention.

"Jesus," he said.

"An old trick," the guy beside me told him.

"What?" I asked.

"Who is he?" The driver was shaking his head.

"Not a truck driver. Just a guy who happens to own a truck."

"But how come he did that." The driver's voice sounded shaky.

"Did what?" I asked. They were talking around me.

The first guy, Joe's cousin, turned to me. "Didn't you ever see him trim a load?"

"What!"

"Truck's messy," the other driver said. "That's what he was saying. Messy. Messy." The man looked half-sick.

I looked at them still wanting explanation. His cousin told me. "Claims he likes neat cages. Takes that knife and goes around the truck cutting the wings he can reach . . . just enough. Never cuts them off, just enough so they rip off in the air stream."

"Those are live," I said.

"Uh huh."

It made me mad. "One of these days he'll find somebody with about thirty-eight calibers of questions."

"Be shooting around that knife," his cousin told me. "He probably throws better than you could handle a rifle."

"But why . . ." It made no sense.

"A long story," his cousin said. "And I've got to be going." He stood up. "Raised in a coal camp," he told us. "That isn't his real name, but his mother was full Indian. His daddy shot coal. Good money. So when Joe was a kid he was raised Indian, trees, plants, animals, mountains, flowers, men . . . all brothers. His ma was religious. When he became 16 he was raised coal miner white. Figure it out." He turned to go.

"Drive careful," I told him, but he was already on his way. Before the summer was out Joe Indian was dead. But by then all of the truck traffic was gone from 150. The guys were routing through Lexington. I did not know at first because of trouble on the Michigan run. Wheel bearings in Sault Ste. Marie to help out the worn compressor in Grand Rapids. Furniture manufacturers run their lousy equipment to death. They expect every cube to run on bicycle maintenance. I damned the rig, but the woods up there were nice with stands of birch that jumped up white and luminous in the headlights. The lake and straits were good. Above Traverse City there were not as many tourists. But, enough. In the end I was pushing hard to get back. When I hit 150 it took me about twenty minutes to realize that I was the only truck on the road. There were cars. I learned later that the thing did not seem to work on cars. By then it had worked on me well enough that I could not have cared less.

Because I started hitting animals. Lots of animals. Possum, cat, rabbit, coon, skunk, mice, even birds and snakes . . . at night . . . with the moon tacked up there behind a thin and swirling cloud cover. The animals started marching, looking up off the road into my lights and running right under the wheels.

Not one of them thumped!

I rode into pack after pack and there was no thump, no crunch, no feeling of the soft body being pressed and torn under the drive axle. They marched from the shoulder into the lights, disappeared under the wheels and it was like running through smoke. At the roadside, even crowding the shoulder, larger eyes gleamed from nebulous shapes that moved slowly back. Not frightened, just like they were letting you through. And you knew that none of them were real. And you knew that your eyes told you they were there. It was like running through smoke, but the smoke was in dozens of familiar and now horrible forms. I tried not to look. It did not work. Then I tried looking hard. That worked too well, especially when I cut on the spot to cover the shoulder and saw forms that were not men and were not animals but seemed something of both. Alien. Alien. I was afraid to slow. Things flew at the windshields and bounced off without a splat. It lasted for ten miles. Ordinarily it takes about seventeen minutes to do those ten miles. I did it in eleven or twelve. It seemed like a year. The stop was closed in Harrodsburg. I found an all-night diner, played the juke, drank coffee, talked to a waitress who acted like I was trying to pick her up, which would have been a compliment . . . just anything to feel normal. When I went back to the truck I locked the doors and climbed into the sleeper. The truth is I was afraid to go back on that road.

So I tried to sleep instead and lay there seeing that road stretching out like an avenue to nowhere, flanked on each side by trees so that a man thought of a high speed tunnel. Then somewhere between dream and imagination I began to wonder if that road really did end at night. For me. For anybody. I could see in my mind how a man might drive that road and finally come into something like a tunnel, high beams rocketing along walls that first were smooth then changed like the pillared walls of a mine with timber shoring on the sides. But not in the middle. I could see a man driving down, down at sixty or seventy, driving deep towards the center of the earth and knowing that it was a mine. Knowing that there was a rock face at the end of the road but the man unable to get his foot off the pedal. And then the thoughts connected and I knew that Joe Indian was the trouble with the road, but I did not know why or how. I was shaking and cold. In the morning it was not so bad. The movement was still there but it was dimmed out in daylight. You caught it in flashes. I barely made Mount Vernon, where I connected with 25. The trouble stopped there. When I got home I told some lies and took a week off. My place is out beyond Lafollette, where you can live with a little air and woods around you. For a while I was nearly afraid to go into those woods.

When I returned to the road it was the Cincinnati run all over with an occasional turn to Indianapolis. I used the Lexington route and watched the other guys. They were all keeping quiet. The only people who were talking were the police who were trying to figure out the sudden shift in traffic. Everybody who had been the route figured if they talked about it, everyone else would think they were crazy. You would see a driver you knew and say hello. Then the two of you would sit and talk about the weather. When truckers stop talking about trucks and the road something is wrong.

I saw Joe once below Livingston on 25. His rig looked the same as always. He was driving full out like he was asking to be pulled over. You could run at speed on 150. Not on 25. Maybe he was asking for it, kind of hoping it would happen so that he would be pulled off the road for a while. Because a week after that and a month after the trouble started I heard on the grapevine that Joe was dead.

Killed, the word had it, by ramming over a bank on 150 into a stream. Half of his load had drowned. The other half suffocated. Cars had driven past the scene for two or three days, the drivers staring straight down the road like always. No one paid enough attention to see wheel marks that left the road and over the bank.

What else the story said was not good and maybe not true. I tried to dismiss it and kept running 25. The summer was dwindling away into fall, the oak and maple on those hills were beginning to change. I was up from Knoxville one night and saw the North Carolina job sitting in front of a stop. No schedule would have kept me from pulling over. I climbed down and went inside.

For a moment I did not see anyone I recognized, then I looked a second time and saw Joe's cousin. He was changed. He sat at a booth. Alone. He was slumped like an old man. When I walked up he looked at me with eyes that seemed to see past or through me. He motioned me to the other side of the booth. I saw that his hands were shaking.

"What?" I asked him, figuring that he was sick or had just had a close one.

"Do you remember that night?" he asked me. No lead up. Talking like a man who had only one thing on his mind. Like a man who could only talk about one thing.

"Yes," I told him, "and I've heard about Joe." I tried to lie. I could not really say that I was sorry.

"Came With Thunder," his cousin told me. "That was his other name, the one his mother had for him. He was born during an August storm."

I looked at the guy to see if he was kidding. Then I remembered that Joe was killed in August. It made me uneasy.

"I found him," Joe's cousin told me. "Took my car and went looking after he was three days overdue. Because . . . I knew he was driving that road . . . trying to prove something."

"What? Prove what?"

"Hard to say. I found him hidden half by water, half by trees and the brush that grows up around there. He might have stayed on into the winter if someone hadn't looked." The man's hands were shaking. I told him to wait, walked over and brought back two coffees. When I sat back down he continued.

"It's what I told you. But, it has to be more than that. I've been studying and studying. Something like this . . . always is." He paused and drank the coffee, holding the mug in both hands.

"When we were kids," the driver said, "we practically lived at each other's house. I liked his best. The place was a shack. Hell, my place was a shack. Miners made money then, but it was all scrip. They spent it for everything but what they needed." He paused, thoughtful. Now that he was telling the story he did not seem so nervous.

"Because of his mother," he continued. "She was Indian. Creek maybe, but west of Creek country. Or maybe from a northern tribe that drifted down. Not Cherokee because their clans haven't any turkeys for totems or names that I know of . . . ."

I was startled. I started to say something.

"Kids don't think to ask about stuff like that," he said. His voice was an apology as if he were wrong for not knowing the name of a tribe.

"Makes no difference anyway," he said. "She was Indian religious and she brought Joe up that way because his old man was either working or drinking. We all three spent a lot of time in the hills talking to the animals, talking to flowers . . ."

"What?"

"They do that. Indians do. They think that life is round like a flower. They think animals are not just animals. They are brothers. Everything is separate like people."

I still could not believe that he was serious. He saw my look and seemed discouraged, like he had tried to get through to people before and had not had any luck.

"You don't understand," he said. "I mean that dogs are not people, they are dogs. But each dog is important because he has a dog personality the same as a man has a man personality."

"That makes sense," I told him. "I've owned dogs. Some silly. Some serious. Some good. Some bad."

"Yes," he said. "But, most important. When he dies a dog has a dog spirit the same way a man would have a man spirit. That's what Joe was brought up to believe."

"But they kill animals for food," I told him.

"That's true. It's one of the reasons for being an animal . . . or maybe, even a man. When you kill an animal you are supposed to apologize to the animal's spirit and explain you needed meat."

"Oh."

"You don't get it," he said. "I'm not sure I do either but there was a time . . . anyway, it's not such a bad way to think if you look at it close. But the point is Joe believed it all his life. When he got out on his own and saw the world he couldn't believe it anymore. You know? A guy acting like that. People cause a lot of trouble being stupid and mean."

"I know."

"But he couldn't quite not believe it either. He had been trained every day since he was born, and I do mean every day."

"Are they that religious?"

"More than any white man I ever knew. Because they live it instead of just believe it. You can see what could happen to a man?"

"Not quite."

"Sure you can. He couldn't live in the camp anymore because the camp was dead when the mines died through this whole region. He had to live outside so he had to change, but a part of him couldn't change . . . then his mother died. Tuberculosis. She tried Indian remedies and died. But I think she would have anyway."

I could see what the guy was driving at.

"He was proving something," the man told me. "Started buying and hauling the birds. Living hand to mouth. But, I guess every time he tore one up it was just a little more hate working out of his system."

"A hell of a way to do it."

"That's the worst part. He turned his back on the whole thing, getting revenge. But always, down underneath, he was afraid."

"Why be afraid?" I checked the clock. Then I looked at the man. There was a fine tremble returning to his hands.

"Don't you see," he told me. "He still halfway believed. And if a man could take revenge, animals could take revenge. He was afraid of the animals helping their brothers." The guy was sweating. He looked at me and there was fear in his eyes. "They do, you know. I'm honest-to-God afraid that they do."

"Why?"

"When he checked out missing I called the seller, then called the process outfit where he sold. He was three days out on a one day run. So I went looking and found him." He watched me. "The guys aren't driving that road."

"Neither am I," I told him. "For that matter, neither are you."

"It's all right now," he said. "There's nothing left on that road. Right outside of Harrodsburg, down that little grade and then take a hook left up the hill, and right after you top it . . ."

"I've driven it."

"Then you begin to meet the start of the hill country. Down around the creek I found him. Fifty feet of truck laid over in the creek and not an ounce of metal showing to the road. Water washing through the cab. Load tipped but a lot of it still tied down. All dead of course."

"A mess."

"Poultry rots quick," was all he said.

"How did it happen?"

"Big animal," he told me. "Big like a cow or a bull or a bear . . . There wasn't any animal around. You know what a front end looks like. Metal to metal doesn't make that kind of dent. Flesh."

"The stream washed it away."

"I doubt. It eddies further down. There hasn't been that much rain. But he hit something . . ."

I was feeling funny. "Listen, I'll tell you the truth. On that road I hit everything. If a cow had shown up I'd have run through it, I guess. Afraid to stop. There wouldn't have been a bump."

"I know," he told me. "But Joe bumped. That's the truth. Hard enough to take him off the road. I've been scared. Wondering. Because what he could not believe I can't believe either. It does not make sense, it does not . . ."

He looked at me. His hands were trembling hard.

"I waded to the cab," he said. "Waded out there. Careful of sinks. The smell of the load was terrible. Waded out to the cab hoping it was empty and knowing damned well that it wasn't. And I found him."

"How?"

"Sitting up in the cab sideways with the water swirling around about shoulder height and . . . Listen, maybe you'd better not hear. Maybe you don't want to."

"I didn't wait this long not to hear," I told him.

"Sitting there with the bone handle of the knife tacked to his front where he had found his heart . . . or something, and put it in. Not in time though. Not in time."

"You mean he was hurt and afraid of drowning?"

"Not a mark on his body except for the knife. Not a break where, but his face . . . sitting there, leaning into that knife and hair all gone, chewed away. Face mostly gone, lips, ears, eyelids all gone. Chewed away, scratched away. I looked, and in the opening that had been his mouth something moved like disappearing down a hole . . . but, in the part of the cab that wasn't submerged there was a thousand footprints, maybe a thousand different animals . . . ."

His voice broke. I reached over and steadied him by the shoulder. "What was he stabbing?" the man asked. "I can't figure. Himself, or . . ."

I went to get more coffee for us and tried to make up something that would help him out. One thing I agreed with that he had said. I agreed that I wished he had not told me.

The Ghost of Dive Bomber Hill

Dead men at the bottom,
A roller-coaster ride,
Smoke 'em if you got 'em,
then hang a right and glide,
with fifty thousand gross . . .
and slide . . .

HEADED NORTH FROM KNOXVILLE, TRUCKS CROSSED INTO KENTUCKY just above Jellico and below Corbin. The road ran two-lane and thin. That was "back then." Today I-75 carries the load out of Tennessee to Louisville.

Bessie has passed into the mists of time, although she lies buried on a rise above Dive Bomber Hill. Her house used to stand where now lies her grave. Her girls have moved away.

But the ghost still wanders the Hill. These days tired farmers see him, or he's seen by highschool kids who get the kind of drunk that mostly happens in places where, each election, bootleggers and preachers get together and vote the county dry. The ghost now seems a little lost, and still beholden to the living. No matter how successful he was in life, he made some big mistakes as a ghost. These days he's got no visible use except to waken tired drivers, or sober up a bunch of fool kids who think they'll live forever, and end up dying in droves.

Dive Bomber Hill hasn't changed. It still runs two-lane and thin. An occasional tractor-trailer still moves along Highway 25 between Corbin and Mount Vernon. The rig rolls beside narrow shoulders, deep ditches and sharp hillsides. Northbound, it labors like a red or yellow smudge through foresty hill country, green in summer, gold in fall, and stark in wet winters. The truck's stacks generally smoke from fouling injectors, and it puffs gray or black on upshifts. When the grade drops hard, the jake causes cracks like rifle shots. Hardwood trees are bright in autumn and creeks still run. The land is alive with deer, varmints and birds.

At the crest of Dive Bomber Hill the driver hangs a right and, whoops, over she goes.

It's a two-lane, mile-long drop with a two hundred-yard flat space in the middle. That long flat space once held Bessie's place, fair-sized restaurant whitewashed, bunkhouse, and a graveled parking lot filled with tractor-trailers. Young trees grow there now.

Coming off the flat space, the road plummets to a short steel bridge that rattles like chattering teeth beneath the tandem. Through the windshield what appears is the shear side of a mountain, a rock face. The road hangs a 90° to the left and points up the next set of hills. What used to happen . . . don't try this at home . . . don't try it on Dive Bomber Hill, either.

Dry freight haulers, and only them because no other type of rig had the right suspension, would hold back a handful of rpms as they crossed that bridge heading at the rock face. Speed, 50 to 60. As they came to the hard left they jerked their wheel left, then right, then left, and goosed out the last thin line of power. The trailer picked up and actually walked across the road, dancing like a truck practicing ballet.

That meant the driver could find himself starting to climb the next hill at 45 or 50. If the curve was driven according to all rules of sanity, he would find himself hitting that grade at only 20. How fast you can approach a grade makes a big difference on a hilly run, especially when you've got a dispatcher who thinks of the world as flat lines on a road map.

A man had to be on his game. Drivers not on their game produced some of the most godawful wrecks and bloody corpses the road has ever seen. Unless, of course, the rig burned. Either way, the guy and truck were pancaked . . . the grim joke being, "Anyone want to buy a tall, thin Kenworth?"

Then, one night, the ghost showed up and there were no more wrecks. Drunks still ran off the road and tumbled down the mountain. Trucks still sometimes ended up in ditches, but that rock face never again took another truck. Could be, it just could be, that the ghost knew he was going to have to pay off a debt.

The ghost knew drivers and their feelings. He seemed to know us better than we knew ourselves. For instance, sometimes a man didn't know whether he was on his game or not. When that happened, and he rolled away from Bessie's, the driver looked for the ghost to appear, lanky, sad-looking and gray as mist. Gray but luminous. The ghost dressed country-style but knew trucking. Under mist or moonlight, he always looked the same; thin face below white hair, the face stern as a ticked-off preacher.

The ghost would do one of two things: he would roll his hand in circles, the old road signal for "road clear ahead so roll 'em." Or he would pat the air, palm downward, like he petted an invisible dog, the old road sign for "slow it down." When he did that we would take his warning and drive like pussycats.

We: Jimbo, Mick and Luke-the-Apostle. I'm Mick, Jimbo is a wop . . . a skinny little ginny with ravioli eyes . . . and Luke, a Christian, but couldn't seem to help it. He didn't drink, smoke, chase loose women (although some chased him), cuss, gamble or do anything interesting except be a lay preacher on Sundays. He was sort of off in his own cathedral-type world. Me? As the saying goes, kiss me, I'm Irish.

Our trucks were '47 White Mustangs, six years old, engine rebuild at half-a-million, but lean and beautiful. They packed five-over transmissions that would keep a guy working in the hills. Men swore that the seat was nothing but a board and seat covers. They were a tough truck, in tough territory, what with hills and hijackings; both of which happened. And, it was a sure bet that unless the schedule was totally shot, on every run those trucks would, soon or late, be found parked at Bessie's . . .

She was in her early fifties and just beautiful. Even the youngest cowboy who ever strutted slowed down and looked. Bessie was a little plumpish, with little-bitty face wrinkles, and always wearing a spiffy housedress. Mostly her dresses were flowery, sometimes plain and decorated with flower-pins. Her three daughters took turns "doing" Bessie's silvery hair. What made her beautiful, though, was how she made a man feel. The minute you walked into her place you just naturally felt peaceful. For one thing, you had to hand your gun to one of the girls. She hid it behind punch-boards over the sink.

Get seated at the counter and knots in the shoulders relaxed, the back didn't ache so much because the kidneys weren't bouncing, and it was like sitting around a country kitchen with country people. Guys talked civilized with no cussing. I've actually seen guys sit and help snap green beans. It's hard to say, even now, if we showed up because of Bessie's daughters or because Bessie's place felt like the home we wished we had.

The girls, so help me God, were named Molly and May and Mary, with Molly being dark-haired, blue-eyed, and cute, May also dark-haired and cutting a fine figure, but more-or-less modest. Mary was quietly pretty. She had the brains in the family; bright, strawberry blonde, and sometimes a smarty mouth. The girls also dressed in clean and pressed housedresses, flower prints, and with their hair fixed like ready-for-church. Without meaning to, they were more attractive, and a lot more sexy, than any of the hookers on each end of the Knoxville/Louisville run.

In the days before CB radios news along the road traveled by truck. If there was a race riot in Detroit, people in Alabama knew about it before radio reporters had time to digest the news. Plus, it wasn't only news. Truckers, some of them, are awful gossips. If a man didn't know better he'd swear that b.s. never existed before the invention of trucks.

We heard about trouble at Bessie's while pulled over in the truck stop just south of Indianapolis. August heat lay flat across cornfields. Asphalt in the parking lot bubbled. Steam rose from ditches.

We'd been rerouted to pick up loads. Rigs ranged along the ready-line; Mayflower Fords, Roadway (roadhog) Express kicking Internationals (known as Binders), a few bright Reos here and there, Jimmys, Diamond T's, an occasional Marmon-Harrington; all in road colors of red, orange, yellow.

"You're an honest man," Jimbo-the-Wop told another driver. "You wouldn't be flippin' bullshit?" Jimbo took it serious. He sat small, muscular, sniffin' suspicious with an Italian beak that had already been busted one time in a fight. His hands were callused and scarred like everybody else.

"I was there," the driver said. "I saw it happen." The guy was short, built like a fireplug, and capable.

We sat before cups of coffee. The place in no way resembled Bessie's. Like most truck stops the counter was three-sided, with kitchen at back. Guys looked across at each other. The design allowed management to overwork its waitress while keeping the boys happy, more or less. It all depended on, was the coffee fresh? Did the waitress look like someone you might have dreamed of, once?

"Turned out there was this old guy at Bessie's, must-a been sitting off to himself. Seemed familiar when we finally saw him. Seemed kind of gray and quiet." The driver paused, like he just knew he was about to be accused of bullshit. "You guys ever see anything on that road? Night stuff?"

"Who doesn't?" Luke said. He talked soft in the hubbub of the restaurant. The jukebox sobbed away on Truck Gypsy Blues, ". . . chasin' that lonesome road . . ."

Everybody sees night stuff. Luke calls them visions, I call them hallucinations, and Jimbo calls them hangovers. Different stuff appears on the road, and not just ghosts. Luke sees angels, I see animals that aren't there, Jimbo sees barns in the middle of the road with doors opening to let him through.

"So," the driver said, "some guys claim they see a gray ghost tellin' them what to do."

"We've heard about it," I said, admitting nothing.

"Suppose there is a ghost," the driver said, "and suppose one night he walked up to Bessie's like any normal man. Does that sound right? That don't sound right."

From what the guy said, we learned that three plowboys from London, Kentucky had showed up mid-week, the week before. They'd been drunk, passing out crap, busted a chair and propositioned the girls, treating them like whores. They left the minute Bessie phoned the sheriff.

"So everybody's sitting there," the driver said. "Minding our manners, mindin' our own business. This gray guy ain't at the counter. He's maybe off in one corner at a table. Then these three sodbusters who didn't learn nothin' show up again. They're drunk and drivin' a crapcrate '41 Buick.

"The very minute they come through the door, Bessie starts moving. She takes a broom like she's gonna sweep those boys right into an outhouse . . . one of the damn fools makes a mistake. Instead of running he raises his arm against the broom. Bessie gets kind of bumped, falls back against a wall."

"Who's in jail?" Jimbo was believing the story. He no longer had doubts.

"I assume that one or more is dead." Luke didn't look like an apostle, really. He looked like somebody who ought to be running a hardware store. Just a quiet, smart guy with thinning hair.

The south has a few things to answer for, but it also has good things going. Nobody hits a woman, or if they do they get dealt with. Sometimes, some sorry fool is stupid enough to hit a woman in the presence of real men. It was damn near a death sentence in older days, and maybe it's changed, but I wish it was the same way now.

"Nine, maybe ten guys on their feet right away," the driver said. "We chased those bastards to their junk car. Just as the driver got the engine started this gray guy shows up. I admit to bein' scared, somewhat." The driver's hand actually shook when he raised his coffee mug. The coffee slopped a little.

"This gray guy, outta nowhere, stands beside the car and there's this spic driver steps up beside him; Spaniard or Mex, or some such-a damn thing. The spic reaches through the open window. He grabs the driver's hair and jerks the head down against the doorframe. Then he lays a knife, honest to god, longer than your wanger, across this hayseed's throat."

"Okay, so far." Jimbo liked it.

"And then," the driver claimed, "the damn Spaniard starts out preaching woe about killin' bulls and visitations and general horseshit."

"It wasn't," Luke said real quiet-like. "What you're saying sounds like Jeremiah. Jeremiah 50:27."

It always seemed strange, talking about the Kentucky hills while surrounded by civilized Indiana, which is as flat as a political promise. In the busy truckstop rigs roared off the ready-line, and there were rattles of air tools from the shops. Guys in the restaurant slugged five-cent coffee from thick mugs while they told stories about themselves being heroes.

". . . sounded like horseshit to me," the driver said. "And the spic kept it up. The other guys stood, the whole bunch of us, watching and listening for maybe ten minutes and not able to do squat. Ever' time the spic made a point in his sermon he'd bang the hayseed's head agin' the doorframe, 'til the bastard wasn't just scared but sober. Ended with talking about evil and upright and bloodthirsty . . ."

"Proverbs 29:10," Luke murmured. "Most likely."

"And then," the driver said, "he drew that knife light across that throat, just enough to bleed. And then he gave the guy's head one more bounce, and let go the hair. And that Buick got out of there, throwin' gravel all the way to Miss-i-friggin'-ssippi."

"And nobody dead." Jimbo sounded indignant.

"Not unless the hayseed bled to death, which I gotta doubt." The driver gulped his coffee. "Then the Spaniard says, 'Mother-of-God, what happened? Did that shit come out of my mouth? I don't talk that way.' The Spaniard wiped the knife on his pants leg and looked toward the gray guy, and the gray guy wasn't there. And the spic says, 'Damn farmer wasn't worth goin' to jail over. How come you guys didn't stop it?'"

The driver tossed a tip on the counter and stood. "Turnin' St. Looie." Then he paused. "The thing is, there was a bunch of guys there, and that meant a bunch of guns behind the punch boards. Nary a one of us thought to go get one." He shook his head like he couldn't believe the memory. "And we watched the Buick leave, and then looked around and the gray guy still wasn't there, and the spic was still sore at us." He started toward the doorway.

"Keep it between the fence posts," I told him as he left.

=

The outfit we drove for tried to keep its trucks running in groups of three. Driving the hills of Kentucky and West Virginia was no joke back then. Trucks that got hijacked were generally whiskey or tobacco haulers, but dry freight or swinging beef was fair game. Our outfit figured that a lone truck was a target, but three together were safe. Nice idea on paper, but hard to make work on the road. On the turn-around headed south, we generally held pretty close together until Frankfort, Kentucky, where a long, long grade leads out of town. The truck stop on top of that hill not only had walls of the can painted gleamy white, it supplied crayons so guys could write graffiti; most of which was on the order of, "Goddamn my truck."

Jimbo always led, Luke second, me at the rear pretending to supervise. When we got into the hills our little convoy fell apart. The only way anybody ever caught up to Jimbo was if some farmer in a '41 Chevrolet got ahead of him, 40 downhill and 30 up. Lots of times, though, another trucker, well ahead of that slow farmer, could see a clear road. He would give a road sign. Jimbo would catch the farmer on a curve. Even some country boys would give you a road sign when they could see clear road and you couldn't.

I trusted the judgment of truckers, didn't trust the country boys. Jimbo took chances with the country boys. He figured if they misjudged, and he got caught looking at oncoming traffic, he could always whip his trailer to the right. He would run the screw-up off the road.

The sum of it was that Jimbo always sat at Bessie's, licking away on his second cup of coffee by the time Luke pulled in, and his third cup of coffee by the time I got there. Made no difference whether summer or winter, we'd all three have wet armpits from busting gears through the hills. And, we'd all three be as tense as a rabbit with a case of the hots.

The parking lot was long and narrow, and when I pulled in there wasn't a ready-line. A gasoline Binder hauling for North American sat toward the end of the lot. Shadows reached toward it, with an August sundown sitting atop the western hills. A flashy new Ford convertible sat behind the Binder. Jimbo's rig sat beside the Ford, engine rumbling. Hot diesels were hell to start. The drill back then was to lock the doors and leave 'em idling. Luke's rig sat behind Jimbo. I set my rig square behind Luke. When I climbed down I was looking directly at the bunkhouse.

It looked abandoned, and was. After WWII trucking had changed. The country could run a war using mostly railroads, but peace caused a need for trucks like nobody had ever believed, and the trucks were getting snazzy. Sleeper cabs replaced bunkhouses.

This had once been a fair-sized bunkhouse, maybe six cots. Now it sat as whitewashed as Bessie's place, but with dusty windows and a padlock on the door. Decaying sunlight shone onto, or into, the dust, and it seemed like there was movement inside. Couldn't be. Seemed to be. Couldn't be. I peered through a dusty window. Nothing. The place was zipped up tighter than the Pope's skivvies.

I crossed the lot to Bessie's and expected Jimbo to be shooting a bunch of bull, depending on which one of the daughters had the counter. With Molly or May, Jimbo was just full of it. He didn't try tales with Mary, because Mary could answer up faster than an alderman. When I got inside, though, and laid my .38 on the counter, Jimbo sat and stared into his coffee cup. The jukebox complained that there was more rain in the road than there was in the sky. Something was wrong. Something dark.

Mary had the counter. The North American driver sat next to Jimbo on one side, Luke on the other. The guy flogging the Ford sat two stools down. Nobody sat at tables, not even that shaded table over in the corner of the room. Or maybe not. There was a little touch of mist over there, like tobacco smoke had collected.

"You're of a marrying age," the North American guy said to Mary. "But are you of a marrying disposition?"

"I think of it not a little," she said, "and a man could do a world full of worse." She glanced toward Luke. Luke blushed. Out there in the parking lot Luke's truck sat registered for fifty-six thousand gross, a truck that could pull the top off a mountain. It was a truck that ran through every kind of weather and every kind of trouble. It was a truck that could only be touched by a full-grown man who was no fool. And, yet, Luke, who was surely full-grown, blushed. Okay. Something going on between them. Maybe Luke spent Saturday nights here, not Knoxville. More than a case of the hots. More like a case of the quivers.

The North American guy picked up. "In which case," he said, "I'm a mite too late." He stood, paid for pie and coffee. He didn't ask Mary for his gun which meant he didn't have one. Furniture guys didn't really need them.

"Keep the rubber side down," Jimbo told him. Jimbo still stared into his coffee cup. He didn't make a move until he heard the North American roar into life and pull away. The dark feeling still covered the room. Windows across the front of the building let in light, but the light seemed defeated.

"Something," Jimbo said, "somethin's going on. Somebody's trying to sandbag this poor dago." He looked toward the guy with the Ford convertible.

"Could be," the guy said, "that it's none of your gaddam bidness." The guy was one of those turning-to-fat heavyweights. He had piggy eyes, and tried to dress city. Checkered pants, narrow suspenders. He looked like a chubby pimp or a used car salesman.

"Could be," Luke said quietly, "that it's some of mine." Luke might look like a hardware store owner, but didn't sound like one. In the south you don't worry when a guy starts yelling. You worry when a voice goes quiet and calm.

"Could be," Mary told the local guy, "that one claim-jumping deputy is in over his frowzy head." To Luke, she said, "Take it easy." She turned and headed quick for the kitchen. When she came back she was followed by May who took the counter. May looked onto the parking lot. "Furniture haulers," she said about the North American guy. "Gypsies. You hardly ever see them twice." She sounded almost wistful.

"Bring your coffee," Mary told Luke. "We'll sit in your truck and talk."

I watched them walk outside, both shy as teenagers on a first date. Waves of heat rose from the road, but was nothing compared to the heat between them. Mary could not have been more than twenty-two and Luke maybe five years older. And both of them virgins, most likely. I wanted to tsk, thought better of it; wanted to laugh, thought better of it.

"Start any bullshit," May told Jimbo, "and I turn you into wop soup." She grinned as she said it. "You could, I reckon, spread just a little."

Jimbo turned to look out the windows. Luke and Mary were still walking to Luke's truck, but now they were holding hands. "What's she want with Luke? Preachers ain't no fun."

"He's smart," May said. "And she's smart. I got the looks, she got the brains. She'll marry a preacher or a teacher, or something. I'll end up with somebody like you." She was right about the looks. May had hair nearly to her waist, but done up high. She had full lips, blue eyes, a smile that could soften rocks. Her figure was like in Esquire magazine, and her sass like Sophie Tucker.

The heavyweight stood up. Looked at May. Looked at me and Jimbo. Made a decision. "I'll be back," he said. "Tell your ma." He headed for the door.

"Coffee's on the house, you cheap bastard." May sounded just a little hysteric.

The guy turned, reached in his pocket for change, thought better of it when he looked at Jimbo, and left.

"Don't go nowhere," May told us. She reached behind the punchboards. "Keep 'em hid. Ma's got a rule and I'm breakin' it."

My .38 was a snub nose. Not hard to conceal.

"Don't go nowhere until another truck comes in. We got no man around this house. Not always." She looked toward the dark corner of the room. Looked through the window toward Luke's truck. "Our daddy was a preacher, and we miss him," she said about Mary. "I expect that's why she's attracted." She turned toward the kitchen. "Fatso is gone."

Movement in the kitchen. Molly showed up, little and cute like a colleen. Lots of Scots-Irish people in these hills. I kept watching the clock and wondered just how far off schedule this would take us.

"Get ma?" Molly sounded like she didn't know whether to be afraid, or get so mad she'd stomp her foot.

"Not now," May told her. "Bully-boys are cowards. He'll wait."

"We're losing minutes," I mentioned. "At least let us know what's up." Through the windows, where dusk already lay across the lot, I could see Luke and Mary walking back from the truck. They walked slow and somewhat pretty.

"We had some drunks run out of here," May told Jimbo while ignoring me. "One got a little bit cut and bleedy. He's the brother of a deputy. The fat boy is another brother, only in construction. He fills potholes for the state. Quite a family." She didn't say more because Luke and Mary came through the doorway.

"Brush your hair, missy," Molly told Mary. Molly couldn't be more than eighteen, but bossy. Mary looked rumpled, Luke looked flustered. Maybe a good bit had happened in that truck, but it was clear everybody kept their pants on.

Luke blushed, Jimbo chuckled, Molly fussed, May winked, Mary brushed, and I turned to the windows when I heard a downshift coming off the hill. A new Mack pulling propane eased onto the lot.

"Pete," May said about the propane driver. She turned to me. "Thanks, guys. Keep it out of the ditches."

Luke was whispering to Mary. "Get rollin'," I told him. We passed the propane driver on our way out.

I figured we were free and clear and not too far off schedule, but figured wrong. The ghost appeared at the top of the hill which surely meant something wasn't right. He'd never appeared all the way at top. This time he gave the road sign for "trouble ahead," the hi-sign; right hand stretched forward, palm out, fingers spread. We took him serious since there was a deputy in the neighborhood.

Sheriffs didn't bother truckers. Sheriffs were elected and needed friends. Truckers spent a lot of money in poor areas. Sheriffs didn't want to get a bad name for running away business.

State cops didn't bother truckers, unless the guy was weaving. They always allowed at least fifteen percent over the limit. State cops were trained.

It was deputies that caused trouble. They were usually young punks who worked cheap, because a red flasher and a badge made them feel like their ding-dong was longer.

This red flasher showed up right away. Sunlight had decayed to twilight, and shadows lay long across the road. The punk came wailing past me in a '50 Mercury, siren yelling high and thin against those forested hills. He pulled in between Luke and Jimbo.

Jimbo flipped his marker lights four or five times, which, knowing Jimbo, told me he was ready to start something; if I was. He eased to the shoulder which was none too wide. The deputy pulled in behind him. Luke pulled in behind the deputy.

I admit to some impatience. Instead of pulling in behind Luke, I stopped right in the roadway beside the Merc. The Merc sat boxed between three trucks, and three drivers who weren't expressin' a hell of a lot of charity.

I didn't even climb down. Just waited for the punk. He came around the front of Luke's rig, already losing his nerve. If he'd been in control he wouldn't yell. He looked to be late 20s, but already had bad teeth. His hat must be minus a sweatband because it was sopping. He had greasy hair hanging out below the hat, the hair all straggly around his ears. He vaguely resembled the Fatso guy who'd been flogging the new Ford. He started yelling at me to clear the roadway.

I spoke low and slow and pleasant enough. I told him that if I moved my rig it would be to push that frickin' Mercury off the berm and down the mountain.

His pistol was in his holster. He touched it, looked around, saw Jimbo out of his truck. The guy considered the odds, thought better of it.

"Stopped you 'cause there's construction," he muttered. "Road's busted up at the county line."

"Appreciate it," I told him. "Nice to know a man who takes care of working guys." No sense pushing it.

He turned and stomped away. We pulled out, rolling Knoxville.

=

Pull the rig over, shut it down, let the warehouse guys have it, and sleep. It wasn't until day after, waking up for another Louisville turn, that we heard of a dead Fatso, though at first we couldn't be sure. All we were sure of was that August had turned to September, and there'd be more ground mist in the hills.

Jimbo and I sat in the ready room with our rigs on the ready-line. We waited for Luke. Eleven at night. The road would be good for the first hour, get knotty in the second, and by two a.m. the drunks would all be off the road. The best hours are two to five when the only trouble is a deer or a razorback hog. Hogs are just short enough to get under the front axle, and tall enough to roll the truck. Rather hit a deer. Rather hit a bull. Rather not hit nothin'.

A driver came into the ready room looking for coffee. His shirt was dark with sweat. His eyes were somewhat benzedrined but not too eggy. Just a tired guy after a long haul.

"Anything worth knowing?" Jimbo asked it, but either of us might. You could only get road information from other drivers. This guy looked like a thousand tired guys I've seen. He poured coffee and sat on a ratty couch with peeling imitation leather. The walls of the ready room were institution-green, and his complexion about the same.

"One-a these days," he said, "I'm gonna buy a little store. I'm gonna sit on my sweet behind and sell all kinds of shit to truck drivers. I might even get married." He stretched, yawned. "Naw, that could maybe be pushing it." He licked away at the cup of coffee he surely didn't need. Habit.

"Helluva wreck," he said, "up by London. Ford ragtop tumbling down the mountain like Jacky and his girlfriend Jill."

"That Fatso guy?" Jimbo looked at me.

"Don't know who it was," the driver said. "Last I heard, they were still trying to figure a way of prying it off of him."

"One a week . . ." It was a road saying. It meant that if you drove for a living, you'd see at least one fatal accident every week. Cars were not well suspended. Roads were narrow, speed limits high.

"Woe betide." Jimbo couldn't help spreading b.s. He looked to the doorway where Luke had just entered. Luke looked like a guy who had been up half the night listening to a complaining wife. He wasn't bleary-eyed, but if it had been anybody except Luke I wouldn't have trusted him. He looked worn to a nub.

"If you wasn't drinkin' and smokin' and speakin' bad words and runnin' around with trollops . . ." Jimbo saw that flippin' it wasn't going to work. "What's happening?"

"I've been up to Bessie's," Luke said, real quiet. "I've got to get her out of there."

"Bessie?" Jimbo grinned.

"You know who."

"This is getting serious?" I pretended to take his news casual. "There's lots of girls in lots of truck stops."

"The Lord's work," Jimbo suggested. "Like predigested?"

"Maybe," Luke told him, "All I know is she's the right one. But there's a dead man now. Fatso's gone. You know what comes next."

. . . the Hatfields and the Coys. Feuds in the Kentucky hills lasted well into the 20th century . . . "You kick my dog, I shoot your dog, you shoot my cousin, I shoot your brother, you shoot my pa . . ." and on and on and on. Revenge. Dark. Deadly. Over in Bloody Breathitt county they'd shot a whole family, plus five sheriffs in six months, or six sheriffs in five months . . . I forget which.

"People are going to die, and all over fifteen bucks and stiff-necked pride." Luke poured half a cup of coffee and looked guilty for doing it. We were supposed to be rolling. "The drunk who got cut went to a doctor who charged fifteen dollars, so the cut must have amounted to something. The deputy tried to collect the money from Bessie. Then Fatso tried. Bessie told them to stick their gearshifts up their tailpipes . . ." Luke almost smiled. "Who would have ever thought that Bessie . . ." Then he sounded sad. "Now Fatso is dead . . ."

"Proves nothing," I said. "Let's roll."

"You know it," Luke told me, "and I know it. But tell it to the drunk. Tell it to that speed-trapping deputy. How many others in that family?"

"If you guys got any brains," the tired and bennied driver said, "you'll keep your sweet fannies t'hell out of it. Them hillbillies ain't responsible types." He stretched again. ". . . got a woman both ends of the line, but think I'll rent a room and try to sleep." He trudged away.

"Sin of pride," Luke muttered. "The deadliest of the seven deadlies."

The road in early September is generally clear. Trees are tired and ragged from summer, but leaves only droop. Few blow. In the hills the moon is often hazy because mist rolls off the tops of hills. The road can get hazy as well. Ground mist rises. Summer fogs turn the road into a mist-smoking path between trees. On downhills you let her roll, because you have to have something for that next grade. When it is late at night on smoking two-lane, trucking is better than best. Your senses are so sharp they actually cut the night. Falling down a hard grade at seventy, you have to be smarter than God, and twice as alert.

And it is on such nights that visions, apparitions, and ghosts appear. Giant moths flicker pure white as they drift high above the road, and an occasional night-flyer, dark and invisible, splats against the windshield. Headlights bore into the mist, and if a man is not a fool he slows. But, he doesn't slow much, because half of what he sees probably isn't there.

The ghost appeared at the top of Dive Bomber Hill, off to the right on the berm. I saw brake lights before I saw him. Jimbo's rig slowed, rolled past the ghost, and stopped. Luke's rig pulled in behind Jimbo. I pulled it over, climbed down.

Did I believe in ghosts? Hell no. Did I believe in this one? Hell, yes. Would I let my guys flail that turn at the bottom of the hill? Not a chance. Not with what had been goin' on.

The ghost wasn't doing anything. He's standing there like a luminescent glow against the black backdrop of the hills. He stood, just waiting, and he wasn't waiting for me, or Jimbo. We three walked up, and stood like stooges in a little circle before the ghost. Our rigs rumbled at our backs.

"The evening's entertainment . . ." Jimbo tried to flip it, but the words died in his mouth.

What we saw depended on who we were. Jimbo says he saw almost nothing but mist, at first. Then he saw a sidewalk preacher, the kind that used to come to town on Saturdays to bang their Bibles at street corners. I saw the figure of a man who raised his hand like a Cardinal, ready to sprinkle holy water while calling for money; pennies for the poor, dollars for the Pope.

Luke saw a father giving him a blessing. Luke saw a father's permission to marry a daughter. It could even be that a bit of scripture passed between them.

Then the ghost looked a little apologetic. Nobody could figure that out at the time. We climbed back up and coasted down to Bessie's. Five-thirty a.m., mist on the mountains, moon already down, dawn threatening. The only truck on the lot was a sixteen-foot van being flogged by a route driver. The sheriff's car stood near the doorway. One window of the restaurant was boarded up. Rock or bullet. Window gone. What with news about Fatso spreading up and down the road, and what with the sheriff's car, it was no wonder the parking lot sat deserted.

When we got inside the route guy was just leaving and it was family day at Bessie's. Bessie stood behind the counter looking cool as the morning dawn. She wore a plain housedress, light green and with a red flower pinned to it. Bessie was usually happy, but this time she was not smiling. The jukebox sat silent.

May, being the oldest of the girls, stood beside Bessie. Mary and Molly hovered down to one end of the counter. The sheriff sat real quiet and thoughtful. He was a perfect picture of a country sheriff, middle-aged, brown from the sun, muscular and capable. If he hadn't been a cop, he looked like somebody you'd like to know.

Finally, he said, "I'll handle Jerry, and tell him to handle Ellis." He sighed, like this was more trouble than it was worth. "A'course, Ellis and his sidekickers are drunks, and you can't ever be sure what a drunk is gonna do. 'Cause even the drunk don't know what he's gonna do."

"Arrest him," May said.

"And let him go," the sheriff said. "Just because we know he did it don't mean much. Best I can do is threaten him." He stood, rubbed his hand through his hair like he was trying to chase a thought. "I'll keep as close to it as I can."

"Tell those boys," Bessie said, "that's it's time to call it even. One cut, one window. I'll cough up the fifteen bucks, and let it go." Out there on the road a downshift cracked, a tanker slowed, then the guy must have seen the sheriff's car. He revved a shift and pushed it on down Dive Bomber Hill.

". . . little late, and Ellis would have blown up even if you'd paid up, right off." The sheriff stood. "I can't tell you what to do, but it would be smart to hire a man to stay on the place . . . so Ellis don't make more mistakes." He looked kindly toward Bessie, and then left.

Luke watched him go, while Jimbo and I watched Bessie. Luke whispered something to Mary that I didn't catch. He had taken a seat nearest Mary, Jimbo beside him, and me beside Jimbo. Luke kind of scooched around in his seat. He put his hand on the counter. Mary touched his hand. I knew right then, that was the moment we lost him.

And so the deputy's name was Jerry, and the drunk's name was Ellis. It felt easier to hate their guts once they had names. Then I told myself that this would have happened, anyway. Luke was the kind of guy who, sooner or later, would leave the road. Truck gypsy blues. We've all had 'em. At one time or other we've all sworn we'd leave the road. Hardly anyone ever does. The road takes hold of a guy. But Luke . . . he might as well run a dinky restaurant . . . maybe better than running a hardware . . . he could keep up his lay preaching on weekends . . . maybe even get ordained . . . with a church . . . become respectable.

"A man?" Bessie said to her girls. "I never had but one man in my whole life, 'cause that was the only man I ever wanted. We'd not find anybody to come close to your pa."

"I have," Mary said. She kind of wiggled, which was sexy, but not what she meant. What she meant is that Luke was a goner, and happy about it. She touched Luke's hand.

"A case of the hots ain't proof." May didn't believe it, even if May thought well of Luke. "You're talkin' about a truck driver, for hell's sake . . ." Then she shut up quick, because Bessie didn't allow cussing.

Bessie, real delicate, reached beneath the counter and pulled out this junky-looking 12-gauge double-barrel. She laid it longwise on the counter, the business end pointing away from everybody. I thought she was about to ask if Mary was in the family way. Then I thought nope, too delicate.

"You'll be wanting this," she said to Luke.

I tried to save him from himself. "We got a schedule."

"I'm quits." Luke said it quiet. "My place is here. I'll scout around and find a man to stay here until I can drop the rig. You guys go ahead."

"Leave it sit," I told him. "I'll bring another driver from the big city. You're done." I admit to being sore.

"Credit to you," Jimbo told Luke. "I never much held with preachers, but it's a credit to you." He didn't ask for his gun, because he hadn't checked it, what with the sheriff having been there. Jimbo looked almost sentimental. He turned to Mary. "You're a nice lady. My mom was a nice lady, and look what happened." He wrinkled his nose which had already been busted once. "Take a lesson, and good luck." He walked away.

"Could be," Bessie said real quiet, and still talking to her girls, "that your pa's still around here somewhere."

=

Maybe I didn't understand wanting a woman so bad you'd leave the road, but I did understand what Luke was thinking. In the south, in those days, a man was expected to defend his family with his life. If he had to kill somebody doing it, nobody complained. These days, if a man tries to rape your daughter, and you shoot him, you go to jail. If you're a bad shot and the rapist lives, he gets counseling . . . I'll tell a little story to show what I mean.

=

Back then, in one of the coal camps over in Knox county, a man got drunk and started beating his wife. She ran to her brother's cabin. Her drunk husband followed her and started banging on the door. Her brother yelled through the door. He said, "John, I know you're drunk, but I got a shotgun. If you come through that door I'll cut you in half. You know I got to do it."

The drunk came through the door. The brother cut him in half. The coroner's jury ruled that when that man came through that door, he committed suicide.

=

So I understood Luke, and I approved. It was just that it made a mess to have a truck stranded on Dive Bomber Hill. Jimbo and I rolled Louisville, phoned Knoxville, and Knoxville said "Leave it sit." They sent two guys in a car, one to pick up the truck.

Meanwhile, Jimbo and I got rerouted to Cincinnati, then back to Knoxville. A week had passed before we got back on Highway 25. By then we'd picked up a third guy, but the guy wasn't gonna work out. His name was Sven, a hunky, and in spite of being Swede he had no Swedish steam. I put Jimbo in front, Sven in the middle in Luke's old place, and I batted clean-up. A couple miles before Bessie's we hit a delay.

The sheriff's car and the deputy's car sat on the berm, flashers twirling. A Chev station wagon, painted like an ambulance, sat with its doors open. It looked like men were scrambling up and down the hill. Somebody off the road. Nothin' new. Happened all the time.

We got to Bessie's at four a.m. with morning still on the backside of the hill. The parking lot lay empty as a bootlegger's morals. Sven asked, "Why we stoppin'?" and I told him, because I wanted. We weren't even inside, yet, when a North Carolina rig pulled in, and behind it a Conoco tanker. Things seemed almost normal. Everybody headed in for coffee.

The busted window had been fixed. The place smelled like morning, the way truckstops smell when one shift goes off, another comes on, and the day starts over. Luke sat at a table in one corner. Mary had the counter. Somebody was moving around back in the kitchen. Luke looked tired as a man can be, like a guy who'd been crossing Kansas at forty miles an hour.

Jimbo and I sat beside him, and I waved Sven off. He went to the counter. Nobody said anything about checking guns.

"Keep this up," I told Luke, "and you lose weight in your behind. What's happening?"

"They won't leave us alone," he told me. "Like flies on honey. Like the plagues of Egypt. I run that Ellis guy out of here at least once a day. Plus his buddies." He looked through the windows. "See what I mean?"

The deputy's car rolled onto the lot, rolled right up to the front door, and stopped.

"Move away," Luke told me and Jimbo. "I'll be needing room." He picked up that junky shotgun from where it lay at his feet. He didn't even stand, just laid it across the table pointed at the door. When the deputy came in he saw the shotgun, and stopped.

"Right barrel has birdshot," Luke said quietly. "It probably won't kill you but it'll hurt. Left barrel has a slug. It won't hurt much, because you'll be dead before you hit the floor. Which one you want?"

The jukebox started wailing about some babe wearing blue velvet. Mary came around the counter and unplugged it. The deputy stood in the doorway and watched three drivers at the counter turn toward him.

"Go away, Jerry," Luke said. "If you have law business here send the sheriff."

"If," Jerry said, "you are the sonovabitch who is running folks off the road, it'll take more than shotguns to save you." He turned away, and walked to his car.

"I want no part of this," the Conoco driver said. He stood, and Sven stood right along with him. They left.

The deputy's car pulled out slow and stopped before pulling onto the road. Something going on out there.

"Go see," I told Jimbo. He slid away.

"Tell me," I said to Mary, "'cause the gent with the gun is kind of groggy." I pointed at Luke.

"We're not married yet," she said, like it was the only thing on her mind. She looked at Luke. "He's gotta trust us to call him if stuff happens. He's gotta get some sleep." She looked through the windows, out toward the parked rigs. "Trouble. Better look. Somebody's about to go to Jesus."

I came out of my chair and was through the door before Luke could react. The deputy's Mercury had already pulled away, but somebody was out there. When I got to the rigs Jimbo had his .45 pointed right at a farmer. Ugly pistol. Sven stood looking like he was about to wring his hands. The farmer gasped, tried to talk, and was too scared. He was built blocky as a farm wagon, and looked just about as smart. An old Chev pickup sat beside the road.

"Cuttin' tires," Jimbo told me. He looked at Sven. "You'd better drive the east coast, pal. This road is too long and mean for you."

"Don't shoot him," I told Jimbo. "Not yet." The farmer whimpered. He looked like only his overalls were holding him up.

"One of Ellis's pals," Luke said. Luke arrived ten seconds behind me.

"I all the time ask the holy saints that I don't gotta use this," Jimbo said about the pistol. "Keep him covered." The farmer cowered. Jimbo moved quick, climbed in his cab, and came back with a tire billy. "School days," he said, "education time." He swung the billy against the farmer's left arm. We all heard the muffled crack as the bone shattered. The guy fell, rolled, and howled.

"You'll notice I picked the left arm," Jimbo said to Sven. "He can still shift gears. Take a lesson."

"How many tires?"

"Three."

I figured fast. If we took the spares from all three rigs we could make it, but good Lord, the delay. The only thing worse than changing a tire is mounting chains when it snows. I figured an hour lost, maybe more. No shop. No air wrenches . . . tire on wheel, 150 pounds . . . block up the jack . . . hydraulic jack with an eight-inch throw.

Take a chance rolling with cut tires? Not if I'm running the show. Not if anyone sane is running the show.

"Put the hayseed in his truck," I told Sven. "Get useful." To the hayseed I said, "Tell your boy Ellis he's done messing with this freight line. Next time the gun goes off."

The guy was hurting just awful, but you could tell he understood. Sven started his pickup for him, got him into it, and the guy weaved away headed for a doc. That's when Jimbo heated up.

He stood along the roadside looking up the hill where we'd seen the ghost. I can still remember it, plain as day. Dawn just back of the hill, the road running blackish-silver, drawing a line across the world, and Jimbo standing there like he was forty feet tall; despite he was short and skinny and tough. He shook his fist at the top of the hill, and he yelled: "You frowzy-headed jack-leg-preachin' old sonovabitch, you started this. If you're any kind of man at all, end it."

I thought he'd gone nuts. We got busy, working, and while I'm working I'm thinking. And this is what I thought.

If, back when Ellis and his boys first showed up, the ghost had not been so hot to deliver a sermon, none of this would have happened. The Spanish guy would not have banged Ellis's head against the door frame of the car, or laid a knife across his throat. It was obvious the ghost was the one who caused the Spaniard to do the ghost's preaching, because the Spaniard claimed it wasn't him. The sum of it was, I figured Jimbo was right.

And maybe somebody or something was running cars off the road. It seemed pretty clear that the ghost might be well intended, but he had screwed up royal.

=

Our dispatcher got the story, and told me not to let the boys stop at Bessie's. He didn't have to tell me, but management generally figures that drivers are stupid. Even Jimmy Hoffa once said, "Any damn fool can drive a truck. I was a warehouseman."

We made another turn, then Sven took a job driving for Greyhound. I think what happened was Sven had finally driven Highway 25 in daytime and saw what he'd been driving through at night. It scared him right down to his gizzard.

The company assigned a Frenchy-Indian guy named Tommy, and Tommy was gonna work out. He could move slick as water running. Plus he had a sense of humor. "Women are just so trouble," he'd say, "'cause they all so cute and they so many of them. Wonder guys ever get anything done."

Which was good, that sense of humor, because otherwise the scene went dark. We didn't stop at Bessie's anymore, but I couldn't just forget Luke. In spite of being the marrying type, he was a friend. We'd put up a lot of miles together. What happened is, me and my guys would drop our rigs Friday evenings and not leave out again until ten PM Sunday. That's when the road is as good as it ever gets. That gave me Friday nights for sleep, Saturday for myself, and also Sunday morning. I flogged a one-ton Diamond T pickup in those days. It was a tough little truck, pretty as a race horse, lots of low end torque, okay in the hills. I drove to Bessie's.

When I parked beside the bunkhouse everything looked normal. A North Carolina straight-job with an attic sat next a Mack pulling a lowboy. A D6 Cat sat on the lowboy. An old Ford stake with hay racks, a farm truck, sat in front of the Mack. Farmers stopped at Bessie's sometimes, and that was all right. Not all farmers were idiots. Just most.

When I got inside Luke looked lots better. At least he'd had some sleep. Bessie had the counter and she was jiving the farm guy about "he should come in Tuesday," what with Tuesday being "wide-pie day," "slice 'n-a-half." The guy looked smart enough, and didn't smell like pigs. The guy chuggin' the Mack looked more like a mechanic than a truck driver. The guy with the North Carolina job looked like he was sick of hauling furniture. From the kitchen I could hear Mary singing to herself.

"Outside," Luke said, "and I appreciate you're here."

I followed him to the bunkhouse. The lock was off the door. The place seemed roomy and had been fixed up. Curtains at the window, a single bed and no cots. A table and a couple chairs. "Staying here until the wedding," he explained, and wasn't embarrassed. "We're looking for a place."

Preachers. Go figure. The guy was determined not to hop into the sack with Mary until after the wedding. At the same time, he was ready to chop up a deputy with a shotgun. Call me dumb, but somehow it contradicted.

"I don't actually believe this myself," Luke told me, "except I have no choice. It seems that I have in-law problems."

"Bessie?"

"Bessie is fine," Luke told me. "The girls are giddy over the wedding. Big deal. Flower girls, long dresses, the whole business. It's taking time." He pushed a curtain aside and looked onto the parking lot. "Someplace out there," he said, "my future father-in-law is a little too busy, and he won't listen. One reason he won't listen is because he's only about as solid as smoke."

I wanted to laugh. Instead, I shut up and opened my ears.

"That guy who got run off the road, the second guy, is one of Ellis's sidekicks. My problem is that he lived. He's in the hospital and the docs say he isn't crazy." Luke looked toward the top of Dive Bomber Hill. "The guy says that he braked too hard and spun off the hill because somebody was standing in the middle of the road. The guy says 'Ghost,' the docs say 'shook up,' and I say, 'Lord protect me from my friends.'" Luke sat on the edge of the bed and talked like talking to himself. "So we got one sidekicker in the hospital, one with a broken arm, and Fatso dead. That means I'm down to two, Jerry and Ellis."

"Those guys who are busted up are going to heal." It seemed to me like the answer was for Bessie and girls to get out of town.

"Not for a while," Luke said, "and that boy in the hospital is a coward. Maybe a backshooter, but he can be handled." He sat, estimating. "The guy with the busted wing is blaming Jerry. Bad blood between them, so he's not a problem."

"The ghost?"

". . . was Bessie's husband, the girls' daddy. He had a little church plus this restaurant. He tried to stop two hot heads from killing each other, and ended up shot."

"Might have stayed out of it?"

"He couldn't," Luke said. "The hot heads were in the parking lot, and his girls were in the restaurant. The girls were little more than kids at the time."

"Protecting his family."

"The problem is," Luke said, "he's still doing it." He stood up, walked to the window, walked back across the room like a man pacing a jail cell. "I don't know how this is going to end, but it will surely end badly."

=

It ended that same afternoon, except this kind of stuff never really ends. Makes no difference if it's between men or management or unions, or even nations; once bad stuff happens it keeps bouncing like bullets off of armor plate. But, at least one ending came along toward evening. I wouldn't have known Ellis from Adam's off-ox, which was maybe a good thing. If I had known I might have prevented something.

Shadows lay real long across the road when I pulled away from Bessie's. Summer heat had faded and in another couple hours ground mist would rise. It would be a slow road because it was the time of year when crops come in. The road fills with flatbed farm trucks carrying side-stakes and hayracks. They are mostly held together with baling wire.

A guy almost feels sorry for the farmers. These are poor farms. If a hill farmer owns eighty acres, forty will go straight up, and forty straight down. There are places that are still farmed with mules because a tractor would fall off the side of the hill. It's said that men plant their corn with shotguns. Mostly, the farmers work narrow strips along bottoms and in hollows where streams always run.

And the farmers work hasty, like the devil is biting their heels, or at least they do in September. The last cut of hay comes in after the August thunderstorms. Farm crews work until daylight decays, then ride home in rattling hay trucks. The truck cabs hold three guys. If there are more than three men in the crew, they ride in back. You see them against a red sundown, tired silhouettes standing toward the front of the truck bed, holding onto the hay rack, and watching road. That's the kind of truck that was holding up progress when I got near the top of Dive Bomber Hill.

I found myself in a little caravan. The hay truck was in front, followed by a beat-up '41 Buick that looked as bald and ragged as its tires. I was behind the Buick.

Rust drew a line around the trunk of the Buick, and rust made the same kind of line around the back window. The junker blew a little smoke, but not much, and it bucked real hard when the guy braked, like a car about to kneel and pray. The driver tailgated up to the hay truck, swung out to see if he could pass, and cut back in. Cowboy stuff. Impatient to get somewhere unimportant. I might have known it was Ellis because Ellis was said to drive a junk Buick, but I wasn't really thinking. Just another slow down. There was a flat run two miles further on. Wait it out.

My pickup felt like a tin can, and, compared to an over-the-road rig, it was. It didn't stand high enough so a man could see much road. It was suspended like a brickbat on a roller skate. And, mind you, it was the best pickup made back then.

The sun stood just behind the hills. Trees, rocks, and cars looked like paper cutouts pasted against a red sky. A guy stood in the hay truck. He was also silhouetted, watching road. I hadn't noticed him before, but suddenly he was there. He steadied himself by holding onto the hayrack. He looked like just another farmer, or farm help, headed home at the end of a weary day. Then it came to me that he looked familiar. I almost hit the brakes.

Things happened fast, and yet it was like slow motion. It was like one of those movies where people get shot and take time flopping. The Buick gunned up to the rear of the hay truck, braked, fell back. An oncoming car flew past like the driver was late for an appointment at a cathouse; sixty, maybe seventy. And it was then that the guy standing in the hay truck, the familiar guy, turned and pointed to the Buick. He gave a road sign saying that he could see clear road. He rolled his hand.

The Buick jumped into the oncoming lane to pass the hay truck, and it jumped right into red lights twirling, because Jerry had been chasing a speeder.

Perfectly square, head-on wrecks almost never happen. What mostly happens is two cars hit on the corners, and the backends rise and twist. Sometimes the cars roll. This head-on was only absolutely square one I've ever seen.

The impact caused Ellis's Buick and Jerry's Mercury to lift straight up, as much as a foot off the road. The sound was too sharp for a normal wreck. No tires squealing. Just explosion, while I ran the narrow shoulder to get the hell away from them.

The front ends of both cars disappeared, and the heads of both men appeared through windshields. Combined wreck speed, something in the neighborhood of 110 mph. Dirt and dust from the undersides of the cars burst above the dark road, and the cars for a moment looked like they rested on a cloud. They settled. The farm truck pulled over. I pulled ahead of the farm truck, because you don't pull in behind a wreck. You don't do it because the road is gonna get blocked.

There's no sense going into how it looked. The front ends were gone. The two heads, what were left of them, seemed to be trying to stare each other down. They did not look brotherly. I stood with a fire extinguisher expecting the worst, but the wrecks didn't burn. The farmer flogging the hay truck came up to me, took one look at the mess, and sicked in the ditch.

"You okay to go for a phone?" I asked.

He was all trembly, but no kid. "I can manage. What would make that damn fool try to pass."

"Because he's a damn fool." I wasn't admitting to nothing. "Go phone the sheriff," I told the farm guy. "I'll set out the flares." When he pulled away I took a moment to look at his truck. There was nobody in back, no man nor ghost, and the land was going darker.

=

I attended the wedding, and for a country wedding it was nice and not too corny. The flower girls were shirttail cousins from somewhere. Molly and May starred as bridesmaids, and Mary was prettier than angels. A country preacher, in a black suit that was slick with wear, and white shirt with frayed collar, managed to be dignified. Bessie looked sweet. Luke looked like a man who didn't know whether he was happy or trapped. I have no doubt that the ghost was in the neighborhood, but I didn't see him.

As it turned out, Luke was both happy and trapped. He worked with Bessie, and through the first few years Bessie's place prospered. There was no more trouble. Luke managed to get anointed, or ordained or whatever it took. He got a small church back in the hills and spent time both there and at Bessie's. He and Mary raised two kids, both kids bright and sassy. Time passes, though, and things change.

May married a banker in Corbin, and Molly went off to Cincinnati. She got a job and went to college. She teaches in a country school. Bessie hired help for a while but things were not the same. She retired and moved into London. Her restaurant stood empty until the fires.

Everybody guessed, but nobody could prove, that the fires came at the hand of one of Ellis's buddies. The restaurant burned, and Bessie's little house burned. Nothing to be done about it. At least nothing was.

Jimbo and Tommy and I ran Highway 25 until the interstate opened. After that, I kind of lost track, except I saw Molly once in Cincinnati. She was just walking along a sidewalk, on her way to a summer class for teachers. We talked for a while. Bessie had passed on, and was buried on the hill where her house had been. Her girls didn't like it much, but they had honored her wishes.

And trucking changed. Lots of fancy rigs. CB radios happened, and that was one of the worst things ever. All of the comradeship came out of the road. There was nothing much left out there but bad mouths, bullshit, and cowboys turning the freeways into fester. Movies started showing truckers with monkeys and big-boobed babes in their cabs.

And, of course, we got old. Tommy went off somewhere, chasing a skirt. Jimbo actually married a nice Italian girl and settled down in Boston. I thought about such matters and decided against. The road had me, even after I retired.

It's a long road, and it winds and turns on itself. It goes somewhere, I suppose, but men who drive often only think they're going somewhere. I was in upstate Michigan near the Canadian border, and pushing a Dodge camper, when I thought of Dive Bomber Hill. Nothing much was happening in Michigan, so I drifted south.

Coming around at the top of Dive Bomber Hill, and hanging a right, the road looked the same. I rolled it easy and pulled off where Bessie's place used to sit. Nothing there but young trees and overgrowth. I slept for a while in the camper, and woke when the sun stood behind the hill and the sky was red. It seemed like the ghost had been waiting to meet me. Out there among the young trees a little pocket of mist moved as deliberate as a man pacing.

I waited. It didn't approach. I kept waiting. It moved up the hill. I waited until it was clear that the ghost wanted nothing much to do with me. It didn't dislike me, but it sure as hell didn't trust me. I waited until I finally understood that the ghost was doing the last thing a family man could do. It stood between the road and Bessie's grave, protecting the grave.

The Souls of Drowning Mountain

[This story is in memory of Andy Strunk,
coal miner of Gatliff, Kentucky.]

MOUNTAINS IN EASTERN KENTUCKY HAVE NAMES: BLACK MOUNTAIN, Mingo Mountain, Hanger Mountain, Booger Mountain, and, among a thousand others, Drowning Mountain which rises above a hollow where sits Minnie's Beer Store. Both mountain and store carry tales, and I'll tell but one. It says too much, maybe, about folks helpless beyond all help, and angry as sullen fires. There will be however, some satisfying murders.

When I first saw Drowning Mountain these many years ago I was 'full of piss and vinegar' as old folks used to say. Thought I knew it all. Had knocked off four years of military duty, then worked my way through college. Took a job with a government agency that was partly in the business of welfare, and partly in sanctimonious advice. My assignment was a railroad town in southeast Kentucky.

I'd seen my share of bad stuff in the bars of Gloucester and in Boston's Scollay Square. I'd seen green water over the flying bridge of a cutter. I'd seen fire at sea. I'd dealt with the dead and dying; figured I could handle whatever came.

The day I arrived trains hooted, ladies gossiped in summer heat while fanning themselves on front porches. They stayed away from town. Hatred, downtown, boiled along the streets like ball lightning. It dawned on me that I was the only man in sight who wasn't wearing a pistol.

"We're in the middle of a coal war," my new boss told me. "Keep your head down and stay polite." His name was Bobby Joe and he was from around there. He'd done army time. Rail-skinny, shrewd as a razorback, but smiling. After the army time he'd come back to the hills. Almost everybody from the hills returns sooner or later.

Bobby Joe assigned me a secretary named Sarah Jane, also from around there. She called me Mister James, not Jim, and we did not warm toward each other for weeks and weeks. Sarah Jane was thirtyish, overweight, pale beneath tan freckles, wore frumpish housedresses, and there was nothing about her that would make any preacher claim her a candidate for heaven. She knew her job front and back. I admired her, but didn't understand her anger.

There seemed no end to everybody's anger. My experience with middlewest small towns and large eastern cities meant nothing. I understood ghettos, poverty, welfare, rich bastards, cops, especially rich bastards and cops.

Yet, nothing matched up. There wasn't a kitty cat's chance in a dog pound that I could understand Minnie's Beer Store or Drowning Mountain.

"Walk easy," Bobby Joe told me. He spoke slow and southern, but in complete control. "If you bust ass you're courting trouble." He kept me on a short leash for two months. I warmed a chair behind a desk and talked to old men and tired women.

Then Bobby Joe turned me over to a field rep named Tip. We visited small towns, took hardship claims and gave advice. We visited people who were shut in. When we drove along thin and rutted side roads we changed from white shirts to chambray shirts, because men in white shirts looked like revenue agents. Men in white shirts got shot.

What thoughts came to pass? These: This is not real. No one lives this way. This place is straight out of medieval times.

Tip was from around there. He looked more like a hill farmer than a government agent. Lank, with longish hair, thin mouth. He could talk tough as barbed wire, and yet the old people we dealt with were crazy about him. "Tell you about Drowning Mountain," he said one day. "Maybe you'll understand why I'm pissed off ninety percent of the time."

We were outside of Manchester, Kentucky, scouting around the top of a ridge called Pigeon's Roost. Huge broadleaf trees covered the hillside, tangles of bramble, little wisps of smoke on a hot summer day. Smoke, probably from stills.

Tip had a way of explaining the world by telling stories. "Didn't used to be called Drowning Mountain," he told me. "But it sure as sweet Jesus earned its name."

Even today, all these years later, it breaks my heart to think of it. I'll condense what Tip said.

These mountains are limestone with seams of coal. Sometimes the seam goes straight into the mountain, but not often. It usually angles in and the coal shaft follows one or more seams. Those shafts are propped with timbers, and generally slate lies above the coal. Take out the coal, slate falls, even sometimes, when propped.

Because the limestone is porous there's always ground water. In those days, when miners hit a narrow seam they sometimes had to lie on their backs in water, underground and between rock, pushing shovels backward over their shoulders to draw out loose coal that had been blasted. In mining camps, even little boys knew how to set a charge of dynamite.

Were these men screwed? You bet they were. Mine owners used up men worse than bad generals killing their own armies. Coal camps were the kinds of hells that made chain gangs look like a vacation. Men actually did owe their souls to the company store. Even if men had enough imagination to leave town they had no money. They were paid in scrip. Plus, they didn't know any better. Lots of those men had gone into the mines at age 12.

So, in a coal camp, way, way back in World War I, they had driven a shaft deep into the heart of the mountain. When the seams played out the shaft was abandoned. Twenty-six years later, no one remembered the shaft was there. The coal company opened a seam on the other side of the mountain. The seam drove in on much the same angle as the old shaft because of a fracture in the rock.

Miners blasted their way in, propped the slate, drove deeper, and deeper; and on a fatal day blasted through to the old, forgotten shaft that had filled with ground water. Seven men died that day, drowning in darkness in the middle of a mountain.

"Ah, no," I told Tip.

"Helluva note," he said. "Makes you sorta sick, don't it?" Tip was the kind of guy, who if he had been a preacher, would have been a good one. He would not have been hellfire, only tough and kind.

"The reason I tell the story," he said, "is because next week we go to Drowning Mountain."

It was a miserable weekend. The office closed. Nothing to do except keep my head down and wait. The town sat in a dry county. Each election, preachers and bootleggers went to the polls and kept it dry. A wet county was just next door and Tennessee was not all that far off, but there was nothing going on in those directions. I hung out at the drugstore, slurped coffee, listened to gossip.

The main rich bastard in town was named Sims. He ramrodded a coal corporation. Sims was one of those sanitary pieces of crap that wear summer suits and carry perfumed hankies as they walk across the faces of dying men.

Sims's chief armament was a guy named Pook. Pook had the reputation of a real nut buster. Pook was an actual killer with at least two murders notched to his gun. Gossip said the sheriff was afraid of him.

The two showed up Sunday afternoon, walking Main Street like they owned it. Sims said "howdy," or even, "howdy, neighbor" to grim-faced men who stepped aside to let him pass. Sims had a bald spot, a sizeable gut, and dainty little feet. He seemed cheery. He had jowls like a pig, and a sneer that could push people backward. On Sunday afternoon he went into the bank. The banker came down and opened up just for him.

Pook stood outside the bank. He looked like Godzilla with a haircut. Or a better description, maybe: he looked like a storm trooper, but with a .45 automatic on his hip, not a Mauser.

People didn't talk to him. Pook couldn't out-sneer Sims, but his look told folks that he figured them for dog dump. When Sims came from the bank the two cruised town in a new Cadillac, snubbing everybody; the Cadillac black and shiny.

On Monday morning Sarah Jane tsked. "You take it slow, now," she told me. "Jim."

It was the first time she ever called me anything but mister.

Bobby Joe talked to Tip, real quiet. Both men looked serious.

"What's the war about?" I asked Tip. We left the office and headed for Drowning Mountain.

"The usual," he told me. "Wages, mechanization, it's pitiful." He kind of hunched over the steering wheel. He kept a low profile in the hills. His car was a beat up Ford made before WWII. "The men only know one kind of work, and there's no other work. They strike in order to go back into the hole at a bit higher pay, which is like asking to jump smack into hell." He paused. "And there's something worse. Stripping."

I'd heard about it. Strip mining was coming into fashion. It destroyed whole mountains. Strip mining made 6,000-foot mountains into smoking piles of rubble. Trees gone. Not a stick of vegetation. Not a tree. Only broken rock. Sulfuric acid rose in the air and washed in the streams. Strip mines were profitable because they needed a few machine operators, but no miners.

"There's something else," Tip told me. "Before we get to Minnie's I gotta prepare you." Even though he was the guy in charge, he looked off-guard and hesitant.

"You might meet some people," he told me, "who you won't know, and maybe I won't either, if they're dead or alive. If you want to stay happy take it for granted. Don't try to study it out. Don't back away."

"Why? Come to think of it, Why and What?"

"Dead or alive, all these folks have is each other. They stick together. There's talk of stripping the mountain."

"Sims?"

"Not all rich men are crap, and not all crap-heads are rich. But, yep. Sims." Tip actually looked relieved . . . probably because I didn't make a deal out of that 'dead or alive' business. I'd come to trust Tip, and if he said don't figure on something, it seemed best not to figure. What he said made no sense. For me, it was wait and see.

"I got more to tell," he said. "There's a history."

He explained that Minnie's Beer Store sat in an abandoned coal camp. Old men were sparsely scattered in cabins along the sides of the hills. Most were widowers, but some had young wives because there were no young men for girls to marry. The young men had gone away, some to the Army, some to other coal camps.

Miners, back then, were more spirits than real by age 40. They moved slow as cold molasses because of black lung, silicosis, violent arthritis. Their hair, if they had any, was white and their faces were black. Coal dust gets under the skin. It doesn't even go away in the grave. When bones become dust, they are still tainted with coal.

"So much anger," Tip murmured. "They're furious about being screwed, but most of them don't know how much they're screwed. They don't know how to fight back. So, they're really furious about not knowing." He slowed the car, making a point. "That dead and alive business. It happened at least once before, and it happened during a coal war."

As we approached, rusting rails ran beside a road of thin macadam once laid by the coal company. The hills were covered with hardwood trees, and here at the end of August a little spot of yellow, leaves changing color, appeared amid stands of green. The narrow road was rutted now. Most of the railroad had been torn away and sold for scrap.

"This is the day when government checks arrive." Tip seemed talking to himself. "Things might get pretty lively."

"How can that happen?" It was an honest question. I didn't see how anything could get very lively. We were, approximately, forty miles from nowhere.

"These folks live off the land. They trap small game. Sometimes they have to dig roots." Tip was always in control, but he was angry. "Every month we send each of them a lousy thirty-two bucks. Minnie runs a tab. She cashes their checks. They pay up their owes, mostly for canned goods and liniment. Then they buy a pack of factory-made cigarettes, called tight rolls, and drink. One day a month they get to act like men who don't scratch roots and roll tobacco in newsprint. Around here, that's the main and only use of a beer joint."

Electric lines from earlier days still ran into the hollow, but not to all the cabins. Here and there shelves of rock hovered above what looked like shallow caves. "The people dig out coal for heat," Tip told me. "At least the people who are not too old."

When we turned off the road and up a rutted lane to Minnie's Beer Store, Tip came off the gas. We coasted to a stop. "It looks," he said, "like we got ourselves a goddamn uprising."

The store stood two stories, ramshackle and unpainted. It leaned a little. Upstairs windows had old bed sheets for curtains. Downstairs windows were naked as wind off the mountain. Not much could be seen through the windows because men stood outside the store, blocking the view.

One man packed a silly old over-and-under, a two-barrel combination of .22 rifle and .410 shotgun. He pointed it at another man who knelt like in prayer. A half dozen other men stood around, watched, like people stuck in church with the sermon boring. Everybody except the kneeling man wore faded patches on faded clothes. The only man who looked fully alive was the guy who knelt. The rest of the men were old and tired. They seemed wispy.

"You are more'n'likely gonna see a shooting," Tip said, "For God's sake keep your mouth shut." He climbed from the Ford. Slammed the door. Knelt like he checked a tire, knelt real easy like he had all the time in the world. He kind of *tsk*ed, scratched himself behind the ear, then turned and ambled toward the men like nothing was going on.

"Shitfire, Tom," he said to the man with the gun, "if you shoot the undertaker who's gonna plant him?"

The kneeling man looked about to faint. He dressed in city clothes. His shoes had once been polished. His eyes were wide and scary. Black hair dangled wet over sweaty forehead. "Tip," he said, "they got it all wrong."

"They probably don't," Tip told him. He turned to me. "This is what comes from too damn much government. The minute we started paying a death benefit, funeral prices went up to match the benefit."

"T'ain't that," Tom said. His arm trembled as he held the gun. It looked like the thing would go off just from his shaking.

His hair was pure white, his face with black circles around green eyes ... green but dulled ... lots of Scots-Irish blood in these hills. Tom seemed feeble, but not at all nervous. "We got graveyard problems," he told Tip.

"Might be fun," Tip said, and sounded droll, "to park him inside. Sweat him a little. You can always shoot him later."

"If you wasn't Tip," Tom said, "I reckon I wouldn't listen." To the kneeling undertaker he said, "Remove your ass. Inside."

I hope to never again see what I saw in Minnie's store. What I heard, I can handle, and tell about. What I smelled was like sweet perfume, the kind that rises from corpses just before they begin to stink. What I saw . . .

A congregation of weary men, white-haired with faces dark, especially around eyes and noses where coal dust painted faces into masks. Eyes, some brilliant, some flat and dull and deathlike, stared at us from the rings of blackness. Here and there a man wheezed. Others sat quiet, and if they breathed no one could hear. The silent ones seemed to have brighter eyes than the ones who drew breath.

Minnie, rail-skinny, gray-haired and sharp of face, stood behind a bar made of plain boards. Behind her, shelves held chewing tobacco, plus some tobacco leaves, little cans of deviled ham, little cans of sardines. There were a few grocery items plus small bottles of aspirin and some patent medicines. Beer coolers ran beneath the shelves.

=

When the undertaker came inside he stopped, even though he had a gun in his back. He went wild-eyed, gasped, and literally fell into the nearest chair. He was worth watching, but there was lots else to see so I just listened to him gasp.

"Don't you dare do any shootin' in here," Minnie told Tom. "It makes a mess and it brings the law." Her voice sounded lots nicer than she looked, because she looked like fifty years of hard times. Her oversize man's shirt made her seem small, like a boy. Her worn jeans bagged. Her graying hair was done in a bun. Her voice sounded alert in the surrounding tiredness.

"Now me," Tip drawled, "I drink whilst on duty." He grinned at Minnie. She looked at me. Tip nodded. Minnie pulled two bottles. The undertaker still gasped, like maybe he would die for want of air.

Tip straddled a chair and looked to Tom. "I ain't come across a good story in a dog's age. Lemmie hear it . . ." He got interrupted.

The undertaker's teeth began to chatter. He kept gasping. Finally, he looked toward one of the sitting men. "Ezekiel, I done buried you."

"And did a piss poor job," Zeke said. Amber eyes flashed like a man alive and angry. Zeke's voice was more like a dry rustle than an actual voice. The rustle did not sound kind. In fact, just the opposite.

Somebody chuckled, but not friendly. Nothing else happened. The undertaker kept gasping. Tom told his story.

"He buried my brother," Tom said. "Buried Ezra. Cheaper coffin than he promised. Coffin got loose. Dropped into the grave, instead of lowered. Cracked open, and Ezra looking at the sky." Tom reached to where he'd leaned the over-and-under. "This bastard threw dirt in Ezra's face, and cussed him."

I couldn't tell whether Tom was dead or alive. He looked mostly alive, and his eyes didn't shine like Zeke's.

"This shootin'-business reminds me," a man said to Minnie. "Give me two cartridges. Might could get a deer."

30-30 cartridges, it turned out, cost thirty-five cents apiece.

"Maybe you wanta wait," Tip said. "Near as I can figure, Ezra might drop in here any minute."

The undertaker was as close to insanity as any man I've ever seen. He hunched in his chair, and when he wasn't gasping for air he sobbed. His face was complete torment. He had badly made false teeth, shiny, but too big and clunky for his face. He whispered to another man. "Why you here, Bill? You're buried."

"The way you laid me out wan't comfortable," Bill said. His voice was a dry whisper. "It ain't right a man's gotta be dead and not comfortable." Bill's eyes were not green, but sharp and glowing blue.

"Preacher," Tip said to another man, "I done heard you'd gone to glory."

"I can't figure it," the preacher whispered. He was a small man. Probably a lay preacher, self-ordained. He wore a frayed, black suit, and his white hair hung to his shoulders. His eyes glowed soft and gray. "Something's goin' on," he whispered. "Maybe the Baptists hogged it all. Might be there's no glory left."

Stillness. From outside a raven chuckled. A cow lowed, a dog barked. It was so quiet I could hear the bubbling of a distant stream that seemed to answer the raven. A way, way off in the distance, maybe two or three mountains to the west, a light plane hummed.

"I reckon," Tom said, like he was talking to himself, "My brother Ezra is out there somewheres and about his own business. Goin' it alone. He had that reputation."

"This all happened once before," Minnie said. "You boys recall that big gom-up durin' the war."

"What gom-up?" Tip sounded just as businesslike and sensible as if he were sitting back at the office. I worked at taking his advice about not studying things. Nobody else seemed troubled. Except, of course, the undertaker.

"When we had those drownings," Minnie said, "it was same time the company cut wages. Those boys walked out of the hole. People swore they saw 'em. Then the tipple burned. The mine office burned. The company store burned. Rail cars burned. Nary a coal car got loaded for three months. Then those boys disappeared into the forest. People swore they saw 'em." She looked at all of the men, some alive, some dead. "Looks like nobody was lying."

"Which means," Tip said in the direction of Tom and the preacher, "that you gents have been called back to do a hand of work. Instead of going off half-cocked, let's wait it out. I reckon something's about to happen."

What happened was Sims and his pet goon, Pook.

A man lounging in the open doorway looked toward the road. In a voice so tired it quavered he said, "Cadillac car a-coming." He sounded discouraged and beaten. To the preacher he said, "Better get to prayin', for what-dog-good it's gonna do."

Sun sat high but westering. The shadow of Drowning Mountain reached into the hollow and across the road. The Cadillac ran so smooth that nothing could be heard, save the bump of its tires in ruts and potholes. Men stirred, uneasy. "Never to be let alone, never free," someone whispered, ". . . not in this life 'ner any other." The voice filled with sadness.

Pook got from the car first. He came into Minnie's place, looked around, turned back toward the Cadillac. He must have given a signal. Sims got out and stepped toward us. He moved dainty on little feet, and his summer suit was clean as his car. When he spoke his voice was soft. "Very well, Pook. I'll be but a minute." He ignored everyone except Pook. Then he turned to Tip. "Still kneeling, are we," he said to Tip. "Still hugging the poor and unwashed. Were I you, I'd vote Democrat."

"Were I you," Tip told him, "I'd take a bath. Wash off a little-a that snot."

"Watch that mouth." Pook stirred. His hand dropped toward the .45.

"You watch yours," Tip told Pook. "When you threaten me, you threaten my uncle Sammy. Unc will get riled."

"They were about to shoot me." The undertaker's voice quavered like a scared baby. "I gotta get a ride to town."

"You probably got a shootin' comin'." Pook sounded real comfortable.

"He probably does." Sims looked at Pook. "But he's the only one around who handles paupers. The company needs him."

"Get in the car," Pook told the undertaker. "Back seat. Don't drip no sweat."

The undertaker didn't run. He scampered.

"Goddamit, Tip." Tom had his dander up, green eyes coming almost as alive as eyes of the dead.

"Could be I was wrong," Tip murmured, "or maybe not. It's never no trouble to shoot a fella if you give it forethought."

Except for Tip, there wasn't a man in the place who wasn't browbeat. I exclude myself, since half of what went on breezed right past me. The death smell wasn't quite as strong, or maybe my nose got used to it. There was one woman there, though, and browbeat she wasn't.

"This is my place," she said to Sims, "and you ain't welcome. Speak your piece and get the hell out." She glanced toward the preacher. "You'll forgive the cuss."

"Yes and no," Sims said pleasantly. "You own the building."

"And the land," Minnie said, "Bought fair and square from the company, deed an' all. Twenty bucks a month. Paid in full."

"And the land," Sims agreed. "But the company owns the mineral rights."

Tip pulled me to him. Whispered close in my ear. "Things are gonna get real bad. Keep your mouth shut."

"This is a friendly call." Sims kind of purred. "Trying to help folks out. You'll be wanting to move. Next month I got machinery coming in."

"Gonna strip," someone whispered.

"My cabin's on that mountain," someone else whispered. "I done bought that cabin, five dollars a month."

"The graveyard's on that mountain. My woman's buried up there." A man's voice broke.

Pook chuckled. Sims tried to look sad. "Maybe move the grave," he said. "Nothing I can do. It's the company. The company calls the shots."

"Not exactly true," Tip said. "Why are you doing this?"

"Those seams are hardly touched," Sims told Tip. "That mountain has been a curse." He looked toward Minnie. "One month." He turned and walked to his car. Pook followed, but walking kind of sideways so as to cover his back.

Silence. The whir of the Cadillac's starter. The engine purred like an echo of Sims's voice. The car pulled away. Somewhere toward the back of Minnie's place came a dry sob. Men sat stunned, old, tired.

"Give yourselves a minute to breathe," Tip said real quiet. "Those of you with breath. Those without are called back for something."

Silence in the room was as deep as silence outside. No raven, no dog barking, no light plane buzzing. With the shadow of Drowning Mountain reaching across the hollow there should have been a breeze, but not a sound. Not a leaf stirring.

Then, a crack, like doom riding horseback and striking flame from the hooves. I sat straight up. Looked around. Never saw so many happy faces. I tried to place the sound. It was like a three-inch-fifty cannon going off. Sharp. Eardrum buster.

"How in the world," Tip said real pleased and casual, "are me and Jim ever gonna get back to town?"

"Five-stick shot sure'n God's wrath." The preacher looked about to start a sermon.

"That Ezra," Tom said. "By God, Ezra had the nerve to done it. Waste of dynamite. A three-stick would been aplenty."

Someone laughed out loud. "What do you figger the law will do to Ezra. Kill him?" This, while everybody headed outside to take a look.

The Cadillac, what little was left of it, lay on its back beside a chunk of road that was no longer there. The car was a shiny hunk of black, twisted metal. A body in a summer suit lay sprawled among weeds, another body big as Godzilla lay without a head, and there were scattered pieces of what had once been an undertaker. Bloodstains mixed with burn stains on roadside weeds.

"That Ezra," Minnie said, ". . . now Ezra was always best at setting a shot. He held that reputation."

"Tunneled under the road. Set his charge. Ran his wires to the detonator, and hid on the hill. When the car drove across the charge, he shot those boys straight to hell." The preacher sounded apologetic. "I can't find it in my heart to pray for 'em."

"And now we're gonna catch hell." Tom looked to Tip. "We're gonna get the law."

"Don't give it a first thought," Tip told him. "I got it covered." He turned to the preacher. "Pretty plain why you boys were called back."

A man whispered. The whisper sounded faint, but pleased. He spoke to the preacher. "I reckon brother Sims and his lot feel sorta surprised. They got no experience at being dead." The voice turned mean. "I expect we should show 'em some things. Sort of introduce them around."

"I got a goodly number of things to demonstrate." Another whisper. The whisper sounded most unpleasant.

"I purely agree," the preacher whispered, "an' may The Lord have mercy on my sinful way."

Down by the road an old man limped off the hill. He wore a black burial suit of the cheap kind furnished to the poor. He stood looking at the broken car and broken bodies. Then he scratched his head and looked like a man who figured he had wasted dynamite. Then he looked toward Minnie's.

"That Ezra," Tom said. "I expect you boys better get down there before he has all the fun."

When those who were called back walked to the road, the crowd in front of Minnie's store thinned. We trooped inside. When screaming and torment went on down there, it was not for the living to know or understand.

"Anybody got a peavey?" Tip looked to Minnie. "Me and Jim have got to fix that road a little."

We borrowed the peavey and used it to crack out sleepers from the broken rail bed. For two hours we tossed sleepers into the torn spot of road. With the sun back of the mountain, the old Ford limped across. We made it back to town considerably after dark.

Next day Bobby Joe pulled Tip off to one side. The two men talked, looked toward me. Sarah Jane looked toward me. Lots of questions on faces. Not much said. It seemed clear I was on trial.

When the sheriff showed up he pulled me and Tip into Bobby Joe's office. He wasn't much of a sheriff.

"Lord only knows who done it," Tip told him. "I can't say who did, but can say who didn't."

"Could have been someone from town," I mentioned. "But I'm new around here. You might say I didn't see anything except a well-used Cadillac."

When the sheriff left it was clear I'd passed my test. Sarah Jane was lots more friendly. Bobby Joe said that maybe, in a couple months, I could go into the field alone.

"Will those dead stay dead?" I asked Tip once we cleared out of the office.

"Can't imagine that they won't."

"And those alive?"

"They are not off the hook," Tip told me. "You kill a bastard like Sims and ten more just like him come to the funeral. "

It fell out that Tip was wrong. The coal company turned the show over to a man wise in the ways of the hills. He wasn't a bit nicer than Sims, but lots smarter. He figured it more economic to strip some other mountain.

I worked out of that office for two more years, then got transferred to Cincinnati. It took all of those two years, a long, long time, for the old men of Drowning Mountain to repair that road. I'm told that they sang church songs as they worked.

Miss Molly's Manners

A Book of Etiquette for Dogs by Miss Molly
Manners as told to Jack Cady & Carol Orlock

*For Rufus and Keeley and Jude,
great bounders and leapers all, in memory.*

Contents

How it All Began

A dog and two humans—a lady and a gent—sat on a front porch one morning and watched children on their way to school. It was a very nice day filled with colorful autumn leaves. The humans chatted as children hopped about and sang, and as a Golden Retriever named Chester Culpepper Bosworth bounced among them. It was Bosworth's job to see the children to the bus, and the humans thought the picture a pretty sight; until the dog on the porch gave a long sigh.

"The world is changing very quickly," the dog said in a quiet voice. She was a brown-chocolately dog with a white blaze on her chest, and floppity ears. "The gentlemanly dog out there tries to do his job correctly, but see how he fails to cover the outside of the pack. He should always herd from the edge of the sidewalk, keeping the herd away from the street." She gave another sigh, and this sigh was definitely sad. "In my day," she murmured, "dogs were rather a bit better at taking charge. These young ones have crude skills and slip-shod manners." Her voice was not, fortunately, as prim as her words.

"In many ways I agree with you," the man said, although he failed to conceal a smile. The man suffered from a waggish reputation, and some people, and some dogs, complained that he was never, never serious. "Perhaps," the man suggested, "you should write a book that explains the finer elements of the dog business."

"That is a case in point," the dog replied. "Ladies of my station do not type, although your idea is sound."

"But people can type," the woman said. "We do that sort of thing all the time. You can tell us what to write, and we will copy it out."

The dog looked at the woman, and the dog's eyes were sparkly with love, although they also held a smidgen of uncertainty.

"That would be very kind of you," the dog said, "but there may be editorial problems." She sniffed the back of the man's hand. "Just as I thought. He is already too excited."

"Between the two of us, I believe we can keep him under control," the woman said.

"He is wry as well as waggish."

"I am the soul of decorum," the man protested, "and I am ready to begin. Let's give it a shot."

And so the three sat around the typewriter through long fall and winter evenings as the dog, Miss Molly Manners, dictated the book that follows:

A Word About Breeding

I am one of a litter of seven, and even before our eyes were open our dear mater began to teach manners. As we pups grew, and embarked on careers, the wisdom of our good parent became evident. Each of my brothers and sisters has gone on to remarkable success. The largest—and I fear rowdiest—of my brothers now owns his own auto parts business; with injured autos stacked in neat rows behind chain link fence. A second brother is a police sergeant, and a third is a captain in the Army; for there is a military strain on both sides of the family. Two sisters own herds of sheep, and one sister (adventure is also a family characteristic) runs a sled team in Alaska. The family functions beautifully across a wide spectrum, and it is largely due to the inner elegance that rises from dear mater's teaching. We early on learned to make the following distinctions:

Protocols between canines are reasonably well understood. Centuries of breeding have allowed dogs of all nationalities to develop civilized communication. It is thus true that the German Schnauzer and the Mexican Hairless are quite capable of discourse, and of enjoying each other's company. Even dogs of mixed breed— or perhaps they especially—are capable of drawing on the best manners of the breeds.

My own family, for example, stems from two proud lines. On the maternal side we trace our heritage through generation after generation of Labrador Retrievers (of the chocolate persuasion), while the paternal side is pure Brittany Spaniel; and it is largely from that side of the family that we inherit a tiddly-bit of British accent. In fact, these pages follow the Englishy tracking style of the true spaniel, zigging and zagging and owning their share of wobbles. One need only trail along in true spaniel fashion. If the trail goes cold, simply backtrack and regain the scent, a scent always flavored with culture and manners. The calm and steadiness of our mater will be complimented by the (sometimes boundless) enthusiasm of dear pater. Thus, it will be understood that when encountering fellow dogs, we are readily able to join in thoughtful communication, or in play.

Problems with breeding do not really occur until we turn to our relationships with humans, and it is toward that relationship that we embark. The book examines the canine-human relationship, including a section for the instruction of puppies. It then considers relationships with other animals. The third and final section discusses specific social situations, sometimes with humans.

We may only say at the beginning that it would be most unkind, and certainly not courteous, to look into the breeding of the human race. The best that may be said is that the human background is a frightful mix. The worst that may be said, will in a book of manners, not be.

Yet humans are a part of our lives, often a welcome part. We assume that humans were first attracted to dogs because, in dark and ancient days, humans feared the night. They also feared lions and volcanoes. Companionship with their own kind was insufficient, and life was obviously dreadful. They turned to the dog, and they became our loyal companions. The human who pledges love and loyalty to a dog is usually answered in kind, and that human is lucky, lucky.

Our relationships with them are far more workable after a bit of training, a subject to which we may momentarily turn.

Despite obvious limitations, humans are surprisingly teachable, and most of them seem eager to please. You'll soon discover that the learning problems your humans encounter have to do with misunderstanding your desires. The dears want to obey, but cannot figure out your meanings. In order to train a human you really have to think like a human; never an easy task, but one that usually succeeds when undertaken in a spirit of patience, courtesy, and kindness. Civilized behavior, after all, is what we seek.

When thinking like a human it is necessary to virtually abandon the most important of the senses. Humans, although they sport prominent and often inquisitive noses, cannot even smell a gerbil at ten paces, leave alone five hundred. They depend largely on their eyes, and moderately on their ears.

Let us suppose, for example, that you wish to train your humans to come to you. Rather than exhaust everyone in a game of chase (at which humans have no chance of success) it is not indelicate to use their infirmity to assist their understanding. I suggest that you feign enormous interest in a particularly lush and grassy spot of lawn or golf course. Show great excitement, as if your own keen sense of smell has detected a gopher. Begin to dig with great enthusiasm. Your human will come immediately, since it appears that the creatures cannot resist the possibility of retrieving a gopher.

Or, perhaps you are sufficiently rested after a nap beside the fireplace, and wish to take a stroll in the cool of the evening. You attempt to communicate with humans and find them obtuse.[1] There is no excuse at this point for ruffian behavior such as barking, whining, moaning, or pawing at the rug or door. Simply get the leash and stand beside the door. Raise your tail as high as it will go, and adopt a puzzled but worried look. Humans, for reasons that are not completely understood, will universally respond to this signal.

In my experience I've found that humans learn rather well in the context of play. When convinced that joy is the object, they are easily taught to throw a ball or a stick. Many of them can even learn to ride a bicycle if you trot politely beside them offering moral support.[2]

These examples, and others we are to later see, should be studied at some length by the dog of refined sensibility. Our society has evolved to a high plane since the days when our ancestors dwelt in dens and caves. It is only right that we cultivate the finest graces of manners, so that these graces will serve as an example in an otherwise troubled world.[3]

If you set the example for humans and for cats (these two comprise the most obstinate of the many species) you may be sure your endeavors will succeed. Perhaps you will not turn your humans into charm school graduates, and cats will never completely lose their sharp edges, but you will have made your world, and theirs, a far more pleasant place. A wonderfully large number of lovely humans have learned most of their social behavior from canine associates.

Selecting Your Human

How sad it is to meet a dog who has shown poor judgment in the choice of a human. In my travels I meet many such unhappy cases: Pomeranians in charge of two-hundred-pound monsters (who the Poms must dutifully drag home from ice cream parlors), or Mastiffs controlling their natural large urges because they have befriended a human who weighs less than the smallest Saint Bernard. Although affection may certainly exist in these relationships, it is an affection with only partial fulfillment.

Remember, the human who first comes bouncing toward you may not be the human who will best suit your needs. The young dog should study the characteristics of breed. It would be the height of folly for Retrievers to choose from the breeds of Bowler or Pool Player, since the balls used in such games are unsatisfactory. Golfers look interesting at first blush, but prove tedious. A human with an affinity for softball is ideal.

Or suppose one is a Beagle. The rule here is: 'Do not adopt a surfer'; a good rule, in fact, for any dog (although a few Newfoundlands who own lower than average morals have prospered).

When it came to choosing my own humans I surveyed a rather large field, for few humans exhibit every characteristic the individual dog might desire. I chose Miss Lovely and Rags because Miss Lovely likes to dance or run, and Rags likes to throw things (especially balls, sticks, and an occasional party), and because he is jolly.

The lesson, then, is one that asks young dogs to review their needs and choose accordingly. It is quite difficult to pass up the soulful look of a hopeful human, but you do yourself and that human no favor by making a poor choice.

Naming Your Human:
Will it be Spaught or Mr. Janders

In naming your human it is well to pay close attention to his or her appearance and propensities. How many, many unfortunate males bear the unhappy name of Ralph, simply because it is easy to pronounce? Ralph is a very nice name, as we may all agree, but it is not suitable for those fleet humans who are best named Shadow or Scout. My own male, Rags, earned his name through his disheveled and comical appearance, as well as his inordinate interest in garage sales.

My female, Miss Lovely, is a welcome contrast to Rags. She is sleek, soft spoken, and cultured. Whereas Rags will burp or even scratch at a dog show, Miss Lovely orders her behavior in a considerate way that ennobles all around her, even the irrepressible Rags. It would be an error, though, to believe that culture and jollity cannot combine. Miss Lovely is greatly sought after by both talk show hosts and Sunday schools, since each is intrigued by her ability to put a wicked spin on any conversation.

In the naming of humans trust to two simple guidelines and you will not run astray:

Overlook any name humans have given to themselves or to each other. These are often based on the names of ancestors, or movie stars, or comic book heroes. Nothing more need be said.

Eschew pet names such as "Cutsie," "Honey-huggums," or "Muffin Mix." Calling out such in public thoroughfares or in parks is liable to bring out other humans with whom you want nothing to do.

The Care of Humans

Research demonstrates human intellectual development as equal to that of an eight-month-old pup, which means that humans are trapped in a continuing state of adolescence; or at least the best of them are.[4] This is what makes them so loveable, and deserving of elegantly descriptive names such as Jolly Boy, and Rompers.

Like adolescents everywhere, they are given to taking chances while showing little judgment. They are especially susceptible to avalanches, swimming pools, campfires, traffic snarls and lava flows. They tend to fall from high places. Most regrettably, they often forget what they are about and wander off, sometimes into snowstorms.

The responsible dog knows that adopting a human is a commitment not lightly undertaken, because a human is not a toy. Too often, after the newness of the relationship wears off, the care of humans is undertaken with a grudging spirit. If, however, a bit of time and thought are dedicated to the care of humans, the average dog will find both satisfaction and enjoyment in the endeavor. The thoughtful owner should follow a few simple guidelines, pursuing them in a kindly and civilized spirit.

EATING: Never interfere with these creatures while they are eating, unless they offer to share. If this should happen, you have an opportunity to train them to good table manners. Sit quietly and accept their donations with simple good grace (if such donations are edible). Sometimes they will offer to share something that does not take your fancy, lemonade or sauerkraut. Decline politely, and wait to see if there are other offerings.

WALKING: They have a frightful tendency to get off leash, and off heel. A bit of corrective action at the beginning of the relationship will save just worlds of bother later.

When off heel you can bring them back by bracing with all four feet and emitting a sharp command. Some handlers feel that a yowl should be used at this juncture, but I have found a precise yip all that is really necessary.

When off leash one must take command immediately, or they are liable to become confused and dash into traffic. It is best to simply lope beside them while searching for areas into which they may be herded. If one stays slightly ahead, and follows standard herding practice of gentle pressure left or right, the creatures are generally compliant. With really difficult cases, it may be necessary to hide their shoes during some period when they are asleep.

SLEEPING: Their patterns are peculiar. They miss the choice parts of the night and stay awake during the dullest parts of the day. They will spend an evening beside a nice fireplace and never blink. Then they will yawn and go to bed for eight hours. A few of them, such as my Rags, understand naps; but very few, I fear. Rags does not, therefore, get the credit he deserves.

Rather than try to change their sleep patterns, it is best to simply take charge of the bed. The courteous dog will choose the foot of the bed. It is possible to nap there with practically no discomfort to anyone.

GOING OUT INTO THE WORLD: You could retrieve the newspaper from that icy front lawn, but if they wish to do so, so be it.

MAKING TRIPS ALONE: Some humans are solitary creatures. They leave the house on most mornings and do not return until evening. This is disconcerting, since it breaks the rhythm and order of the pack. It is proper to make a bit of a fuss when they leave, but do not scold when they return. Remember: the recall must always be a pleasant experience, no matter if it follows an admittedly shabby performance.

HOUSECLEANING: You can help by barking at the vacuum cleaner. It is a cheery business to joust with the thing, and it makes your humans laugh. Thus is a dull chore brightened.

BATHS: People take so many baths because their bodies are not supple and their tongues are too short. Humans are good at a great many things, but they cannot lick worth a snip. Some dogs like to participate in a bath by hanging over the edge of the tub. The main hazard is a dab of soap on one's nose if one associates with a human who has clownish propensities.

UNDER-PETTING: They occasionally become preoccupied and do not give enough ear and brisket rubs. Do not nag. Simply sit before them and whine in your most plaintive manner. They are relatively intelligent creatures, and rapidly learn this command.

DEPRESSION: You are at your best when they are depressed. You should first recall their loyalty to you, and give some indication that it is respected and well received. The simple gesture of placing one paw on their knee as they sit, or bringing them a squeaky toy if they are standing, works wonders. You cannot always make them happy, but you can almost always make them less sad.

MOVING TO A NEW HOUSE: They are such creatures of habit that any move is traumatic. It is imperative that they not be reminded of good times at the old address, but be enticed by the promise of good times at the new address. Your best gesture is to root around behind the refrigerator. Draw forth your hidden treasure of old socks and well-seasoned bones. Stack them beside the doorway.

EXERCISE: This is one of the tedious arenas in which we and our humans perform. Some humans, such as my Miss Lovely, are fleet runners and bouncers who present few problems when it comes to conditioning. Other humans, such as my Rags, require daily attention. If Rags is not walked, and vigorously, he tends to drift about the house while talking to himself and bumping into things. It is a bother on wet or cold night to take him around the block, and sooner or later all dogs face similar situations. Remember the happy times, however, and you will gladly give the small personal investment it takes to keep your human reasonably fit.

A Primer for Puppies

The joys of puppyhood are greatly enhanced when the young dog receives the careful guidance all youth deserve, and it is never too soon to lay foundations on which may be built that cultured and dignified presence the well-mannered dog displays. Even the youngest puppies may be introduced to principles of good behavior. While each parent will wish to interpret what follows with his or her own emphasis, we may generally agree that the young dog should have knowledge of the following:

CROTCH SNIFFING: As we all know, the dog, through superior intellect and sensory ability, communicates with information supplied by the nose. The normal and desirable sniffing that goes on between dogs is, however, denied the human species. There are a goodly number of reasons (most of them more or less unmentionable) why one should not attempt to communicate with a human in this manner.

PUPPY LOVE: There is nothing more comprehensive in the world than puppy love, but as the young dog grows and gains weight the following formula will eventually obtain:

$$\frac{\text{Strength} + \text{velocity}}{\text{Love x trajectory}} = \text{"OFF"}$$

And when this happens, you can injure someone. Humans have extremely slow reflexes. Their ability to dodge and weave is mostly intellectual. Puppies will need to temper their actions if not their affections. With other dogs, of course, a puppy may bounce at will.

EATING: The inhaling of food is simply not done. We are not wolves, after all.

PICNICS: differ from normal eating situations. In order to communicate one should adopt an orphaned look. Concentrate on sorrow. Think of all the balls you have lost, and of the taunting of cats. Think of how you have forgotten the sites of buried bones. As your gaze fills with limpid sorrow your humans will beg you to join them. When you accept the choicer portions of the scraps, your humans will feel ever so much better.

LICKING: Nothing is sweeter than a puppy lick, and all dogs know this, as do many humans. Be discreet around humans, however, as some of them are insensitive. It is probably wise to avoid any creature that does not love a good lick.

GROCERY BAGS: Almost always contain something of interest to the young dog. Perfectly sound practice dictates that one may dance beside the person who carries such a bag. Nipping at the bag, or attempting to jump inside, betrays a lack of dignity. Until the age of one year, drooling is marginally acceptable.

BATHS: please humans so much that they wish to share the experience with you. This may involve tubs or buckets or hoses; all aimed at your enjoyment, but generally unpleasant. Humans hold the farfetched idea that the young dog wishes to be rid of his wonderfully natural smells.

It is only courteous to join in their game because they, as we, should daily experience the joys of play.

One should jump right in. Do not shilly-shally in the shallows or dilly-dally in the shadows. Immerse yourself with pretended enthusiasm and splash like the veriest trout. When sudsing occurs remain passive but alert for the precise moment when fingers massage your backbone. At that point give a jolly, jolly shake—a very large shake—then turn and give your human's nose a lovely lick. If they are acute, they will come to realize that two can play this game.

TOILET BOWLS: are attractive hazards that will fool the inexperienced youngster. The cultured dog regards the bowl as an emergency water supply reserved for occasions of need. On the other paw, uncultured but pretentious dogs will chatter endlessly about the qualities of bowl water. A good rule is to listen for expressions of veneer-thin sophistication. If the young dog hears such statements as: ". . . chilled natural water replenished several times daily", or "A truly regal bouquet, carrying full-bodied aroma and a bold nose that makes a strong statement," it is well to avoid the speaker whose company will prove too fast, and who obviously associates with very odd companions.

ELIMINATION PROTOCOLS: If humans understood the glories of nature they would surely stop hiding in small rooms during the performance of desirable functions. The puppy will soon discover that his or her human is almost unreasonably obsessed with a desire to be discreet in these matters. An honest dog cannot really offer understanding, but any courteous dog can offer aid. In a spirit of charity, and when walking with a human, avoid deposits in:

a) The doorways of banks.
   Crosswalks, when walking with the light and in front of stopped motorists; and even more so when jaywalking.
   Tennis courts.
   Lawn parties.
   Ornamental fountains.
   Before mailboxes.
   Play fields, and
   In front of Police Stations.

b) Marking territory: Inexperience usually betrays the young male who has not been advised that there is need for precise and definitive movement. As the dog grows, and the lifting of the leg is required, the careless youngster will stand slightly skewed and will bear the disgrace of sporting a very damp foot.

   c) Tall grass is not only a comfort, but should be sought out of consideration for your human.

COWS: The chasing of cattle is a lowbrow characteristic displayed by the uneducated dog. It is, however, perfectly acceptable (and also rather grand) to frolic with horses.

COMPANY: No matter how well you have trained your humans, the training will sometimes slip. They will become fanciful or flighty and not pay enough attention to you.

Wait until they bring strangers home for dinner. Behave as if you adore the strangers. This will get your humans' attention and they will take you seriously. If you begin to hear such statements as, "I'd like to take this furry little thing home with me," you've probably overdone it, so be careful and beat a hasty retreat. After your humans have chased the strangers away you will be rewarded. I prefer steak and kidney pie.

TO CHEW OR NOT TO CHEW, THAT IS THE MASTICATION: As all puppies know, you always eat the thing you love, the thing you shouldn't eat . . . etc. Thus the question has as much to do with love as it does with chewing. The careful parent will point out that furniture is not really lovable, and that there is a difference between squeaky toys and the human toe.

Why Mirrors Have No Scent

We all recall our first encounter with a mirror, and recall the combination of uncertainty and thrill that shivered down our spines and even to the tips of our tails when we met a dog who gave no scent. Canine lore holds a number of possible explanations, and those explanations range from rational to mystical. No one denies that smell-less dogs exist, but there is as much disagreement about how they exist as there is disagreement over some of the mysteries of humans; as, for example: why does a human choose to talk to himself by holding a piece of plastic to his ear, after the plastic has made a disagreeable ringing sound?

Or, for that matter, why does a human sit before a box of moving pictures that talks to him? Some canine thinkers claim that the box is actually alive. Others, and this seems more likely, claim that the box is the human's substitute for a nose.

The dog in the mirror, according to the more rational argument, is not a dog at all but is our alter egos displayed at their hopeful best, and the mirror itself is an as yet unexplained expression of natural and universal force, since cats, people (or at least parts of them), babies, and an occasional mouse are all viewed at some advantage from time to time.[5]

If this theory proves true we are certain to discover that the world, already complicated with a virtuosity of smells, is far more complex than anyone has ever before imagined. We will have to accept the idea of the existence of a world within a world. In fact, we may have to learn, as have humans, to operate equally well in a smell-less universe.

The mystical answer serves many dogs, and it may well contain part or all of the truth. The legend goes as follows:

In the beginning our forebears lived in caves, and life was crude, brutish, and short. These first ancestors lived in a twilight world, because the sun had not yet been discovered. For this reason the nights were always cold, and it was always night. The packs got together and appointed dogs to travel north, south, west, and east in an attempt to discover a land of warmth.

The eastward bound dog was named Cosroe, later celebrated in primitive society as the Hound of Heaven. It was his lot to discover the sun, which, while attempting to rise, had gotten wedged between mountains. Cosroe set it free, and life forever changed.

As the sun rose dogs began to cast shadows, and fear rose among some members of the species. One could not really play with a shadow, could not smell it, and shadows do follow one around. Some dogs, who declared themselves sons and daughters of the moon, or Moon Dogs, fled into mirrors where they were mainly free of shadows. The dog in the mirror is thus a descendant of our mutual ancestors, and is vaguely related. In matters of courtesy, such dogs are entitled to the same consideration given shirttail cousins. One may bounce before them, and even woof (for it may be that they hear), but any attempt at intimacy, or other social discourse, should be foregone.

Balls, or Siren Song Sing-Along
and Matters Concerning the Moon

The first ball was invented in antiquity by the legendary Armbruster T. Licksmaster, a Cocker Spaniel and contemporary of Alexander the Great, although their politics differed. Licksmaster, himself an adventurer, understood that messages about the future lay in the past. Instead of studying prophecy he became engrossed in history.

He saw, and clearly, that the wolfish ancestry of the soon-to-be modern dog sent a message that, if translated, would change the lives of dogs forever. Licksmaster was especially taken by the ancients' fascination with the moon. After years of study he could still not say whether that fascination rose from moonlight, or from the positions of the moon in the sky, or from some combination of moon and clouds.

As age came over him he experienced despair, for indeed he had spent a lifetime on what seemed a fruitless task. As so often happens in the history of great discoveries, the intuitive moment occurred when least expected.

He embarked on a trip through the Greek Isles, retracing the steps of the famed Odysseus. His vessel touched the eastern end of Crete which in those days was still covered with trees. It was through the silvering branches and leaves of an olive *Olea Europa* that the great realization struck.

It was *not* as he had supposed, the illumination; and it was *not* the position in the sky. Licksmaster—and how often had he felt sorrow at the waning of the moon and joy at its full return—how often, in fact, had the very essence of his being leaped forth during the fullness of the moon—Licksmaster realized that all along it had been the shape. The roundness, the completeness now stood among the branches of the olive as Licksmaster, in one rare, intuitive leap of genius, understood that what was two-dimensional in the sky could be three-dimensional on earth.

... and all of nature had been trying to tell him this, the roundness of rolling stones, the curling of leaves ... he immediately canceled his trip and returned to his study. The rest is the stuff of legend.

Today we have as many different types of balls as there are types of dogs to chase them, and we even have balls for our humans. We have balls that bounce and balls that squish. We have furry tennis balls, smooth soccer balls, and the textured surfaces of basketballs.

With these balls a mythology has risen. As with any great idea, there will always be those who hope to make a reputation by interpreting (in their words) what the inventor 'meant.'

One cult of dogs (fortunately small) holds that balls are alive, and that balls have rights, and that any dog who chews a ball to excess should expect to be hauled into court.

Another group believes that the ball, while not alive, does serve as home for living creatures in much the way that the Mexican jumping bean harbors insects.

In addition, there are mystics who believe that balloons are the disembodied spirits of balls, and those spirits return to earth for brief periods when they either pop, or sail away into blue sky. There are, of course, various interpretations of the messages those spirits are supposed to bring.

My own educated feelings (for I have no small experience with balls) is that life can exist in a ball when the ball combines with a dog and a human. This is not mystical. The otherwise dormant ball actually comes to life, and is both plaything and companion.

The point of this in a book of etiquette is, obviously, an explanation of correct reactions to the moon. Your reaction is an atavistic trait, and it exists among dogs in the same way that singing exists among humans. Any dog may howl and any human may sing, but only those who hold atavistic talents are worth hearing. It is wise to sternly evaluate your own howl, and unless it has a touch of genius, use it only in remote areas where there is no one, except squirrels, to be annoyed.

Approaches to the Ball

The proper handling of a ball poses questions so complex that they can only be dealt with in a full-length work, and such is not possible here. A work does exist, however, in which philosophical matters are discussed, with special attention to metaphysics.[6]

My own small contribution consists in acknowledging major categories and approaches to them.

THERE IS ONLY ONE general principle: Does the ball enjoy the play? I have known many that do. They leap joyfully to me, and in my mouth give a satisfied squish as they express delight. This, dear friends, is a happy ball. It bounces, therefore it is.

BASEBALLS: are exceptionally enthusiastic, and rather more firm of spirit than one might desire. Do not catch them on the fly.

TENNIS BALLS: emit a lovely, swishy sound when they are happy, and tennis balls, like daffodils, are always happy. They are best chased on closely mown grass or on baseball infields. These venues yield the highest bounces.

SOCCER BALLS: should be awkward but are not. The rule is to play them at a distance, because in their enthusiasm they may bruise your nose. Once you have picked one off, however, you may with nose and paw soccer it right back to your kicker.

THE FRISBEE: is not a flat ball, although some frisbees make claim to aristocratic origins. They are actually instruments of flight and not for the inexperienced. Whereas a ball is predictably dependable, a frisbee is a creature of the wind. I advise a course in aerodynamics.

BASKETBALLS & FOOTBALLS: are either too large or too clumsy for a clean retrieval. They are delightful companions, though, when one merely wishes to tumble about.

VOLLEYBALLS: are first cousins to Soccer Balls. Difficult to say which is nicer.

RUBBER BALLS: these cover such a wide range that one must become intimate with each individual ball. Taste it, test it, measure the bounce. If you pay close and respectful attention the ball will tell you what it wants.

SNOWBALLS: Challenging questions rise regarding the nature of snowballs. All we can say is that their nature is transient, and sometimes wispy. They flee before us and are gone, like the passage of mayflies, or the disappearance of hares into tall grass. Always treat them kindly for they are not long among us.

SOFTBALLS: are the royalty of balls. They are heavy enough for distance, small enough to make a nice mouthful, and yet light enough for a graceful retrieval. I once met a highly spiritual

Weimaraner named Gertrude B(ertha) Schmidt. She owned a
great reputation as a mystic, and was a proponent of reincarnation.
We will, according to her, enter onto the highest state of being only
on that happy day when we are reincarnated as softballs.

A Word Concerning Squirrels

Perhaps the most distasteful and distressing sight it has been my
share to witness occurred one sunny autumn day among the
grasses and trees of a lovely park. My male human, Rags, and
I returned from a rousing game of fetch. We were both in fine
fettle. A lovely hillock rose beside us, and on the rim of this hill
suddenly appeared a handsome Samoyed, who, I am sorry to
report, turned out to be a rather giddy fellow. All would have
gone well, no doubt, had it not been the season when squirrels
come to ground.

An enormous tree stood at the bottom of the hill, and halfway up
the hill a squirrel foraged, tail a-flip. The Samoyed strolled down
the hill, the squirrel tended up the hill, and it was clear the two
would meet. Here was a fine opportunity for a display of civilized
behavior on the part of the Samoyed. Nothing of that sort might,
of course, be expected from the squirrel.

I am grieved to report that no civilized behavior occurred.
The squirrel, on seeing the Samoyed, immediately rose a foot
in the air while reversing his field. It would be a fine thing to
report that the squirrel actually called on his Maker, but the
most that passed his lips was, "Oh, sweet . . ." and then he began
cursing. He ran like a road thing for the huge tree at the bottom
of the hill.

The Samoyed had been thinking of other matters and was
actually in a bit of a squat when he first observed the squirrel. He
rose from the squat like a small jet exhausting a contrail of effluvia,
tapped his heels together three times before he hit the ground,
and enthusiastically turned into a flash of white as he pursued the
loudly cursing squirrel.

The squirrel reached the tree and dashed upward. The Samoyed,
shortening the distance of his angle between hill and tree, leapt

into the air with the lightness of witchery; until, of course, he missed the squirrel but captured a very large portion of the tree (the splat being the only impressive feature of the event).

The Samoyed slowly slithered down the tree, shook his ringing head, and wandered off in search of safer game; moose or cougar. The squirrel sat on a branch and turned the blue sky a deeper dusky blue with those obscenities of which only the most depraved squirrel is capable. The fact that my human, Rags, had dropped his leash and leaned against another tree in a paroxysm of chuckles, did nothing to lighten a truly tasteless situation.

The question now rises: what should the Samoyed have done, and why?

Three courses of action were available:

1) IGNORE the squirrel while concealing any natural aversions for rodents.
2) WOOF once, but sharply, to alert the squirrel and thus avoid unseemly confrontation.
3) TROT in a wide circle. The squirrel will still be alerted, and confrontation avoided, but the squirrel will also be puzzled. If puzzlement causes him to mull on the meaning of life, then a good deed has been achieved.

Why should confrontation be avoided?

a) There can be no communion between souls so radically different as dogs (capable of noble thought and deed) and squirrels whose universe looms no larger than the next nut.
b) One is only demeaned by association with low fellows. When a human named Mark Twain wrote of the bad language of bluejays, he might well have gone on and mentioned the truly original observations made by squirrels. Remember, when you lay down with squirrels you catch sleaze.
c) And finally, it is awfully difficult to behave in a cultured manner during a day in which one has made an absolute fool of oneself. That Samoyed, we later learned, was last seen chasing his tail in the lobby of a Federal Building.

In the Dubious Matter of Cats

Every so often evolution has a bad day, a fact to which the feline, *Felis Catus*, or common housecat, is simple testament.

Some dogs choose to befriend them. Unlike squirrels, cats are highly complex creatures who, in the manner of humans, are occasionally capable of utmost grace.[7] A creature who holds so much potential cannot be dismissed in the way one may dismiss bunnies.

If one keeps in mind the main characteristics of cats it is possible to live comfortably beside them, although my observation suggests that such a life is like living in a mild stage of siege. Along with other characteristics, cats are devious.

Not many days have passed since I heard the unhappy tale that follows, a tale made even sadder because it promises to be unending. It came through chance acquaintance on a playfield. The Poodle's name is Jacques Jean Louis, a graduate of one of the most prestigious obedience schools in the nation; a school not named here because Louis, I am sad to report, momentarily discredited it. No opprobrium attaching to the distressed Jacques Jean should reflect on his alma mater. But, let me report the sad affair in his own words, for it seems that I can nearly see him now as he rested on mown grass (and not among weeds which might have contributed burrs to his gleaming white coat). It actually seems that I can hear his voice, albeit thanks to his mellifluous French accent, he delicately spiced his story with an herbs garni of "*Mon ami's*", "*Mon chere's*" and an "*Au contraire!*" now and again. Put in proper English here is the essence of it:

"In a whimsical moment, but with all good intent, I adopted a cat. This was a big bull cat, one of the stripey kind that one sees guarding the back entrances of bistros, or sitting in the cheap seats at soccer games. I know something of the nature of cats, n'est pas?—and therefore named him Gladstone. I knew from the beginning that there would be a few problems, but figured I was dog enough to handle them. Gladstone was at first a welcome addition to my pack which also includes the humans Bastion (a rather large fellow) and Twinque (especially light on her feet).

When the four of us rested around the fireplace on cold winter evenings it seemed that life could offer little more in the way of comfort and joy.

"Gladstone, however, was of a cat's normally devious nature. I recall his initial approach on a spring day when Bastion was out wandering through side streets, and Twinque played hostess to a bridge party that was a-slap with cards, a-tinkle with tea things, and a-chirp with the voices of female humans; altogether a combination of light and wholesome sounds.

"'Louis, old chap', said Gladstone (who is something of an anglophile) 'are you up for a bit of sport?' He then explained that he knew a nearby spot where the hunting was 'a rum go.'

"No Poodle ever born could turn down a good hunt. I was intrigued. I supposed that Gladstone had located a covey of raccoon, or the cave of a bear. I forgot that no game is too petite for a cat.

"He led me to the back of a neighbor's house where sat a motley pile of boards. 'Louis, old man, just you climb onto the stack and bounce. Let us see what comes to pass.' He then trotted about twenty paces from the stack, went into a crouch, and his tail flicked like a quartermaster's semaphore.

"And I, like a fool, jumped onto the stack and bounced. I expected a porcupine to emerge, or perhaps one of the smaller catamounts; or, was it too much to hope for the emergence of a fox?

"Instead, there was a series of small shrieks, and then a cacophony of squeaks. At the very moment that I realized I had been taken, a gray flash tumbled from beneath the boards and dashed across the lawn to the accompanying cry from Gladstone of, 'Tally Ho, the mouse!'

"A tawdry scene ensued. Gladstone easily captured the mouse which he held pinned by the tail.

"'Topping good show, lad,' Gladstone said to me. To the mouse he said, 'Bit of a shame, chum. But, you're in time for lunch.'

"In all of my days of hunting I have never encountered a creature so bold as that mouse. He looked into Gladstone's eyes, and pity shone from his own.

"The mouse made explanations. He claimed himself sole support of a family of seventy-three, and he claimed to have a number of incurable ailments of which all were transmissible through stomach lining, and he claimed to have a secret treasure to which only he could draw a map. The mouse waxed eloquent. He claimed close friendship with the chief of police. He asserted that certain members of the Mafia would greatly resent it if he turned up missing. He was passionate, intense, and magnificently persuasive. As I turned away in disgust, I heard Gladstone saying, 'Ah well, then, matey, perhaps we can cut a deal.'

"Even then I did not realize that the affair was a highly sophisticated set-up. Who would ever dream that a cat and mouse were capable of collusion? In disgust, nay revulsion, I repaired to the house. The bridge party was at full tinkle. The female humans were having a wonderful time. As I stood in the doorway to the living room and watched the players at their game, I did not sense the shadow of Gladstone (who carried the mouse gently in his mouth) approach from behind.

"'Shipwreck,' muttered Gladstone, in what was obviously a code. He released the mouse which ran between my legs and into the living room. At the same time Gladstone gave me a small poke in the behind, and naturally I jumped forward. As I jumped, the mouse began a dizzying performance. He scampered here, there, amid shrieks and flurries, among falling playing cards and between running feet as the humans fell over themselves getting out of his way.

"And I, knowing my duty although detesting it, gave chase. The mouse dashed up the draperies, a small gray streak against blue velvet; and from the top of the draperies did a swan dive onto the back of an easy chair. The mouse stood on that chairback as on a stage while singing a few bars from *The Hallelujah Chorus*. He sang most lustily, then made a lewd gesture as he ducked beneath my hurtling form. I came down in a plate of avocado dip, while the mouse disappeared through the now open doorway. Gladstone sat leering.

"And so ended my days of quiet joy. My leadership of the pack has been challenged. My humans are confused, and the detestable Gladstone now tries to pre-empt my favorite spot beside the fireplace. I do not know how long it will take to once more cement my friendship with Twinque; and worse, I fear that I've not seen the end of duplicity in my pack. Gladstone is not ill-named. Mon Dieu!"

Louis, poor fellow, then wandered off muttering to himself. He was not the first Poodle ever betrayed by a cat, and he will doubtless not be the last; for Poodles are a rather innocent breed, although their courage is never in doubt.

Perhaps most of Louis' troubles might have been avoided by following a few principles that would have kept the relationship within the bounds of civility. These are:

THERE ARE two kinds of cats; indoor and garbage can. The indoor cat amuses herself by being svelte. The garbage can cat specializes in raids. You can get along with either by addressing their interests. It pays to regard the indoor cat as a mere ornament, and the garbage can cat as a vagrant.

SCOUT the terrain and know your territory. Cats are notorious for lying in wait and cuffing the innocent passer-by. They claim to do this in the missionary spirit of keeping dogs on their toes, but one suspects some sort of low self-gratification.

WHEN A CAT HOPS onto a human's lap it is important to exhibit no signs of jealousy. One may chuckle, but not sneer. The cat knows that you know what is going on, and the human knows that you know what is going on, and you and the cat know that the human knows—in other words, the whole business is a stalking horse. If the cat cannot make you jealous it will hop off that lap and try other methods.

NEVER ARGUE. The feline point of view is generally warped, and the cat will force you to take the moral high ground. The moment that happens, the cat will declare itself the winner on the basis that you are not practical.[8]

IT IS A WASTE of time to chase a cat. If you catch one you'll find that you really do not want it. If you tree one, then it will be the treed cat, and not you, who gets all the attention.

WHEN CATS YOWL at night you should remain quiet, dignified, and aloof. The automatic comparison between your conservative behavior, and their loss of all claim to decency, will become obvious.

Control

CATNIP: can be one of your best friends. Keep a small supply in reserve while hoping that the cat waits for a rainy day before becoming too obnoxious. Leave a light trail of catnip from living room to outer door that should be open. With a little luck, and superb timing, it is possible to arrange for kitty to take a real bath.

WHILE POWER PLAYS are usually poor tactics, you can always control a cat by threatening to spread its kitty litter about the house. No cat wishes to get blamed for this, and no human will ever dream that the dog did it. Use only as a last resort.

The Dog Who Owned a Harley
A Cautionary Tale

Jackson J. Jodphers was a confirmed car chaser throughout his callow youth, and by the time he gained his full weight and strength had become an errant rogue who ignored his cultured training. His lack of manners, and generally dissolute performances were the principal sorrows of his parents. His mother, Prudence Elizabeth (nee Adams of the New England Adams), was a quiet and retiring Great Dane, while his father, Chesley, took pride in being a gentlemanly Doberman of the old school.

The opinion of all decent dogs held that Jodphers's destiny lay beneath the wheels of a pink '57 Rambler, or perhaps something not quite so quaint. No garbage can within ten miles was safe from him, and his collection of clothing dragged from clotheslines became legendary. Jodphers bragged on any and all street corners that he had persuaded entire litters of pups away from the paths of righteousness, and onto the straight and easy road that carried aught but high times and Hell's Angels. It was a Hell's Angel, in fact, who contributed to Jodphers's undoing.

When he finally got around to adopting a human, Jodphers chose the hottest motorcycle in town, and resolved to take whatever human came with it. That human carried the appellation of Goat Breath Jones, a man famed and feared throughout the countryside. With Jodphers in a sidecar, and with Goat Breath dressed in leathers, the two were a diabolic sight before which even the sheriff fled.

Night after night, and through the wee hours of morn, dogs huddled in their houses as the sharp crack of the Harley roared beside the howling of Jodphers and the crazed shrieks of Goat Breath. The two cruised highways and byways, and became familiar in roadhouses and other bawdy places. If a dime store was robbed of its candy, or a meat market of sausages, heads wagged and paws pointed to Jodphers and Goat Breath. The Harley, although never asked for an opinion, or giving one, was also held culpable.

A dissolute life is usually short, but among some scamps and scalliwags a distorted worldview functions like vitamins. Instead of meeting a wretched end, the duo used their travels to gather a pack of followers. Before long Goat Breath and Jodphers were selling motorcycles and sidecars. The business grew. Soon the entire county blazed with yells and howls and the snapping of bike engines. Just before the authorities moved in, Jodphers and Goat Breath moved out.

They now live on a ranch in west Texas, where they run cattle, and indulge in every luxury. Theirs is a gold-plated existence, but crudity has taken its toll. From his climate-controlled doghouse, Jodphers occasionally strolls; and for long moments he sometimes sorrows over what might have been, for he knows he has lost touch with common dogdom and his roots.

The Moral

This tragedy of moral corruption carries the stern and awful message: "You can't go home again." Perhaps even worse, when you try to go home again, you may end up in west Texas. To avoid traveling down the road to gilt-plated obscurity, it is well to memorize the following principles:

NEVER court a friendship based on material possessions. If Jodphers had been willing to settle for a Honda, he would no doubt have found a companion of slightly higher quality.

ALWAYS dare to dream. Why, one wonders, did Jodphers not aspire to a Triumph, or, lacking that, a BMW?

The Car

Your people have gone to a bit of expense in furnishing you with your auto. The thoughtful dog will wish to set an example of care and maintenance. The exterior may be disregarded, inasmuch as only the most raffish dogs actually chase cars or engage in other mongrel behaviors. If tires are to be watered it should be done in an unostentatious manner at curbside while the machine is not moving.

On the other paw, the interior of the car is quite another matter. A simple checklist will allow you to keep the auto in tip top condition for as many as two or three weeks. Your behavior will also reflect credit on those who ride with you.

NOSE PRINTS: while it is essential that the nose be pressed against glass when riding, the thoughtful dog will place nose prints only around the borders of windows. This allows the driver a clear view to sides and rear. If you are a larger dog, please recall that your bulk should only block the driver's view before and after—but not during—lane changes.

OPEN WINDOWS: when riding with the head out the window it is courteous to defer your position to the back seat. This will show other passengers that they are appreciated, and it will protect the seat covers. After all, even the most discreet among us will release at least some slobber into the windstream, and your people probably do not need their faces washed.

REST STOPS: are designed for canine research. Proceed to the pet area with dignity and self-control. You know ahead of time that it will be impossible to read all messages imprinted on grass and trees and refuse containers. While your human engages in idle conversation, such as: "Hurry up" and "If we don't get going soon we'll hit commuter traffic," take your time and savor a few of the messages. Remember that intense and careful research of a small area is much better than generalizations covering a complete hill or dale.

COMFORTING: the driver during a traffic jam. A simple lick behind the ear will elicit sufficient response to determine the driver's mood. If the driver is crabby, take a nap. If the driver giggles, then another lick may be appropriate.

BARKING: indiscriminate barking is an embarrassment to all involved, thus barking should be limited to occasions of joy or warning. One is almost obligated to bark while on the way to a picnic, and one should certainly let the world know about the presence of cats sitting on porches, but barking at funeral processions simply is not done.

WOOFING: carries a good deal more authority than barking, and should only be used to assist the driver. When parallel parking, for example, one really should center oneself on the seat and peer though the back window. Woof with authority. This will clear the way for your driver.

DEFENSE: when defending the car it is well to remember that one can get caught up in the enthusiasm of the moment. Try to claw your way through the upholstery on only the most important occasions. What follows is a list in descending importance:

- Pekinese in another car sneers.
- Great Dane passes along sidewalk while minding his own business.
- Kindergarten class on field trip to fire station.
- Stewardess pulling luggage carrier that contains a suitcase.
- Covey of ducks strolling in park.
- Urchin stealing hub caps.
- Suspicious looking stranger lifting hood.

And always remember that the armrest may be used as a headrest, but should never be mistaken for a rawhide bone.

The Veterinary Visit

It is the rare dog who actually enjoys a trip to the veterinary, but such trips are necessary. It is true that they are tedious, but is also true that some dogs have come to regard them as frightening. Because of mixed emotions, it too often happens that otherwise respectable dogs make a dreadful fuss about 'The Vet' who, they declare: "Is not my friend and never will be and I am going to brace myself against the posts of doorways never to be moved vetward world-without-end." Such dogs strike me as namby-pamby, incapable of understanding duty, and are decidedly lacking in pride; for there are few other times in life when we may so truly encourage others by our display of elegant manners.

If a visit to the veterinary is broken down into its several parts, it will be easy for the sophisticated dog to analyze and develop the finest manners for all varieties of veterinary situations:

Preparing for the trip

YOU NOTICE that your human is behaving deviously. My Rags, for example, always begins to whistle *Tangerine*, and Miss Lovely dons socks that carry happy pictures of giraffes or pink pigs. Odd actions always mean a trip to the Vet so prepare your mind. Think noble thoughts; pretend you are an English Bulldog. It may help to mutter such things as 'make a good go of this, chum' or 'stiff upper lip, old chap.'

Remember that your human already feels horrid, and you have little reason to complicate the situation. Tell yourself that the universe is really rather large, and this matter is actually a bit small from a celestial point of view. Do not:

Cower beneath the bed (one does encounter dust kittens)

Hide in the cellar

Roll onto your back and scream

Run up walls and across ceilings.

ONCE IN THE CAR silence is the best option. Silence allows you to brood, and it may well render your human both guilty and thoughtful. If your human is sufficiently thoughtful, some very nice things may happen after the visit.

Arriving

STEP FROM the automobile with dignity. If anyone is to betray nervousness, let it be your human. They are, as we all know, fairly emotional.

KEEP your human at heel. They tend to bolt at the last minute.

The Waiting Room

YOU are here for a booster shot, but remember that others may actually feel ill. Do not bounce.

IF other humans exclaim, 'What a sweet dog. How pretty. What kind is she? What is her name?' bear with it. They may be under stress and their clamor may be doing them some good.

BE CORDIAL. Exchange pleasantries with any other dogs, but do not inquire about their health. There is always a chance they will wish to discuss personal affairs about which you really do not wish to know.

IF CATS ARE PRESENT it is the worst possible manners to sneer, or go "n'yah, n'yah, n'yah." It is cruel to scoff because the creatures have far-and-away enough problems even when they are in good health.

The Examination Room

THE VET'S HAND is not a pork chop, you know that. In addition, aggressive tactics betray low breeding.

WHEN RECEIVING A SHOT one should adopt a military stance while retaining a wholesome state of mind. Repeat to yourself something on the order of "Dad drat the torpedoes . . ." etc.

WHEN HAVING YOUR TEMPERATURE TAKEN stare into the distance and ruminate on how Gloria Vanderbilt's dog might handle the situation. If the situation is extreme, substitute Gloria Vanderbilt.

WHEN LEAVING it is not necessary to thank the Vet. However, if the visit has been conducted in a professional manner, the gratuity of a very small tail wag is not inappropriate.

The Reward

WHEN returning home, display mild brooding. This will help your human work though guilt, because your human will search out a tennis ball. This is known as compensatory play behavior.

ACCEPT all treats with subdued pleasure. Refusing them, or snapping them up eagerly, will shorten the supply.

The Faux Paw, Or
So You've Attacked the Mailman and Other Peccadilloes

It is almost inevitable that even the best-bred dog will some day confront an awkward situation. I recall, for example, a Labrador Retriever (fortunately, no relation to my own family) who resided in a duplex. Since no other dogs lived there, and since he was more than a little possessive, the gentleman assumed that the entire duplex and surrounding greenery constituted his territory. Much to his chagrin, he woke one morning to the scent of another male who had just moved in next door; and, even more interesting, the scent of a female.

A tense situation developed. It seemed that the other male was never outside at the same time as the Lab, and the Lab began to brood. The more he brooded the more he forgot that the cultured dog is always discreet.

And so it was, that on a day much like any other day, beneath a warm sun and with fierce joy in his heart, he encountered on emerging from the house another dog who had tarried too long outside; a Border Collie, she was, but the Lab did not take time to discover that truth. All he knew was that this invader of his territory would not slip from his grasp.

The chase was short; the climax disgraceful. The slightly portly Lab overtook the smaller Collie, brought it to ground, and flipped it over with a snarl . . . and discovered it was not the hated male, but a female.

There are, as we all know, Chocolate Labs and Black Labs and Yellow Labs, but our gentleman of misplaced passion was probably the only Red Lab in history. His embarrassment was so great that he slunk home with his belly bruising the grass. It was of no help, whatever, that the Border Collie, once freed of fear, proved herself ready for a game of chase.

The Lab went to his room and spent the next three days taking mighty vows, vows large of vengeance on the invisible male who had sent a girl outside in his place, vows so heartrending and filled with fury, so powerful with truth from a being felled by a wrong, that it is a wonder the entire house did not fall to flinders.

To no avail. In less than a week the strangers next door moved on, and a cat of the garbage can variety took up permanent residence.

=

This story, while sad to relate, at least happened between dogs, and can thus be kept secret within the canine family. Our actions, however, become the stuff of legend when error reaches its fumbling paw into the realm of human endeavor. It is not exactly cozy to find that one is the butt of anecdotes told at cocktail parties. One may never completely salvage an embarrassing situation, but correct behavior can, at least, mitigate some of the damage done your reputation. Improvisation is usually required, and the following examples will provide a guide toward that kind of creative work:

HAVING ATTACKED THE MAILMAN: Plead temporary insanity. Wait until the mailman next appears, then run in circles while barking madly and feigning unrestrained joy. Continue running until you become dazed, then fall on your side and roll over a dozen times. Retreat to the furthest corner of your yard and cover your eyes with your paws. This will allow the poor fellow a feeling of security, and, if you are lucky, will make him wonder if he should not also be feeling a bit of guilt. If he does feel guilty, he may bring a dog biscuit next time.

MISSING SLIPPER: You recall that you buried it in the garden, but have forgotten the exact location. While your people scurry about in search of the slipper, assume your most noble stance. Face the doorway as if guarding the house against slipper stealers.

BRUISED PETUNIAS: You have gone mole hunting in a flowerbed and the only dignified apology is to give something of value in return. I suggest that you pre-empt the kitty's dish and place it in the hole. Your people will still hold you responsible, but at least they will treasure your attempt at good will.[9]

BROWN BAG PROBLEMS: You knew that the ham and cheese sandwich was not really made for you, and you knew you were going to leave telltale crumbs. The only way out of this is to convince your people that, by absconding with their lunch, you have saved them from the horrible trauma of food poisoning. Stagger to your bed and pretend to a seizure.

NUDGEY NOSE SYNDROME: Your human sat watching the television, and you nudged his elbow upward just as he raised his glass of soft drink. Dash immediately to the bedroom and fetch his robe and slippers. He will wipe away moisture while believing that there has been an error in communication, and that the error is his.

And, of course, the best corrective behavior is to learn and practice manners, and thus avoid such sticky wickets as the examples above.

A Dream of Fair Beaches

There is naught so lovely as a day at the beach, and there is probably no beach in the world that will not interest the average dog. We welcome the opportunity to stretch our legs, press our noses to their limits, and, if we are water dogs, engage in a virtuosity of splashing unequaled in all the lakes, puddles, and children's rubber pools on earth. A dog on the beach experiences the high tide of existence. All else, while not dross, pales.

Hazards to correct behavior exist at nearly every turn, so it is well to think of potential problems before-paw. This is especially true for those who are lady dogs. After all, the proper lady only gets her name in the newspaper three times during her life. One must always avoid the least breath of scandal.

That hazards exist, and that enthusiasm can get your name in the paper, is best illustrated by the really untoward and bizarre story reported by Gwendolyn K. P. Perkins-Monmouth. Perkins-Monmouth is a Great Pyrenees who fell under the thrall of the wind.

She tells me that all was well with her pack. Her male Heathrow, her female Bluebell, and their children whom she had named Piddle and Poppins, accompanied her on a visit to the sea in southwest Washington State. It was a breezy day with gusts coming out of the west. She picked up scents from Japan, Russia, and the Aleutian Islands.

"A really normal sort of ocean day," she reported, "with just a hint of Canadian scent to leaven the mixture. Winds do swirl and try to trick one along those western shores."

"The nose of the Pyrenees is legendary." I said this through sympathy for her tale. Perkins-Monmouth is a proud and aristocratic dog who displays a touch of Castilian accent. To her credit she took full responsibility for her actions. She did not blame the wind, although to my mind she would find some justification for doing so.

"The tide changed in mid afternoon," she reports, "and the wind went swinging along with the tide. Before I even realized what was happening, scents of a kind I'd never known began to assail my nose. The wind had shifted and was coming exactly from the south."

The scents were rare beyond belief. The smell of grease paint mixed with the sweaty smells of humans galloping on horses, or trekking across forty years of wilderness, or holding shootouts in saloons, or having light romances. The smells told of talking mice who wore pants, and of Ferris wheels and gorgeous castles. There was gaiety in those smells—the arc of skyrockets above magic kingdoms, the pop of ten million popcorns, the promise of illimitable reams of hamburgers—compelling smells, they were.

"It was a strong and steady wind," she remembered. "A freak of nature, one supposes. At any rate it blew and continued to blow, its promise irresistible to a weak vessel such as myself. A Chow Chow, being of a somewhat cynical nature, might have resisted."

In sum, she ran into the wind. The ground-covering ability of her breed may be assumed, and miles passed as if she sped on a magic carpet of scent. She does not recall breathing heavily, only recalls that she floated along the sand, paws barely touching, while wind ran over her fur and spoke to her nose. She recalls that the sun went westering, then disappeared, and she recalls running by moonlight. She recalls sunrise over tawny mountains, and the gradual appearance of humans arriving from seaward, riding surfboards. She now knows that she was crazed, but does not recall hunger or thirst. She ran and ran and ran and ran until—and we may be grateful that her fate was no worse—she collapsed in a faint; and when she awoke a sign before her eyes read:

HOWDY STRANGER
WELCOME TO PISMO BEACH

She had heard of the place, true; but thought it a myth. It was only then that she understood the seductive power of California.

Hers was a long trudge home, and a trudge not unmixed with danger. A scant trot above Monterey brought a covey of windsurfers who she had to avoid on pain of becoming a mascot. Hunger took her to the edge of desperation in Mill Valley where she sat outside a hot dog stand wearing her most mournful look. The ploy worked, but a little snip of a Cockapoo caught onto her act and became quite snooty. To be cut in this manner seemed to her a reflection on the Cockapoo, but such knowledge did little toward salving the hurt of the snub.

In Oregon she became so fatigued that she rested for two days and nights in a barn, becoming fast friends with a Guernsey named Maude. It was the only rewarding part of the trip. By the time she arrived home she had lost ten pounds and gained a considerable weight of wisdom. She confided to me that the whole business was a great adventure, but she would not wish to try it again, no matter how seductive the wind.

MORAL: Seduction has its downside.

A Main Principle

Perkins-Monmouth might have avoided a good deal of unpleasantness if, when arriving at the beach, she had searched out a point of reference for her nose—a clump of tangy seaweed, or a deceased fish. Reality, after all, is a stern companion that can overwhelm most illusions. Let us now discuss general approaches to the beach.

Definitions and Protocols

STICKS: are to the beach what balls are to a park. In the surf they become open game. Do not begrudge sharing your stick with other dogs. You are under no obligation, however, to share with fur seals or sea lions.

FRISBEES: do not catch another dog's frisbee. It confuses the humans.

SURF: is the sea wagging its tail. You will probably encounter mermaids as you dash about in the foam (for they are much smaller than is generally believed). Treat them with courtesy and respect.

SEA GULLS: are feathered squirrels. The girls are named Flotsam and the boys are named Jetsam; or perhaps vice versa.

SANDPIPERS: you might as well chase smoke, so only chase if you can accept the knowledge that your efforts will be greeted with wry smiles.

UMBRELLAS: avoid kicking sand in the neighborhood of umbrellas because they usually shelter a human, one who is often caustic.

PICNICS: are certain disaster for the dog who forgets his manners. Think of how a raccoon would handle matters, then do the opposite.

TIDE POOLS: are a delight, and one should hit with as large a splash as possible. Some dogs, however, are jaded. I once met (on a beach with some of the world's finest tide pools) an Airedale named Abner Ptjer Wyczknowski, a Chicagoan, who claimed the tide pools rather shabby compared to Chicago's potholes. He could not get it through his head that no contract would be let for paving.

OTHER ANIMALS: all beaches have been constructed with a dog in mind, but sometimes one meets a walrus. Inquire politely about the weather in Anchorage and Nome, but be on your guard. Walrus have many adventures and have been known to expand on the truth. Gullible dogs, after listening to tales told by a walrus, have been known to run off and join the circus.

DUNES: always dance on top of dunes, thus avoiding dune buggies and undertow.

KITES: kite flyers are gentle folk who will weep copiously if you foul their strings. They may also do other things. If you find yourself being zoomed by a stunt kite, you are entitled to nip at its tail.

Travels—With Particular Emphasis On Camping

There is no such thing as the standard camping trip, because surroundings dictate infinite possibilities. A trip to the mountains, for example, alerts one to the presence of bears; a trip to a fine motel yields room service. If one travels to a river or lake, the possibility of otter and beaver is present, and a trip through high desert yields roadrunners and weasels. The fauna will call to your senses, and some of that fauna can send a dog into dangerous ecstasy. The scent of a skunk (which one would think most noxious) is as attractive to some dogs as catnip to a Manx.

All trips, however, hold some requirements in common. It is well to review these in a general way:

Preparations

You will need to chew while on the road, so bring something substantial, a shoe or tennis ball. Otherwise you will be tempted by the tastes of sleeping bags, tent pegs, and flashlights.

If you own an animal carrier, see that it is included in the load. If you do not own one it will be necessary to improvise a bed. Some dogs enjoy snuggling beside a human, while others complain that a tent is too confining. "Suppose," they argue in a voice of sweet reasonableness, "suppose an elephant stumbles through the camp, and there you are trying to untangle yourself from a tent." No, these dogs explain, it is a far, far better thing to camp rough and tough—so be sure to bring a pillow or two. These may be wedged into the mouths of caves, or in hollows beneath the roots of trees. It is raw comfort, but allows easy access to the wild.

On Site

If this is your first camping experience be prepared to sleep a bit extra during the day you arrive, for it is nigh certain you will be up all that night. The new camper finds herself awash in sounds and smells, with the sight of moving shadows, and the feel of breezes in her fur. She may see a raised snout silhouetted against the moon, and hear a drawn out howl. In canine lore this is known as The Call of The Wild. My recommendation in such cases: If The Wild calls, do not answer.

Such experiences are novelties to the dog accustomed to plush carpets and tended lawns. I have heard (but can scarcely credit) tales of dogs so overwhelmed by wilderness that they could not catch a wink until they climbed into the back seat of the automobile.[10]

If you camp with humans, as most of us do, choose a level campsite; humans tend to roll around and skid. It will be just lovely to have a nearby source of water, a crystal lake or rushing stream, but do not scorn a faucet. As humans argue with their tent in growly tones, and as the tent answers with a rustle while falling flat, you should mark your territory. Check all scents, making certain no animals of a pushy variety, such as cougars, visit the area. If cougars do visit the area, arrange to sleep in the car.

Suppose, however, that you have decided on a hiking trip and the car is not allowed to come along. The cougar problem becomes serious, and you should think long and carefully about any possible encounter. I suggest a review of everything you know about cats. Think of their hopes and fears for their children, their aspirations, their aversions. Armed with useful observations and questions you will then, if a cougar appears, be prepared to start a discussion group.

In some forests the problem revolves not around cougars but around bears. According to some experts, the bear has an atavistic fear of dogs. These experts believe that in the far, far distant past a race of giant wolves existed on this continent. The bear's instinct of avoidance was formed at that time. In theory (according to these experts) a bear can be treed by a sturdy Fox Terrier, and—since there is no Fox Terrier tale of this type extant—I would be most pleased to hear from any Fox Terriers who survived. Their stories will be contained in future editions.

At this writing, however, I must express doubts. Unless you are a dog bred to understand bears, the courteous gesture is to pass by with only the simplest salutation. If the bear is inclined to offer sass, as some are, remember that you can twist and turn faster than the bear. This is one of the few occasions in canine behavior when a bit of impudence is permissible. Say to the bear that he is shamefully overweight, and that his nose should be ticketed for incompetence. Explain from a distance that bears are not really very bright, and that you have known squirrels who were less easily distracted. This will make the bear grumpy.

The grumpy bear will want to play tag. Lead him to a cliff, get him to charge, step aside.

Other Animals

AVOIDANCE: is a good rule when encountering any wild animals. Skunks are humorless, and there is very little difference between a badger and a hand grenade. Remember, these are wild animals unaccustomed to the gentle graces of civilized and domesticated behavior. They have no manners, desire no manners, and actually enjoy being crude.

Getting Lost

Your humans, having at first taken a short cut that landed them in a rather tacky shopping center, had a hard time finding the forest in the first place. You may be sure they will get lost. Whilst they wander the trails and mutter phrases that would offend a chipmunk, it is your opportunity to take the lead in a jolly game of 'Let's find the car.'

Your nose tells you exactly how to return, but the human's noses do not. If your humans suffer from intellectual pride (as most of them do) you may be sure they will ignore you while talking about blasted trees, rotted stumps, 'crinkly places in the rocks', and other such landmarks. They will rapidly discover that one rotted stump looks very much like another, and that most of the rocks in the region have crinkles. At some time during their inventory of blasted trees, they will turn to you as a last resort.

At this point you'll discover that you have a dreadful tendency to 'show off.'[11] Pretend you are a Basset Hound. Place your nose no higher than a leaf's thickness above the trail; sniff with authority. If your people do not follow, you have options. Some dogs bark. Others tug at pant legs. Persistence pays, because sooner or later they will understand your message. Keep your nose nearly flat against the trail. You do not need it for your own information, but it makes your humans feel secure. Once you have led these urban children out of the wilderness you may anticipate a great deal in the way of a reward. I once met a Corgi, Clandestine S. Dangerfield, who secured for herself a full month's supply of steak bones for what amounted to no more than a routine rescue.

Evening

THE CAMPFIRE: is the biggest event of the day and customarily begins at dusk. You may, if you wish, assist in digging the fire pit; but one should control wanton urges to possess oneself of the sticks. Remember the rule: no sticks, no fire—no fire, no leftovers.

LATER: as the humans converse and tell stories, of which a very few might have some small basis in fact, you can warm your fur as you sit beside them. They seem to enjoy that.

How It Ended, Or
Nips and Tucks

The dog and the two humans worked through long winter evenings, but in early March icicles along the roof began to drip. Before anyone really became aware, snow banks drizzled while crocus raised perky heads to springtime sun. The gent at first became a trifle giddy, then downright irresponsible. He wondered aloud why reasonable folk still sat typing when the world outside was sunny and muddy and skiddy and wonderful.

The dog and the lady remained resolute. Finishing touches were required, and it was clear the book could be much, much longer. The lady retained her discipline for quite a while, but her feet started to get dancey. When the first daffodils appeared the lady became inattentive, and finally, wistful.

The dog, Miss Molly Manners, whose brow had furrowed through the thoughtful, chilly months, regarded her humans with no small amount of compassion.

"You have done wonderfully well," she told them, "and I am grateful. With your help we have at least covered the basics. Perhaps the finer points of conduct could be dealt with at another time."

This made the humans happy, and they began talking about pumping up bicycle tires.

"But we should end with a few little advices," the dog told them. "Let us make a closing list."

And this is what the lady copied down:

FURNITURE: humans are sometimes possessive. Capture furniture by extending paw and brisket a little bit at a time, rather than all at once. Gradual control of a chair, for example, will eventually earn human gratitude since you have warmed it nicely.

SO YOU THINK YOU HAVE A FLEA: Elbow pounding, foot kicking, snout snorkling, and rolling on your back are all recommended. Do not attempt to chase the flea through the weave of the carpet. They are deceptive creatures who, given half a chance, will once more hop aboard.

A 12 STEP PLAN TO CURE DEPENDENCE ON SLIPPER CHEWING: Imagine the slipper as a vegetable, a very large zucchini, for example. Would you want to chew that zucchini? Certainly not.

Of course, you may very well be aware that it is a slipper, not a zucchini. Imagine it as a different vegetable, possibly a pumpkin. If the first two steps fail, you can surely think of ten more vegetables.

THE DOORBELL: Pavlov wrote about this, and we dogs were not amused. Whether the bell causes people to appear at your front door, or people arrive—thus causing the bell—is a matter still under study. In either case, barking helps people materialize. It offers the added advantage of preparing them to greet you, and pet you, a courtesy they might overlook.

IMPOLITE HUMANS: will occasionally visit. Do not answer rudeness with rudeness, but simply define the situation. Point your nose away from them and lower it so that it rests between your paws. This will place your rump in the air. This done, raise your tail.

SLOBBER: some humans find it distasteful. When faced with an overly meticulous human, remove the offending liquid by a gentle nuzzle along the pant leg. Or, if dealing with a female, a firm nudge of the muzzle onto the lap will prove successful. The human will exclaim mightily. Probably in gratitude.

GARBAGE CANS: even if they belong to you it is socially incorrect to stick your head in one. Some dogs of the rough and ready variety hold the opinion that anything that can be tipped should be. In polite circles, however, this is regarded as pushy.

CHILDREN: the dog and child have much in common, and most of what they have centers around affection for each other. One agreement should be made, however: You do not pilfer the tot's candy; the tot doesn't steal your bones.

And one might go on and on. As any intelligent dog can see, the nuances of etiquette are endless although their general shape is universal: Honor doghood.

There is, however, one addition. To illuminate it we need turn to the world of humans and their books. One human, a writer of excellent Brittany stock himself, wrote a book similar to this one. It was directed to humans and their writing. He listed numerous rules, yet wisely ended with a final and important rule: "Break any of the above rules rather than say something barbaric."

We practice etiquette in order to honor doghood, but it is well to keep human needs in mind. They are dear creatures who, properly trained, obey nearly every command. They are greatly loved, though limited. Thus, break any of the above rules sooner than do anything inhumane to humans. They are, after all, only human.

NOTES

1. Humans often display an obstinate streak and are at first hesitant to take to leash. Some humans have been known to fight the leash for months before they finally acquiesce.
2. Bears can only be taught to ride tricycles. This, I believe, is the principal difference between humans and bears.
3. With the exception of squirrels, of which more later. Squirrels, one fears, are the tipped-over dominoes in the cosmic plan.
4. J. Bugle Danforth, A Comparative Study Of Intellectual Functions Between 2000 Subject Canines and Humans, *Journal of Canine Psychology*, Vol. XI, #7, pgs. 94-107.
5. I am indebted for this argument to the editors of *Dog's Quarterly* who offered extensive coverage of the theory in their January issue, Vol. XVII, #1. Also see, *The Conundrum of The Mirror*, Rumples J. Smythe, The Doghouse Press, '93.

6. *An Inquiry Concerning The Principles Of Balls*, A. Arnold Waggenstein, University of Chesapeake Press, 1994.
7. Also the utmost depravity, for they are known to yowl their emotions beneath the dark of the moon.
8. Never fret about the morals of a cat. They have none.
9. The human race simply does not understand that there are times in history when the universe has a distressingly painful need for a particular hole in a particular place.
10. For exceptional conditions, see next paragraph.
11. Setters almost always overdo things, as do Dachshunds; who you would think would be more serious.

Now We Are Fifty

THE NIGHT THROB OF FROGS AND CRICKETS LAY LIKE A TUMBLED blanket across the valley and mixed with the humid vegetable odor of the wet forest. I sat with Frazier in his comfortable house. He remarked that it was still possible to find windowless cabins in these mountains. Not all feuds were dead.

"I never expected it to change." I listened to the pulse of the night. Owls called. Predators and scavengers ranged. In these hills death was direct. I wondered at the compulsion that made Frazier return to this place. In the last few years his poetry has dealt with spirits of dark, voices of shadow, and the gray mystery that intersperses with dappled sunlight on a trail. Such things are the business of poets, but I feared that he was becoming a mystic.

"The mist will rise soon." Frazier stepped to the doorway and looked into the hot night. He was framed by the dark. Frazier is tall. His nose hooks and his brows are wide and thick. His face is hollowed and creased. The gray eyes hold either an original clarity or an original madness. They burn bright and sometimes wild. We have been friends all our lives.

Frazier laughed. Erratic. He turned from the doorway to take a chair.

"Now we are all sitting," he said. "You and I sit here. Mink is crouched in his cabin beyond that far ridge. He will be like a night-bound animal. Erickson sits and pilots a broken plane through a tangle of blackberry. A great pilot of great affairs was Erickson."

"The man was your friend." He had no right to talk that way about Erickson. I did not need his sarcasm. The situation was more than bad. It was grotesque.

A year ago our friend Erickson had checked out on a flight to Ashland in one of his company's planes. He had been engulfed by the forest. Every evidence showed that a man named Mink had killed the injured Erickson. He had waited to report the wreckage for a year. He had robbed and mutilated the body. The remains were incomplete. The lower jaw was gone. In my briefcase was film I had exposed after a long trek into the mountains.

"Not a friend," Frazier said. "I last saw Erickson in Ashland long ago. It was only for a moment. He was in a hurry."

"And you were not?"

"At the time I was," Frazier said. "Didn't I spend all those years playing the same fool as the rest. Erickson manipulated, you argued law, and I circled poetry like a hawk while wearing a mask of simplicity. These hills, from whence cometh . . . and yet, I believed it, believe it."

"You complain about what work costs?"

"I'm not complaining about poetry. Where in the hell are my smokes?" He rose to fetch them from the fireplace mantle at the end of the room. "You're wrong," he said. "Erickson had ceased to be a friend. Still, it was strange to see him today. That was a quiet, sober meeting. Erickson was in no hurry."

"You've earned the right to be eccentric, not the right to be cruel."

Frazier ignored me. He returned to the doorway and to the pulsing dark that was filled with death and movement. "It was probably a night like this," he said. "It's almost exactly a year since Erickson went down." He flipped the just lighted cigarette into the darkness. "We were told right away. The sheriff sent a man thirty miles. Name and age and aircraft number. As if that had any special meaning here."

"It had no meaning to Mink."

Frazier tapped at the doorframe. Stepped into the dark. Stepped back inside. He wore conventional work clothes of the hills with the shirtsleeves rolled. His forearms were tense.

"It had meaning to Mink," he said. "Erickson was Mink's problem."

"And he solved it with a rifle." I did not try to hide my disgust.

"You're the lawyer. Do you think you have a case?" Frazier turned to gesture to the room which was well furnished and held stacks of current journals, magazines and books. Recordings were shelved across one end of the room. Work by known painters hung beside sketches by a local artist. The sketches were of drift mouths, blackened faces, and abandoned cabins. Frazier's house was built of native rock and timber and resembled a small hunting lodge. The differences were subtle. In this house the ceilings were peaked and high. The windows were narrow and heavily draped.

"Identification numbers are out of place here." He gestured again at the books. "Do you think I would be allowed to live in this place if I were very different? I mind my own business." He turned back to the doorway.

"I've been a long time away," I said. "I wouldn't be allowed to live here any more, and when there is murder you don't have to mind your own business. I don't understand you. I don't understand Mink."

". . . that the meek are blessed because they get to stay meek. What is there to understand?"

"You've been here too long." I was convinced of that.

"Don't change the subject. What offends you? The death, or your long wait in the city to confirm the death, or some missing bone? Mink is not that much different from the rest of us."

"Yes he is," I said. "Are you saying you didn't search?"

"We all searched. There are thirty-seven men and boys in this community and all of us searched four days." Unseen, but in the direction Frazier looked, Hanger Mountain was a ridge rising above slightly lower hills. A trail ran halfway in. It was used for weekly mail delivery by mule.

"We covered every slope beyond this hollow to the three adjacent. We searched until it was a fatality. You could lose a herd of elephants in these hills."

"Something as foreign as a plane?"

"One could crash now within a quarter-mile and you would not hear. The mist is rising."

"But you did not search Hanger Mountain?"

"The folks from Haw Creek searched that mountain. We trust them."

"Always?"

"In matters such as this, and others not as stupid. And this is not a courtroom. The mist is heavy. Come to the door."

With the proof of death on film the estate could be settled. I was attorney for some of the heirs, and it might be that Frazier would be poet for the crashed plane. I did not want to think of that. I did not want his mist and his bitterness and that humid night.

"You need to be more generous."

"And you more brave. Come to the door."

It was like looking at a black shield. The darkness lay flat as paint, the night voices dim. They were a mutter. A jumble. The stream that during the day filled the clearing with the rush of water now blended with a gurgle, a liquid hint of motion behind the black shield. As my eyes adjusted I saw the mist. It hovered and crawled at short distance. It rose slowly toward the lighted doorway and our feet.

"It will rise faster now," Frazier said. "Let's walk."

"Enjoy yourself."

Frazier turned to me. "You're angry because you're afraid."

"You are the one who is angry."

"Yes," he said. "You are afraid of Mink. Erickson. Twisted metal and twisted lives and skulls that either talk or don't or can't. This is dull. An incident between aging men."

"An incident of murder."

"Only an incident that's a little mysterious. Erickson would have understood."

"There's no mystery," I said. "The plane crashed and Mink took all he could get and then waited to see if a reward would be offered. So Erickson's affairs are delayed for a year."

"Erickson attends to his affairs," Frazier said. "He is doing it now. Doing the only business he has left."

This sullen, intellectual son of a bitch. He was asking to do battle. Arrogance. My mind is as good as his.

"And you are not afraid?"

"No," he said. "Beleaguered. You people will not leave us alone. You will not leave the hills alone. Erickson helped destroy these hills with his mining. You and your precious business." He stepped through the black shield and into the night.

Without him I would be lost within a hundred feet. Between his mood and mine it would be crazy to make myself dependent on Frazier. I walked the length of the room to sit by the fireplace, which was clean and gray from fires of the half-dozen winters Frazier has lived here. The mist was beyond the heavy drapes. The voices of frogs and the mutter of the stream were like a murmur of the mist. The night was hot and wet but I felt almost cold.

Murder. I hate this land where we were raised. It was my old acquaintance with Frazier that brought me back. Ordinarily we would have sent a younger man.

Erickson had hated this place. It is dark, wet, hot, violent. Erickson's life was spent trying to deal with the waywardness of boondocks Kentucky.

Murder. When Erickson checked in missing, it caused the interlocked directorships of three coal corporations to start earning their pay. No one knew this place like Erickson. Erickson could talk to men who wear overalls and do business while standing in small-town streets. When Erickson disappeared I had written to Frazier. He had written back and told me to stay away.

The heirs became impatient and offered a five-thousand-dollar reward. The results were on film.

"A hundred dollars would have gotten the same result." Frazier had said that on the morning two days ago. On that morning we began our trek in to view the crash. A guide walked ahead of us. Silent. Although Frazier owned a mule he said that no suitable mules were available. The silent guide carried a machete.

Along the trail were deep slits in the rock where coal seams had been entered. They were good seams.

"They still risk their lives for that," I said. People around here have always scrabbled free coal. Sunlight reached toward the black veins. The bracing props were stout, but this had nothing to do with mining. Even from the trail we could see fallen slate.

"They do not have much money," Frazier said.

The trail branched down through a streambed bridged by logs, and then wound across the base of the first mountain. Laurel grew like trees. Shrubbery and sapling growth was brushed greener by the humidity. It would be a full day's hike.

In a mile the trail narrowed and in five miles it was overgrown footpath. Under foot was the give and slight backward pressure of deep moisture. Our guide shouldered through brush. Silent and sullen. Since I arrived I had spoken to no one but Frazier. The suspicion of these hills. It is redneck, hot, hillbilly, and righteous.

"There is a mixture of spirits in these hills." Frazier was musing to himself. "The Cherokees left some, for they were an ambitious people with emissaries north and south. The Scots Presbyterians brought some along, and the first evangelicals invented some."

I said nothing. He did not want conversation.

"Spirits of mist, thunder, wind and spirits of the dark." He laughed, low, brittle. The man ahead slashed at blackberry. The trail rose and then again descended. It was hot and getting hotter.

"Spirits of the dark," Frazier said. "Well, and we are getting old, and most mystery is only a contrivance." There was a sudden flurry ahead. A kick, the sound of the machete striking the forest floor, a hush.

"Stand still," Frazier said. "There's often a nest of them."

The guide pushed at foliage with the machete. He kicked the brush. Then he motioned us forward. Blood lay on the trail, and the pieces of a hacked snake.

"Always where it's low and wet," Frazier said. The reptilian blood was almost black on the humus. The head was split, the body chopped. Though he walked heavily our guide had been swift.

We walked. After the fourth hour my body passed from revulsion to acceptance and the trek was mechanical. Mine is a good body. Even under pressure I could depend on my movements. Part of it comes from early training. Erickson and Frazier and I had all been trained to movement and the use of tools when we were young. It was not until we arrived and met Mink that it occurred to me how much Frazier resembled Erickson and how much I resembled both of them.

There are hill people and there are sorry people. Between the two there is as much difference as between a stump preacher and a theologian.

Mink was well named. I have known a thousand like him. Sly, shifty, and with long teeth. He moved with no dignity of age or experience. His clothes and cabin stank. The permanent coal dust that gets into the skin of miners circled his eyes; and his eyes were dull and clouded and suspicious. His gaze only seemed vacant. He looked more like a dying raccoon. One that could still bite.

His shack was empty but there was the mark of a woman and children. Pictures had been clipped from catalogs and religious magazines. A worn doll was tossed in a corner. The family was away visiting. They would return when we left.

"Let's unroll the sleeping bags outside," I said.

"Mosquitos," Frazier told me. His voice carried a warning I did not understand.

We ate from our packs and lay bundled on the floor. The trek in had been exhausting. There would still be the inspection of wreckage and the trek out. The coroner was old, Frazier told me. When the wreck was more than hearsay a deputy would bring the body out by helicopter. The inquest was a rubber stamp.

Two days of heat and fatigue. Now I sat in Frazier's long, low timbered room and stared at the shield of dark. To have to consider murder after two days of fatigue and fear and wreckage.

The wings had sheared from the plane and were tossed far enough that they did not burn. The identification numbers, white on the red wings, were like remote signals from a space of trees. The forest was dull in late summer. The pines held no gloss. Deciduous trees were chewed and ragged from August storms and insects. The fuselage lay on its side and was half-gutted by fire. I had not wanted to do the necessary work because it was terrible, and because I had known the man.

Where steel was exposed there was rust, and the aluminum skin was curled from fire. I watched twisted metal and tried to keep my hands from trembling. A year's accumulation of dirt lay in tiny pockets and waves of metal. The engine twisted away from the cockpit. I looked, tried to speak, motioned to Frazier.

"No animal would do this." I turned to check the forest. Where was Mink? I felt the place between my shoulders where a bullet might enter, turned, felt the same place in my chest.

"Spirits of the dark," Frazier muttered. "No animal could."

"Where is he?"

"Keep working. Lawyers don't get hysterics."

There had been only silence, and the silence lasted all through the long trek back. Now I sat in Frazier's living room, my thoughts scattered. Mink would get by with it. There was no love here for Erickson. There was no proof that a scavenger had not gotten to the body. Of course, Mink was stupid. He would betray himself if questioned. But who would bring him out unless there was some old grudge?

How stupid was he? I rose from the chair. Had he thought it over in his dull-minded, murderer's way and thought of his danger? Had he followed us? I know these people.

The muffled sounds of the night pulsed. The door stood open to the darkness, and the black shield seemed to move. The dark soul of the night. The dark heart of these people who have always bred revenge and killers. There was no mystery here. There was only fear and greed and violence.

I wanted to call to Frazier and stepped toward the doorway. Then I stopped. He had said that he was like them. The night was a glowering spirit of fear. It was the only spirit in this place.

Terror passed slowly. By the time Frazier returned I felt under control. Resignation replaced fear.

When he stepped from the dark it was like the appearance of a specter. His hair and face and clothing were shining with mist. He brushed at his sleeves. His shirt was damp and showed the mark of his hand.

"Why do you defend Mink?"

"I defend no one," he said. "That's in your line."

"I defend what I can understand."

"Then understand this."

"Impossible."

"No," Frazier said, "it's possible. You have been away too long. If you were in a foreign country you would be more generous. Man, this is not Madrid or Paris. These are the hills."

"Murder is murder."

"Tell Erickson about it." He crossed the room to choose a recording. The room was designed for music, the measured address of an orchestra perfectly transmitted. One did not think of volume. The room lived in music, and the music was surely Bach. Frazier walked the length of the room to sit by the cold fireplace.

I waited for one more lecture or protest. This had been going on most of my life. It would have been better for both of us if we had never been friends.

"Erickson may have been hurt," Frazier said. "Forget what's missing because Mink hid some bone broken by his bullet. It's twenty miles from anywhere on Hanger Mountain, at least two days to a doctor."

"But to kill . . ."

"Sometimes around here a dog gets snake bit. We shoot it quick."

"And to rob."

"Dammit, how do you know? He's ignorant and was afraid and had to try to burn the plane, but Mink is a decent man. At least as decent as the rest."

"And he did not report."

"Yes," Frazier said. "That's what really bothers you. On the other hand, why do you intrude with your five thousand dollars and pure intentions?" He leaned back, stretched his long legs and waited. The music surrounded us. I remained silent to force him to speak.

"Erickson was dead when he took the first course in engineering at that cow college," Frazier said. "He was dead the first time he spent ten cents on mineral rights."

"All three of us went to that college."

"And all three of us chose how we would die." There was a rush of music. "Illusions," he said. "Such a splendid choice of illusions, and so we made our choices."

"We're talking about Mink."

"It's dark out there." Frazier motioned at the now-closed door. "Mink is not much different, and most of the darkness is only natural darkness. It cares nothing for our concerns, law, poetry, business, what does it matter?"

"My friend . . ."

"Yes," he said, "but the rest . . . it's the darkness of the mind. Toy monkeys on sticks. A dime a jump if you jump high." He broke off and sat watching me with neither judgment nor affection.

"You remember when I came here," he said presently. "All of you, my friends, cautioned me against being a fool. You cautioned me. Yet, you have known me longest. You know how high I climbed my stick, did my tumbles, tipped my hat and mumbled and grimaced out there." He motioned to the closed door.

"You are famous."

"Enough to choose. I spend my time with a mule, a cow, a few chickens and a small garden. I occupy myself sorting Presbyterian ghosts, spirits, devils and haunts that are all illusory because they cloud the few real mysteries of these hills. My death is on my face, wrinkled, hawkish, and I feed my beasts and listen to *The Art of the Fugue*."

"Are you dying?"

"Yes. Listen. Erickson was no different. I speak of dying. All of us, all of our lives tied to these hills. We left because our fathers had jobs in the city. Erickson became rich, I became famous, and you . . ."

"Have done my job."

". . . have also chosen."

"And Mink could not choose? Pity is a poor thing."

"And waste is a lousy thing, but you are right about pity. Mink spent his life in the mines."

"Which belonged to Erickson. You are getting childish. Are you really dying?"

"Hell, the mines belong to whoever owns mines, and I am getting angry. We do not speak of equity or irony. The whole lot of us are only representative props in a two-bit melodrama. By God!" His lips were drawn and white.

"Props," he said. "Whatever we do, whoever we are, but the props fail because of the human heart . . . Mink's work was harsh work."

"I don't want to feed your anger," I told him, "but everyone works and gets old."

"Yes. Except Mink had no pretense about work or the hills. We were trapped in illusion. Trapped in the immemorial darkness that will always be one of the true mysteries." He paused. Glanced at the closed door. "Your life was worth the price of a bullet a while ago. You were vulnerable. No pretense. No illusion. I sat beneath a poplar and watched. Had you come for the right reason . . ." Frazier stood, but did not walk to the record shelves. He crossed the open room to the kitchen area and began to brew tea from a local herb. With the door closed the night sounds were muted but still present. For a moment the room seemed like a lighted cave.

"This whole matter was none of our affair," he said. "Erickson intruded. He had no right to be here with those intentions and his pitiful business. He had no right to come sailing over Mink. He had no right to crash on Mink's place and leave wreckage to plague another man. Will the concerned heirs pay to have that junk removed? Erickson's last intrusion on Mink was just one of a thousand."

"What in the hell are you preaching?" I felt that he really must be dying and raving in the face of it.

"You don't see it," he said. "Forget it. But, man, you are alien. You have interfered and have no right to interfere further. Come on a true visit, or send me your letters, but stay away from these hills with your intrusions. This tea is always a little bitter."

"As bitter as the host?"

"Even now," Frazier said, "you intrude on Mink. You are going to give him money."

"Or press charges."

"Try to understand."

I felt that I should be angry and was not. The murmur of the night lay just beyond the heavy drapes. I could hear it, restless, throbbing and certain.

"The wreck looks worse than it was. Maybe Erickson was hurt. Maybe he was only unconscious." Frazier sipped at his tea. "There is no way to know what Erickson thought, and there is no way to know what Mink thought because his mind is heavy and dead and he would not remember. He would tell you that Erickson was snake bit, and around here that is a cliché."

"The man is an animal."

"The man has become an animal, now an animal with five thousand dollars."

"You object to the money?"

"The immemorial darkness," Frazier said. "Already folks call it blood money. They would not lend a mule to help in the matter.

I would not myself. Mink might have lived in that hollow for the rest of his life and been buried by his children. Predict his future now? I would not dare." Frazier motioned to the delicate porcelain cup that was as strange in this place as a mule would be in a law office.

"My anger passes," he said. "When I die the people here will bury me. Then, without discussing it, they will divide the plunder. I have made provisions for the manuscripts and a few of the books."

"What does that have to do with anything?"

"Everything. It's what remains from all the things that happen, and which we believe and which have no meaning. Are you so layered with illusion that you do not believe in revenge, which is another of the true mysteries. Man, I'm not just talking about the spirit of these hills."

". . . that they will destroy or steal your property?"

"That Erickson had his, I have had mine and you are engaged in yours. It's sodden revenge. That's all. There is no heat to it. We are old."

"Maybe you are."

"We are old. Old as revenge."

"And you are a fool," I said. "I do my job."

"Yes, yes, and well, there is the Bach. Sometimes, even now, there is poetry. Around here people can sing very sweet. They do that. Some make their own musical instruments. There are new ways to mine and new ways to build airplanes. The quality of rifles improves each year from army surplus. I listen to the Bach, walk through the natural darkness, and protest against intrusion. Sometimes when there is a gray dawn the forest and pasture are silver when I walk down to feed the mule, and those dawns always happen in winter. The chickens are safe behind wire fences because the valley runs with hounds and foxes."

He looked at me and his face was creased, gaunt, shadowed in the low light and filled with his particular madness. "You leave in the morning," he told me. "File your report, send Mink the money, ignore the rest. It is none of your business." He walked to the door.

"Will you stay?"

"Here," he said. "Yes, right here, but for now I go to check on the beasts." He opened the door, stepped through the black shield and was engulfed. I saw him no more that night and he was uncommunicative in the morning.

I left in a dawn that promised high humidity and heat. We rode in Frazier's old car along broken road. My driver was yet another silent man from the community. We bumped along and connected with a state road. I was carried to Ashland.

My plane flew over mountains that were like waves of green light and glaring heat. They shone in the sunshine and reflected the shadow of the plane. The shadow ran beneath the left wing and appeared and disappeared below us. The cuts between the mountains, the hollows and ravines, the dark gullies and slashes on the landscape swallowed the shadow only to throw it onto the next bright mountaintop. The shadow traveled like a gray imp, a faded demon, and for those stretches where the landscape was altered it was nearly invisible. Erickson had been dead for a year. Frazier was dying in his chosen place and time and manner, and I was responsible for the affairs of others . . . but damn him, to be told that I had no right to be here.

The pilot banked above a river and followed it north. The shadow ran beneath us and only a little forward. It pointed toward the world that I had chosen.

All right. Maybe the son of a bitch was correct in his madness. I would respect it enough to respect his wish about Mink: and let him be correct. It was his world that was helpless, not mine. But he still had no right to tell me that I had no right to be here.

Seven Sisters

I

IN THIS WORN TOWN ON THE WASHINGTON COAST, RAIN SEEPS through darkness and turns silver on fir needles when dawn rises gray as tired spirits. Rain washes thick clumps of black moss from decaying cedar roofs. On the edge of town stand the Seven Sisters; mansions once gay with lights and finery, now silent and nigh-lightless except when sounds of rain are overcome by sounds of weeping.

To understand Seven Sisters, one need know somewhat of the town. In the long ago, back in the 1890s, buildings along our main street rose elegant as Victorian architects could contrive. Turrets soared, ornamented. Lamplight gleamed through stained glass windows. Our wharves bustled with offloading of goods from the Far East, including bond slaves and opium. Money flowed with the abundance of rain.

Harlotry, shanghai, and murder were common. Yet, though many people died, at the time no specters were reported. It has taken a bit over a century for haunted figures to congregate in group portraits of anguish.

Some of us see these creatures during gray dawns, and in gray sunsets when black clouds cover the sky but leave a streak of blue along the horizon. As the sun sinks, and blue sky turns orange, long shadows cross our streets. Faces appear through mist, whorish faces, bookish faces, and a few young girls. Some of the faces seem fragmented, as if these spirits have pieces ripped away. Others hover and seem howling; their fear beyond our imagining, their gathering power a dread force.

And to further understand the town, one need know something of Gentleman Julian ('King Julie') Babcock who was a renegade religionist, a renegade showman, a business mogul, and a scamp. During the meetings of this town's Historical Society (there are three of us, I, Peter Green, once haberdasher to gentlemen, and costumer; the barrister Jabez Johnson who once sat on the bench; and our female member, Catherine 'Cat' Peterson, actress, who in her age has become less scandalous) we find ourselves still musing over Gentleman Julie.

"A finer tomkitty never yowled from the top of a fence. A more randy hound pup never bayed at the moon." This from Cat who, though old, cannot help being beautiful, if bawdy. It is true she will not capture the eye of youth, but experienced men find themselves reassured. She proves to them that they could still make fools of themselves over a woman. Her silver hair gleams more brightly than our silver mist. Her face is creased rather than wrinkled, and her gray eyes are alight with potent life. She dresses in ornamental silks, long skirts sweeping to occasionally display a well-turned ankle. She remembers King Julie well, as do I and the Barrister.

"A silver tongue had Julie. He was a charmer. A spellbinder." The Barrister, like Julie, also strode the speaker's platform in his day. He was once a powerful orator. "We can thank every star in the firmament that Julie never went into politics." The Barrister's voice seems bigger than his body. Age has shrunk him to a mite of a man, although he remains formal in dress. In the days when he was on the bench he was strict. He was known for his standard statement to the guilty: "For you, sir, a spot of jail will be instructional." In fairness, it can be said that if he was firm with miscreants, he has always been equally firm with himself. People joke that he wears suit and tie when he sleeps.

"We can also thank every star in the firmament," Cat adds, "that our Julie was sterile. Otherwise, we'd be up to our eyelids in third-generation-Julies." And, she shudders. "Tomkitty."

"He made my fortune," I am forced to admit. "He dressed like a star of moving pictures, and the demand for costumes was endless."

"Costumes that still hang in place, and in darkness," the Barrister mutters. "One shudders to think of it."

He refers to closets and dressing rooms in number five of the Seven Sisters, known as Thespia. Julie, who built Seven Sisters, had a fondness for highflown names.

When Julie came to our town, the town was surprised into shaking off its infancy. The story of the town is not unlike the story of King Julie who entered the frontier just as the Klondike gold rush opened in the 1880s. He did not own one plugged nickle. Equally, at the time, this town was a dismal settlement, wet and gray.

Julie began his career in Seattle, which was then a small town clinging to the shores of Puget Sound. Seattle rapidly turned into a frontier city where money flowed like wind in the sails of clipper ships. Seattle supplied adventurers who headed for the gold fields of Alaska.

Julie started building his fortune with cats and chickens. No vessel left for Alaska without a shipment of felines because the gold camps were alive with rats. No vessel left for Alaska without cages of chickens, because on the Klondike a single egg sold for as high as five dollars.

Julie quickly widened his vision. During weekday evenings Julie offered lectures on Phrenology, Women of the Bible, Modern Prophecy and The Secrets of Egyptian Immortality. On Saturdays, outside of taverns, he sold snake oil (Dr. Julian' s Elixir and Miracle Tonic).

On Sundays he preached.

"A wonder he wasn't hanged," the Barrister murmurs. "And buried under the jail."

"It was frontier," I suggest. "The frontier allows wide margins."

"No it doesn't." Cat always smiles when she offers a flat contra-diction . . . part of her charm. "The frontier is only liberal about murder and whoring."

Julie preached an early form of sexual permissiveness and community. He spoke with passion of a new Zion where each belonged to all, and all to each. His message was not completely new because communes were then a feature of Northwest Territory.

What made Julie's message different was its emphasis on immortality achieved through communion of bodies. Although young at the time, he seemed particularly tied to notions of immortality. Strangely (or perhaps not) most of Julie's congregation were women.

"Can you imagine," Cat muses, "being Julie, and alive, for all eternity; having to feed his awful hungers and that god-awful ego? Gives a girl a bellyache just thinking of it."

I understand Cat. I would not even wish to be me for all eternity, because I think I can do better. But, bellyache or not, there is no denying that Julie was obsessed with not dying. The obsession would become nigh maniacal as he aged.

"He sold stock in a railroad that was never built." The Barrister tends to lay one finger alongside his nose, and sniff in the face of rascality. The Barrister cares naught for life everlasting.

"And then he started a bank." I pause, thinking of my own rise in fortune because of Julie.

"He had the gift of business," the Barrister mutters. "Dirty business. He was not political, but he bought politicians."

"And then," Cat murmurs, "he discovered Romance, big 'R.' And then he discovered Art, big 'A.'" She sounds uncertain, ready to sigh, or giggle. "Bloody fool," she says. "I'd be the last to keep a man from chasing a skirt, but there are limits."

Art. Big A. In ten years Julie became scandalously rich. He entered this town while freely spreading money, and when it came to sex, he was as wanton as a mink.

And, like a mink, he was small and slim. I remember his body well, having tailored to it for years. He had a large head, a high rump, and thin legs. His shoulders were narrow, but his arms heavy. His Scots blue eyes could cut like razors, and his thin lips curled with power. And yet, Julie was not first-of-all mean, only, perhaps, desperate. He dressed as meticulously as Beau Brummel, but had not the suaveness of that English gent.

II

The terrors in our streets ebb and flow from Seven Sisters. Spirits manifest when mist embraces mansions and hovels, or when

shadows from the setting sun darken the land. In darkness some
spirits weep, but others howl. We cannot hear the howling, but we
see faces as they drift toward Seven Sisters. Along our streets pass
more than sorrow, because, while some weep others seem intent
on violence. Vengeance is as vital here, and as real, as rain.

When he arrived in our town Julie was thirty-two, rich as
Croesus, and enamored of a modern dancer named Gabrielle.
She brought her dance company with her; a company
described by the famous dancer, Isadora Duncan as "Crazed
but beautiful ladies." Gabrielle, more practical than kiln-dried
boards, gave her all to Julie. Nor did she mind when Julie
bedded her entire troupe.

It is not known if Gabrielle adhered to Julie's religion, but it
is known that Gabrielle knew how to play her fish once he was
hooked. Gabrielle had tested the frontier's crude halls, found them
wanting, and wished for a permanent stage where audiences would
come to her, and not she to them. Seven Sisters began as Julie built
a mansion to house his harem; a mansion named Forte.

We, of the Historical Society, do not remember the early years.
The Barrister was born in 1913, I in 1914, and Cat? No gentleman
speculates on a lady's age.

By the time we matured, Julie was old: 72 in 1930, filthy rich,
disgustingly active and too vital; plus (it was rumored) in his
age, obscene. Gabrielle had long since ceased to play the part of
mistress. She called herself 'artistic director'; but in truth was a
procurer for Julie. Gabrielle's troupe, some of them, had remained
but were no longer seen. It was as if they danced their ways into
smoke or mist. By the time we, of the Historical Society, reached
working age, Seven Sisters stood at its height.

I must tell what it was then, before saying what it is now.

In my youth Seven Sisters stood in a semi-circle surrounded
by rolling lawns and cascading fountains. A dark forest of fir and
cedar framed the background. The houses were massive, three and
four stories, and in their prime were masterpieces of Victorian
architecture. From left to right they were:

Forte, four stories bracketed with four turrets and painted in
lilac with royal purple trim. The first floor held a thrust stage for
dancers, the top floors held apartments.

Muse, a brooding mansion with small windows of crystal, the windows lodged in walls painted black, and ornamented in gray. It rose into our gray skies like dark poetry.

Maestro, a concert hall with a ceiling forty feet high, and with practice rooms and living quarters. It stood three and a half stories, the colors bluegrass and teal.

Gaudens, the tallest and most narrow of the seven, it stood more like a tower than a house, and was itself a sculpture in marble-pink. Its balconies displayed busts of the famous, but in chaotic order . . . Socrates beside Mendelssohn.

Thespia, a theater lodged in the largest of the mansions. By 1920 gaslights had been replaced by electricity. The massive stage, and seating for a thousand, carried paint of red and black; was colored auburn and black inside, with rose-colored stage curtains. The mansion stood four stories and included small practice stages, closets of costumes, and, of course, living quarters with many beds.

Greco, more neo-classical than Victorian, stood brilliant and unornamented in white behind massive pillars. At three stories it was the smallest of the mansions. Its architectural statement posed simplicity among mansions ornamented with Victorian roses.

Michelangelo, was a museum, and was thought by those whose business it is to know such things, an architectural failure.

Natural light in the northwest runs to gray more than gold. The enormous windows of the mansion helped illuminate its display galleries and studios. Had the builder allowed the structure to remain plain, what a success might have been had. Instead, where clear glass was not needed, stained glass was added. The mansion stood like a patchwork quilt of color, sporting unneeded turrets and widow's walks.

When we of the Historical Society were young we strolled the well-tended lawns. We watched beautifully dressed ladies and gentlemen pause as they chatted before fountains. In the mansions craftsmen and artists worked. The place seemed a small city and we, young and untested, could not imagine the dread force hovering above the silver crash of water from the fountains.

"I surely believe," Cat says, "that we appeared on the scene just as decline began." She shifts lightly in her chair. In this old library there are now musty smells as books begin turning liquid. Frames of windows have long since lost their paint and are swollen with Northwest rain. Beyond the windows decaying houses are themselves like a congregation of ghosts adrift against the gray sky. Those that still have paint have been repainted. Nothing original and bright remains. Only here and there, from a distant chimney, smoke from woodstove or fireplace rises above narrow streets.

Cat looks askance at the Barrister. She almost does not want to say what she is about to say. "One of the Popes, long ago, grew old. He tried to stay alive by suckling the breasts of women."

The Barrister sits stunned and does not see the relevance. He is not surprised, because the Barrister reads history. Mostly, he is shocked because someone, even someone as scandalous as Cat, would speak of such a thing. "Pope Innocent VIII," he murmurs, and his blush is vivid.

"Because," Cat says, "if we talk about Julie, let's cut the guff."

"Men live by symbols," I say. Better to say something innocuous than put up with this shocked silence.

=

Perhaps Cat is correct. Decline may well have started in the 1930s. Seven Sisters took decades to fade. The houses had been too well built. Many artists lingered. They made livings by working in this town, even as the town faded. And, with passing years many lived to old age and died. The town, however, has no record of the deaths of Gabrielle or Julie.

"And yet, we were certain they died," I told the others. "I recall the rumors. Some said that Julie was murdered by an angry husband. Some said that he traveled to the Orient and never returned. The most likely rumor claimed that he stepped into eternity attended by the best physicians in the nation, and that the body was embalmed with rich spices and oils."

"Artists died as well," the Barrister said. "As did others."

"It's the manner in which people died." Cat allows herself another shudder. "Think of the deaths, then think of the mansions."

"Few deaths were normal." I am uneasy admitting what is so obviously true. "Most were not. Bodies did not develop dread

155

disease. They withered from within. Something siphoned life. Life seemed purloined."

=

Today, at the beginning of a new century, Seven Sisters stand like crazed echoes. Our townspeople do not go there because of fear. The decaying mansions are now immersed in a forest of young fir and cedar, as untended lawns allowed forest to reclaim the land. The darkest and ugliest and completely broken mansion is Muse, black paint washed away so that remaining boards are sodden and gray. Chimneys have tumbled, and the crystal windows have been shattered by vagrants, or, even more likely, by storm. Bare rafters decay in the rain.

The others are in great disrepair. Gaudens has scattered its busts of the famous. One steps cautiously through young forest and is sometimes surprised by a marble face staring upward. Busts lie on the ground, Rembrandt and Beethoven.

Perhaps the strangest is Michelangelo. Its large windows hang cracked and crazy before its galleries, and its stained glass windows are now clear. Color, for over a century, has drained from those windows. In the galleries hang empty frames, or sometimes frames holding canvas that is blank. The frames no longer hold gilt. A stark place, it is devoid of color, form, and even, some would say, perspective.

The only sister that still shows color is Thespia. Perhaps the color only comes because of rusting iron railings. At any rate, Thespia stands intact and stained. On the darkest nights, lamplight still shines from high rooms of Thespia, and for a generation, now, people have assumed that vagrants camp there.

Of late, however, we are no longer sure. Our qualms are the reason for the meeting of the Historical Society.

"Because," Cat says, "we are still alive." She shrugs. "No big deal because lots of people live long lives. But we are too active. We move like fifty-year-olds, and you gents are approaching ninety."

I am not happy, thinking what I'm thinking. "We are the last people alive," I say, "who not only knew Julie, but who had intimate dealings with him."

"My accomplishments with men are private. My accomplishments with theater are sufficient. I have played alongside the Barrymores." Cat speaks with quiet dignity. "I trod his stage, but Julie never came within a country mile." She turns to the Barrister, and Cat is ready for a scrap.

"I," says the Barrister, "handled much of his legal work, but none of his dirty work."

"And I," I tell them, "never cut a corner, never compromised a task, never substituted cheaper material, and never padded the account." Since it sounds like bragging, I add, "It would have been poor business."

=

When I wake in gray mornings it is always with a surge of untoward energy, like the twinge of static electricity. Or worse, it is like a false stimulus, the kick of concentrated caffeine or some other drug. It is not normal, this I know.

When I step into our narrow streets the town stands slanted, crazy and askew. One does not know whether to admit that this a ghost town, or, more likely, a town profoundly under the control of spirits. Victorian houses stand like colorful ghosts. New paint peels, but wood is silver, and not the muddy gray of Seven Sisters. No original color remains.

Municipal buildings show a few lights. The town still owns a working fire truck. An aging policeman monitors our streets. The mayor runs the general store that sees fewer customers each year. Perhaps the town survives because of eternal mist.

Perhaps gray coastlines are most amenable to tormented and tormenting spirits.

And, approaching the library, one's heart cannot help but sadden. Weeds rise high around the windows. Library hours, these days, are from 10 to 2, Tuesdays. A volunteer librarian fights her losing battle against moisture, mold, and rot.

"We find ourselves in a pickle," the Barrister muses. "I had not realized we were the only ones left who had close dealings with Julie."

"Julie was morally venereal. Fully corrupt," Cat tells the Barrister. "We have just confessed that we were not. Something to think about."

"It is true that I am too spry for my age," the Barrister says. "Since we are granted this energy, let's use it. I'll research records at the courthouse. There'll be no answer, but there may be clues."

"I will research sunsets," Cat says, and I am not sure what she means.

"I will walk the night," I tell her. "I'm far too old to be playing it safe."

"Think of the arts," Cat whispers, and I am certain she is talking to herself. "Think of sex, or rather, its reasons."

III

In a land of tormented spirits it's easy to be cowardly. I walk through twilight and admit to cowardice that has kept me from watching haunted movements. As twilight fades, and darkness thickens our streets, whispers become palpable. Perhaps the whispers have always been there, and we have not listened. While turning away from soundless screams, we have ignored the whispers.

Black moves against black. Beneath a shrouded moon, and far away, dark figures manifest then fade to black. In yellow light from street lamps, movement appears where light melds to darkness. Something in our streets is not dead. Or, if that something is dead, it is propelled.

Faces congregate, but seem separate from the black-on-black movement. I sorrow to think that I am used to faces of horror, of shocked children viewing injuries they cannot believe belong to them, of the faces of the murdered or the raped.

And through the years, too many faces have been costumed— Pilgrims and Plantagenets, Harlequins and Hamlets. Faces fanciful, but crippled: a belled cap invisibly jingling above blind eyes, or stern eyes staring from beneath eyebrows above which the skull is broken and missing. These forms have appeared and rapidly faded. Perhaps their transience is why we ignored them.

But, it comes to me, walking our nighttime streets, that I may ignore them no longer. Survival of the body is not the question here. The question is survival of the soul. Their souls, if they still have them. Mine.

"Think of the arts and sex," Cat had said, "or think of their reasons."

"Better yet," I murmur to the night, "think of a bad Pope, plus a corrupt opportunist. What had they in common?"

And, I answer, "They wanted to live past their natural span."

Our streets meander, but all eventually wend to Seven Sisters. When I stand among young trees and look at the mansions it is almost always beneath a shrouded moon. Mist rises with the night. Clouds that form in the Aleutians roll down our coastline sometimes bringing storm and wind.

Whispers in the forest rarely assert. Instead, they consult. Movements which earlier seemed random, I now understand are direct and with purpose. It has taken two weeks of nights to understand that this town is the site of a ghastly war.

Vengeance rides the wind, but it is not vengeance, only. The dead make direct assaults on Seven Sisters. The assaults have something to do with survival. Survival of whom? Survival of what?

I only know that as darkness seals the forest, movement focuses on Seven Sisters. While some apparitions momentarily appear, I now know it is necessary to follow whispers and murmurs, not apparitions. And, slightly distant, but always present, dark forms move like jet-black ink scrawled across the night.

Whispers encircle Seven Sisters and wage a war of attrition, of surrounding, of gnawing. I was stunned at first, because I quickly understood that the collective army of whispers can actually direct the wind. Wind rises above treetops and concentrates on a single mansion. The concentration doubles the force of the wind, so that glass panes crack and shingles fly.

Young tree branches are torn by wind. They are hurled against the mansion; a bombardment.

Equally impressive, during nights of rain I huddle in my water-proof and watch funnels of rain whirl crazily through the darkness, to crash precisely on weak points of a mansion. Rain centers on cracks in windows, siding, roofs. Having no other weapons, the army of whispers directs weather like a conductor before a symphony.

=

"Maybe it isn't war," Cat says. "Maybe it's theater." She sits again in the library as the three of us consult.

"You're joking."

"Maybe," Cat says, ". . . but theater is involved, so maybe not."

She is particularly beautiful on this gray day, and hers is an unconscious beauty. There' s witchery in her smile. Her flowing gown of greens might seem showy on other women, but on Cat it seems only casual. It occurs to me that I have lived a passive life. What might it have been had it been lived beside a woman like Cat?

"I'll ask you to explain that theater-business soon enough." The Barrister studies notes on a yellow pad. "I have interesting information. It seems Julie once had plans, and his plans went astray."

The Barrister has never owned a reputation for vengeance.

He owns a reputation for being just. Now, though, he smiles, and his smile is not kind. His small and wrinkled face seems as formal as his suit and starched white shirt. His dark tie is held in place with a diamond stickpin. The diamond glitters only a little sharper than the Barrister' s eyes. "That old saying . . . 'you can't take it with you' . . . Julie tried. What he didn't count on were other men just like himself."

The Barrister explains that Julie set up a foundation to administer his great fortune. The mission of the foundation was "To maintain and advance the aims of Seven Sisters in perpetuity." As the 20th century rolled past, ambitious men contrived to load the foundation's board and directorship. They stole the fortune.

"Not a drop left," the Barrister says with some satisfaction. "Not a dram. In his grave, Julie lies as a pauper."

"If," Cat says, "he is buried. Because, if one is buried, it pays to be dead."

It is the second time she has shocked the Barrister. Of course, the Barrister has not been walking our midnight streets. He has not stood in sunrise and sunset.

"If alive," Cat murmurs, "he would be a desperate, desperate man. If alive, then what's happening is both theater and war."

"If alive," the Barrister whispers, "he would be more than a hundred forty years old. Do not make jokes." The Barrister knows full well that no one is joking.

"You don't get it," Cat tells the Barrister. "The arts are not simple entertainment. They are life, itself. You don' t get that, do you?" Cat is angry, though managing to seem only annoyed. She turned to me. "If there' s a war there's two sides. What is the other side doing?"

"I don't know. The notion never occurred." I know that Cat is going somewhere with this, but it lies beyond comprehension.

"Find out," Cat tells me, "because what's alive at Seven Sisters is after us. At least part of it is." Her anger still lives, but is now subdued. "The war is now our war," she says quietly. "It is defensive. Julie is still alive. He is suckling symbolic breasts." To the Barrister she says, "Did you think the arts are male?"

The Barrister sits confused, as am I. Why this anger?

"After us?"

"In dawn and sunset the horrors of this town appear." Cat sounds like a grade school teacher. "There is not a rape, a murder, a disemboweling or a lynching that is not recalled. Those are most of the broken faces we see. That kind of manifestation no doubt happens in other places, places beyond the town. Manifestation probably happens in any place where the past is as dark as hate." She shifts in her chair, pauses, and I can tell that she still controls anger. "Apparitions are all around us. Call them ghosts. Call them history. Makes no difference. But, what happens at night is different."

"He is after us?" The Barrister, for perhaps the first time in his life, actually sounds fearful. "After us?"

"Shakespeare had it right." Cat once more muses to herself while ignoring the Barrister. "Storm and winds, thunder and Lear. War."

"I'll find out what the other side is doing," I tell her.

=

In darkest night spirits may, or may not, endorse my movements. One thing is certain. The wind drops. Night is as still as glass, but like glass, it may shatter. Mist flows away from the forest and the sky. Stars appear like streams of cold fire. In this depth of darkness Seven Sisters sit like hulks thrown on a rocky shore. Candlelight, or lamplight, glows on the fourth floor of Thespia. It is small illumination, but increases during an approach through the forest. Someone, or something, wields light.

Forte stands at the edge of the semi-circle. It is the oldest of the mansions. Starlight reveals broad and broken steps, and one can only pass up them by use of a flashlight. Covered porches encircle the mansion, and, in olden days, served as a promenade for beautifully coiffed ladies and tailored gents. It is on these porches that an intuition arrives.

The living have power here. It would be possible to step inside and strike a match. Words from an ancient book seem to echo along the porches, something on the order of "What's born in fire belongs to fire, so I fear hell's certain."

Whispers surround, question, hesitate. Fire is an option, but the whispers wonder to each other, debate.

On the other hand, one does not casually destroy the past, even those parts that are toad-ugly. At least one does not do so on a whim. It is wrong to destroy without knowing what is being destroyed.

From the porches, the main doorway leads into a foyer. The foyer leads to the auditorium and long, thrust stage where Gabrielle and her troupe once danced. My flashlight illumes furnishings now turning to dust. Upholstered chairs are pale as mist. Color has left or been stolen. A simple touch on the arm of a chair, and the thing crumbles. Overhead, ormolu roses hang like thin ice as copper alloy turns to dust. The very floors are without color. Missing, even, is any hint of carpet or varnish.

Drapery fragile as cold breath divides the foyer from the auditorium. And, in the auditorium the mind goes numb.

On the huge stage a single figure dances, ghostly as mist in dark forest. The stage dwarfs the figure, so that she seems no more than a child. Slow and rhythmic, she moves against paleness. There is no music here, except in her movement which suggests music. It seems, though one cannot swear to it, that as she dances, she weeps.

And so, it would seem, fire is out of the question.

After five more nights I am able to report that, with the exception of Thespia, figures inhabit each mansion. I have not yet found the courage to enter Thespia.

In Muse the figure is dark. It slumps over a desk, quill in hand, but the pen does not move. In Maestro, fingers caress a harp that holds no strings. Gaudens carries the sound of gentle tapping, like chisel and hammer, but the echo says that it is not marble being worked, only brick. Greco is perhaps most fearsome, because figures clothed in Athenian style seem in pursuit of philosophy, and the figures murmur: "Gordian knots of ice cream," and, "When the Jersey-moo arrives the point lies proved", and thus, are the figures insane.

And, Michelangelo I doubt not, is most bizarre. In all the mansions there has been no life, but Michelangelo hosts a mouse. One walks the galleries where pale walls stand empty, except where an occasional frame still hangs. The frames are stripped of gilt, and are gnawed.

As one strolls through the galleries, the mouse scurries ahead like a guide telling the story of each empty frame. There is only one mouse. Perhaps it is an incarnation of some sad spirit, condemned to gnaw until Michelangelo falls to dust.

=

"Desperation," Cat says, and she talks about Julie. We once more sit in the library and look at mouldering books; and look through windows beyond which Victorian houses lean crazily against the sky. "Madness. What awful, awful hunger."

The Barrister whispers. "I have lived here all my life. A man ought to be allowed to die where he has lived."

I listen to the Barrister. Does his mind wander? He was in strong mental control only last week. Is he now senile?

"I'm beginning to think the same thing," Cat tells him. "It may be half-past time to get the deuce out of town." She turns to me. "Run or stay?"

"We are duty-bound to see this through." The Barrister still whispers. He does not look well. His small frame, already shrunken, seems like fragile sticks clinging to the inside of his suit. He is only a trellis for clothing. "My energies," he apologizes, "are not what they were."

Cat and I look at each other, and our looks ask the same question.

Trust Cat to choose honesty. "You are the first of us to be attacked," she tells the Barrister, and her voice is gentle.

"You are physically smallest. The thing that was Julie, or maybe is Julie, is running out of options." She again looks through the windows. "There's nothing left of the original colors out there. Surely those were stolen first."

Sometimes, even in my great age, I am reckless to the point of stupidity. "I'll confront him," I tell them.

"We'll confront him," Cat turns to me. "You still don't 'get it.' I expect you'll be needing help." To the Barrister she says, "Keep close to home. Rest. One way or other, this is soon over."

=

Death is a fearful problem for the young, but people who are truly old do not fear it. We fear other things. I think about this as I wait for Cat. I stand at the edge of the young forest.

We, who are old, fear the death of our worlds. Each of us has known the world in a particular manner. As we grow old the world gets revised. We, who are old, mourn the passing of ways that sustained us in youth. In my case, I mourn loss of formality and custom and honor. The Barrister, who is admittedly starchy, is one of the last men alive who I truly admire.

Cat approaches through gathering darkness, and there's magic in her movements. No one, and certainly not the young, move with such grace. The approaching night seems to fall away like a discarded cloak. She moves through the dusk as a small essence of light.

"Forte," she says, and leads in that direction. As she moves, whispers from the forest congregate. They no longer question. If anything, the whispers endorse. Mostly, though, they seem excited in ways that only belong to the living. But, a whisper can't be alive . . . how can a whisper be alive?

"Do you hear?" I feel like a young kid tagging behind an older sister.

"Shush," Cat says. She is focused.

I follow in silence. When we stand in the foyer, dusk lingers in the windows. Sunset seems unwilling to fade. The last time I was here the foyer was viewed by flashlight. In this gray light it stretches long and wide and barren.

Cat looks at crumbling furnishings and muddy-gray walls. "Tomb of lost dreams." Her voice is quiet. Whispers surround us. On my first visit, the whispers stayed on the porches. Now they have moved inside. "Lost dreams," Cat repeats. "Let's see if we can find 'em."

=

I follow her to the auditorium which has no windows. It is darker, even, than most of our nights. In the darkness gray figures move. They are the same figures that moved black-on-black through streets and forest.

"It's been a while," Cat murmurs to herself. She watches the enormous stage where a pale figure dances, ghostly, slow, dancing with its own silent rhythm. "I never was much one to hoof it," Cat whispers, "but since we're here."

When she ascends the stage and joins the dancer, pale light trembles on the edge of darkness. If there is music in the air it lives on the edge of hearing. And, if it is music, it is in three-quarter time. One thinks of Mozart.

The living figure bows, the phantom curtseys. Both the bow and the curtsy are as delicate as music that now reaches to surround, but not touch the dancers.

"Quick study," Cat says in a soft voice, "I was always a quick study. So show me."

And they dance, slowly, in classic minuet; Cat learning as she goes. And as they dance the specter no longer weeps, although Cat does. And, she smiles. And dances.

Gray figures turn luminous. Light attends the stage.

Whispers become murmurs, and I feel separated from Cat, from the phantoms, and from the luminous shadows. Something is alive here, and beyond my understanding. All around, murmurs speak of form, color, sound.

". . . a bit more light . . . blue filter . . . make it soft."

". . . that snare drum's in front, not back of the music. Get it where it belongs . . ."

The figures on stage gradually meld. What was once a specter fades toward Cat, and it is impossible to tell whether it becomes

part of her, or simply disappears. Cat stands on the stage, trans-
fixed like one seeing visions.

"If those two were trying to impress me," one murmur says,
"they've done it."

"The drum should have gone to a deep tom-tom," a second
murmur insists. "The snare was too sharp."

It seems a private discussion held in public, but I do not
understand. When Cat speaks it is not as I expected, which is to
say, gently.

"Act two," she says, her voice brisk. "And it's only a two-acter. Let
us proceed." And—by the Lord Harry she giggles. To me, she says,
"If you still don't get it, watch what happens next."

What happens next is that we leave Forte accompanied by
murmurs from luminous shadows. In growing night the shadows
gain color. I feel sure that they will soon materialize.

Once clear of Forte we turn and watch. It does not, like a house
of legend, sink into the tarn. There is little spectacle in the death of
Forte, although it is interesting. The four high turrets bend slowly
inward, like dancers bowing to each other; but unlike real dancers
the turrets continue to fall. Dust raises its smoke above walls no
stronger than paper. Destruction takes its time. It is methodical.
The building shrieks as rusted nails pull from worn boards and as
walls collapse inward.

By the time of complete collapse not a salvageable piece remains.
"I'd be the last," Cat murmurs, "to keep a man from chasing a
skirt, but there are limits." To me she says, "Julie never made the
connection. All that this meant to him was a roll in the hay."

"And Gabrielle?"

"There's art, " Cat says grimly, "and then, there's bad art. Those
who can't dance well can always dance on their backs." She turns
and heads for Thespia.

IV

Nightmare lay ahead. No grotesque vision of Hell ever burned
more brightly. I write this record on yellow legal pads as I sit in the
library. My writing instrument is a black marker; wide, dark lines

against the soft glow of the paper. The lines seem thicker than my fingers. My sight fades, and the vivid ink seems insubstantial. The Barrister has died in peace, and I am soon to follow.

When Cat turned toward Thespia I could feel tension gather as shadows gained substance and wind began to rise. The Harlequins and Pilgrims and Plantagenets who strode stages in other days, now showed no blinded eyes or ravaged skulls. Their murmurs were alive, and they seemed alive as well. As we strode forward I found myself in company with a band of costumed men and women. They were not yet corporeal, but they were no longer creatures of shadow. "I've saved, your Grace, a pocket full of wind . . ."

". . . warriors or cartoonists." Cat spoke to the forest, or to the company, but not to me. "I expect we'll have to decide which."

Thespia seemed to gather night as it loomed into darkness. It was always too massive for a house, too massive, even, for a theater. In many ways it resembled a castle, but one of wood more than stone. True, the widely sweeping steps were of marble, and the foundation was of granite, but all else was wood. I did not then know that marble and granite can burn.

=

Gaiety accompanied our approach, ready to whistle, or break into song. Cat hummed, and seemed ready to whistle, or break into song. She moved with such grace that I did not at first realize what else was happening.

From the other mansions black shadows emerged. They staggered, fumbled, and gradually gained strength. As they grew stronger, black turned to gray, and gray to luminosity. We walked in light as freed spirits congregated.

Thespia loomed so huge I could only feel intimidation. As wind began to bend trees, light from the fourth floor of Thespia brightened. The first three floors then illumed with glow like electric storms against clouds. As light grew, wind became stronger above the forest. It blew through my clothing and chilled my spine.

When we entered Cat paused. "Welcome back, " Cat murmured, probably to herself. After all, she had once walked the stage that opened before us. Cat looked around the immense auditorium that contained not one shred of color.

"No wonder it attacked the Barrister." Cat finally spoke directly to me. "It's so hard up that life is even being drawn from the place where it lives."

"It?"

"Julie was always an 'it,'" Cat says. She reconsiders. "Maybe not always, but that's what he became." She sees that I do not understand. "My dear man. Wake up. You once fashioned cloth into beautiful things."

All around us spirits hovered silent but poised. Those crippled spirits that had joined us from the buildings remained shadowy, but Cat's company of materialized spirits gained even greater substance.

"Black-and-white must buy color, or steal. Thus, do I give you Julie." Cat turned to ascend broad stairs.

Wind thumped against Thespia. The building did not shake, but from upstairs rooms came moans as wind poured through broken windows. Wails rose as wind probed cracks between boards and window frames.

Second floor displayed dressing rooms, and a shock. In closets were products of my own hands. Costumes hung in tidy and colorful rows; costumes to bring forth aviators and princesses, churls, beggars, merry wives, or Spanish dancers.

"Their colors have survived," I whispered to Cat.

"I think," she said, "that they have been preserved. I think I'm beginning to understand this."

The second floor was also used as storage: coils of cables, dry and decaying manilla rope, tools and other appurtenances of stagecraft. Below us, down in the theater, echoes sounded. They were not whispers. The echoes spoke in large outstanding terms, proclaiming the awakening of dreams. Cat listened. Smiled.

As we climbed, color became more than a suggestion. It had not completely drained from walls where fading white had turned to yellow, and where ormolu held traces of pastels. Third floor was given over to private chambers, and it was on third floor that one knew that first taste of absolute fear. The fear is not so terrible one cannot bear it, but it lives like copper on the tongue.

Some of the doors to private chambers stood open. And, what lay in them might have once lived. Wind swept the rooms and rustled faded gowns.

And less fearful, though like echoes, walls carried notatations and graffiti; a record of what had once been positive about Thespia. "H.R.H in Hamlet, spring 1897." "Ferrill, 1918, the Armistice just announced. We're playing a George Ade." "E. Barrymore, Ah, Cassandra, 1932." The notations were normally faded, yet still seemed alive.

"Think on't, milord," Cat muttered, "Think ye longish and well." Around her, materialized spirits became more physical. Murmurs turned to soft speech; not confused, but questioning.

"We are stronger, are we strong enough?"

"The lion in its cage now mews," Cat said to the company. "Let's bait the lion." To me she said, "He built his own cage. Let's see what the fool has done with immortality."

Steps to fourth floor wound crazily, as if the builder had grown tired of symmetry. They were broad, solid, and burnished with soft light that at other times might have seemed seductive. At the head of the steps a massive door stood open.

"The play's the thing," Cat said to the spirits. "Improv emptiness and wind."

"That," said a cultured male voice, "is a quite well-studied role." The fully manifested speaker stood beside Cat, and he was costumed as a strolling minstrel. His hair curled dark, and his brown eyes flashed. Jerkin in cloth of green.

We entered and I stood amazed. I looked at a throne room, and two massive thrones. I saw gold roses in the gilded ceiling, and draperies of royal purple. I saw cloth of gold. Tapestry in rich reds ornamented walls, and yellow and violet rugs of Arabian design covered russet floors. Sculptures guarded corners and doors, forms of naked warriors and women; only some of them obscene.

"Engage him," Cat whispered to me. "We'll handle the rest." Her confidence served well because I have no great reputation for courage.

It seemed impossible to talk to the thing before me. Julie sat enthroned, the throne tall and chaotic with color. Paint did not chip or fade. Every color that could come from a pallet twisted and curled; the effect demented.

I looked upward. Julie's blue eyes peered peevish through lids heavy with bloat. The once-narrow frame had expanded beyond possibility of fitted clothing. A light and transparent robe covered pendulous breasts, and fingers were so enlarged they seemed all-of-a-piece. Arms looked thick as rolled rugs, and legs were swollen like fleshy balloons. This was not fat, but bloat.

On the second throne sat a corpse. Gabrielle had mummified and seemed no weightier than tissue paper; her once strong frame dwindled to thin twigs. When she spoke her voice echoed from elsewhere, because her lips did not move. She had been drained of life, but not of speech. "Betrayed." The echo ran the ranges of despair like a chromatic scale. "Betrayed."

In this high place northwest wind gained strength. It buffeted the walls.

I heard Cat's voice. It sounded loud or faint, depending on where she moved in the huge room. "'Tis here, 'tis there, 'tis everywhere; but nowhere do I see it."

"What seek ye, mistress? Wither we away?" A male voice boomed and I nearly turned from Julie.

"A sack of moonlight. Possibly a poem." Cat's voice sounded distant. "A wreath of music and a flight of bird."

"Peter," Julie said. "You're looking well." His voice remained the only thin thing about him. The voice issued from swollen lips. The snideness that was always his had increased. It held contempt, but it also held a hint of fear. He turned his massive head as much as he was able. "For that you'd better thank me."

Cat had skipped beyond his vision. I saw her standing in a far corner, arms akimbo, and her gaze enraptured as she watched a man in green cloth cavort. "Buds of May 'neath pale winds dance, and on yon hill fair lambkins prance. Hey nonny nonny."

Wind crashed against Thespia, and now the building trembled. From the forest branches of young trees were cast. They hit with ballistic force.

"Better explain that," I said to Julie. "Before thanking people, I like to know what the conversation's about." Oddly enough, my voice remained calm.

"I've stored life in you," Julie said. "You're nothing but storage, and you, I don't need." He listened for Cat. "But at least you brought the woman." Julie turned to look at Gabrielle. His lips were too bloated to curl, but scorn filled his voice. "This one has become a burden."

An ornamental suaveness had always been Julie's trademark, but now it was replaced by something savage. He sat enthroned, too bloated to walk, and he sat beside a corpse. Color whirled crazily around us, as far across the room Cat and a company of spirits cavorted. The spirits were now as substantial as when they were alive.

"Betrayed." Gabrielle' s voice seemed made of dust. It faded, as a last rustle of her being departed.

"Betrayed." The word dwindled, and the mouth which had, until then, not moved, gaped. If Gabrielle was not free, at least she had been released.

"You were always a milksop," Julie told me, "thus useful. I control vitality here. I control life. If I invest in you, and keep you vital, I persuade myself that you're insurance."

And finally, after nearly ninety years of life, I began to catch on.

I made connections. Vitality was stored with us for use in keeping Julie alive. That was the reason for the Barrister' s decline. Julie was feeding on his capital.

Poor fool. I finally understood, then understood something more. Cat was not scandalous. I was, or had been. I had played it safe, not knowing that poverty of spirit is defensive, but life isn't. Poverty of spirit only shapes more poverty. Creation shapes the world.

"I believe," I told Julie, "that your policy just lapsed." Beyond the mummified figure of Gabrielle, a ring of dancers circled a Maypole. Cat skipped nimble as a child.

"Give way," I told him. "The woman behind you has lived more, in any five minutes of her life, then you have in a hundred-and-forty years."

A sneer. And yet, the bloated figure above me moved uneasily. "Behind me?"

"My mistake," I told him. "You're way behind. She does not give two snips about you."

"Soupçon of breeze, a stir of air, and rises lordly wind." Cat's voice sounded like a child at play. Dancers began to flow around the room, and from the first crack in the walls of Julie's bastion entered a movement of air. It was but a breath at first, but definitely a breach. Dancers pantomimed the wind, swooping, eddying, while laughter deepened.

"She'll care soon enough. What I can give, I can take away." Julie watched the actors as they danced. "I took what I needed from them once, I'll take again. You idiots have done a favor."

"Release the Barrister."

"Already done," Julie told me. "There's fatter game here."

"And a fatter hunter." I thought myself mad to bait him.

Then I thought that he was the one who was mad. For a century he had run roughshod. Now, with a breeze ruffling that tent-like and transparent robe, he could not imagine his hazard.

He was like a man trying to pick up a stone that he thought was a prop, an imitation made of paper; but instead had turned out to be a real stone. He paused, perplexed. He concentrated, strained, and his eyes were portraits of fear.

"What cruel revenge they are taking," I said about Cat and her company. "It is the revenge of unimportance. They tell you that you were, and are, king of nothing, nothing more." In defiance, I wet my finger and held it aloft to determine the direction of the breeze. "Observe as they create the wind, because you look your last."

I thought I could not care about Julie, and yet as his struggle began I felt small sadness. "If you were truly evil I would rejoice," I told him. "But you're only arrogant. What you do is evil, but to be truly evil . . . you're not man enough."

Now the actors formed a cortege behind a casket borne on a donkey cart. They were costumed as clowns, and they cast flowers in the air; and flowers threw petals into the wind. A shower of petals blew toward us. Actors near the coffin sang a funereal song, although they smiled and their clown shoes flippity-flopped. At the end of the procession, like mischievous children, actors pranced.

"The king is dead," I told Julie, "and he was only king of a room that is about to disappear."

Fear, like none I have ever known, now lived on Julie's face. I doubted not that fear lived more vibrantly than any other emotion Julie had ever felt. At first I thought he was trying to steal life, then realized he was in struggle to hold onto what he had already stolen. "You could offer help," he choked. "You owe."

"Nothing I can do." I thought of a hundred years of theft and exploitation. I thought of our dying town and the murder of people, and the murder of dreams. "Nothing I want to do. No one owes anything, even simple courtesy."

"I'll pay. I offer life."

I think he believed he spoke the truth. For all his many years he had fed, and fed. He had controlled. He could not then grasp that his control was gone.

He began to wither. At first, he only seemed to shrink, and for a moment I did not understand that the lives and colors he had hoarded were escaping. The bloat decreased. In the distance actors postured, declaimed, and their play was grimly comic.

"A little life. Save a little." The plea was to me, or to fate, or to some god unknown; and it was frantic.

It was then I became cruel. "None," I told him. "You're not important enough for Hell, and so you simply disappear. You will not even be a bug, a mote, or any incarnation. Neither earth nor heaven will know you more." I had no notion whether I spoke true, but it seemed true. Mine were the last words Julie heard before succumbing to fear.

He did not shrink, but like Forte folded in on himself. As the bloat disappeared, and as blue eyes grew wild with insanity, Julie appeared as he had once been. His thin-legged, high-rumped form writhed on a throne now devoid of color; and as color departed he screamed. He was momentarily young, and in torment.

As he departed he aged. Faded hair, faded but tortured eyes, creases beginning, then deepening. His fingers grasped uncontrolled as he screamed. When dismemberment started its slow and bloody progress I had seen enough.

Cat took me by the arm. "At the very outside," she told me, "We have ten minutes." She tugged, and I was not loath to follow. My last memory of the place is of screams and the stench of decay.

We moved quickly and without speaking. Cat's band of actors accompanied us, and I could not for the moment believe that they were spirits. They trod the stairs, and the stairs drummed beneath their feet.

Past dusty rooms, past fragile bones, while we were chased by wind that scoured hallways. We moved quickly, but slowed as we left the building and stepped into young forest that danced in the wind. I felt age begin to creep upon me. Life was not stolen, but the vitality Julie had invested was now leaving. Soon I would be weak and tottering.

Cat stood beside me, sisterly and protective. Actors gathered about as we watched a consummation.

Fire started in a hundred or a thousand places from small torches of light. Wind wrapped around the building. An actor's voice muttered. "'Blow winds, blow and crack your cheeks.'"

"I mourn its passing," Cat murmured to the actors, or possibly to me. "The theater couldn't help who owned it." Then she brightened. "But then, one does not need a building. The street is a stage."

It is a formidable sight to watch any large building burn.

When the building is nigh the size of a castle, the sight inspires awe. The small torches of light appeared when lives trapped in that building flared in their escapes. Wind fanned the tiny fires, so that in only moments the entire mansion alighted with fire. Wind flared around fourth floor where, if Julie still existed, he lay in an immense crematory. Fire illumed clouds and mist flowing from the forest. Wind searched, expanded, and the burning of Thespia was like a dry stick dropped into a blast furnace.

"Time to leave," Cat whispered to me. "Good job you did in there."

I turned to her. In the fire-glow her face seemed young as a girl, although age crept across her body. Her hands trembled. She smiled, happy as an excited child, and reached to touch my cheek. Beside her, spirits faded as they began to move into the forest. "I leave with them," Cat said. "It's where I belong. But you, I'll miss." And then she turned, walking slowly, and disappeared into the forest.

There is little more to tell. I had enough remaining strength to leave the forest. Our town's policeman found me trudging the road to town, and took me home. It was a week before I ventured out.

It seemed that with the passing of Forte and Thespia any fear that locals owned was gone. When I stepped back into our streets the remaining mansions had been raided, with little of value recovered. The buildings stood stripped and bare. A constant wind guaranteed their passing. The story was over, but the record still needed to be made.

The library is a cool, sometimes cold place, but I must close the record here. I want nothing of Julie, not even a notation, to enter my own rooms.

I note the passing of the Barrister. He died in peace, and in a hospital bed. He was conscious and only a little ill, but his illness was not Julie. He was his own man.

And I proudly note that I am mine. In nigh ninety years I learned trade, and craft, and even artfulness; but never art. It took Cat to teach me. One need not regret lost years when one has learned great things.

The Twenty-Pound Canary

In memory of Damon Runyon

[*Two sentences in this story were adapted from* The Mauve Decade, *by Thomas Beer, Alfred A. Knopf, 1937: a book that English teachers do not read, but should.*]

IF COUSIN MURPH HAD NOT EXPANDED HIS LAB, AND IF CANARY Clarence had not developed a glandular condition, then Miss Janice would not have scored a husband. Uncle Willie would not be muttering confused rhymes in his sleep and writing poetry in the attic. Aunt Easy would still be a member of the Temperance Union, and forty duck hunters (more or less) would not have thrown down shotguns to take up crappie fishing.

The unhappy mess started on a winter morning when Aunt Easy wakened in her front bedroom, from which she could see neighbors scooping snow from their walks, and four-wheel drives making doughnuts in Wisconsin streets. The house was still warm from wood stoves in living room and kitchen. Aunt Easy shuffled along with her usual, early morning cheerfulness. Until she hit the kitchen.

Pearly curtains with blue duckies hung straight. A clean and greenish tablecloth covered the round oak table where Aunt Easy did crossword puzzles and Uncle Willie read dusty books with yellowing pages. A patchwork cover over the birdcage shielded Parakeet-in-residence Harold from prowling night breezes.

Aunt Easy stoked the kitchen stove, made a cup of tea, and lifted the patchwork cover. She found Parakeet-in-residence Harold flat on his back, toes pointed heavenward. Her wrinkled but pretty face went blank. Her shoulders raised as she gave a light sob, and brushed curly gray hair from her forehead. Her worn bathrobe, once purple, now glowed faded pink.

Movement behind her. Uncle Willie, silver-haired, yawned into the room, took one look, paused. Whispered. "Gone to a better place I expect." Uncle Willie is a Rosicrucian and didn't believe a word of it.

"What was wrong with the place he had?" Aunt Easy was not going to be consoled. At least, not by a Rosicrucian.

She had a point. No other place in the world was as nice as that kitchen. Compared to that kitchen, Versailles was drafty, Monaco was loud, the British Museum was stuffy, and Disneyland was a laugh. Nothing, nowhere, was as warm and friendly as that kitchen. Compared to that kitchen, Harvard U was a muddle and the White House was a mess.

Then Cousin Murph showed up. He came fumbling out of the basement where he lived among cages of rodents, antiquated computers, Bunsen burners, test tubes, and flowery little notes from lonely spinsters. Cousin Murph is moderately red haired, thirty, lean and lank, works at the bank, and is about the only bachelor left here in Chedderburg.

Come to think of it, he's also the only redhead, the only mad scientist, and, until he got kicked out of the league, the only guy who owns a radio-guided bowling ball.

"Hummm-m-m," said Murph. He walked to the cage and got his hand smacked as he reached. Aunt Easy could see autopsy in Murph's eyes. She could sense dissection.

"Sorry," said Murph. "I'll build the coffin."

Parakeet-in-residence Harold was laid to rest in an intricately decorated box lined with velvet. I had to chip ice and frozen dirt for an hour to make a foot-deep grave beside the garden. I'm Kissing Cousin Effie, sweet sixteen, and extra smart. Smart enough not to fall in love with Murph, which is more than I can say for some.

Of course, being extra smart, I hang around Murph's lab from time to time. When the late Parakeet Harold went to his rest, one of those times happened. I'd bail from school, do homework early, and be at the lab when Murph came home from the bank. He almost always brought a plate of cookies with him; gifts from local trollops looking for a husband.

The problem, as I explained it to myself, is that Murph is just too nice. He tries to fix things that won't fix . . . like build a designer bird, the kind that cheeps and doesn't die.

The problem, as Murph explained it, is, "We gotta have birds. You can't breed birds if you don't have birds. Where do you get birds in Wisconsin in the middle of January?" He cleaned an empty cage while all around us stood cages filled with mice, white rats, voles, and something outstandingly huge. It looked like a hamster on growth hormones. "Name of Janders," Murph explained, and his voice held apology. "Sort of a mistake." Janders twitched a nose bigger than a pig snoot. He looked sarcastic, like maybe Murph, not hamster, was the mistake.

"Dime store in Wausau, pet store in Oshkosh, where else?" I told him. It's a good thing Murph has me, because he can't solve the least practical problem. Just the experimental stuff.

"Saturday," he said. "Assuming snow's not tail-high to a Hereford." He turned back to work on the cage. His lab is helter-skelter, but clean. Shiny counts, neatness don't.

The trip fell flat because it turned into a family occasion. Murph drove his ratty old station wagon which might have once been manufactured by a car company, but which had been improved. It now sported four-wheel drive, and all identifying marks had been removed. From a junk pile somewhere Murph had found a nameplate he'd proudly soldered to the front of the hood—Maytag.

Uncle Willie sat in front with Murph. Aunt Easy and I sat in back. Most cars can't dawdle, but we did. As we passed through town Murph slowed from ten mph to five. He watched Miss Janice clump along the sidewalk on her way to work at the library (hours 10-3 M-F, 11-2 Sat). Miss Janice dressed for the weather and did not look slim.

"Picked up weight." Uncle Willie has no right to talk. Not with that tummy hanging over his belt.

"Wearing a parka on top of a parka," Aunt Easy told him. "Janice is a lovely girl."

Janice is not a lovely girl. Janice is an adventuress. She wears her hair up at work, long skirts to hide long legs, and glasses that make her eyes look cloudy. The minute she visits the lab, though bearing cookies, the hair comes down, the skirt hits around the knees, and there's just enough cleavage to knock a preacher put of a pulpit. No glasses. Lovely, my dear: I think not.

Once clear of town snow fences lining the road were banked high. Frozen lakes lay dotted with fishing shacks. Trees stood naked as windmills, and a polar wind scoured.

"Pretty day for a drive," said Willie, and quoted something out of Tacitus that made no sense at all. I mean, how often does it snow in Italy?

". . . maybe a pair of finches," Aunt Easy murmured. "Or a nice canary. I can't handle another parakeet. Not just yet."

We all took a moment of silence. Parakeet-in-residence Harold had been somewhat adorable. For a bird.

The heater hummed, Maytag churned, and we finally got to the big city. We dropped Uncle Willie at a poolroom where, being adroit at the game, he figured to hustle wintering-over cheese farmers for a few bucks.

The sum of it was canaries: Aunt Easy bought one named Sylvester, and Murph bought some breeding pairs, especially a betrothed couple named Sally and Grogan. He also bought something that looked parrotish and South American. Uncle Willie won twenty bucks at pool and caught holy heck from Aunt Easy for sampling local brews. Murph drove faster going home than coming because he wanted to work with his birds. The subject of Janice did not reappear. We were all real happy, except for sweet sixteen, here, who was feeling strangely lonesome.

Things that winter got speedy, at least at the lab. Each day after work Murph committed science. Everything went fast and biblical. Grogan begat Jonathan and Jonathan begat Peter and Peter begat Cosroe, and Cosroe begat Clarence. Girl birds were involved, of course, mostly not biblical: Claudia and Shirley and Sandy and Tangerine. By the time ice began to break on the lakes, there were enough canaries singing through that lab to challenge the Mormon Tabernacle Choir.

And there were women. Winter in Wisconsin makes people want to cuddle, bundle, stay close as paint on woodwork. That lab was infested with visiting babes wearing flimsy fashions beneath ski jackets, and not a stitch of underwear. Lady things jiggled beneath raw silk blouses. It was worse than the locker room for gym class.

"And Murph pays no attention, not a-tall," I told Uncle Willie, telling him about the floozies. We sat at the kitchen table where I did homework and Willie read the witticisms of Charles Sumner. Frost rimed the windows, and from his cage Canary Sylvester cleared his throat.

"You're still a little young," Willie told me. "It's the breeding season, but Murph is letting our species down. He pursues a sterner mistress. Murph is all confused with science." Willie paused. ". . . as for the ladies . . . young women hit a certain age and get compulsive about marriage." He looked toward the living room where Aunt Easy was doing something-or-other. "I think I'll not go into it." He glanced uneasily out a window. A church steeple stood like a small blot on a flat horizon.

I understood. In this town everybody is Lutheran, except the few who are Methodists, or worse, Baptists, or worse, Presbyterian. In this town the only Internet service filters the crud out of everything, and the only movie features nothin' but G-rated. This town figures it's the only pure place on earth. This town thinks that Oshkosh is Sodom and Wasau is Gomorrah.

Things changed, though. Murph caused it, and didn't even know it happened. When it comes to being a theorist, Murph is worse than Willie, and Willie is almost worse than anybody.

"My masterpiece," said Murph, as ice broke up on the lakes, daffodils sprouted, and he sat before a cage containing a chick, which sat beside a cage that held giant Hamster Janders. "Name of Clarence."

"Didn't know baby turkeys hatched that big."

"Not a turkey. Might be a small mistake in there, someplace." Murph looked a little guilty.

"He's got this look in his eye . . ."

"He'll feather up," Murph said. "He'll be buttercup yellow." Then Murph muttered to himself, something about "You got to train them young . . ."

Bird training. Oh, you bet.

The parade of cookies dropped off as spring progressed and Clarence grew. And grew. And grew. Fewer cookies was good. I stopped gaining pounds and growing zits.

Janice still showed up, though. It was either Janice or Uncle Willie who ran off the other babes. A rumor circulated through town. Rumor said that Canary Clarence was only bred for practice. Rumor said that Murph had a contract from the Marines. He would breed a race of giant warriors. The babes, who had more-or-less taken the huge Hamster Janders for granted, took one look at that massive Canary Clarence. They thought of marriage, and of carrying a kid seven times bigger than a wheel of Limburger, and opted out.

Meanwhile, training progressed. Flight school for Clarence. Murph enticed him from one end of the lab to the other using huge chunks of birdseed.

"He's sorting through his genes," Murph explained. "He's too doggone big to flutter, but flutter is what canaries do. He's gotta rise above it."

". . . got a pleasing voice," I muttered. Clarence did not have a pleasing voice. For one thing, he could sing loud enough to shake plaster from the ceiling. For another thing, he was a baritone.

"I built in just a tad of duck persuasion," Murph explained. "When he hatched I was right there, waiting. I was the first thing he saw, and now he's fixed on me . . . thinks I'm his mama."

"For why?"

"So when he flies, he'll still come back to the nest. I'm his flock."

There's nothing anyone sane could say to that, but sanity is not real big around here, anyway. When word about the duck persuasion got out, Murph was denounced from every pulpit in town. The Lutherans thundered that Murph played at being God. The Methodists yelped about building flight paths to heaven. The Baptists whimpered over the Book of Revelations, and the Presbyterians claimed Murph was predestined for the hot-squat. Uncle Willie, with a Rosicrucian point-of-view, tried to keep a straight face but was constantly caught giggling. "Clarence bothers members of societies for suppressing things," Uncle Willie said. "I find that charming."

The public appearance of Clarence pretty much stunned the entire town, plus dairy farmers for a radius of forty miles. On a day of sun, and above green, green fields, Clarence rose buttercup-yellow on a summer breeze. He cruised the town. He swooped around city hall. He flapped like an eagle, coasted like a gull, and drifted high above, hovering like a vulture checking out the action. He was a huge yellow streak as his shadow flirted with chickens in farmyards, chased a red-tailed hawk in gyrations through the sky, and seemed searching for the best way to be obnoxious. It is gloriously recorded that he succeeded.

Because Clarence, with no spiritual training at all, chose the highest steeple in town for a perch. He was a buttercup-yellow vision of enthusiastic feathers, and as the sun went west he cast a real long shadow. He sat up there for the best part of a late afternoon singing, and trying to flutter, and warbling, and pooping. You think a goose can poop? Well, a goose can, but don't show me a goose when I'm talking about Clarence.

And loud? Bull horns are more quiet. Loudspeakers are mere whispers. That bird could make more noise flapping his wings than a Piper Cub racing its engine. On the best day of his life, Caruso would have sounded like a whisper next to Clarence. Clarence made a name for himself that day, and by the time he came home at dusk he had also made a name for Murph.

There are those who have always doubted Murph. The Ladies Aid could not stand the thought of an eligible bachelor remaining eligible, when so many solid Lutheran girls were lonesome. The Temperance Union felt that owning lab equipment is evidence of a still. And Janice (who could have her pick from most of the married men in town) was wondering if Murph was actually male.

"I am drop-dead gorgeous," she confided to Uncle Willie, "and I make a tolerable cookie. What's wrong with him?" Janice sat at the kitchen table and dealt with Willie. I sat beside Willie and dealt with algebra.

"The depth of the human psyche, about which we know so comfortably little . . ." Willie began.

"Don't go there," Janice told him. "Just give me your take on the problem."

"You work in a library," Willie told her, "but Murph works in a bank."

"So?"

"You wanta work in a library all your life?"

"A girl could do worse."

"You wanta work in a bank all your life?"

"I think I'm catching on." Janice looked alarmed but hopeful. For a moment I almost liked her.

"Dear, dear Janice," I said.

"Ah, youth," she said. "Drop by the library and I'll introduce you to Krafft-Ebing."

The likable moment passed.

"Murph doesn't want to be stuck in a bank," Willie told her. "If he marries, there's a ninety-nine percent chance he's stuck."

"I can fix it," Janice said, and she sounded dreamy. "Gotcha." And she was out of there.

Janice moved quickly, but not as quick as the Ladies Aid whose members demanded that Murph be fired from the bank. That happened while the Temperance Union hounded the sheriff. The Temperance Union wanted someone arrested, and didn't much care who, although Murph didn't make the cut. Three things came to pass:

A new rumor floated through town. It said that Murph had caught on to the critter-construction business. He would build a Guernsey who could yield ten gallons of milk from a mouthful of grass.

The Rotary then jumped to Murph's defense. The Rotary knows what is good for the cheese business, and what ain't.

A sharp and nasty dust-up between Aunt Easy and the Temperance Union ended in red-hot letters-to-the-editor, and revelations about shortcuts in cookie recipes. A fearful number of American mothers were involved.

Meanwhile, Murph kept Clarence on a tight rein. No more outdoor flights. After the church steeple debacle it seemed best if Clarence dropped out of sight.

Other rumors surfaced. Murph could quadruple tourist traffic because he would build a real Babe, Paul Bunyon's Great Blue Ox. Rumor had it that Murph had invented a way to make all mosquitoes disappear from the face of the Earth, a real big selling point in Wisconsin.

While all of this went on Murph fielded questions from bank customers, denied everything, and hurried home each evening to play catch-up in his lab. I felt obligated to help. He was obviously a hunted and very lonely man.

By then the lab had burgeoned into canary land. There were enough birds, and many of them strange, to fill an aviary. There was a giant hamster porking up through a lack of exercise. Clarence occupied a perch, like a bird of prey, and shouted down other boy birds that started to sing. It was bedlam, and beyond. Clarence was becoming obnoxious.

Hamster Janders wasn't much better. When I tried to train him to leash he wasn't having any part of it. It took him exactly two seconds to chaw through the leash. He headed for Aunt Easy's garden where he grazed on all of the cabbage. Janders is no bigger than a Great Dane, but he isn't a whit smaller, either.

"I've created a monster," Murph confided, and he didn't mean Clarence, and he didn't mean Janders. "The birdseed bills are killin' me. I get no work time, what with cleaning cages."

"You'll think of something." But I didn't believe it. Instead I checked in with Uncle Willie.

By then June had turned to July and July to August. On a Sunday afternoon when lawns were fried brown and even the trees seemed to pant, Willie lay crumpled in a hammock sipping cream soda and reading Petronius. As I approached, so did Janice.

Janice looked at Willie's book. "In Wisconsin?"

"At my age it's the best I can do."

I have to admit that Janice looked pretty good. Her long hair kind of fluffed around her face, and her blue eyes did not look like members of any religious sect. They looked downright ornery.

"I'm taking one last shot," she told Willie, "and if it doesn't work I head for a job in the big city." She didn't look like someone ready to take a last shot.

She dressed casual, in slacks, and no cleavage.

"Seduction doesn't work," she told Willie. She turned to me. "Take a lesson." She turned back to Willie. "I've set it up. I got enough success rumors running to promote investment. I can put together a Murph corporation that gets him loose from the bank."

For some stupid reason my heart sank. If Murph was a success, and risk capital built him a real lab, and if he could hire real lab assistants . . .

"Don't do it," Willie told Janice. "Worst thing in the world."

"For why?"

"Ah, youth." Willie rocked gently in his hammock. "Take up the violin. Write poems. Inscribe the story of your life in pictographs. Study astronomy." He scratched himself behind one ear and blinked upward at tired leaves of an oak tree. The tree sort of rustled.

"Science and art have lots in common," Willie told her. "Scientists and artists expect to fail. They know they're gonna fail. Our boy Murph is a little of both."

"This better be about something." Janice looked toward the house, where, in the basement, Murph cleaned canary cages and whispered cuss words.

"Because they go for the big picture," Willie explained. "They go for a grand statement and only end up, with maybe, something like the Mona Lisa. Great, a little grand, but not the big one." Willie also looked toward the house. "Scientists the same . . . put together the theory of relativity, then spend fifty years trying to dope out what it means."

"You're talking about success," I told him, not a little sarcastic. "No wonder you're confused . . . all those books . . ."

"And when they don't even get a Mona Lisa, or relativity, they crash in flames." Willie reached over and patted Janice's hand. The pat was grandfatherly, teacherly, and he looked like everybody's papa. "History is filled with great men who fail, stare at the cold idol they pursued, the idol with dead eyes, and end up weeping while kneeling before a woman and clasping her knees. Great women generally just fall into the arms of a man. You want love? Court failure."

"Gotcha." Janice looked ambitious.

"You court it by doing nothing," Willie told her. "Right now Murph is sure-fail. Don't disturb the balance." To me he said, "Stay out of it. Study basketball or candle making. Adopt a cat. Learn to play harmonica." But, he grinned when he said it.

If failure was what Janice needed, then success would block it. "Garage sale," I told Murph. "Sell canaries. Sell cages and toss in a canary. Start a canary society. Sell memberships. I'll handle the whole deal."

I printed a sign for the front lawn. We sold three canaries, with cages, for a tenth the cost of the cages. I thought my idea had gone west, failed, flopped. I searched for a new idea. Before I came up with anything, we hit big.

Of the canaries we sold, one turned out scandalous. A preacher's wife bought him and waited for him to sing. Instead, he started to cuss . . . real stinky little mouth . . . something in the genes, something about Murph installing a dash of parrot. Murph got a little overboard on that one.

The preacher's wife sat cage and bird outdoors while she opened windows to air the house. She even washed the walls. When a mildly inebriated Swedish person passed down the alley, she sold him the bird and made ten bucks on the deal. The Swedish person took the bird to the town's only tavern where, even today, it charms the customers. Very popular, that bird. Name of Oscar.

Word got out that Murph's canaries were sleepers. We sold out, except for a breeding pair, Jimmy and Cleopatra. Jimmy has a tuft of feathers on top of his head and a confused look. Cleo lives up to her name.

The lab returned to normal. One oversize hamster, one oversize bird, plus white mice and other varmints.

"Don't do that again," I told Murph. I might as well have been whispering in a hurricane. He was already looking dreamy.

"County fair," he muttered. "I can regain my reputation. Blue ribbons. Yes, indeed."

I could sense that failure was once more in the wind, but felt helpless.

"What do girls do," I asked Aunt Easy, "when guys don't listen?"

She smiled and looked around a happy kitchen where Canary Sylvester sang. Aunt Easy motioned toward the living room where

Uncle Willie diddled with a radio. "Ignore them," Aunt Easy told me, "but stand by to pick up the pieces when they crash." She smiled, even happier, and anyone could tell she was actually fond of Willie. "The dears have to be good at something. At crashing they are experts."

"Even Uncle Willie?" I was astounded.

"Especially Uncle Willie." Aunt Easy looked both sweet and tender. "He spent twenty years researching and writing a history of Wisconsin. When the book was published he was blacklisted by the State Historical Society."

"Because Uncle Willie lied?"

"No, dear, because he told the truth . . ."Aunt Easy is such a nice lady. She looked at me with real concern. "You're growing up. You'll soon have a birthday. And, oh Lordy, I'm afraid you have talent."

Yeah, well, talent for getting into messes.

Autumn covered the land and Murph's crash, plus the big Janice victory, happened at the county fair. On a day of changing leaves, but with lots of sun, Murph sat Clarence on the front seat of Maytag and put Janders in the rear. About the best you can say is the two critters put up with each other. There were accusations but no fights.

Autumn lay across the land. Oak leaves were going brown, the last cut of hay was in, and the farm implement dealer displayed snowmobiles. Birds were flying south, churches held "harvest home" services, and the Ladies Aid quietly bragged of canned beans, canned corn, cherry preserves, and freezers stuffed with beef. Woodpiles rose high as chainsaws roared, and chimneys were cleaned. Yet, in the middle of all this wholesomeness dwelt something rancid.

That rancidity came from the Fin, Fur, and Feathers Division of the Brotherhood of Exalted Beagles. That elite division of gun toters was known, far and wide, as the best justification for the existence of the Temperance Union. The Beagles were generally a red-nosed lot, often glassy-eyed.

When Murph arrived at the midway a Ferris wheel twirled, and kids yelped as they rode a baby roller coaster. Rides and booths lined the midway; pop a balloon, win a stuffed skunk. Colorful streamers flew above the booths of boat dealers, feed and implement dealers, car dealers, and a make-believe Indian selling patent medicine. Popcorn laid underfoot, a calliope clanged, cotton candy smeared cheerful faces; but then, of course, there was also the booth hosted by the Exalted Order of Beagles: the Fin, Fur, and Feather Division.

These are the guys with rifle racks in their pickups, Jim Beam in the glove compartment, combat fatigues, tattoos reading "Poopsie" or "Mama," plus an occasional swastika. Their booth was just short of a full-fledged gun show. The only thing missing was ammo. These guys know each other well enough not to trust their buddies with weapons that work.

So, here comes Murph, red-haired, smiling wide as a cornfield and just as corny, towing two cages on wheels and heading for the livestock show. Hamster Janders, overweight and with an attitude, is banging the side of his cage. Clarence sits silent, checking out the action, but with a gleam in his eye that should have been a warning.

Fin, Fur, and Feathers were standing in a group before their booth pretending they knew something. As Murph's little caravan passed, one of them worked his mouth real hard, tried to think, and was finally able to form words. "Hey, Murph." It was a real victory.

Murph stopped. Fin, Fur, and Feathers gathered around his cages. They regarded Janders.

"Ought to dress out at around two hundred. Be purty gamey."

" . . . ever fried up any of these?"

"Reminds me of my first wife. Looks like her, a little."

You could tell that Janders's attitude was getting even worse.

Fin, Fur, and Feathers looked at Clarence.

"This is the steeple-pooper."

"Got to admit, he looks purty tasty." A Fin, Fur, and Feathers guy stuck a finger into the cage. Clarence pecked it. The Fin, Fur, and Feathers backed up yelping. He still had a finger, but barely. He choked back a sob.

"We got shotguns for guys like you," he whispered, and no one, including him, knew whether he talked to Clarence or Murph.

"I'll be going," Murph murmured.

"Nope," the Fin, Fur, and Feathers guy said: "You'll be staying until I wring a neck." He reached to open the cage.

"Better not," Murph said.

"Don't say I didn't warn you," Murph said.

"Oh, well," Murph said.

Clarence came out of the cage singing. The Fin, Fur, and Feathers guy tumbled on his fanny, hollering. The rest of Fin, Fur, and Feathers stood with mouths open as they watched Clarence become a disappearing yellow spot in the blue sky. Clarence sang anthems as he cruised, and he would sing them again when he returned.

Meanwhile, though, all heck broke loose on the midway because another guy had opened Janders's cage, and Janders was primed. He lumbered down the midway, stopped at the first hamburger stand he found, ran everybody out and ignored all the hamburger. He grazed the lettuce, scorned the pickles, and moved on to the next stand. He clicked his teeth as he worked, and if you've never seen a hamster's teeth well, imagine a pair of scissors big enough to snip through a bale of hay.

By the time the sheriff arrived Janders had mopped up every piece of lettuce, carrot, spinach salad, and okra on the midway. He had cruised the Homemaker's tent, licked up a few preserves, threatened the President of Ladies Aid, snarled at Murph's attempts to lasso him, sniffed the rear end of the Temperance Union's president as she fled past, and chewed the tassles off the Methodist preacher's shoes. Janders then raised his snout to the wind, picked up the scent of a distant cabbage patch, and his bottom was last seen charging over the horizon like a brown and hairy sunset.

The sheriff has a sense of humor. In this town you gotta. He drew Murph aside. They talked about payment for lettuce, general damages, and where, by all that is holy, did that blamed bird go?

"I'm afraid," Murph admitted, "that he'll return."

The sheriff looked along the midway, looked at tumult and confusion. ". . . Temperance Union lady got her bottom sniffed. Maybe protective custody?"

"I'll tough it out," Murph said. He looked toward the sky. "Oh, Lordy," Murph said.

Imagine, if you will, a massive V of Canadian geese, a V filling the sky from east to west. Imagine the honking of a thousand geese. And high above the honking, the celebrating song of a giant baritone canary calling the shots.

Imagine, if you will, a midway in total confusion as children flee screaming and adults stand stunned before a sight that nobody, nowhere has ever dreamed. Nightmares are made of such sights, at least the really bad ones.

Imagine, if you will, dive-bomber geese descending on the booth of Fin, Fur, and Feathers. Imagine a gray and green rain so constant that the fastest windshield wipers in the world could not keep up. Imagine men in combat fatigues huddled in a collapsing tent beneath waves of shimmering gray and green slurry, while high above, a baritone canary sings something out of George M. Cohen.

If you've imagined that, you've gotten hold of about ten percent of what was happening.

The bombardment lasted for something less than half an hour, after which Fin, Fur, and Feathers emerged from a mountain of gray and green, to see Clarence leading his V of geese south, migrating.

"I should have thought of that," Murph whispered. "It's the duck gene influence. He's gone. My masterpiece." Murph sat, head in hands, while all around him people stood and whispered. The members of Fin, Fur, and Feathers were also migrating to the nearest lake.

People were confused. They had a sense of tragedy, but couldn't figure who or what was tragic. They looked at each other, looked for a preacher or a president to tell them what to think. They looked at Murph, slumped before a sagging Homemaker's tent as he tried not to weep.

They watched the bank president approach. The bank president is a dapper little man, always well dressed, always well groomed. "You're fired," the bank president said to Murph, although his voice was not unpleasant. "Business is business."

Murph slumped further. He stared at spilled popcorn, while noxious odors coasted on a breeze. He did not notice when Janice pushed through the crowd and took a seat beside him.

"We could emigrate until this blows over," she whispered. "Go to someplace new and crazy, like maybe Albuquerque."

"You'd go along?" Murph whispered.

"I expect," she said thoughtfully, "I'd better lead." She snuggled a little closer.

"Witchery," I muttered to me. "Pretty dumb," I told myself. Nobody answered.

The wedding took place in Oshkosh because there wasn't a single preacher in this town who dared to touch it. Uncle Willie, Aunt Easy, and I rode in Willie's '49 Studebaker. Janice and Murph piddled along in Maytag.

"There's not an epic here," Uncle Willie said to the Studebaker, or maybe himself, because he sure wasn't talking to me or Aunt Easy. "There are elements of epic, but somehow the damn thing is allegory. How best do we handle allegory?"

"Niagara Falls," Aunt Easy murmured. Then she explained that with Murph comfortably married, the Ladies Aid would leap to defend him. "If Murph and Janice can hold out for a month," Aunt Easy told me, "they can come home." Aunt Easy's eyes shone misty with romance.

The wedding didn't amount to much. "Do you take this woman, etc." "Yep." "Do you take this mad scientist, etc." "Yep." "You're married. Pay the cashier on your way out . . ."

Okay, so it was a good bit better than that. They had a real preacher and, unfortunately, Janice looked just smashing. Murph seemed a little less confused than usual. Before they left on the honeymoon Murph pulled me aside. "I'm worried about my critters," he whispered.

"Trust me," I told him. "In spite of everything, I have a good heart." Then I stood and watched Maytag towing old shoes and sprinkled with rice as it became a diminishing spot along the highway. That darned Janice waved a hanky just before Maytag disappeared over a low rise.

"It can be done in eight cantos," Uncle Willie muttered. "Or certainly no more than ten." He kept muttering all the way home. Aunt Easy sat beside him, but turned to me once in a while. She smiled and gave an occasional wink.

Matters were quiet for a couple days and then reports began to surface on the evening news. Janders was seen here, there, always grazing. When he was shot at a couple of times, he began feeding at night. In less than a week he had raided cabbage patches as far south as Peoria, only to be adopted by a nearsighted lady famous for collecting stray cats.

Other reports came from down around Redondo Beach where airline pilots reported a giant, buttercup-yellow bird sporting among clouds, and, apparently, singing. Pilots were amazed. They had never seen a bird that could outfly a crop duster. No one else paid much attention, because in California, stuff happens.

Our town has settled down as we coast toward winter. Uncle Willie spends his days in the quiet of the attic. Willie forgets to eat sometimes, and he talks to himself in iambs, and his silver hair frizzes, and Aunt Easy sometimes has to lead him in from the garden that apparently now grows symbols. Aunt Easy thinks he's cute.

And Aunt Easy is cute, herself. Now that she has shut out the Temperance Union, she takes a little white wine with supper. When she's not doing crosswords she does picture puzzles. She and Canary Sylvester hold down that warm kitchen, while she waits for Willie to crash.

And I sit in this lab surrounded by forty-seven white mice, fifteen white rats, a frowzy parrot, two exhausted rabbits who have been fulfilling their duty to their species, as I suppose Murph is fulfilling his. I oversee three guinea pigs, of whom one seems to be a good bit bigger than he oughta, plus Canary Jimmy, and Canary Cleopatra; and, oh, Lordy, Cleo has just laid an egg.

And sweet sixteen has now become disillusioned seventeen. I think of Murph and Janice doing fulfillment, and wonder if all that householdy stuff is worth a snip, anyway. What I don't wonder is what I'm gonna do, because this is my senior year.

I'll graduate and then I'm just plain gone. The big city. I'll go to college, or become a poet, or a philosopher, or maybe a biologist, but two things are certain. I ain't gonna do it in no attic, and I ain't gonna do it here.

The Art of a Lady

WE KEPT UNCLE GEORGE ALIVE DURING THE SUMMER OF THIRTY-TWO by asking him how was business, which in his case and despite the depression, was excellent. About Miss Chloe Johansen we stopped asking. It would have been as tactful as inquiring of Lady Macbeth if something was bugging her.

Unc was thirty-two in thirty-two, having hit the world at the turn of the century when social stability was beginning to be regarded as a hazard. It worked out perfectly in his case—the whole philosophy, I mean.

He was fair-haired, tall and kind of skinny. Friends wavered over his looks which were between reflective and confused, although Chloe's drinking uncle, Willie, described him as 'Deeper than a gallon.' Despite the increasing dabs at his freedom by the dedicated Chloe (he had given the engagement ring, she kept up the payments) he remained a bachelor.

His main persuasion was that of an artist. Not a paint artist, but a carver of wood. Even though I was only a kid I knew that he was the best carver outside of the Orient, and is to this day. He could whip off a horse for a merry-go-round, shape down the reeds for a bassoon, or do your portrait in the grain of your choice. He did one of Pop in mahogany one time that caused a family scandal. The color of the wood got to him and he made the old man's nose a little flat. Nobody had ever noticed the resemblance before.

But that was his only venture to impressionism if you discount Chloe and Geraldine.

Chloe was just fine. She wanted the same thing other girls wanted, which Unc thought was a glad and good attitude, but she also wanted a wedding band.

Unc would look at her departing form as she moved down the road from his store and hum around in 'Die Valkyrie.'

I'd mutter "Freedom." Unc would take a hitch in his belt and another look, then pat my head.

"Yeh," he would say. Sadly though. Very sad.

He was right. Chloe had a great deal of everything. Geraldine, Chloe's sister, also swung. With her it was mostly mental. She was twenty-eight and had the intellectual nudge on Chloe as well as on the rest of the town. Willie was also her drinking uncle. She claimed to understand Willie. But, while she was intelligent and pretty it was just not in the grand manner so she had plenty of time to think. It was whispered that she thought about Unc.

Reality got them all in trouble. Mostly reality got to Uncle George. When he decided to do a piece of work he did it with the absolute conviction that he would fail. It was a part of his philosophy, one in which many great artists are trapped. He wanted to duplicate experience and nature. He wanted to show exactly how and what a thing was. If he carved a horse—I mean real horse, not merry-go-round, he wanted to be able to sit that horse beside a real horse and let you guess which one was breathing. About half the time you would guess wrong, but Unc always believed you were humoring him. Perfection was his long suit and perfection is what crossed him up in the big 'Figurehead order,' as it came to be known.

Like all artists: painters, writers, perhaps even musicians and acrobats, Uncle George thought of the passing of sail as a loss to part of the soul of man. Being from small town Indiana, he had only a passing notion of what constituted a seaworthy vessel or of the practicality and beauty of a steamship. He just knew sails were beautiful and smoke was not. Also, in the time of sail woodcarvers were in their heyday. Perhaps that had something to do with the figurehead compulsion because he did not really know much about the sea. His only experience with water was the lake where we fished, which on a stormy night would whip up a trough of maybe an inch and a half.

He had a picture book of ship's figureheads that I used to hook while he was at the store, mostly because there were three of the figureheads who (or which) were ladies who (or which) were undressed on top. Uncovered tops were interesting to me. These were well done. Later, when I arrived at high school age I remember being vaguely disappointed.

Chloe and the month of April were surrounding the store at the start of the trouble. Unc had a little house on the highway where he sold antiques, old magazines, his carving and pottery by Geraldine and Chloe who were part-time instructors of the 4-H Club. The pottery was splotchy jugs, vases and decorated souvenirs of Hereford City, Indiana. People who had never heard of Rorschach tests became uneasy. Most of the antiques were not really antique, just old. It seldom mattered. Nearly everyone who came in bought something, usually carvings by Unc or pottery by Geraldine which had the most brilliant splotches of all. I guess Uncle George grossed as high as fifteen dollars most weeks, and it was clear profit since he closed at dark. Taxes on the place were a dollar sixty-three cents a year. He did a fair mail order business with regular customers and worked at finished and rough carpentry around the county. I judge he made as high as three thousand in most years. That was good business then. In terms of what it would buy he was no pooch of a marriage prospect.

I was at the store with Chloe and Unc when the Duesenberg pulled up. It was a beautiful car, painted a lovely money-color green. The youngish looking man and woman who got out and traipsed up the path were obviously accustomed to having doors opened for them, so George did. Later, he said he should have locked it.

Entering the tiny, over-stuffed house, the lady tripped over a replica of Doc Sams's prize Poland sow. She staggered here and there, then sat down with a pretty good bump for one so apparently frail. She ended up looking the sow in the face and letting out a fetching scream. I told you Unc had realism cold.

The greasy-haired little guy who was dressed like a house pet and who, we learned later, was a house pet, cursed and kicked the sow in the snoot, chipping it a trifle. He nearly chipped his meal ticket at the same time. To make up for it maybe, he started to threaten a lawsuit. She shut him up pretty quick.

"This man is an artiste," she said, in a phony, rhubarby way that hit Chloe fairly stiff. There was a kind of threat mixed with the rhubarb, even while the lady was still on her can facing the sow. Chloe held herself in, but her blue eyes were hot and she mixed up her blonde hair trying to get it smooth. Who could blame her? She was twenty-three and had given her best years to Unc, the way she figured. She meant in waiting, of course. Maybe it occurred to her that she had never called Unc an 'artiste.'

"An artiste," the lady smiled as George gave her a hand up. She half-whispered to him, asking if he had ever done a self-portrait.

Chloe looked about the way Delilah would have looked if someone told her that on his way over, Samson had been scalped.

After a lot of bazazz from the little rich lady Unc sold the sow on discount because it had a chipped snoot. He also sold a small carving of Chloe's drinking uncle who was his best friend. Willie was county judge and town drunk, held both offices. After two successes, Unc tried to get the lady interested in his impression of an ill duck which looked exactly like an ill duck.

It was just then that the gigolo rolled his eyes and smacked his hand to his forehead so hard he staggered.

"Godiva," he yelled, "he can do Godiva!" Everyone stopped what they were doing to admire the performance. The little woman smiled and nodded.

He had bought her a one hundred-ninety foot schooner to celebrate their great love. Her money, of course, but it was the thought that counted. The vessel had been a bargain. It was the last important thing left from an ex-millionaire's estate who had engaged in 1929 sky diving.

Deceased must have been as bad at seamanship as he was at margins. Before the big crash he had worked up a pretty monumental one of his own. Coming alongside he moved the port of Boston as much as three inches out of line when he hit the entire town. They had the schooner *Exchange* in drydock for major repairs including bowsprit and figurehead. The plan was to rename her *Godiva II*. Unc was courteous enough not to ask who was *Godiva I*. The old figurehead would not have been fitting anyway. It had been of a broker in a derby hat.

While Unc loaded the chipped sow in the backseat of the Duesenberg (it was a chore, but as he said later, you could get by with almost anything in the backseat of a Duesenberg), the lady bargained with Chloe who had snapped up the role of agent. They agreed on a commission figure of five hundred dollars, two hundred of which the lady paid along with eleven thirty-five for her pig and a buck, six-bits for Willie. Willie, the original, later demanded a snort for modeling. George bought him a tub full.

Chloe was sharp. Unc would have done the job for thirty dollars. He did not realize the value of art. Most artists never do until they bump someone like Cecil B. DeMille. It was not until the pig was loaded that the situation began to fester.

"Five hundred!" Unc yelled, almost silly happy.

The lady looked worried. "You can do it?"

He watched her as if in devout belief that there would always be a gold standard. She took it for devotion, that was clear. "For five hundred I'd . . ." He was thrashing around in his head for ultimates.

The lady looked pleased and thoughtful. "You would?"

Chloe interrupted and tried to raise the price.

Then it occurred to Unc that any yacht named *Godiva* had to have a figurehead that would put the front end of a Rolls to shame. A little hesitancy flickered across his face. The guy and woman insisted on a full-length woman, nude to the waist. The lady insinuated coyly that it might not hurt if the figure wore a satisfied smile. The guy kept looking at Chloe, stating that a very substantial type model should be used. Chloe blushed and kept trying to stop up my ears.

They left it at that. The lady and her escort eventually arrived in Boston and started writing letters to Uncle George.

The first was from the man with specifications for length and mounting. Unc did not allow anyone to read the next letter which was from the lady. He started to walk around with a worried look. Whatever was in the letter could have made little difference because trouble happened before their car had disappeared.

Unc had to have a bare model. You can joke about it now, but in thirty-two in small-town Indiana; or now when I think of it, the prospect of a nude would have caused a riot, a church burning and a jail delivery.

If Unc had been a normal man he could probably have done the job from memory. I mean he was pretty grown-up and had once visited a relative in Indianapolis for a week.

But he was not normal. When he did doc's sow he borrowed the sow. When he carved the duck he had given it a good kick first and then worked like stink before it died, but *that* part had been unforeseen and unfortunate. If he was going to do a nude woman he had to have a nude woman. He was in a bind. As always when in doubt he sought out Willie.

"Marry Chloe," Willie said, tipping the jug. "Art is the iron wrought from the hot forge of suffering." I had tagged along to the courthouse with Unc who packed a prohibition quart. Willie leaned back grinning at the flaking walls of his courtroom. He looked a little flaky himself. Willie was a middling large man with scraggy gray hair and more than a wink for the law. He was also a philosopher, especially with the quart sitting on the bench.

"That's a helluva sentence," I told him. Unc said nothing but I knew I would catch a word or two about that 'helluva' later.

Willie slowly waggled a finger. "Art," he said seriously.

"Art?" Unc said.

"Art," Willie repeated.

"My masterpiece," Unc murmured.

"Freedom," I said. "From every mountaintop, let . . ."

"Go home," Willie told me. "Have another snort of your whiskey, George."

Unc had several. Then he and Willie went to the pool room and talked. There were a lot of people around. I guess that explains how Chloe found out.

The short, sharp and nasty little brawl that developed took place at our house when Chloe stormed in after Unc. I am not sure what had her most angry. It seemed to be the idea of getting her man because he needed to see her naked which is maybe the whole point anyway. But it may have been the idea, as she said, "Of parading my everything over seven seas for every porpoise and dockhand to admire." Chloe could be quite conceited at times.

Whatever the reason she threw the ring at him, then remembered that she had made most of the payments and grabbed it back. She never married Unc although she tried to make him suffer. That succeeded for about two hours until further developments slugged him. The same day another letter came from the rich lady. Three weeks later Chloe was holding hands with one of the Rileys. The turkey growing Rileys, I mean. Not the dirt farmers. Geraldine split her time between the store and Willie's courtroom.

Uncle George was heartbroken but he went back to work. All summer he turned out figureheads that looked like wadded burlesque handbills. They would not have startled your grandmother. I think he finally jointed arms on the whole lot and jobbed them to Si Hansen for scarecrows. It was then that Geraldine came strongly to his aid. The sewing circle started whispering that she had always been a willful child.

Geraldine was always so pretty and so kind. I was nine and planned to marry her myself if she would only wait, even if she was on the rail-skinny side.

She was nearly as tall as Unc with beautiful brown hair and a good eye. But, like I told you she was twenty-eight and an old maid. She must have suffered for Unc a good deal that summer, because finally, as autumn rolled in, she slipped down to the store with her heart in her mouth and her hand on her zipper. It had good results. Unc went enthusiastically to work, sometimes late at night with the blinds pulled. I went catfishing and pondered.

Chloe could never have gone to the store at night, but even the sewing circle was not about to lock horns with Geraldine. Everyone makes at least one mistake in their life and Geraldine had that real good eye . . .

When the work was done Unc was wearing a sort of dazed look. He decided to deliver the figurehead to dockside himself. He had thrown away none of the rich lady's letters.

He packed the figurehead in Willie's casket without showing it to anyone, then took a train to Boston. The casket was a demonstrator Willie had picked up in 1925, figuring to need it sooner or later. He could never pass a bargain which is the reason it was lent. In payment for its use Unc promised to install a built-in bar.

Despite the letters Geraldine did not protest his leaving. She showed neither doubt nor hesitation. When I asked her what she thought she smiled and said, "Lots."

Everyone else thought exactly what they pleased which was not a little. Geraldine was not fretful. No letters came for her, but she kept busy pricing yard goods and occasionally slipping Willie wet goods. About December she took to hanging around the courtroom. Lectures on philosophy, maybe.

Unc was gone until the following January when he pulled in with the coffin bolted to an old truck chassis. It looked sort of avant-garde and was. He later realized that he had invented the trucking industry's sleeper cab and with it made a fortune.

It was late Saturday morning. I was the only one to meet him. He whirled me around, set me back on the ground and headed for the house. I pried up the lid of the coffin and there was his figurehead dressed in a real bathing suit and a satisfied smile. It was too many for me. I headed for Chloe and Geraldine's house and hid behind the woodpile.

As soon as Unc cleaned up he rushed over. Chloe met him at the door waving a fresh engagement ring.

"Ha," she said.

"Ha, hell," he told her, real frantic, "where's Geraldine?"

She arched a little, pouting, and said that she didn't know. Unc hollered around for a while fairly desperate, then began to believe her.

"Pete Riley," she flourished the ring.

"Really," he seemed interested, "short fellow, dark hair, talks nice?"

"Him exactly."

"How 'bout that?" He dug around for his billfold, opened it and shook his head sadly. "You didn't get any rebate on the other one?"

Chloe disappeared inside the house to come back with a hot stove lid. By that time Unc was on his way to town.

I took a shortcut and made it to the courthouse ahead of him where I ducked behind the rail of the jury box. Unc and Willie adjourned to the courtroom.

"What happened?" Willie breathed into an empty glass and pulled out a shirttail, giving the glass a high polish.

"Where's Geraldine," Unc wanted to know. He leaned forward, scary-like.

"Get my letter?" Willie breathed at him over the rim.

"I'll . . . Why did she do it? Leaving with a poet . . . I'll—!" Unc was screaming.

"Easy," Willie told him. "She didn't. I lied. You figure you're the only one with the license?"

"You drunk?" George was stumped. "License to what? Drink?"

"Lie."

"Oh."

"You need a drink."

"Not now, Willie. Where is she?"

"Where she's been all along. Right here in town, be home if there isn't some errand." I figured Geraldine had finally gotten a price on yard goods.

Willie poured one reverently. "What happened," he came at Unc again.

Unc looked worried. "Nothing I'll tell. Well, no, one thing. *Godiva II* got back to sea."

"With your figurehead?"

"Not the one I took, another one. My masterpiece—I brought the first one back."

"You need a drink."

"No! Now Willie, dammit," he paused sort of uncertain. "I've been busy and I kind of quit." He said it and said it meek.

Willie gave a real horrible laugh followed by a giggle. "Didn't need to," he told Unc. "All you had to do was grease your hair and buy cake-eater shoes."

Unc jumped halfway up. "It's okay," Willie settled him, "*I* need a drink. You're okay, George, you're okay. Who is on *Godiva II*?"

"Emma . . . Uh, the rich lady." And, he said that meek too.

Willie leaned back in his chair gasping with laughter. "Couldn't put her on the bow, huh? Had to go all the way to Boston to trip over yourself."

"Ah, George," Willie waggled his head philosophically, "you're a product of the time. Love one woman while you're with another . . . don't realize it 'til you find you can't flaunt the first one. Whyn't you borrow a swimsuit?"

Inside the jury box I doubled up biting my fists. Unc stood up yelling horrible, kicked the chair from under Willie and took off. Willie lay for a while looking thoughtful. "Puck," he said, "dusted em both, by God." He reached to pull the bottle down for company. By that time I judge Unc had found Geraldine.

They were married in less than three weeks which pleased several old ladies. It gave them something to talk about. They were disappointed at the sewing circle. *Cousin* George did not arrive for two years and *Uncle* George used to stop the busybodies in the middle of the square on Saturday night. He would introduce Cousin George to them as the baby Geraldine carried for twenty-four months. My cousin took after his parents for skinniness and grew up a copy of the rail-splitting Lincoln. He never made it as far as politics, being side-tracked by the wholesale fertilizer business.

What happened in Boston was anybody's guess for a long time. Unc told everyone that the rich lady had given her boyfriend some money and a from-behind kick in the right direction. Everyone theorized that Unc was the replacement but it could not be proved. Since Willie elected to keep quiet I figured it was splendid judgment if I did the same.

However, I did find a notice from a Boston paper in Unc's luggage which told about the unveiling of the figurehead in the rich lady's honor. It was at the time of the official renaming and return from drydock. There was an apologetic reference to some kind of disturbance that was in language I later learned was used in Boston to describe a riot. They have a different way of handling sportive material up there.

The mystery remained for a while and then was forgotten. It was only by chance that I learned a little more some ten years later when *Godiva II's* captain at the time of the refit came through town on his way west. He was retiring and looking for a little patch of desert or whatever retired captains are chasing. Perhaps because he was getting older, or because he knew no one to the westward, he stopped to have a drink and a yarn with Unc.

I was pretty well grown then, sitting on the porch beside them while the captain had a cold one and settled himself deep in a rocker. They chewed over old times for a while, then talked about the rich lady who had married a Portuguese Admiral. Presently the captain eased a look at Unc and said, "George, I'll never understand an artist. There you were with a death grip on two and a half, maybe three million dollars and you settled for a bust on the head with a bottle that knocked you off the platform. You passed, George, you just plain passed. I *know* you could have married that woman."

Uncle George allowed that it was probably true. In the house Geraldine was singing and Unc just kind of eased back and hummed along on the same tune.

"It's your cussed persistence for exactness did it, George," the captain said. "I'm sorry I've got to say it, but it is. You fouled up *Godiva II*. You really did."

"Reality," said Unc, breaking into his own humming. "Art is the evocation of reality."

The captain worked that one around pretty sad-like. While he did he knocked off another cold one.

Finally, he said, sort of lumpy and dreamy, "The soul of a schooner is like the soul of a little bird. Under the weight of its own wings it soars, but the soul of *Godiva II* is dead."

He paused, as if studying for a soft way to say something and hawed around for a little bit, then must have decided to heck with it. "I know you did your best," he told Unc, "but my hand to heaven," (and he lifted it) "you hurt her best by at least three knots and her feeling of joy. We'd get her offshore with a fair wind and following sea . . . I'll swear to you George, she just kind of sagged."

Weird Row

WE DRIVE THE RENO STRIP BEFORE DAWN AND IT'S ALL BRIGHT LIGHTS and casinos: gin and tonic at five AM, fancy ladies with drooping eyelids, the clank of old-fashioned slots and the zippity hum of electronics; an occasional rattle of coins. Dawn sees some gamblers weary with defeat and completely busted. They park before used car dealers and wait for the lots to open. They sell their cars cheap in order to get breakfast and bus fare home.

Me, and Pork, and Victoria (my comrades) drive through this glossy city as morning rises quick above the desert. We say very little, because Pork is dreamy and Victoria is crazed. We flee like refugees, though we don't flee far.

Storyland sits at city limits, between the town and the desert. When we approach, it looks like a hangar for monster airplanes, being of round metal roof and immense. It does not look like a book barn, though it is.

Once inside, Storyland stretches into distance like a stadium with fluorescent lights. Lights hang way, way up there, sending glowing messages from an awkward heaven. This is a freakin' church, a financial cathedral.

My comrades and I take our places before stainless tables, with dumpsters at our backs. I'm in the center with Pork on my left. Victoria giggles on my right. Dust collectors hum, conveyer belts slide slicky-sounding, and we snag packages from conveyors which trundle before us. We open packages. We work like dogs and are paid like dogs. Employee turnover is fantastic. Still, a few genuine nut-cases hang on; plus us. We like it here. We say we're on Weird Row. We're talkin' revolution.

The packages contain books, audios, videos, but mostly books. Thoughts and amusements of two thousand years trickle through our hands.

It works like this: The Corporation owns Storyland and sends books to every country in the world. Packages go out, but packages also come in. Packages arrive because when The Corporation receives orders it shops the Net. It finds needed books at small bookstores in Denver or Ashtabula or Cape Town. The small stores ship the books here for Storyland to resell. Workers who are higher paid repackage the books and send them to customers. Those workers get higher pay because what they do is boring. We, here on Weird Row, get the best part of the job.

Books on necromancy mix with Bibles, and children's picture-books rest beside dusty philosophies from two hundred years ago. History, evolution, how to raise a family cow . . . you name it, we open it . . . all kinds and colors of books spit forth, plus: there is packaging.

"Plus," Pork reminds me, "there's Package Police." He checks the terrain with heavy-lidded gaze as he speaks. Conveyers hum all around, and other teams open packages. We don't speak to other teams. Who needs 'em?

Pork looks rested. Many years ago there was a song titled "Mr. Five by Five." That's Pork. Five foot tall and five foot around, like a giant bowling ball with a fluffy head. He has hazel eyes and the kind of beard you find on billy goats.

"There's also denouements." Victoria generally sounds cultured. She is virginal and sweet and only slightly insane. She has no business in a candy-fanny town like Reno. Victoria should be gliding along marble halls while wearing a satin gown. She should be waving a wand that casts sparkles. Victoria is knock-down-dead gorgeous, little and cute, like a movie queen, like Hepburn. "There's visualizations," she says, "and actualizations and excite-ments. There's also a certain amount of stardust."

I make no big claim to sanity, either. If I am sane, why am I in Reno? My name . . . ? It seems a guy would remember . . . I'm sure my mom recalls it, but she lives in New Hampshire. Around here they call me Smoke. Because I do, whenever I can sneak a butt. I'm skinny and going on thirty with bright eyes and yellow teeth; a nice smile to go with it, a tidy little cough. I lust after Victoria. Fat chance. Lotsa luck, buddy.

"Package Police," Pork says, again. Even wide awake and rested, Pork sounds dreamy. Dreamy is dangerous. When he gets too dreamy, Pork fondles books.

The Corporation can't allow that. A man who fondles books is liable to steal something: a notion, an essence, an idea. A man who fondles books might learn a trade, develop a philosophy, found a religion. All through history, book fondlers have been known to commit creative acts. Around here, Book Fondling is a godawful sin.

After all, those books belong to The Corporation, and The Corporation has its own philosophy. The Corporation not only wants its fair share. The Corporation wants to own Everything. The Corporation will not be stolen from. Thus, the Package Police.

"Our plot marches forward," Victoria whispers. She is excited. She places a book titled *Teach Yourself Celtic in Your Spare Time* on the conveyer, then slowly turns to dispose of packaging. Recycle goes in one dumpster, reusable packaging in another. The Celtic book had been wrapped in newspaper. A headline flatly states:

VAPORS EXCITE CAT SHOW
PULCHRITUDINOUS KITTY DEEDS FURBALL

"No story enclosed, just headline." Victoria speaks with some chagrin.

"None needed," Pork whispers. "We got enough to work with." Pork sounds as excited as Pork ever sounds, which is to say, real dreamy.

"Put a sock in it," I tell them. "We got problems."

A Package-Police cruiser has just pulled a U-ey at the end of our conveyor row. It heads toward us. The cruiser is electric and only big enough to hold one cop and one prisoner.

"Pulchritudinous," Pork says, and says it real dreamy. I give him a good nudge. He sort of wakes up.

This cop has missed his place in history. He's a perfect model for a Storm Trooper or an Alabama Deputy, an Adolph or a Bubba. He chaws on a toothpick and wears short sleeves to show his biceps. His brush cut stands spikey above blue eyes that can't help looking at the front of Victoria's shirt.

"You creeps, again," he says, and gives me a shove just hard enough to mess up what I'm doing. "Keep workin'."

I place a book titled *Ergonomics and Policy Reform in 13th Century Mesopotamia* on the conveyor. The packaging was bubble wrap. I toss it into the reusable material dumpster. Pick up another package.

This particular cop always shoves me when he's after Pork . . . something, Victoria always explains, that they teach you in cop school.

"You moved your lips funny," the cop says to Pork. "Say it again."

"Cheeseburgersforlunch," Pork tells the cop. It's one of our ready made words. We have ready-mades for occasions like this. "We were talkin' lunch," Pork says. "Before that we were talkin' breakfast."

"And now you're talkin' bull." The cop knows full well he's in the presence of subversion. He knows we're stealing thoughts, but doesn't have enough to hang us.

We got rights. The cop doesn't even have enough on us to justify a mild beating. He's one frustrated jockstrap.

"With French fries," Victoria says, and says it most sweetly. She zips open a package containing *Pachyderms Of The Circus: Their Wit and Wisdom*. This one is wrapped in newspaper. She deftly, and with no seeming regret, tosses the paper into recycle. We who know her, though, feel her sorrow. We caught a fleeting headline, something like:

SYMPHONY GOES O AND 1 AGAINST MENDELSSOHN

Something to think about. And we will. As soon as we get rid of Adolph.

"We'd ask you to join us for lunch," I say in a loud whisper, "but then we'd be fraternizing." I figure the cop is so dumb he'll think it's a compliment. I think rightly.

"Another suck-up," he says. When he finally leaves we shelve Mendelssohn for the moment, then once more discuss a question of law.

It is true we steal words and thoughts, but we're not stealing them from the books. We're taking them from the packaging. Plus, things fall out of books: pressed flowers, locks of hair, clippings (usually obituaries or marriages), bookmarks, snapshots, postage stamps, love letters, receipts, and postcards. It's all throwaway stuff.

So, if it's junk, who owns it? The Corporation says, "Throw it away."

"You can't steal something that's been thrown away," Pork always explains. "That's our fall-back position. When we finally get caught, and finally heal up from the beating, and find ourselves in front of a judge, that's our defense."

"Pulchritudinous," Victoria murmurs. "Nobody is gonna throw something like that away. That'll be their claim."

"Plus," I say, "they got lawyers. They own the judge. We got minimum wage."

"And the joy of combat," Pork tells me. "We got the pleasure of taking stuff right under The Corporation's drippy little nose." Pork can talk vicious when he wants.

"Every day," Victoria murmurs, "I take an idea, or an image, or a word away from here. I set it loose in the world. That, I believe, is Pulchritudinous." Victoria sometimes gets a dazed look whilst talking philosophy.

She is describing our mission. Our mission is not to defy The Corporation, but to subvert. We are warriors. That's the truth.

When books go out of here, headed for Bangkok or Plymouth-in-England, or Carrolton, Kentucky, they look just great. The Corporation has slicked them. Spots on covers have been cleaned. Torn dust jackets have been repaired. Lots of them look new, and all of them look snazzy. Like Reno.

But, I've seen inside some of those books. The words are still there, the ideas, the theories, the stories; but somehow life is gone. It's like everything in them is written on a dying desert wind. The books show color but have no heat of impassioned brains or beat of loving hearts. It's a giant gyp. The Corporation keeps the life of the book and sells the husk. Just like Reno.

Our subversion comes because we hijack words, ideas, dream-stuff, and yeh, occasional stardust. We hijack entire concepts, plus screwball visions. We can take a headline, a cat show, and talk it through. Then, we take it outside of Storyland and set it free. If our new idea or vision can make it beyond the city limits, it has a strong chance for a healthy life.

"Lunch," Pork says, and really means it.

We get takeout burgers at a roadhouse, then roll the car a mile into desert. The land is flat and covered with sage. In some places small hills rise, also sage-covered. We choose our spot with great care because The Corporation has spies. If we get caught, doing what we're about to do, the least that will happen is fractures.

I smoke a butt, smoke another. In the distance Reno seems to dance through heat waves, a tired and faded dance. The Corporation fits right into Reno. The Corporation came here because of tax stuff and central shipping. Birds of a feather.

We chaw on burgers, pretending that we hold a conversation about nothin'. We look here, there, every place. When we spot no spies, Victoria murmurs a little chant, tosses in a small but mystical spell. Then Victoria moves her delicate hand as if she waves a wand. She opens her hand. Pulchritudinous flies free.

Pulchritudinous dances like a tiny blue flame beneath desert sun. It rises above desert sage, skimming like a splendid little bird. It bounces playful. It dives, circles, and sports around us as it seeks a destination. It finally heads out in the general direction of Tennessee. It's gonna have one whale of a hard time making it in Nashville, but at least it's free of Reno.

"What is the difference," Pork murmurs, "between Storyland and The Strip?" He's talking, of course, about the Reno Strip.

"Us," Victoria says quietly.

I know what she means. Of course, Victoria is crazy, even if she does have smart brains. I search across the desert, but nothing out there moves. It looks like we've pulled off a successful stunt, but a day will come when someone spots us. Scary thought, but I don't think that any beating we get, or even any jail sentence, will allow The Corporation to reclaim Pulchritudinous.

"Time to get back to Weird Row," I tell my comrades. "We still got to deal with Mendelssohn."

Tattoo

This tale was written for Ella Rappé and Lillie Schmidt.

TODAY SHE IS A GOOD WOMAN, AND ALTHOUGH YESTERDAY IS GONE and so is she, an awful illumination hangs about her memory. It is the mute dread of unforgiven sin, and it exists like the rumor of weeping in our pecuniary and jiggling-breasted day. I walk through the strobing center of the blare and recall the silhouette of a coiffed woman, the bright gleam of a new coin, and imagine many rows of dead faces; paleness surrounded by ebony caskets with the nose-numbing perfume of mortuaries hanging like drapes. She was my aunt Edna and she was good. Everyone says that now.

I see one other thing that exists as vividly in my mind as the black Sunday coats of a dozen rural preachers. It is a small grave marker of coarse concrete, the figure of a kneeling lamb. The eyes are round and ill cast, the ears curved like dull and circular horns above configurations of molded fleece. The feet are tucked under. Altogether, a blob of cement sitting on a small slab among tall and dying weeds. In a way the lamb is the whole story. I think of pathos and the success of small hopes. I did not think of such things when my sister and I were small and vied for our aunt's favor as she took us to movies or Sunday school.

We were not unusual children. There was no magic in the rattle and spit of electricity from trolleys that passed beneath my aunt's window. The rain that swept the panes of the dying restaurant below her second floor apartment was cold. Always cold. I wonder if we grew too quickly in defense against the cold; leaving to find our American fortunes in the clatter of roads, the quarrel of classrooms and in the busy sales of marketable goods under dangling bulbs.

We grew in an Edward Hopper world. To this day the painting of the Nighthawks reminds me of that restaurant. There is a harmed, sharp-faced woman in that painting. There is also a hawkish man who, externally at least, sometimes reminds me of me. A second man with a washed-out face tends the counter and doubtless serves chopped-up portions of the American head on the platter of the 1930s.

I grew and went about other business. My aunt continued to work. Her picture would not vary in my mind for many years. It is a childhood picture of a large woman with sedate clothing and enormous bosom who emptied treasures of gum and pennies from a black purse. Lately the picture has changed. The sin hovers. I did not even know of the sin until I was thirty and deemed old enough to forgive. Forgive whom?

She was born in 1890, was pregnant with an illegitimate child in 1906, and in early 1907 the child died at birth. The concrete lamb has been kneeling over that child's grave ever since; and this is the 70s and the lamb has knelt for more than sixty-five years. Past the death of cousins and the disappearance of high-peaked farm houses shedding snow in the midst of eighty acres of corn-stubbled fields. My aunt left the country town after the birth and moved to a small midwestern city twenty miles away. She was not a stranger there, but in 1907 it was probably as far as a young woman could flee. The lamb remained in the family plot, the stone nameless and accusatory.

Sometimes I imagine that it rose on cracking joints at night to frolic. Sixty-five years.

Her first man and the father of the child was a medical student who was the son of the town doctor. The doctor delivered the child and it died. The son quit medical school and disappeared. Death hisses through the past, and the seeds of ancient springtimes root deep and live long.

Her second man. And now here's the tale. A mindless, vicious and tongue-wagging malcontent with arms tattooed in celebration of motherhood and tall ships. A sanctimonious ex-adventurer who stood with God and coveted virginity. My uncle Justin. In 1918 he had just returned from the war. A Navy Man, and he sailed in a battleship around the world. A gunner's mate. It was enormous. He was grand and tattooed and muscled and he had *just sailed around the world.*

They were married after six months and after her confession about the lamb. Two years later, at age thirty, she bore a son who would be their only child.

Tattoos do not change. When my sister and I were young we watched the snarled anchor, the leaping panther, the pierced heart and the full rigged ship vibrate over muscles that were hard and capable. Later the muscles changed. In the depression there was no work. There was only the radio, the systematic soap opera fantasy that drained a perhaps stupid man's will. Much later, when he was old and lazy; a man pale and of no muscle, the tattoos were brilliant in red and blue, palpably etched against a canvas of pallid flesh. Only the tattoos were real. The man in every way failed to become his symbols.

Was there ever a chance? I was in awe of him when I was little because he ignored me and yelled at his wife and son, but I loved my aunt dearly.

"Buy yourself a present. You're so big now that I don't know what to give you."

I was seven years old in thirty-nine. I had seen a half dollar several times, but to own one, to be given one . . . the gleam of the huge coin she passed to me made me gasp. I did not realize that the coin would buy nothing as great as its own lustre and so I bought an airplane. We carried it to the mortuary for my aunt's twice-weekly appointment with the dead.

This story is so short. She lived eighty-two years of days; a tiresome round that included cold lips above jaws frozen in rigor mortis, above manipulated eyelids; the work upon work that always returned her to the apartment where her unemployed ex-sailor boomed platitudes and sat by the radio among mugs emblazoned with the pictures of ships, medals for righteous conduct, souvenirs of crossing the equator. "Til death do you part." She worked with death.

The days of torn scalps. The days of mending and knitting and patching above breaks in heads that were soon to be skulls. My aunt was a hairdresser for the dead and also ran a small beauty shop for the living. Death paid twice as much, and it was work that was available in the depression. She had a son who she hoped would finish college.

". . . and Justin never let her forget it. If she complained about anything he always came back with nagging about that." My mother's eyes when she told me the story of the lamb were without judgment. Indeed, my mother knew our entire family so well that the knowledge placed her beyond the requirement to judge.

By then the depression was gone, the Second War was over, and my young world was a memory that had faded before the second American reconstruction.

"You really mean that she has lived with Justin all these years and suffers from something that happened before he knew her?"

"Right is right."

"And wrong is wrong, but we both know better."

"So does Justin," my mother said, "or maybe he doesn't."

It was amazing, this evil perpetuated by zealous righteousness. The occasion was my first big experience with time structuring itself in my mind. I believe it is my aunt who has made me an amateur historian.

My mother told me the story and then turned away to other business. My family has always worked hard, and on this occasion my mother's work was to help feed forty people. The year was 1962, the last family reunion we would have in that small town that is still as raw as new boards; a town enclosed by iced December fields which have been cleared for nearly two hundred years. I wonder at the rawness of small towns and think that nothing man-made and beautiful was ever constructed at the bottom of a mountain.

The family arrived. One of my cousins was the local Packard and Farmall dealer. A second cousin, a man of the hearty variety, announced that he was in the pig business and we all laughed. Children swirled between our legs. I took a position in a corner of the living room and knew that what I watched was the last gasp of an anachronism.

Reunion. Had there ever been union? I remembered my childhood, walking excursion with my aunt, the perfumed smell of waiting rooms where I looked at pictures in magazines while my aunt worked in a back room. In a little while Edna and Justin arrived.

Their son had driven them. When the purple and white station wagon was parked, his children joined the throng. The son came next, walking ahead of his wife. I had not seen my aunt and uncle in several years. She was helping him from the car. With the story of the lamb fresh in my mind I watched and took a small and criminally vicious pleasure in noting that my uncle limped. She supported him as he walked to the house. His hands dangled.

I glanced at the son who had taken a soft chair; graduate of a business school and a Navy destroyer, loud with assertion. He was sitting, legs crossed, and over a rumpled sock the red eye of a tattooed cat stared from above the ankle. I hurried to the door to greet her and help her with her coat.

My aunt. My dear aunt, beloved of a childhood that had contained some hope of wizardry, some belief in prestidigitation if not in magic. I talked to her for a long time that day. Saw the sagging wattles of a once full and healthy face, the drooping flesh of the upper arm, the implied immortality of a single gold-capped tooth. She smiled and was happy. I grinned like a clown performing in pain and wondered. What was this resolve that lived so long, worked so tediously, forebore joy in this world with complete confidence in a supposed next, and resulted in happiness? I judge. Frequently I judge wrong. Did she judge?

"I'm so proud of you. We all are." She spoke of my university education as I might speak of my son's report card.

Later she rambled. ". . . after the war . . . you remember the shop."

"I remember. There was a sign with the silhouette of a beautiful woman." I also remembered the machines that temporarily set hairstyles that came from movies where instant orchestras appeared on 1930s side streets. Black and silver machinery that twisted over heads to make all women into temporary Medusas.

". . . after the war. The home permanents came out. I had to sell the shop. Still work some. Anderson and Hittle still call."

I shuddered. Listened. Felt the sweep of guilt and work and time.

"... gets his Navy pension ... it's really Old Folks pension but it don't hurt if he calls it Navy. We get by. Oh, look at the children. It tickles me pink to see everybody here and look so good."

We were called to dinner. Uncle Justin, by virtue of being a deacon, said grace. He properly thanked Jesus the Lamb of God and slobbered the Amen because he was hungry. A customary thing, but I excused myself as soon as possible.

I saw my aunt and uncle once more and that was two months ago. I am forty years old now and do not understand my age, only that I have it. Passing by plane from the west coast to St. Louis I rented a car and drove to spend a weekend among the streets of the clanging city where I had spent my childhood.

"You must see Edna," my mother said. "She's failing."

Failing, and I am forty. I went to see my aunt.

The apartment was hardly changed since I was a child. The picture of a battleship with curling spray from a rainbow was yellow with time. It hung over my uncle's bed. His souvenir mugs stood on a strangely feminine whatnot that had been the high school shop project of the son. A framed good conduct medal was glassed over but was still dusty and faded. It hung beside the picture. Painted sea shells with brave mottos, bits of coral ... the man lay flat on his back, pale and thin, a neon of tattoos with breath as light as the passage of a ghost. My uncle was already a spectre, but my aunt still lived.

She made instant coffee with trembling hands. She was so thin. The enormous bosom gone. The strong hands faded, but still somehow alive, like weak light through waxed paper. She had not recognized me at first and was ashamed.

"How is he?" I stopped, silently cursing myself for the stupidest of all questions. The man was dying. Fool. Fool to ask such a question.

She was not offended. The coffee cups were dimestore ironware. Plain. The coffee was bitter because trembling hands had spilled some, added more.

"Jimmy, Jimmy." She looked at me. Proud. I, who have violated scruples she held dear. Then she remembered my question.

"I pray for one thing," she said. "I never asked for much ... no, sometimes I asked for a lot, but I pray that Justin dies first."

I could not answer. She knew. All along she knew. For her whole life of submission she knew.

"No one . . . they would not take care of him," she said. "He's not the easiest man."

She knew. Maybe she even loved him, but she was not fooled about the man. She was not fooled about the idiot chase of an ignorant's repetitive ethic over a lifetime. She had forgiven herself. She had forgiven him.

I sat holding the cup, the bitterness of the coffee as immediate and vital as sharp words. A question rose in my mind, stood like anguish in my head because I could say nothing, could of course not ask that question.

I took both her hands and spoke innocuously around the question which was, of course, "Dear aunt, *dearest lady*, what can I *do* for you before you die?"

Later that evening I changed my plane reservations and lost a business day. The next morning, just before dawn, I drove along country roads that were gravel when I was a child, that are now clean-surfaced macadam.

It was not easy to find. The entrance was different, and on the slightly rolling slopes the new section of the cemetery changed the perspective. I parked the car, opened the trunk, stood watching the early glow of dawn over the distant fields that year after year expressed vegetables and occasional wildflowers. The practical, hard-working American land.

A swarm of birds crossed the beginning day like salt superstitiously flung backward over the shoulder of the fields, and dew-heavy bushes crowded fencerows and over-grew old graves. The bottom of a ditch was mudsodden, with occasional shallow pools of stagnant water. I walked through tall weeds, searched, found it.

The marker was smaller than I remembered, and the base was sunk in earth; the curling horn-like ears canted forward increasing the kneeling and submissive posture. I rocked the marker back and forth. It came free, the base mud-clotted.

A hundred pounds, perhaps. No more. It was possible to get it to the trunk of the car, close the trunk, and leave. There is little more to tell.

My uncle died a month ago. My aunt died yesterday, and the circle is closed. The family will erect a marker, and the family will continue its various judgments and forgiveness, its successes and errors . . . as I will continue mine.

My judgment is this: I dropped the marker into a deep but muddy river that runs through tamed land and beside tight-fisted and narrow minded towns. It will never, through the rest of time, interrupt the wind that blows cold over that finally unmarked grave.

Tinker

THERE WERE TROUBLED AUGUSTS ONCE, BACK WHEN OUR GRAND-
mothers were still alive, and when dog days panted slowly toward
busy Septembers. Narrow roads overlaid old Indian trails, cutting
through squared-off fields. The roads were white gravel. In
midwest August dawns, the roads turned orange. Later in the day,
they flowed like strips of light between green and yellow crops.
Along these roads the tinker followed his trade.

We would see his wagon a mile off. Children began to holler.
Women on the farm, mothers and grandmothers and cousins,
exchanged glad looks behind the backs of any men who happened
to be around. The tinker was a ladies' man, but not in the usual
sense.

This was the time of the Great Depression. Farms were flattened.
People were broke. Gasoline was used only for the tractor, or, once
a week, taking the Ford to town. In those days horses were not
spoiled little darlings. They worked the same as everyone else. Our
people lived on hope, religion, the kitchen garden, a few slaugh-
tered swine; and chicken after chicken after chicken. Even now,
fifty years later, I cannot look a roasting hen in the eye.

The tinker had a regular route through the county. We saw
him twice a year. Most tinkers were older men, but this one was
middling young. My mother claimed he was a gypsy, my grandmother claimed him Italian, and the menfolk claimed him an
Indian/mulatto who was after someone's white daughter. But,

I'd best explain about tinkers. In today's throwaway world they are extinct.

The tinker's wagon was a repair shop on wheels. It resembled a crossbreed between farm wagon and Conestoga, but light enough for hauling by two horses. It carried torches for brazing, patches of sheet metal, patches of copper. It held soles for shoes, and grinders for knives and scissors. It was a-clank with cooking pans hanging along its sides. The tinker repaired worn pots, glued broken china so skillfully one could hardly find the crack, fixed stalled clocks; in fact, repaired anything that required a fine hand. This tinker also repaired worn dreams. That was the seat of his trouble. And ours.

I remember all this, not only through the eyes of a child, but through the eyes of a historian. I sit in my comfortable workroom where carpet is unstained, unstainable, and unremarkable. I look at it and remember wool rugs of a farmhouse. The rugs carried stains as coherent as a textbook: the darkness of blood when a younger cousin lost a finger in the pulley of a pump; a light space from spilled bleach; or unfaded bright spots beneath chairs—the signs of living, or (as the poet says) "all the appurtenances of home." I type on an old, old typewriter that was made in the 30s. At least that much respect can be shown the story.

When the tinker's wagon appeared on the road it caused a temporary stop in the work. That August when the trouble arose was as tricky as all Augusts. In August the last cut of hay comes in. Farmers gauge the weather sign, cut quickly, watch the horizon for storm as the hay dries. The baler comes through, the men following the tractor and wagon. They buck the bales. In the August when I was nine, the tinker appeared along the dusty road. I was too small to buck hay, was thus driving the tractor.

"Jim," my father said to me, "get the hell up to the house." He stood beside the wagon, shirt sodden with sweat, and sweat darkening the band of his straw hat. My father was a big man with English-blue eyes. He could be kind when he was unworried, but, what with the depression, he had not been unworried for years. My uncle and a cousin stood beside him. My uncle was from my mother's side. He was German, with eyes a thinner blue, and face a little starchy. Another cousin, my eldest, perched on top of the wagon where he stacked bales.

"I'd have thought," my uncle said about the tinker, "that the bastard would have hit jail by now. Or made a little stop out there at the cemetery."

"Bullshit," my eldest cousin said from the top of the load. "He's working. He ain't a tramp." This was a cousin from dad's side. He was known for a smart mouth and radical notions.

"Bullshit back at you," my other cousin said. "Best you can say about him is that he might be a dago." This was a cousin from mom's side, and he was defending his father, who didn't need it.

I climbed from the tractor and headed across twenty acres to the house.

In the days before World War II a boy of nine was not a man, but he was treated as if he soon would be. He had responsibilities, and most boys that age took themselves seriously. If the tinker suddenly decided to rape and pillage there was not a whole lot I could do. That, however, was not the point. The point was that I represented a male presence.

Manhood comes in peculiar ways depending on where you grow. I recall walking across that field of hay stubble in bare feet. No town kid could have done it, although in the small towns boys shed their shoes with the last frost. By August their feet were as tough as mine. The difference was that they had no feel for the land. They did not know that land is supposed to hurt you a little. Weather the same. A farm is real, not pastoral.

An apparition stood at the edge of that twenty-acre hay field. Even today you occasionally see them in the midwest. Solitary black walnuts stand like intricately carved windmills. They spread against the sky, trees spared when the land was cleared. They grow slowly, and spare themselves. No other tree can root within their drip lines. Black walnuts spread poison through the soil.

This tree was a youngster when men and their families forged through the Cumberland Gap, or spread along rivers from a backwoods settlement called Chicago. Now it had a bole thirty feet in circumference. The first branches began at forty feet, and the total height was over a hundred. It ruled the fields, too majestic for human use. It would not serve for a children's swing, or for a hanging tree. Before first snow, when the guns came out for hunting season, we always gathered walnuts beneath spectral branches.

The tinker's wagon pulled into the lane as I passed the back door of the house. My grandmother saw me, looked toward the hayfield, and murmured to herself, probably a verse from Isaiah. At age nine I had small appreciation of women, did not understand that my grandmother was the most beautiful woman I would ever know. She was a storyteller, and she was tall in a time when most women were not. Her white hair fell below her waist when she brushed it. During the day she had it 'done up.' Her worn housedresses were always pressed by flatirons. Her dresses fell to the tops of her shoes. My grandmother had been a young wife on the Oklahoma frontier when Indians roamed. The depression of the 1880s brought her back to Indiana.

The tinker's horses were wide from summer's roadside grass. One was bay, the other black. Color radiated from the wagon, red, white, and blue paint, green canvas, sun leaping from polished pans that clanked at every jolt in the rutted lane. Sun sparkled and danced against colors. My mother stepped from the house, my least cousin beside her, a girl of fifteen.

Did I understand what was going on? I doubt it, although I surely felt the men's displeasure and the women's pleasure. For my own part, the tinker's visit was exciting. Days on the farm are long. We had a telephone party line, but we had neither radio nor electricity. Townfolk had both.

It was a shy welcome the tinker faced, although he was accustomed to it. Since he moved from farm to farm, he met such welcomes all the time. Families learned how to comfortably handle each other. They had little experience with strangers.

"Missus," the tinker said to my grandmother, "I think of you last night and turn the horses this-a-way." His smile was a generalization among the sun-flashing pans, but he tipped his hat exactly toward my grandmother. His face was dark from either summer or blood. His brown eyes might have been those of a young Mediterranean girl. His eyes held no guile, and his face was—no more, no less—permanently relaxed and happy. In memory he seems a man without needs, an enlightened monk.

Even before he climbed from the wagon my least cousin passed him a dipper of water. Her young breasts moved beneath her housedress, her bobbed hair (which scandalized my grandmother) shone almost golden in sunlight. She had a pretty but puckish face, and lips that sometimes tied themselves with confusion. Although I had little appreciation of women, I was fascinated with what was happening to my cousin. Her body seemed to change every day. No doubt she was self-conscious as she became a woman, but to me she moved with confusing mystery.

"There's marriages all over," the tinker said. "From here to the county line." He drank, then climbed from the wagon. His horses stood placid as a puddle. The tinker not only repaired things, he also served as the county's newspaper. "The Baptists over in Warren bought a bell for the church. You can never tell what a Baptist is going to do." He said this last with a sort of wonder, but with no malice. He passed the dipper back to my least cousin and thanked her.

In the hayfield the men reached the end of a row. The tractor turned, headed back toward the house. I recall noting that another row would make a wagonload. The men would bring the load to the barn. Leaves of the black walnut looked ragged this late in August. The leaves carried no dust because the tree stood tall.

"It sounds like a busy winter," my mother said, and smiled at my least cousin.

"She was raised better," my grandmother said about my mother.

I had not the least notion what was meant. Now, of course, I understand that my mother spoke of the marriages.

"If this isn't the prettiest place on earth, then the Lord is fooling me." The tinker looked across fields toward the hardwood grove. Beyond the grove the river wound among rushes. At this time of year the river ran nearly clear. In spring, or after August storms, it ran brown with rich mud. The tinker looked toward our small farmhouse, then toward the barn. There was no hunger in his eyes, only happiness. He busied himself at repairing dreams.

The Great Depression, in spite of the softening that comes with years, was gray. We were an ambitious people, but ambitions were set aside as we struggled against hard times. Grayness arrived because hard times did not end. Women lost color and men lost creative fire.

The tinker owned only his wagon and team, yet he magically wished for nothing. Because of this he allowed us to see our lives with new eyes. That was at least part of his magic. He did not want what we had, but he showed *us* how to want it. Looking back, I almost understand the other part of his magic.

"There's so much time for thinking," he said to my grandmother. "I wonder after your quilt while I drive." Copper-bottomed pans reflected sun, and the wagon seemed alight with the warmth of mighty candles. The black walnut stood indifferent as a tower. In mid-afternoon it threw a shadow shorter than itself. "Quilts take such a fine hand." The tinker did not say that he also had a fine hand.

"Margaret is growing up," my grandmother said about my least cousin. "She helps. Some day she'll be teaching me."

"She has a delicate way. That's a sign."

My cousin, strong enough to help with the heavy work of slaughtering, looked at her feet and blushed. In the everyday life of the farm my least cousin was no more delicate than a post, but that is not what the tinker meant. "Times are changing, but a lady will always show herself a lady." He turned to my mother, who had just made that unladylike and licentious comment about marriages. "She is also musical?" he asked about my least cousin. At the turn of the century farms had gained a few luxuries. Many farmhouses had pianos, but in the whole county only my mother excelled at music. She had a warm touch better suited for blues than for church. However, in those days we knew nothing about the musical blues.

"It takes a while to learn," my mother said. She did not say that my cousin took little interest. My mother actually blushed. Somehow she had been taken back into the fold of respectability, and the *how* of the matter seemed beyond explanation.

"There's so much to learn," the tinker said to my cousin. "Takes a year, anyway, to rightly do a quilt."

Looking back, I understand that the tinker's magic truly was magic. At least it was magic in any terms we knew then, and certainly in any terms since.

I recall standing there, my bare feet as hard-soled as soil and callus could make them. I recall feeling that mysterious matters lived around me. The values of a farm are stern. I understood clean fencerows and upright dealing. I had been shown no other values. The word 'grace' had never entered my thought beyond its use in sermons.

The tinker's magic was to restore mystery and value to farmwomen. No small undertaking.

Imagine a Depression farm. People lived close. A tyranny of custom was our only defense against wide knowledge of each other. When we dressed beside the kitchen woodstove on cold mornings the women dressed first. Then the men entered and dressed while the women went to the parlor. In unheated bedrooms temperatures might fall below zero.

It takes time and privacy to be a lady. The farm offers only hog butchering, kitchen gardens, interminable days of canning, the tedious daily round of cooking and splitting wood and cleaning poultry sheds. Men's work is brutally hard. Women's work begins before dawn and ends with a nightly reading from the Bible.

"I saved back some mending," my grandmother said. "It's only a little."

In those days pots and pans were continually pushed from the hot to the cool side of the stove. Pans wore thin through years. We did not throw away a leaky pan.

I watched the tinker apply the patch, while from the barn came sounds of work as the men began to unload hay. The three women surrounded the tinker. The tinker drilled a clean hole through the leak, snapped on the pan patch, and worked to flatten it on an upright anvil. Deft fingers smoothed that patch into the pan with the skill of a carpenter using a finely set plane. As he worked he spoke about a book of pictures from California. He tsked, then smiled. He mended a boot, and told about a new preacher. The preacher's wife was winning over the congregation, not the preacher. My memory calls back sunlight and quiet, above all, courtesy—an old-fashioned word.

"The sewing machine needs tinkering," my cousin said.

"I'll be but a minute," the tinker told his horses. He followed the three women toward the house. The horses stood almost as solidly as the black walnut. Shade spread dark beneath the wagon. My mother's shoulders did not slump as she walked. My grandmother, always busy, now seemed to stroll. My least cousin, clumsy with her growing up, was lithe in her movement. My heart pounded like rifle shots. I stood knowing I should follow, yet was somehow daunted. Even at age nine I understood that privacy lived in this encounter. A loud curse came from the barn. I looked to see my German cousin leap from the hay wagon and stride toward me.

"Are you ever going to grow up, Jimmy boy?" My cousin passed me, not running, but striding. Over by the barn the other men hesitated, then decided my cousin could handle matters. They returned to work, could not admit the work was hopeless.

Jaws of depression gnawed. No matter how hard men struggled, failure and despair were triumphant. Some years we did not make seed money. The bill for land tax stood dark as that black tree.

The sewing machine sat in a corner of the invaded parlor, and the tinker knelt. He removed a worn sleeve from the treadle. He spoke of a neighbor's daughter, studying at Ball State Teacher's College.

My cousin stood in the doorway. I stood behind him, embarrassed to be there, unable to not be there. The three women watched the tinker. My mother laughed. My grandmother said that college would be good for that particular girl. My least cousin yearned after the tinker's words. To us, college was a grand and remote place. I fidgeted. My grandmother turned, saw us in the doorway.

"Ralph," she said to my cousin, "this is not your place."

I do not know how scorn and sadness can combine in such a low voice. The tinker knelt above his work, but for a moment he fumbled with his wrench. My mother turned. I had never seen such anger from my mother, never saw such anger afterwards. My least cousin blushed and stood silent. The man in the doorway stiffened. He stood rigid as a rifle.

"You'd take away what little joy there is," my grandmother said. "Get about your business." She turned back. My mother looked at me, and I did not understand her quick sadness. Nor, probably, did she.

I sat in the kitchen with Ralph as the tinker finished his work. The man sat with fists closed. His blue eyes turned pale as his face. He fought shame with anger, and while his eyes remained pale his face gradually heated. "We'll see," he kept muttering. "We'll see about this."

That night—with the tinker long departed—marked the crossroads of my growing up. A curious silence lived in kitchen and parlor. We were isolated hearts. My mother avoided speaking with my father. My grandmother murmured to my least cousin, had nothing to say to the men. My least cousin worked in complete silence. Darkness lay across the fields by eight o'clock. Exhausted and sullen men made thin excuses to get out of the house, then made no excuse. They piled in the Ford and left on the road to town. For the first time in memory, I went to bed without hearing my father read a passage from the Bible.

No one spoke because no one knew what to say. A stranger came among us. He wielded the power of appreciation, and the power of unheeding affection.

Night passed. Morning arrived with sullen silence. Haying continued, although on that day the men were dragged-out. We made slow progress. When we went to the house for dinner at noon, the women spoke indifferently. An awful resignation dwelt among the women, a permanent tiredness of spirit. I never again remember spontaneity in that house.

The telephone party line buzzed with news. The tinker's wagon had burned. The tinker was intact. His horses had been unhitched and tied. They were also intact, but the wagon of red and white and blue and green was in ruins . . .

I wish this story could end here. I would be compelled by its darkness, would feel such sorrow, but would not have to feel the rest. I sit in my comfortable workroom and type on this antique machine that was new when the world went spoiled. The tinker was not a man who would seek revenge. Perhaps he taught what old mystics knew, that wisdom arrives on the breath of inexplicable pain.

We got the hay in, and we had three days of storm. Sunday came with church and Sunday school. Cornfields stood bright, dust gone from leaves washed beneath August thunder. The land expressed grain, but lives turned dull as sermons. We left church and drove the graveled road that lay like a glowing path, but our way led back to the farm.

We were met by sparkles of light dancing among the tattered leaves of that spectral walnut. My mother gasped, remained silent. My grandmother chuckled. My least cousin was so confused she seemed about to weep.

"Get to the house," my uncle said to the women. "I don't want to hear a word." He climbed from the car and stood staring at the walnut. "How in the hell did he do it?"

The tree was alight with polished pans. They hung far out on branches. Pans glowed silver and copper, iron and enamel. No one could climb that tree. Even if a man could, it would be impossible to inch far enough out on the branches.

"He must have nailed boards like steps, then took 'em back down," my English cousin said. "He must have used a pole and hooked that stuff out there. The man is slick." My English cousin, known for radical notions, was not about to defect from us. At the same time he could appreciate what he saw.

"Jim," my father said, "go get the goddamn rifle."

In a sense it was I who defected. Over the next two years I grew closer to my mother and grandmother. My least cousin turned seventeen. She married. The men became silent and critical, but we still worked. Trapped in questions, I became silent. We avoided our confusions.

At the end of two years we lost the farm to taxes. The world started talking about war, but even that most hideous of wars leaves no memory this enduring:

The tinker used piano wire. Bullets only glanced, causing the pans to dance. We shot at the handles, broke a few pans loose. Work called and we worked. The crops came in.

We fired, and fired, and fired; pings, rattles, the sound of bullets. Autumn departed into winter, and shotguns cleared the walnuts. We spoke of cutting the tree, but did not. We fired as new leaves budded in the spring. Guns tore away small branches, and until we lost the farm they tore at my understanding.

My uncle was tight-lipped when we left the farm. My father wept, but my mother did not. I remember the tractor standing silent in the fields, and a few straggling pans hanging in the walnut. I remember our farm truck loaded with household furnishings, and wish that this were all. It is not, however; for what I remember always, can never forget, are two years of wasted ammunition and the sounds of firing, the silhouettes of raised weapons, the rattle of bullets as men sought redemption; through all the seasons shooting guns into that tree.

Kilroy Was Here

He dreamed his feet were so cold that he ran to the battalion aid station, and there were his mother and sister fixing him some hot food over a wood fire, and poking up the fire so he could warm his feet. But before he could eat the food or warm his feet he woke up—and his feet were still cold.

—Ernie Pyle, "Brave Men"

THE V.A. HOSPITAL SITS SOLEMN AND GRAND ABOVE THIS TOO BUSY northwest city where traffic rumbles and rain mostly pours. Darkness lies between this place and the city, a darkness we've but noticed lately. I totter at a red-hot half-a-mile an hour along lighted halls and Burnside generally outruns me. Burnside drives a wheelchair and his motto is, 'Leave no nurse's butt unpatted' because, as he says, "Waste is a sin and I'm practicin' to be a preacher."

And this V.A. hospital, itself, is no bad place for a Burnside type of ministry. The hospital stands like a temple, and through its halls and secret passages and operating rooms eternally pour shapes of human hope and pain; shapes of mystery, dread, high times and low. People stride or tippy-toe or cakewalk these halls depending on who's got what share of joy or trouble, and where that trouble lives. Talking about the geriatric ward, Burnside says to me, "It ain't altogether a noble occupation, Ross, but it's three hots and a flop. It is, by God, a livin.'"

"It's a dying," I tell him. "It's the jump-off place where the world takes its last shot, and Sarge, the world is gonna win." When you talk to Burnside you have to mix good sense with a touch of facts or he won't understand. Burnside has flung b.s. for seventy-six of his seventy-eight years, having been somewhat slow as a baby.

He rolls that wheelchair like a Hell's Angel of the geriatric ward; a wheelchair with racing stripes, a foxtail, an ooga-ooga horn, and the remnants of a Japanese battle flag fluttering from a stick of the kind you see on bicycles. Burnside has arms and shoulders like a dwarfed goliath, and legs so thin his small feet look like powder-puffs attached to toothpicks. "It's a real adventure being in this kind of shape," he tells me. "You learn to crap in a lotta new ways." Burnside has about three red hairs remaining along each temple, his dome is bald, his moustache gray, and hair sprouting from his ears approaches maroon.

The kind thing would be to let him pass away in silence, and the smart thing would be to pass away myself; but days stretch long when the brain is good and the body is shot—and for too long, maybe, we've been silent. My hands no longer hold a pen, but thanks to the mysterious East I have a tape recorder that works. My hips almost don't work. I've got hips like cracked glass.

My tape recorder purrs like a Japanese cat as I tell about what happens, or has happened, and as I concentrate on Burnside. Burnside was okay until, some years ago, he bounced a Honda Goldwing off a phone pole and into a lady's petunia patch. She stood wailing over bruised petunias. He claims to have hammed it up over a busted motorcycle and a busted pelvis, taking advantage of the situation in an attempt to lure her into the sack.

Other people around here are lucky, maybe. They fester in a vegetable state. They've disconnected from the world, have dreamed their ways into the past, and become ghosts who sit before the dayroom TV; listening to chatter, patter, gossip, and lisping cartoons. The TV spooks are more ghostly than the real ghosts who plague this hospital. This place is a ghost factory.

It was the real ghosts who started things. We lifers were peaceful enough telling lies about our different wars, and about our lives in and out of the military. We were happy checking obituaries each day, and chortling over the passing of generals and presidents.

"The main difference between dead and alive," says Burnside, "is that 'dead' means off the payroll."

Then the ghosts got into it. They generally hang around the cemetery out back with its brightly glowing slabs, or else jungle up in broom closets or under beds. They wisp their ways through these halls, rolling along silent as the soft paws of dust kittens. The orderlies don't see them. The nurses don't see them. We can hardly see them.

"It's a perfect setup," Burnside says. "Plenty of company, cafeteria, television, bed, and a cemetery right at hand." Then he tells a Burnside type of story. Once, in the days after he retired from the Infantry, he worked as a groundskeeper in a corpse farm called, Rest Eternal. "They had amazin' discounts for employees," he tells anyone who will listen. "I was losin' money every day I stayed alive."

But stories about Burnside's past didn't amount to a pastel damn once the present took over. The ghosts in this geriatric ward began manifesting. We didn't know what was happening at first. We did know our ranks were thinning . . . around here the ranks are always thinning. In a little over a month two beds opened up as sgts. Smith and Sanders passed to the great beyond. Their empty chairs in the dayroom quickly filled with a couple of retired Marines still dumb enough to believe they were assigned to temporary duty. Plus, another bed was knocking on empty. The door to corporal Harvey's room stayed closed. Nurses came and went, came and went. Doctors avoided the place. All signs read 'Farewell, Dan Harvey.'

Darkness started to roll along the hallways, and darkness clustered in the geriatric ward. The dayroom clouded, became blue like a 1940s bar filled with jazz and tobacco smoke. A clarinet wailed as the TV ceased its quack and faded without a flicker. Darkness fell in individual rooms and squelched the common sounds of people puking, or gasping and sucking for breath, or whimpering as pain pills wore off.

Not a mother's son or daughter in that dayroom missed a thing, although nurses kept scampering back and forth, back and forth, unseeing.

Ghosts appeared tricked out in their best things, and so solid you could see them. The men wore '40s uniforms, and the women looked like Greta Garbo, except more fun; American, English, other kinds mostly Oriental. Some of the gals wore uniforms, most wore dresses. The clarinet wailed like the love-ridden and lonesome voice of a transport leaving dock, the voice behind final waves, final goodbyes. The clarinet talked about Lili Marlene, and in the background a trombone sobbed. The ghosts seemed trying to tell us something. A sailor ghost flagged semaphore; colored flags whipping around the alphabet, but the only man on the ward who knew how to read it was a blind quartermaster, so that was a loss.

The halls became bluer, smokier, like lukewarm passions in the dusk of an old man's mind. Chill air moved through the halls, and the door to corporal Harvey's room opened. A nurse stepped through the doorway, her shoulders slumped, her hair astray, and she carried that beaten look the nurses get when they have lost.

"Janet," Burnside said in an abstract and irrelevant way that for the moment held no b.s. "Susan. Yukiko-san. The girls we left behind." He watched another dejected nurse leave corporal Harvey's room. "That poor sumbitch is so dead," he muttered, "that he really ought to go on sick call."

=

We sat blinking. No one here ever thought of ghosts as more than shadows or memories, fragments of aged imaginations. The past adds up as men age, and remembered voices come from everywhere. Now it seemed there was more to it. I thought of reasons for being in a haunted place. I thought of history, of how things begin . . .

We credit tuberculosis with the building of this hospital. In the early parts of the century the 'tee bees' took lives in breathless manners as lungs turned to shreds of dangling tissue, as lesions and excrescence sought out final gasps behind lips stained with choked-up blood. Tuberculosis is not the most vivid of diseases. That score goes to cholera; but unlike cholera, t.b. spelled equal opportunity. It killed schoolteachers and bankers and captains of industry.

Our government, being enlightened, warehoused victims instead of shooting. It built hospitals in remote places. This hospital towers on a long hill overlooking a city that was once a place of neighborhoods if not a city of light. The hospital is thus downwind from prevailing weather patterns. The hospital is huge, serving as a landmark for airplanes, and even a landmark for ships cruising Puget Sound. Its outside displays yellow brick, and its inside glows mental ward green.

By 1940 the docs found ways to beat tuberculosis. Some hospitals closed for lack of customers. Then, as Burnside points out, the happiest circumstance occurred. World War II arrived and spelled a blessing for the medics. "Gave them something to do," Burnside says. "Kept 'em off the streets and out of jail. I never heard of a single doc who got vagged."

A great mixing of ghosts began as the hospital resurrected, first under the military, then under the V.A. Spirits whirled, like in a Waring blender. On this west coast most casualties came from the South Pacific, although a lot of freeze and burn cases came from that snafu in the Aleutians. Men died in colorful ways, or were launched to new adventures from the O.R.s; adventures in learning to walk without legs, work without hands, see without eyes—adventures in sipping beer through a straw when too sad and drunk to pick a glass up with a G.I. prosthesis. Brain cages cooked like French fries as electricity zapped, shock therapy being a hobby with the best medical minds of the day. A grateful nation, loving its loyal sons, did its damndest to sweep the warped remnants of men under the shaggy shagrug of history.

Fortunately for the hospital, as Burnside points out, the country discovered a conscience. "War saves people from themselves," Burnside says, "and we found how to save the slanteyes. We can shoot in any Asian language."

The hospital did not finish sweeping up WWII before Korea vets began to hurt, and Korea did not get swept up even after Vietnam. Around here, docs still sweep, and nurses slump with fatigue and failure when another soul goes west.

=

What with soldiers and sailors and jarhead marines, it is no surprise this hospital seems loaded with ghosts. I say 'loaded' and not 'haunted' because until corporal Harvey checked out, the ghosts saw us the same way we saw them, which is to say, insubstantial. Ghosts didn't give a hang for us, nor did they give a fat rat's behind. And, we didn't think they were any too loveable.

I sat, still blinking, and thinking of history and ghosts and blue light and 1940s bars; of transports and tears. Our ghosts had just held a real shindig, then disappeared. The ghost waving semaphore was last to leave.

"Sarge," I said to Burnside, "what in the world was all of that about?" I eased into a chair in the dayroom, sitting among TV stiffs, and looked around. Twenty old soldiers parked there, including a couple of Wacs . . . during WWII one of those kids helped run an ops center in jolly old Liverpool, the other did time in a supply room in Norfolk. There are not many women in V.A. geriatric wards. We only have these two.

Now the Wacs nudged the guys beside them, and the gals made dry-throat giggles of the kind that say, 'catch me if you can.' Tallulah Bankhead had nothing on these kids, and who would've ever suspected?

"Ross, old buddy, that's amazin'." Burnside watched the women, watched the surprised but suddenly interested men. "If that's the best they can do, okay. I've got my sights a few clicks higher."

"No b.s.," I told him. "What was all of that about?" I looked around the dayroom. No clarinet, no blue light, nobody waving semaphore or goodbye. The door to corporal Harvey's room remained closed. Come lights-out orderlies would steal in with a gurney, play body snatcher, and by dawn's early light corporal Harvey would become a fading memory. This hospital never snatches corpses in broad daylight. It depresses the troops.

"I can't figure it. If the corporal's on the far side, why is the far side waving goodbye? Makes me right uneasy." Burnside popped a wheelie. The wheelchair rared like a pony with ambition, then hit the floor as Burnside spun in a circle. He would catch fire-breathing hell if any nurse saw that wheelie. Staff does not like wheelies. Wheelies mark the deck, cause scuffmarks the buffers almost can't erase, and wheelies are traces of rebellion by patients.

Plus everyone would know it was Burnside's wheelie. He's the only one of the wheelchair bunch strong enough to pop a good one. He spun the chair in three intersecting circles, like an ad for Ballantine's. "A snort before lunch, and a snooze after." He pointed the chair toward his room.

"It's the solitary drinkers who end up doing time," I told him. "You shouldn't drink alone." I followed Burnside, and I followed slow. On good days I can make it through these hallways leaning on a cane. Most days I chase a walker. This place is—this place. If we did not have bullshit, we'd be dead. Let me explain.

Pain around here is real. Around here bodies do not heal, and exercise does not work out stiffness. Doctors can mask some serious pain with pills, and people can hide from pain a little bit by using sedatives and drugged sleep. Pain here is eternal, like sunrise and sunset. It's a part of conditions, part of a deal which says: if you live long enough, you have to hurt.

In this place puke is nasty, sour, bile-filled, vomit that more often than not travels along raw throats from guts that can no longer work a full shift. Puke comes laden with blood. In this place hip bones are so fragile one dares not stumble, and people who fall out of bed do not survive. When one is very, very old skin becomes thin as tissue paper, and cartilage around the nose disappears causing it to retract. The face looks like a skull with skin.

This is human stuff; the human thing we do not like to think about, not even when it's happening. Sooner or later, though, it comes to a lot of us. The only people who are young forever are the ones who early on have the bad luck to get in the way of bullets or trucks or killing disease. The message in this place says: you weren't smart enough to die young, so get it figured out.

Some people don't figure. They become TV stiffs, and TV sucks them into its own darkness. Some people do figure, but they mask their figuring with bullshit. Bullshit is the first line of defense against pain, or, as Burnside says of corporal Harvey—"All that poor bastard had was cancer. I've got cancer *and* a Combat Infantryman's Badge."

"You've only got the prostate kind," I tell him, "and Harvey had it in the gizzard. Prostate comes from frigging around with preacher's wives. Anybody can get it."

The first line of defense against pain . . . the other secret about pain is that it's easier to handle if you don't feel sorry for yourself.

Burnside and I, and most of these geriatrics, learned about not feeling sorry for yourself during grade school. Of course, all of that happened some years ago. The reasons for our learning are now in history books. As Casey Stengle used to say, "You could look it up."

So I followed Burnside as he headed for our room. We bunk two to a room in this place, until it comes time to die. Then they move us into solitary. As I followed I looked forward to a jolt of bourbon, either Burnside's bourbon or mine. Burnside could find whiskey in the middle of the Sahara, and I could find the beer chaser.

Our stash hides in what used to be a dumbwaiter. This hospital has been redesigned so many times even architects lose track of how everything fits. At one time or other dumbwaiters were plastered over. We opened this one, flushed plaster piece-at-a-time down the latrine, and I hung battalion colors of the 120th Engineers over the hole. The 120th is not my outfit anyway, and screw the 120th.

"That was one swell party. Harvey must have meant something to somebody." Burnside uncorked the Jim Beam. We were both having a tough time because of Harvey. Dan Harvey had been a good friend.

"I always thought those ghosties were just part of your imagination," Burnside said. "Ross, you're getting elderly."

He took a belt, wiped his mouth, then took a little sip and passed the bottle. I took it from him just in time to keep it from getting dropped. Burnside looked up, fumbled, saw something standing behind my shoulder. His face went white as a corpse. Then his mouth twitched, and his hands dropped to the wheels of the chair like he was ready to lead a charge. "What are you doing here?" he whispered, and for the second time in a single day his voice held no b.s. He looked at me. "You'll want to take a lick outta that bottle before you turn around."

A Japanese soldier stood behind me as I turned. He seemed polite. He looked almost solid, nearly real. This kid couldn't have been more than twenty-five, though with Japs it's hard to tell. He wore one of those dink uniforms with a sash. He bowed. I bowed right back at him, or at least as well as a stiff back and hips can. Old shapes took me over. The courtesy seemed downright civilized after bunking beside Burnside. The bow seemed to please the kid. He smiled, then vanished. Puff. Little blue mist. Nothing.

I turned to Burnside, and Burnside was so bleached I thought he died. His bald head shone, and fluorescent light lay across it like polish. Those heavy shoulders slumped, and his mouth formed what I feared was a permanent 'oh'. Then his hands stirred. "This is serious," he said. "Pour another shot, but don't pass the bottle. I'll drop it surely."

I sat on the bed, and my hand, which naturally trembles, really trembled. The whiskey, which is one of the last good things in life, roiled my gut, but was worth the roil. "Tell me," I said to Burnside.

"It happened on the Canal," he told me. "At the time he was a better man than me. We accidentally bumped into each other while mutually retreating. I shot him in the gut and my M1 popped its clip. Empty. He leaned on a tree, slid down to sit on his butt, and pointed a pistol at me. He studied the situation, and saw how we'd all been reamed. I could see it in his eyes. He just plain said, 'Aw, screw it,' which is 'shiranu ga hotoke' in Japanese. Then he flipped the pistol away, tipped on his side, and declared peace on all the world."

Rubber soles padded in the hall and I hid the bottle beneath a pillow. Burnside's ears are not as sharp as mine. He took my signal, though, and had his face more or less composed by the time nurse Johnson entered the room. "There's a little more to it," he whispered.

"This had better not be happy hour," Johnson said as she entered. Nurse Johnson is on day shift, and that improves our days. "You deadbeats don't fool anybody."

Johnson gets more dejected than most of the other nurses when she loses a patient, and she'd just lost Harvey. Sometimes she hangs around us, I swear, just because we still show a little life. It perks her up. We do our best to behave indecent.

=

In this geriatric ward doctors outrank Jesus, who, as the Navy boys will tell you, was only a carpenter's mate. Doctors, though, stand with God at their right hands. Nurses range in rank from cherub right on up to holy saint.

And how, one may well ask, did all this come about? And where, one may well ask, does nurse Johnson fit among that celestial chorus? And for how long, one may further ask, has Burnside been trying to put the make on her?

Take it by-the-numbers, because Burnside isn't going to score anyway, so there's no big hurry:

Some people here are dark towers of pain, and some are small, dense, compressed mounds of pain. Burnside, for all his fanny rides a wheelchair, qualifies as a dark tower with flares burning at the top. You don't become a compressed mound, around here, until you lose sight of everything happening beyond your own body. When the body is all that's left for the brain to think about, doctors become the center of the universe. If Burnside did not cuss presidents, and chase women, and originate reams of originals and copies in the way of bullshit, he'd become a mound. I would myself, except, of course, nothing about me hurts except my walker which has four legs and thus more opportunity.

And who am I to judge? At this age everybody has his own pain and his own ghosts, or his own memories; and perhaps ghosts and memories are all the same. People wrap themselves in the past, spinning cocoons around pain. Memories insulate against the ice of death creeping upward from their feet, against eternal cold entering their veins. Men dream of childhood, of crystalline winters warm by woodstoves . . . although ice flowers form on windowpanes of the soul; and they dream of a cherry tree in blossom, and perhaps the welcoming smile of a girl they met but once, yet dreamed of always.

So who am I to judge? I'm just another dogface who rode the G.I. Bill. A dogface who became a high school history teacher who became retired, who became adjudged incapable of living alone; and maybe the judges were right. On the other hand I've seen Europe and Asia, and know how to run B.A.R.s, 30 m.m. m.g.s, mortars, and tests in American history given to teenagers equally endowed with hope and beauty and zits.

And nurse Johnson, who is she?

She's one of those dreamers for whom the world has no time. Let's call her early thirties, which is kindly, and beautiful which is true. She tucks her long hair up under her silly little cap, and walks long-legged through these halls in a way that makes you thankful for the memories of women. Her nose is a little too sharp for the cover of fashion magazines, and her look is too kindly to ever get her hired for television. Her eyes are hazel, her mouth generous, her body enticingly slight. She moves like a girl when she's happy, and the soul of tiredness when she's not. Nurse Johnson cares too much about her job, and is going to burn out. I hope she holds on until Burnside passes. Burnside claims to have spent his whole life in debauchery, and nurse Johnson, who is his greatest challenge, should also be his last sight when leaving this vale.

And thus, in the ranks of heaven, is nurse Johnson a one-ring Warrant Officer, which is just enough gold braid to sing alto in the chorus of the Lord.

"It's these fast machines," Burnside said to me and patted his wheelchair. "They always get the girls." To nurse Johnson he said, "Sergeant Ross was just leaving."

Johnson stood beside the bed where I sat, smiled a sad little smile, and pretended to ignore Burnside. "The dayroom's in an uproar. You guys did something that upset everybody. What?" Her hair is kind of dishwater blond, but gleamy. It fluffs and softens the effect of that sharp little nose.

"Nothing much," I lied. "Burnside told a couple sea stories. Corporal Harvey kicked. Burnside sang something about Minnie the Moocher. Burnside's the man you want." No good could come from telling any nurse about an infestation of ghosts.

I hate to see so much sorrow in a face, and Johnson's reflected about as much sorrow as anyone could bear. She can't get it through her head that being dead is not that big a deal. Toward the end Harvey's pain out-paced the drugs. He was bed-ridden. He wouldn't put up with spending his life in bed, nor would I, nor would Burnside . . . at least not alone.

"He left messages for you both," she said. "I liked corporal Harvey, even if he did hang out with you guys." Johnson should work in a maternity ward, not with geriatrics. "Minnie the Moocher," she said to me. "Do you guys ever tell the truth?"

"On Sundays."

"Or when it don't cost a red cent," Burnside said. "Sergeant Ross is cheap, but I know how to show a girl a good time." As he spoke he kept looking around like a man searching the jungle for snipers. His Japanese ghost would probably not show up with a nurse nearby, but with ghosts who can tell?

"Both of you are going to hate this, or at least I think you are." Nurse Johnson's mouth held just the littlest bit of a sad smile. Her eyelids were a little blinky, a little teary. It came to me that maybe we're more to her than pluses or minuses on a nurse's score sheet. On the other hand, no sense getting too emotional.

"Corporal Harvey understands why the Buddha smiles," she said to me. "He told me to say that to you. He also told me that he has been instructed not to explain it to you." She turned to Burnside, and she sort of bit her lower lip.

I tipped and nearly fell off the edge of the bed. Nurse Johnson was flipping it right back at us. Men dying of cancer do not leave final messages. Men dying of cancer live in great caverns of pain, caverns illumed with the unrighteous fires of infernos real as those of Dante. Men dying of cancer writhe internally, the violence and chaos of tumor overreaching any last intelligence. Pain becomes pure, probably, and maybe such purity has something to do with the Buddha, but sure as hell men don't talk about it.

"And for sergeant Burnside," nurse Johnson said, "and I quote verbatim: Harvey said, 'Get off your goldbrickin' butt and find an honest job.'"

"Got the last word didn't he?" Burnside's voice filled with admiration even as he continued to scout the room. "Harvey always could pile it on." Burnside was not exactly distracted, but his attention went toward shadows in corners, or any other place that might hide visions and worries from the past.

I sort of blinked at nurse Johnson, and she sort of winked at me. Burnside sat between us, and Burnside was stupidly buying every ounce of it. I figured this day marked a turning point in nurse Johnson's career. This was bigger than Paul Bunyan. She had just bullshitted the most noted purveyor of b.s. ever to appear in the history of the American West.

=

For three days the geriatric ward fell back into the drone of routine, except for occasional sorties by TV stiffs. The lads, and two lasses, made tracks to the back windows of this wing beyond which lies Memorial Gardens, the military cemetery, or, as Burnside puts it, The Old Soldier's Home.

Burnside and I went as well, but we did not settle for looking out the windows. We inched through the doorway, onto a concrete terrace, and looked over the terrain. It was not a position I'd wish to defend, and not a position I'd wish to take. From a tactical point of view it's an infantryman's nightmare.

There's a narrow strip of lawn bordering the terrace, then a narrow cemetery with gleaming markers running crosswise the hill; as if some wiseacre had pasted a decorated bandage on nature. At the lower edge of the cemetery there's third growth forest, gently sloping over desolate ground, the last undeveloped area. Beyond the forest a rickety footbridge spans a ravine, and, when across the bridge and at the bottom of the hill, there lies the remnants of a Victorian park. The park was once a place where ladies and gentlemen strolled, and where children played. When this hospital went military in the long ago, something happened down there. Maybe it became off limits. Maybe the darkness we've but lately noticed has dwelt in that park among shadows of neglect. The covered bandstand is broken, the roof cracked, the steps rotted. Ornamental iron fences are rusted, and ornamental trees stand unpruned, while hedges are overgrown. From a distance, though, it still looks like a spot of sanity in all that desolation.

No one goes there anymore, not even to cut firewood. Our V.A. ghosts don't go there. If it is a haunted wood, a haunted park, a haunted spot of history, then it's haunted by something more hideous than ghosts, and more dangerous than guns. This hospital has its safe side, with roads and lawns. It has this dark side, dark nearly to black, empty of life. Not even a bird chirps, and the only way you could defend that position would be with light artillery. If you attacked it you would get nothing but tree bursts from mortars.

Burnside and I, along with the resurrected TV stiffs, gazed across rows of glowing white cemetery stones beneath the flowing flag of a great nation. We gazed toward the forest, the ravine, then toward a city that once exported food and manufactures to the world, a city that now exports only noise and entertainment; and imports everything else. Not one of the TV stiffs, viewing that lordly flag and chronically troubled city, had enough gumption to rub his crotch.

"There's more to tell about that kid," I later said to Burnside, reminding him about his Japanese ghost.

"He was young, and I made him dead. You'll recall there was a war goin' on. I was only young. I figured to score information about the enemy. I went through his pockets." Burnside motioned upward to the remnants of the Japanese battle flag. "They carried these personal battle flags. He can have it back. I only use it to get the girls. Women can't resist that kind of accomplishment." Burnside's voice seemed a little forced, like he was having a hard time spreading it; and that was another first.

Change filled the air like low-grade electricity. Everyone, except those in the final stages of senility—and maybe even those—could sense that the far side put together its own routine.

Shadows drifted along the walls, although nothing solid enough to cause a shadow appeared. Murmurs hovered behind everyone's ears, little whispers from the past. After the first day, newsreels began running in our minds, newsreels of the passing parade, a parade of history and war. I heard voices of people dead and gone, some of them loved, and some despised. I heard mutters of cannonade rumbling behind broken horizons. I heard terrified squalling of children, heard the voice of the enemy speaking crackling kraut language; and I heard the sobbing of women, because, yes, it is possible to sob in German.

I heard again, sounds from the invasion of Europe and sounds from emplacements in Korea. Burnside heard things a little differently. Being ambitious, Burnside tried to square away the whole Pacific theatre before doing occupation duty in Japan.

"I always feared you were a little feeble-minded," he told me, "but never thought you'd run around with someone who's hearing things. You're a nut case, Ross."

Meanwhile, routine droned right along. Nurse Johnson remained busy, distracted, continually ignoring the pain of her job as she tried to reduce swelling in lives around her. Nurse Johnson heard no ghosts and saw none, perhaps being too busy. Routine sustained her and steadied us; and this is the way routine runs, even in a geriatric ward invaded from the other world as—we may assume—most of them are.

Day begins at four AM when pain pills wear off. Very old people sleep but indifferently. We wake and wrestle whatever greets us, be it suppurating sores, or unknit bones. From four until six most lie in the stupor of half dreams. Voices from the past congregate, argue, complain about our attitudes. Brothers, long dead, appear as in their youth. They bandy jokes, or present intense situations that never really happened, but could have if everyone had been smarter at the time. Fathers cuss and mothers explain. Sometimes a favorite aunt appears . . . but, sometimes, the hours between four and six breed monsters. Men see faces: of people they have killed, or women they betrayed.

At six AM pill time begins. Lights up. The stage opens to the day's comedy—or tragedy if that be the will of the Lord. At six a.m. everyone coughs a lot, and if one is destined to die choking, the odds are best around six. Pills run the range of the pharmacopoeia. Drugs take on personalities. Most are plebeian, some even duller, but some are simply splendid. Some drugs cause dreams to run a riff, a coda, a trumpet ride like Ziggy Elman playing *And The Angels Sing*.

Burnside, with a big reputation for going off on his own initiative, and being independent as a hog on ice, waits for no nurse or orderly. He has a system of stainless steel pulleys rigged over his bed. It's like living next door to a circus. Still, it's tough to see him swing here and there. The man would have made a fine elf or gremlin or leprechaun, or even a grown-up pixie, and he's reduced to swinging like an ape. He lowers himself into his seat and heads for the latrine, the tattered battle flag like a broken sun above that rolling chair.

Breakfast comes at seven. You can take it in your room or hit the chow line at the cafeteria. Among geriatrics the chow line carries a message: line up here and tell the world you're still kicking.

Our troops break bread in the company of younger patients, guys in their 40s to 60s who have their own specters, but who were not seeing ours. These are leftovers from later wars. Nearly all are cripples, and not a few are crazy. I wouldn't trust a one with rubber bands and paper clips, leave alone a dull knife.

Physical therapy starts at 8:30 and lasts until you drop, which in most cases is 8:45. Burnside doesn't need it. His jaw works just elegant, and his legs are nearly ready to fall off, anyway. He gets plenty of wholesome push and pull from that chair. "I'd get a Harley," he complains, "but they don't build 'em."

Doctors pull rounds from ten to lunch. They detail hip replacements, spinal taps, and 'ectomies to rearrange the innards. The docs make time-tested jokes, and are capable of their own b.s. After all, what are wars created for?

"Other hospitals ain't this nice," Burnside explains to anyone who bitches. "In Japan the nurses are all dykes. In England the docs sound like Mortimer Snerd. In Frogland . . ." he then rolls his eyes and tries to appear lewd ". . . which is why DeGaulle had that tremendous big nose. DeGaulle was damn popular."

Before lunch, and especially during uncertain days, we grab the Jim Beam, 'have a little sip' as Louis Armstrong used to say, then chase the whiskey with a bowl of soup. "It ain't like South Dakota," Burnside explains. "Back on the farm we never drank after four AM." Burnside credits South Dakota as the place that made him famous. After putting in his time, and drawing retirement from Uncle Sugar, he went back home. "The only available job in all of South Dakota was with a porta-pot outfit." He worked and really strived. In just three months he got promoted to head poop.

After lunch and a nap, some patients receive visitors, be they relatives or social workers or church ladies or a chaplain. Some visitors bring photos of great grandchildren, as if anyone here pretended to give a hang for the precious tykes, or photos of great-great grandchildren who will not need this ward until the back half of the next century. Visitors talk valentine talk. I listen and imagine those kiddies as they will become, dressed in spandex uniforms, lasers at the ready, enduring fleabites as they crawl through mud, or lie chilled and sleeping on frozen tundra. I imagine them in trenches along some MLR, huddled behind a super sonic zap gun, and they have their shod feet tucked in sleeping bags to avoid going lame from freezing. Enjoy your childhoods, youngsters, because as long as there are humans there'll always be the Infantry.

Burnside and I ran our visitors away more than a year ago, old age being a private occupation—and at the time we thought our reasons made sense. I honestly told my visitors to shove off, but Burnside waxed eloquent. He pretended to discover religion. His wheelchair became a pulpit. He preached, favoring Moses and Abraham, and Burnside scared himself half to death. He ran his visitors away all right, but among the TV stiffs he actually made a convert, a gunner's mate named Hawkins who was, anyway, on his road to glory. "Packed him off to heaven," Burnside mumbled, ". . . no good deed goes unpunished . . . stars in my crown . . ." The power of the Word scared the living bejesus out of Burnside, and that's the truth of it.

Visitors leave by mid afternoon, and then arrives The Hour of Charm. Until ghosts got into it, this was the hour of apparitions sliding just on the edge of perception. We could almost see days of our youth, hear the clatter of new model T Fords, or the very first singing commercial from the domed cathedral of a radio aglow with vacuum tubes. We listened as fathers and uncles bulled widely about World War I, while grandfathers flipped b.s. about Gettysburg and Shiloh, or Cuba, or the last of the Indian wars. The Hour of Charm brought a rustle of cornfields beneath midwest sun, the whisper of great rivers: the Mississippi, the Ohio, the Columbia; the heartbeat of a nation's land, salt soil, mountain, prairie, thin fields of cotton, hardwood forests.

Everything changed as ghosts put together their own lash up. Burnside's Nipponese soldier was first, but not alone. By the third day our ghosts had their drill down pat. The far side stepped forward as a Burnside story progressed:

Burnside parked in the dayroom and told how his uncle Henry saved a church after its congregation came up busted. The preacher buried uncle Henry in a likely field, then called the field a church cemetery and free of tax. As prices rose he sold the field, moved uncle Henry to another field . . . ". . . and Unc tax-exempted more land through the years than Alexander the Great. The preacher finally quit when the coffin wore out. Unc was holding up just fine . . ."

At that point doors and windows opened. They moved methodically, not slow, but no snap to it either. Some doors and windows were real, and real weather blew like a natural broom through the geriatric ward. From the freeway came rain-ridden breeze carrying car fumes. Puget Sound contributed a little whiff of salt, and northwest mist became a sheen of moisture touching us like a thin coat of protecting fur.

Nurses closed windows, hissed at orderlies who closed doors, and staff had Burnside singled out for blame before the last breeze choked. Burnside, caught mid story, sat blinking, silent, his tale-spinning out of balance as surrealism took over; because another door opened in the center of the dayroom, and this was a door of tribulation through which only we geriatrics could pass. Staff saw nothing.

The door opened on a scene, like rushes for a movie in which no one would want to star. An enormous room lay before us, and ranks of coffins shone dull and black before the backdrop of night. Silence as profound as eternity lay within that night. Silence resonated with power, silence that could be broken only by some mighty force, because the power of that silence swallowed all ordinary sound.

This was death, or at least part of it. Silence and darkness surrounded frail boxes containing remains even more frail. No spirits lay enclosed there, only corpses embraced by that greatest of all silences, embraced by final darkness.

Nurse Johnson sat as the single mourner, and her low sobs were the only sounds powerful enough to break that silence. Her face was barely composed, her lips trembly as they moved in prayers or confusion, her eyes red from weeping. She seemed such a small figure huddled before eternal night. We sensed her confusion, her loneliness, failure, sorrow; and we knew that each of us in that dayroom rested in one of those coffins. We knew the future by recognizing we were the past.

Nurse Johnson is a very good kid in a very bad world. We fight pain with pain, but she does not understand that, and sometimes it doesn't work all that well, anyway. The coffins sent a message, or seemed to, and the message needed figuring because it said: Take care of this young one, and maybe you are not lost. There is one more job to do. Figure it out, you sergeants and corporals and warrants. You once stirred the depths of history the way bakers stir cake mix. Get it figured, Jerks.

The enormous room, standing before eternal dark, now became shaded as if night pulled the curtain on dreams as well as life. Light drained into dusk, and movement began among the coffins. They did not open so much as they peeled away, like the droop of decaying flowers. The coffins vanished and we, the congregated souls of the V.A. geriatric ward, lay coffinless. Old bodies stretched frail as tissue across bones fragile as the frame of a child's kite. We, a museum of the dead, lay in diminishing light. Then, sinking into darkness, our bodies disappeared and only a touch of light remained, like a wisp of smoke above dead faces; old faces; closed eyes behind which lay departed hope. The curtain of dark came down. Our faces vanished. The only sound to register through eternal night was the sound of nurse Johnson sobbing.

II

"Come out of it. Please do." She gently shook my shoulder, because she is used to dealing with frail things. Nurse Johnson stood beside me as, it seemed, half the staff of this enormous place flurried around the dayroom. Shocked patients muttered to themselves, or turned toward each other with looks of belief, not disbelief; and belief had us running scared. Even senility cases looked in touch, and no damn quarrels started over what was illusion and what was real. People looked at each other, and silent messages passed. Nobody had seen anything. Pass it on. Make it clear even to those dumb Marines. Semper Fi, jarheads. Zip your lip and your fly. Shut down the detail.

"It's okay," I whispered to her. "At least I think it is." When she takes my wrist for a pulse, or Burnside's wrist, her touch is firm but gentle. When she's troubled her touch is that of a woman who loves. I do not say 'lover,' but one who gently—whether motherly or sisterly or even as a lover—touches with perfect knowledge of how affection is shown. At such times Burnside stops his mouth with stutters. He turns a shade once known as panty pink, which is the most blood he can summon for a blush.

When she takes my wrist I remember my first young love. Years shrug away like scabs from the skinned knees of youth. I feel weak as a ten-year-old who coasts his Western Flyer into a tree.

"We had hallucinations," I whispered. "It happens among cripples and sad sacks. I blame it on the New Deal. I even blame it on Eleanor. There was a time back in Indiana when we let the cats out . . ." Then I began to mumble. Nurse Johnson is used to geriatrics wandering in their minds, but she's also accustomed to me and Burnside.

"Don't do this," she told me. "Dementia is bad enough when it's real."

I would never say 'bullshit' in front of a lady. "After Harvey passed you kidded Burnside," I whispered. "Did it help?"

She whispered back. "Are we really talking? Are you serious?" Her whisper is like dandelion down riding warm breezes. Where was this woman when I was her age and lonely? Not born yet. Ships pass, and I would rather die than put up with being young again. Since that's what's going to happen my attitude is wholesome. At the same time, ships pass in history and not just on ponds.

"I'm serious," I said. "You conned Burnside. Did it help you? Not, did it help Burnside, or me. Did it help you?"

"It made me sad. It was fun for a minute, and then it made me sad."

That was not the answer I expected, and sure as gospel didn't want.

"All suffering is wrong," she said. "Dog suffering is wrong. Even bug suffering is wrong." She struggled with some sort of nursish ethics, and decided in my case to make an exception. "Corporal Harvey . . ." She honestly choked, a genuine chokeup.

"It hurt him." I tried to make my voice kind. "It's supposed to hurt. Part of the rules."

Around us staff moved with the caution of a combat patrol. They whispered to patients, and glanced at doors and windows. V.A. hospitals are not supposed to be weird. They are supposed to be palaces of dependability, dull as prunes.

"You beat the Bible," I told her. "The Bible gives us three score and ten. You helped Harvey make it for ten years beyond that." I stopped. She did not want to hear that. Her thoughts lay elsewhere.

"His spirit died," she said almost timidly. "Something awful is chasing you guys."

I sat frozen. Someone turned up volume on the television. Soap is soap, but terror has some shape to it. Around me staff settled patients back into manageable routine, and patients looked at each other with unspoken promises to talk as soon as we got rid of staff.

Something awful chased us. It was not only what Johnson said, but the way she said it. Something awful.

Memories flashed. We once had our m.g.s dug in on hill seven-twenty in Korea, losing more men from freeze than from enemy fire. Ice. Snow. Blood on snow. Chinese corpses lay strewn across roads and fields and ditches like seed, frozen, mouths open, ice on their teeth. Here and there smoke plumes rose where our troops burned farmer's houses in order to stay alive. Oil on the m.g.s froze, making their action sluggish. Hill seven-twenty spelled hell on earth. Nurse Johnson talked about something worse.

Nurse Johnson is a kid, but a kid with experience. She hasn't seen as many men die as I have, because that would amount to several, but she may have seen a couple dozen. If Harvey died differently she would know. I shuddered before a chill. I sat feeble and helpless. My teeth clicked.

Hill seven-twenty was a comfort because you knew that for the rest of your life you would never be more miserable. This was different. We now spoke of something after death, and my chill came because of Johnson's words, and because ghosts waved goodbye. Burnside said those goodbyes made him uneasy. I wish to God I could settle for 'uneasy.'

"I'm not a preacher," I told her. "What do you mean, 'spirit?'"

"I'm not a preacher either, but when corporal Harvey died nothing happened. Nothing."

"I don't read you."

"Absolutely nothing."

"You were tired."

"Absolutely nothing."

When men die they sort of expire, assuming they are not blown to bits. Something happens. The person leaves. Nothing romantic about it, nothing impressive. They just go until they stop, and then stop. Sometimes the body ticks on for a second or seconds. The point is, no matter how minuscule, something always happens. There is a stepping off, a final sigh or choke or spasm. Always. When you turn out a light bulb you are aware that light departs. It goes quick, but there is a 'going away.' Same with men who die.

And with Harvey nothing happened. Something nailed him before he could give a final shrug. I mourned Harvey for exactly two seconds, and would mourn more later—if there was going to be a 'later.'

Nurse Johnson trembled. "I should keep quiet when I don't know what I'm talking about."

In general that's true, because it stands her in the ranks of the rest of the world, but in this case it wasn't true. "You did me a favor," I told her. "Maybe you did all of us a favor. Will you help me to my room?"

Helplessness is the lousiest of lousy feelings. Around here we pretend independence, but could not defend ourselves against a bouncing puppy; and at our age a bouncing puppy can kill. One stumble, one fall. The clock was running. If something popped Harvey, it waited to pop us. We had little time for defense, were physically capable of squat. This would take brains, and half the brains in this asylum are covered with dust.

Ghosts accompanied us as nurse Johnson led me to my room, wispy ghosts who made no points. These were people I never knew or even shot at. They were vaguely oriental, maybe Malay, and small but pretty. They went nervously about their business, but even in these polished halls I could smell, like an echo, the sharp scent of cordite. If they were Malay the cordite likely came from Japanese artillery. These Malays sort of chirped in that soft, island language that seems all vowels, and nurse Johnson led me through packs of them. You can get used to anything.

I wondered what Burnside saw, and waited in the room knowing he would come a-rolling any minute. Nurse Johnson parked me, patted my shoulder with a gentle hand, and went about her business.

Ghosts passed before me, around me, and it really didn't matter. They are around us, always, and we pay no attention. These are spirits of the past, and the past is friendly. The reason to understand history is not to avoid the mistakes of history— because some fool will make those mistakes for you. Some maniac will start a war, and some other maniac will drop an atom bomb, and you'll be the poor bastard who gets to drop the bomb or be hit by it.

No, you understand history so you can understand yourself.

When Burnside wheeled into the room he looked like a man who needed the chaplain. His chair moved slowly, the tattered battle flag not lifted by any breeze, and Burnside was a man who had the crap knocked out of him. He swung into bed like he aimed to stay for the duration. Not a good sign.

He turned on his side. Then he fidgeted, didn't like the idea, turned on his back and stared at the ceiling. He didn't like that either, so he sat up and did some truly magnificent cussing. He swore quietly, like a man talking to a jammed carbine while fearing the enemy is in the neighborhood and close. He didn't repeat a word. It was stupendous cussing. Inspired.

". . . like a garage sale at a mortuary," he said finally. "Ross, we're boogered on this one. We got a Chinaman's chance in Tokyo, that's what we got."

I didn't contradict, but if ghosts wanted to nail us, why bother to get elaborate? Our ghosts seemed trying to help.

"They're trying to tell us something," I said to Burnside. I did not say anything about Harvey. No reason to send Burnside into deeper funk. "Plus," I told him, "other ghosts seem trying to help. Your Japanese kid was never on staff around here before."

From beyond the doorway the hall filled with murmurs, and from the dayroom a voice raised in a thin cry. One of the senility boys sang ". . . you don't know what lonesome is 'til you get to herdin' cows . . ." followed by, "here's to the captain, here's to the crew, and here's to the girls . . ." and somebody hushed him.

"I copped my first feel, at least the first feel I remember, when I was six." Burnside seemed about to become senile himself. Either that, or this was more b.s. I waited for a Burnside story—waited for the end of the world—for the dead to rise—for the second coming—for a face-to-face with whatever dark evil waited to axe our spirits.

"... there was no call to kill that kid," Burnside whispered. "We could have worked something out. We could have both kept running." His voice became harsh and controlled, the kind of voice a noncom uses when he reads out a total screwup. We take pride in not feeling sorry for ourselves, but Burnside took it a little too far. He had bullshitted around this issue for his whole life, and now the b.s. didn't work. He would not be talking harsh if he was not eating away on guilt. You'd think, after all these years, the Japanese kid would be at peace. You'd think Burnside would have come to terms with it. Instead he sat, wiped, totally blown out of town.

"Shish kata ga nai. It can't be helped," I said to him. "It was a fatality, a fatalism. Forget it."

"He was skinny at the time," Burnside said in a voice just above a whisper. "They were on short rations. Skinny and sick and dirty in that crappy way you only get in jungles. He had diarrhea. Even after he died."

The kid looked better as a ghost. Clean uniform, healthy smile. Death seemed to agree with him. I wasn't proud of the way I thought. There is b.s. and there is sick b.s. I whispered, "Good luck, soldier."

"You know how it goes," Burnside said. "He maybe wasn't the first, but he was the worst. Dammit, Ross."

I knew what he meant. I also owned problems in that line, but didn't want to think about them ... and thanks for the memories.

"Both of you were wrong," I told Burnside, "especially him. He was a soldier who acted like a priest. He sentenced you to life. You lived it. He didn't. You're both kicked in your ornaments." Some kind of flak erupted in the dayroom. A quavery voice began reciting poetry in the sing-song-y manner of school kids. The guy tried a passage from *The Wreck of the Hesperus*. Memorized in about sixth grade. He got it wrong, but mostly right.

"I'm so damn popular," Burnside said, "because I overcharge and do poor work." He lay down, turned his back to me. "If something's gonna happen, let it."

Men sometimes acted this way in Korea. Temperatures dropped. Chinese artillery pounded. Chinese attacked. They came in swarms, and there did not seem enough explosive in the world to stop them. After the heat of attack, and as sweat began to freeze deep in our clothes, a man might climb into his sleeping bag where he would not be warm but could keep from freezing. And, the man became pupa, determined not to hatch. Men did that when they gave up. You couldn't even kick them out of those bags. Men died in attacks because they lay snugged in, refusing that last ration of hell the world so generously served.

"I got a problem," I said to Burnside. "I don't have the strength to club your sorry butt."

He grunted. "I know a guy," he mumbled, "that when he dies is going to have his ashes sprinkled on a farm in South Dakota."

". . . a thumbnail history of the Japanese on Guadalcanal," I told him. "Courage, combined with stupidity, does not make successful soldiers. Think about that before you check out." Here he was, talking about his ashes while I'm sweating his spirit.

Still, it was spirit. One man, one vote.

I sensed movement in the far corner of the room. Mist slowly gathered, and movement in the mist did not seem occidental. If our ghosts tried to help then Burnside lay as perfect fodder. The mist might contain a clot of Burnside's personal ghosts. I didn't say a word. Just shuffled away on legs not exactly inspired, but feeling less worse than usual. The Japanese kid, and maybe an entire slew of ghosts, formed up to do a number on Burnside. Either ghosts are a metaphor for history, or history is a metaphor for ghosts.

=

Nurse Johnson would think I was a real gad-a-bout. I moved back toward the dayroom feeling grim. Absolute Evil exists. As kids we geriatrics learned all about it, and no damn social worker had better come along and blame 'evil' on 'conditions.' Evil is a force in the universe, a force using any weakness it finds to do its dirt; and with Evil, Hell is just a sideline.

My mind sorrowed. Harvey had been snatched. He was an old, old soldier, but inside him lived a spirit that was blithe. If his spirit lay hostage, or destroyed, even ghostland took a loss.

Besides, Harvey was a good friend. We weep no tears, knowing he would be too proud of us to weep for us. Still, there are such things as invisible tears. Nurse Johnson weeps them, as well as the other kind.

And then there is nurse Johnson, a good kid in a bad world. Her world reeks with folk who hold no beliefs, or cheap beliefs; people who hope, when they die, to report to Saint Peter with clean bowels. They worry about cholesterol while their kids shoot each other down in the streets.

Nurse Johnson lives in a nation that whines over self-inflicted wounds while claiming itself a victim. At least the people I walked toward did not have minds filled with that kind of shinola. Like everyone else we are filled with a certain amount of crap, but not *that* crap.

. . . something feathered around my mind, almost like the touch of inspiration portrayed in Victorian pictures, or the whisper of someone long dead who wanted to pass me a tip. I almost understood our final act, and why we must act. Then the feathery thing went away. I started counting backward from 100; it's the classic test to see if you've got Alzheimer's. The feathery notion might return, because 99 went to 98, and so forth . . .

Evil uses Hell as a parking lot, and you don't have to die to park. Evil sets people in the middle of war, famine, excess prosperity, or other of Hell's appurtenances, then stands back as people freeze or sizzle; and screw themselves. The main interest of Evil is destruction of faith in gods and ethics, knowledge and honor. When faith is destroyed people create their own hells, and a sign stretches across the universe writ large for all to see. It reads: The Future Is Cancelled.

Maybe it was not simply our spirits at risk, because, as the world turns, faith these days is doing hard time. Maybe nurse Johnson, and all the other fine people I didn't know, but who must be in the world, were at risk. When faith is destroyed, what happens to those who are faithful to their trust? I tottered along figuring that if evil was after me I could stand it, but if it came for nurse Johnson then this pilgrim was pissed.

No sound came from behind me, but ahead sounded a mixture of querulous voices. Mortar fire, properly timed, sounds like tearing paper, and so did the voices. Distance to the dayroom is sixty feet. At flank speed I could have made it in two minutes, but my own ghosts picked that moment.

I leaned against a wall and found myself looking down at a misted valley-plain of rice paddies, and for once I owned the high ground. Rocks lay scattered around a low crest of hills. Behind me rose a stark mountain blasted black by gunfire. My squad had our light thirties dug in across a broad ridge in Korea, early in the war. I watched the plain, watched ground mist rise from the paddies, and knew this was a rerun. I fought against doing this twice, because no one sane would want to do it once.

Five white specks appeared in the distance and moved toward me. I knew them, did not know their names. They were patriarchs, five old men dressed in white, men who should have died in the quiet security of their homes, surrounded by sons and daughters and grandchildren. They were men who had once been the man I would become, old, not wise, but smart for their day and time.

They moved slowly through mist, as reluctant as I to again confront madness. In mist behind them, like on a movie screen, rose pictures of a few faces of Hell; reels of Pathay News, the March of Time; buildings breaking beneath artillery, walls crumbling about women and children crouching in cellars. And from the far, far distance, far at sea, tattered life jackets still afloat, bobbing, the heads of sailors so thriftily held above the waves now turned to bleached and polished skulls.

The old Koreans moved toward me. Armbands with Korean writing showed them as Rok, Republic of Korea, allies. Two carried old-fashioned, long-barreled squirrel rifles, because there were bandits in these mountains. The other three walked with staffs. As they approached they smiled, but that is not the way it went the first time. The first time went like this:

My squad dug in behind a low ridge overlooking a valley. We had a long, thin line not well armed. We did not have enough men across a broad front, and North Koreans banzaied one section of the line, then another. They kept it up all afternoon. We stacked them up like cordwood, and they stacked us.

Night came down moonless, darker than the bottom of a nighttime sea. Only our ears hinted at movement in the valley.

From far, far away an occasional moan or sigh sounded as dying men lay alone, because neither side of the line so much as wiggled. There might be wounded out there, or it might be a trick.

The North Koreans hit again at midnight. They banzaied the left of our line, then banzaied again. Night came alive with tracers, and action rolled beneath flares as our mortars illuminated the valley. The attack was too far to our left to mean anything, except indignation. The attack made so much noise we could not tell what might gather right in front of us.

I froze to the pistol grip of the m.g. We heard nothing. No flares danced overhead. Night seemed concentrated, pointed, directed at our very sanity. Night seemed ready to explode with oriental voices, faces, the screams of a mindless horde, hell-a-poppin', Hell incarnate.

Then, to our left, the second attack stopped. Flares snuffed, darkness returned. The valley once more seemed covered with the dying.

"My momma didn't raise me to be a ground pounder," one of our guys whispered, "so what are we doin' . . ." and then he shut up.

Slightly to our right and so close as to seem underfoot, a noise clicked. Wood on rock, like a rifle butt carried too low. To my right the other m.g. opened at that first snick of sound. Riflemen fired blindly, hysteric. I fired like one insane, like a man trying to kill the night, finally forcing my finger off the trigger before the barrel melted.

From right in front of us came a cry, "Ai-gue! Ai-gue!" Then a torrent of words, and then a single voice, "Ai-gue! Ai-gue!" I burned the rest of the ammo belt, the m.g. bouncing like a mad instrument as I rose, trying to get further depression. The voice sobbed. "Ai-gue. Ai-gue."

"*Do* that sonovabitch," someone yelled. "For Chrissake stop the noise."

One of our guys hopped over the ridge, stumbled, then emptied a carbine in the direction of the voice. Silence. Silence. We shivered until dawn.

Korean bodies are no more remarkable than Chinese bodies, but they wear different clothes. As first light crept across the sky lumps of white shone nearly luminescent on the downhill slope.

Light gathered to show the banzai attack we fought so hysteri-
cally was no attack at all. Five old men, two nearly headless from
repeated hits, lay with white beards running red. White clothing
shone black-stained with drying blood. The corpses lay small and
tangled. They lay like the death of history.

Our company commander appeared through morning mist,
checking the line, doing his job. He looked over the ridge, looked
at the corpses, said, "Musta been one whale of a fight," and walked
on down the line. We sat fully ashamed, wondering 'what the hell,'
when along came a corpsman who knew a little Korean. He said
'Ai-gue! Ai-gue!' means 'My Lord. My Lord.'

=

Now they stood before me. Koreans are taller than most Orientals,
and these old men stood straight but not stiff. I leaned against the
wall, waited, wondering if this was going to be death or a dry run.

They waited as well. Very polite, but not Jap polite. Koreans take
a different fix on good behavior.

"Don't think I haven't thought about it," I told them, and did
not know whether words ran from my mouth or only from my
thought. "You guys were probably trying to cut a deal for your
village. Maybe with us, maybe with the North. You carried two
flags, depending on which army was in your neighborhood, and
you did it to protect your kids."

They smiled. Koreans are not inscrutable, at least not when
they're being honest. One nodded. I actually saw them relax, like a
sense of relief swept over them.

"And you heard all that fighting to our left, so you skirted the
action around the base of that ridge." I watched them. So far, so
good. They watched me with interest. "But your mistake was to
move at night. You could not tell where the lines were dug in."

The tallest one framed the word, 'anio,' 'no,' with his mouth. No
sound. Just the shape of the word.

"Then you had to move at night?"

The mouth framed 'neh,' 'yes.'

"Then you were the advance . . ." I broke off, knowing after all
these years, why those men suddenly appeared under our guns.

Their entire village must have been fleeing south. The enfiladed valley could not be crossed. These old men led, trying to find a way across the ridge and onto the mountain before the sun rose over their women and children. Their young men would have been gone, pressed into service by the North, or held prisoner by the Allies.

"I pray your people made it," I said, "and I honor you."

They turned to look across the valley where people worked in rice paddies, where farmers' houses sat small and distinct, and where raised paths carried the normal traffic of normal living. I heard music few occidentals can really understand, saw forms and shapes of costumes and dress, saw children sitting beside grandmothers. I saw old-fashioned cities, quiet streets, small shops, colorful flags and ornaments and decorations—life before machine guns, before communism and capitalism and the ambition of generals.

And then the scene changed as across the valley rolled a totality of darkness. It came crashing like a tidal wave, and, churning like a wave in the darkness, were flashes of neon, the static of electronics, the buzz and hiss and crackle of a brave new world. The old men stood facing the surge and thump of modern times. They stood squarely, waiting the approach of darkness, then stepped toward the darkness for all the world like men headed into an all-out fight. Darkness rolled toward them, the valley disappeared, and the scene faded, dispersed; and I found myself leaning against a hospital wall and pointed toward the dayroom.

It was about as much action as this child could take. I inched forward looking for a chair, even one before a TV. I would park my carcass and take a blow. Unreal spooks lived on television, electronic spooks with names and haircuts; mindless noise. It wouldn't be the same but it might be restful. I wondered how Burnside made out back in our room. I wondered if Burnside's ghosts were having any luck. I halfway wished he would show up.

In the dayroom patterns of light swirled, illuminated faces, cast shadows; and nothing looked restful. Light danced phantasmic as aurora borealis, flashing across old faces, wattled necks, scraggly limbs. Where normal light should fall through large windows, darkness glowered. Oppressive gloom lay beyond those windows.

Even as I watched gloom fell to darkness, impenetrable, empty, deep as reaches of space. Black was not simply a presence, but an aggressive absence of light. It backgrounded weirdly illuminated figures of my companions, made them into pictures surreal as effusions of Dalí—fearsome as improbable laughter issuing from the depths of mausoleums.

Each person in that dayroom was surrounded by his own ghosts. Ghosts of the enemy mixed with ghosts of the Allies. Reinforcements seemed to be coming in from everywhere. I wondered if this was a last bastion, a place of some fateful and final resolution. I lined myself up in the direction of a chair and putzed forward. I heard the swish of a wheelchair.

"Be thankful for baldheaded people," Burnside said. "Ross, I got a problem." He wheeled his chair in front of me, twirled a couple of circles, and Burnside's mouth might be tossing a minor load of b.s., but the line across that mouth was firm. The old sarge was back on top of things.

"You're looking better," I told him. "Have you gained weight, or have you done something with your hair?" It was obvious that Burnside's ghosts had given him some sort of reason to quit pouting.

". . . getting stuff settled with that kid. It cheered him somewhat." Burnside looked around the dayroom. ". . . like old home week at the pearly gates," he muttered. He watched some of the action, shook his head; steered his chair between me and the goings-on like a machine gunner covering a retreat. "The Good Book says 'This too shall pass,' and I've found that's always true, except in the case of gallstones."

"Welcome back," I told him and found a chair. The TV bubbled mindlessly as I watched the dayroom. What with all the silent messages between ghosts and geriatrics, what I saw was wild and less than wonderful—like a Chinese fire drill—the Greek air force—the Estonian navy.

Mostly what I saw was blood and neon, history and the present, everything mixed; and, as everything mixed, darkness grew as people and ghosts became diminutive. We were getting cut down to size by darkness—and where it came from—what it wanted—I could not tell.

"Did you ever hate anybody you were shooting at?" It was a dumb question in Burnside's mouth, the kind of question an old soldier is not supposed to ask. There are standard attitudes toward the enemy, and old soldiers are supposed to know them.

I was still pretty shaken up. My breath came fast and shallow. "Only when they shot back." That was not strictly true. I did not hate the standard Kraut or standard North Korean, but the German S.S. would never rest peaceful in my mind.

"Because," Burnside mused, "they were just dog soldiers. Doing a job. Nothing to get hateful about."

Either Burnside suffered a conversion, and angelic wings were about to whisk him to heavenly realms and walls of gold, or else his ghosts told him something that made him confidential. He talked about pretty personal stuff.

"The Bataan death march," I told him. "So much for your dog soldiers."

"You're a man of many parts, though somewhat scattered. Don't crap me about the Far East."

What I know about the Far East mostly has to do with broken cities and broken bodies. I did not spend time on R&R, and did not spend time on occupation. "History itself is scattered," I said, "and don't crap me about Bataan. I reckon you've been in touch with the far side."

We watched the dayroom, the encroaching dark, as the show began to fade. Geriatrics stood wiped out. Ghosts winked out. People stared at empty space, then turned to each other; murmured, touched hands, checked the 'realness' of people and things. They jiggled chairs before sitting, just to be sure the chair existed. They did not sit quiet. Each and every one of those kids started beating his gums.

"Tokyo and peanut butter," Burnside said, "and if that isn't the damndest?" He watched our troops jaw at each other. "Makes you yearn for South Dakota."

Darkness faded, but glowered as it faded. Darkness might disappear along with our haunts, but it seemed to wait just beyond the daylight windows. It was there, pressing, and it would come for us in its time.

"Get a little more exact," I said. "Peanut butter?"

"We're sitting pretty here," Burnside said, "and Ross, you've become neglectful. What I'm gonna tell you is straight dope."

I waited for another Burnside story, figuring he would bull around some little while before getting to the point. It was a mistake. If you hit Burnside with an expectation he'll usually exceed it.

"Our fifty-first state," Burnside said about Japan. "We raised a whole generation on peanut butter."

Oriental diets are generally thin on protein. During the occupation some very bright people used peanut butter to raise protein levels among children. The kids, being kids, lapped it up.

"One thing led to another," Burnside said. "By now those kids are hurting and don't even know it. I find it less than fascinatin'."

"You and the far side had a go-around. Then you haul out of bed and get cracking. Now you're blowing smoke. What?"

"The Japanese kid showed me Tokyo. Tokyo ain't Tokyo anymore," Burnside said. "It's a damn party. Something's dying in the Jap spirit. The past is dying, but something else is dying." Burnside has never been real subtle. Furrows on his forehead did not stop where the hairline had once ended. "I don't get it," he told me. "My ghosties said the same thing Harvey said: 'get off your goldbrickin' butt and get an honest job.'"

That would have been an interesting conversation, except our ghosts weren't talking. Burnside imagined things.

"Pay back time," he said. "It's the least I can do for the kid."

He really fretted about his Japanese soldier. Bad enough we tried to figure a message, now Burnside had to get his morals in gear.

"I got roughly the same message from Korea," I told him, "but it came from the countryside, not the city."

Burnside looked like a man in mourning. "Her name was Yukiko. I should have brought her home with me." Burnside was saturated in guilt up to his starched little dickie. "During '44 she lived in a cave with her family, avoiding bombs. Her best memory was when they caught a stray cat. It was the only meat they had in '44."

"The rules would seem to indicate," I told him, "that if you start a war you really can't complain when people drop bombs on you."

"She didn't start it, you didn't start it . . ." Burnside wallowed before an abstraction, and Burnside is not Houdini when it comes to abstractions.

He tried to say something more, and failed, but sparked that feeling in me that I somehow knew our final act.

"You're the guy with the gift of gab," I told him. "Check around. See what's up while everybody's still talking."

I had a piece of thinking ahead of me and didn't need help, especially Burnside's. "Get it right," I told him, "because we won't know what to do until we know what we've got. The time-line of history is getting a little thin."

Burnside nodded, checked me over to make sure I sat firmly settled, and wheeled away. Sometimes he reminds me of a kid in a soapbox derby.

III

No one recalls the names of dog soldiers who fought beside Leonidas at Thermopylae, or with Charles Martel at the Battle of Tours; but how they fought, and what they fought for, lives through centuries. Without those forgotten men western civilization could not have come into being. They put it all on the line, because there are times in history when universal evil crawls from its cave of darkness.

When those battles happened, though, what did anyone know? The dog soldier only knew that some fool Persian had it in his head to whip the world, or a Moorish chieftain was on the prod.

And the dog soldier stood. He stood between the enemy and home, standing before a way of life that was particularly his. If in his home he was boss during peace, then during war he paid for the honor. The male of the species defends his land and home. It will always be that way. At least that is true of the Infantry.

Some such thoughts flicked through my mind, more certain than the flickering of television. Around me people who hadn't spoken to each other since they arrived started talking. Some who never talked at least tried to come from behind a camou-flage of silence.

There are not enough of us here to make a platoon. We are a small group, and like other forgotten soldiers are about to become a mere dot on the wall map of the past.

Yet, the far side charged us to step forward one-more-once. I asked myself: what did we have to give that could be of any possible use? If anyone here was rich he wouldn't be parked at V.A.

So what use are we? Burnside hopes to die exhausted in a cathouse with the sweet, sweet taste of bourbon on his tongue. My own ambition is less raunchy. I want, at age ninety, to be gunned down while storming the Congress.

And that, of course, is so much bull. Burnside will die in bed, or of stroke in his wheelchair. Considering the remnants of his prostate, he wouldn't make any kind of show in a brothel, anyway.

TV light flicked here and there about the room. TV doesn't claim me much, but sometimes I watch light flicker on darkened walls. The rest of our troops face the screen, but I'm engrossed with flickering. Sometimes it looks like distant shellfire, and sometimes like cities burning. Sometimes, though, greens and blues chase reds away, and walls of the dayroom seem mysterious as haunted woods, or, when yellow happens, like meadows on a spring morning.

I watched the flickers, thought of modern times, and it came to me that we've never stopped fighting. When our wars ceased a rearguard action began. We fought against deterioration of order; and lost as an old culture died and society went crazy at the funeral. Yammer got crowned King, with chatter its Queen.

At least bull keeps us from becoming maudlin. We do not deify the past, as the flickers rise upward. No one here believes in Lawrence Welk or Eisenhower.

I watched our troops clam up whenever a member of staff approached. Even nurse Johnson had trouble getting more than a simple greeting. At the same time, people hard-of-hearing talked confidentially at the top of their voices. In a little while staff would decide that something on TV had driven us nuts, that their personal worlds ran normal; and they were doing their jobs. Humans, being creative, can rewrite anything.

. . . which is a coy way of suggesting that each young generation invents history according to its own bigotries. The rewritten history gets quoted to show that one or another special group has perpetually saved civilization while suffering abuse known only to holy saints. The justification for historians is the same as the justification for janitors. Both sweep up the mess when the public gets done trashing.

Nurses and orderlies mingled, picking up a bit here, a bit there. Nurse Johnson acted smarter, which is usual. She hung back and listened. She touched people's hands, arms, and moved like warm music. Nurse Johnson is the best of what remains good about the world. She should work in pediatrics, not a geriatric ward . . . except, I've already said that, and it isn't true. I suggested it once and she said she prefers geriatrics. What she actually said was, "You guys talk ornery as skunks, but you take care of each other." Then she said she had already worked in pediatrics, and some people don't love their children.

=

Nurse Johnson comes to me in dreams and I am young. Curiously, she comes as a long-loved friend, or as a wife of many, many years; although in the dreams we are both too young for that. Or, she comes like innocence that was once adolescence, of hand-holding in movies, the dark screen flashing images of love or action while hands, not yet fully grown, twine fingers in an ecstasy of inves- tigation; learning that this—this touching in this sweet way— explains all there is to know about the word 'happiness.'

=

I must have dozed off. Old men do that, fall into bemused sleep. Then flaccid muscles cramp, joints scrape like bone against sandpaper, and we awake. Pain is nature's way of mentioning that pharmaceutical companies enjoy an array of opportunities.

The Hour of Charm was underway. Our troops sat pooped, worn, busted and beat from all the excitement. If any mouths yapped they yapped to themselves. If consensus had been reached I hadn't heard, and half of these palookas had forgotten it by now. The dayroom sat solidly quiet except for TV. TV spooks discoursed as if believing it meant something. As I came fully awake the main show stood in the windows facing the cemetery. Ghosts no longer impressed me, but this thing did.

The figure stood like a hologram of black on deeper black, standing more needful than the king's ghost in the rampart scene from Hamlet; and like the ghost of Hamlet's father, the figure beckoned. Worse, it waved me forward in the time-honored infantryman's signal to advance.

I needed this the way guys in trenches need head lice. At the same time, who could pass up such an opportunity? I made it to my feet. My walker trembled, although, natch, I walked steady as mountains. The figure in the window waited, and maybe the dayroom stayed bright but darkness rose before me.

Something resembling corporal Harvey stood in irons, like a man foot-bound on a chain gang; but only Harvey's eyes told any kind of story. They shone not wild, not crazy, but were great pools of sadness, a sadness portending universal judgment, universal sorrow. Worse, it seemed the figure stood in a steadily increasing wind.

That Harvey, who was once so smart, was now mindless, also showed in the eyes. Only sorrow lay there. Intelligence, if it remained, hid inaccessible, remote to Harvey, forgotten by Harvey who now stood as the ghost of a ghost of an old soldier.

The ghost of a ghost must surely be a walking memory. I felt the many memories of darkness surrounding this hospital, this century, the lives and deaths that skip or trample or stumble across time; and darkness stood before me like a slab of slate.

. . . sooner or later one of us had to get brave as well as smart. I edged past the windows and onto the terrace. The terrace seemed normal; tables, chairs, a long-distance view of the city that swelled like a boil between Puget Sound and the Cascade Mountains. From distance came the roar that attends cities, and it pounded and twisted, cooed and pulsed. Light flashed above dark streets, light from skyscrapers, aircraft, and searchlights dancing above used car lots.

The cemetery started about fifty yards away, and ran across the face of the hill as ordered as a bank statement. The poor bastards kicking daisies were still lined up in ranks. White slabs

shone dazzling in surrounding darkness. I wondered, as I had
wondered before, if flunkies or gremlins came at night and
polished those slabs.

Further down, the woods began, and beyond the woods the
bridge, park, bandstand; all broken now, but in the distance still
giving the appearance of sanity and order.

Darkness stained but did not obscure the landscape. It fell
backward as I advanced. Darkness moved slowly, sullen, like an
animal on defense but not cowed; or it moved with calm assurance
that my days were short and its patience long. I searched the face
of darkness and Harvey was nowhere seen, but I right away saw
how Harvey had been snatched. When men die—and I nearly
have a couple of times—they are occupied. Dying is what they're
doing, their job. They don't pay attention beyond the job, and that
happened to Harvey. He was taken while his attention pointed
elsewhere.

"I try to run a couple months late. That way I avoid the crowds."
Burnside whispered as he wheeled next to me. "We got a merry
little hell on our hands. You'd better take a seat." It is not like
Burnside to whisper.

"Something's coming clear," I said, and did not know whether I
spoke to Burnside or Harvey or darkness. "You can only picture
the future based on what you know about the past. If history dies
the future can only be hideous."

"I owe my brains to my poetic nature," Burnside said, "because at
least one of us is sensitive. Sit."

I hovered above my walker and regarded darkness. I now knew
what it was, but just because you can name a thing does not mean
you understand it.

"Fan out to my left," I told him, "like you're going to flank." I
moved toward the edge of the terrace, where the concrete slab
stops and grass begins. Burnside wheeled left, then rolled slowly
along the edge. I watched darkness pause, retreat, become sullen as
a spoiled child, more dangerous than a teenager with a Mauser. It
backed five or six yards downhill. "You're right," I said to Burnside,
"we do have a merry little hell, and a firefight's in the offing." I
turned, found a chair near the edge of the terrace, sat. Darkness
ceased retreating.

"Tell me a story," I said to Burnside.

"Nurse Johnson calmed the troops. The kid is a peach." Burnside looked downhill. In the center of darkness stood mean terrain; a gentle slope that begged for enfilading fire, a young forest to distribute shell bursts, a rickety bridge crossing a ravine that only a torrential river could love; and a haunted park. I listened, really listened as Burnside turned factual. For the first time I understood why he made top sergeant in the old Army.

"The situation ain't just tactical," he said, "it's strategic. If the damned thing was solid enough to put a fork into, you'd see the movement of armies, and they'd move across hemispheres."

"Not that I'd doubt someone who's saintly . . ."

Burnside raised a hand to shut me up. "The dayroom has guys who have been everywhere, and it has ghosts from everywhere. This is no crap, Ross."

"How solid is it?"

"That's the trouble," Burnside said. "You can't lay a glove on it. But, what we're up against is dark as the inside of a snake, and that's not a bad picture. It throws coils."

As he talked a theme repeated over and over: darkness cut with flashes. Our men saw Rome and Madrid, Paris and Berlin, London town and Athens. They saw Hong Kong, Sidney, Bora Bora, the Falklands, Murmansk, Tunisia; and every place looked the same: thundering noise mindless as carnival rides obscured all silence, and fires rose not above military encampments, but above schools; not above shipyards but above mosques, cathedrals, meeting houses, while ceremonial dragons fled before encroaching night.

I looked into distance at the city, a dark city cut with flashes. Nurse Johnson lives somewhere in that city. Somewhere, in an apartment with a roommate or a lover or perhaps only a cat, nurse Johnson irons dresses, fixes dinners, perhaps listens to light rock or jazz. She grows an ivy, or, more likely, a philodendron, and her kitchen curtains are a happy color, red, or orange, or blue with yellow ducks. Beyond the glow of that apartment darkness crouches. Nurse Johnson probably does not know it is there. Or, because she is young, she does not know how fast it can hit and how hard.

"You've been to college," Burnside said, "so what the hell is happening?" He rolled back and forth along the edge of the terrace, and he watched his movement cause slow waves in the darkness. "The kid's gonna be here any second, so spill."

I did not know if he meant his Nippon soldier or nurse Johnson who would be about to go off shift.

"You're a cupcake," Burnside said to the darkness. "A Nance, a lollipop, a Shirley Temple; you're a pint of pup pee, and your ma remains disappointed . . ." I raised my hand. When Burnside starts on insults it can take a while. He looked at me. "Why are we worked up? It runs from us."

What to tell him? Should I tell about the burning of the great library in ancient Alexandria?

"It doesn't give a damn one way or other for us," I told him. "It's come after what we remember and believe." Behind us a door swung open. Nurse Johnson, about to go off watch, stepped onto the terrace.

She stood silhouetted against darkness, and did not see the darkness. Her mouth pursed, and her face became a study in determination. Her slight form concentrated on immediate tasks. Her thoughts shaped to tell us goodbye. I wondered how it was for her working in a place where every goodbye might be a last one—which is a cliché—but around here really true. How often had she said goodbye to a patient, only to come to work next day and find he was dead?

"I saved you gentlemen for last," she said in a low voice, "so don't try to snow your girlfriend. Something is happening and it isn't nice."

"Mickey Mouse is only Mickey Mouse," Burnside told her, his voice grim. "Old Mickey ain't supposed to be a national hero."

She looked my way. "You're the one who keeps this guy on a leash. Does he make the least smidgen of sense?"

"He misses South Dakota and the Dust Bowl. Burnside's turning into a duffer . . ." It wasn't going to fly. Nice try, but it didn't work . . . "When we talked about Harvey you told me something awful. You were right."

She straightened, looked around, stepped to the edge of the terrace. Darkness pulsed, moved uphill toward her. If Burnside and

I did not sit on that terrace darkness would engulf her. Burnside muttered something about darkness, so low she could not hear, something moderately filthy.

"What I tell you stays between us," I said. "If it gets out we'll have shrinks and social workers. Our people see ghosts. We see what snatched Harvey."

"And 'scared' ain't in it," Burnside told her. "Our guys feel mean as mange. They're talking 'fight.' They're growing new teeth and toenails . . . one of the curses of being sober."

"I almost don't believe in ghosts."

She was stating part of the problem. If ghosts are a metaphor for history then belief is a leap into reality. If history is a metaphor for ghosts, matters get really serious.

"You believe the part about Harvey being snatched." I watched her and cursed my imagination. The fires of history burn hot and long, but memories of fires do not burn long enough. Nurse Johnson does not know that women and children are always first to be devoured. They do not die by ranks and squads and armies, but helter-skelter, the casual victims of forces headed elsewhere; forces blowing aside populations like chaff. Nurse Johnson is one strong young woman, and she knows more about suffering than almost anyone else her age . . . and she ain't seen nothing.

"I know what I saw." Now nurse Johnson whispered about Harvey. "I have to do something. We can't . . ." and she stopped, because she about said 'we can't have any more getting snatched,' and she about said it while standing between seventy-eight and eighty-year-old guys. She bit her lower lip, tried to grin, made a poor show. "You're right," she said. "We don't need social workers."

We had a doomed situation. Nurse Johnson was going to go through her share of pain and sorrow. No way out of it. No way to break it gently. I decided not to break it at all. At the same time, I couldn't betray her. "Keep staff off our backs," I told her. "It's our problem." Not true, nurse Johnson, it's your problem too. "And if we can't handle it we'll give you a ring."

"You're really seeing ghosts?" The nice thing about nurse Johnson is her ability to stop being a nurse and start being a woman when anything important happens. "You sound okay."

"I wish it was d.t.'s," Burnside said, "but it ain't."

"You've never seen a bad case of d.t.'s," she told him almost absent-mindedly. "What are you guys going to do?"

"Fight back," I told her, and then lied. "I'm not sure how. Keep staff off our backs. We'll work it out in a day or so, maybe more."

"You'll tell me?"

"I will." What a liar. I'll tell you after it's over, nurse Johnson. News from nowhere.

She patted Burnside's bald head, which made him blush, touched the back of my hand, and left.

"Hard to win a war unless you win the battles," Burnside said.

"If we just sit still we'll get picked off one by one."

"I never made notches on my rifle or my bedpost. Seemed like cheating, somehow."

"Now I know for certain the world is gonna end," I told him. "You just confessed to being a gentleman."

"I can stand being decent," Burnside told me, "for as long as we keep it private. Plus, the fickle finger seems to be pointing our way." I could not tell if he understood what he talked about, or if this was more bull. On some level he knew we had to go into this clean, no jam on our face.

It is a creature of dissolution. It wakes when minds of men become narrow, secular, vengeful; and at some point it turns foul and crawls among us remembering flames of Inquisition.

I spent my working life patrolling the past. Now I patrolled the future. "One more battle," I told Burnside.

"If it makes sense."

"When did any of this crap ever make sense?"

"It can't be worse than the Canal."

It couldn't be worse than hill seven-twenty. I looked across the terrain. Hill seven-twenty was worse, but the enemy had only been North Koreans. I thought of them, thought of how they banzaied, courageous as madness can make a man, running into the mouths of guns because a politico told them their country was attacked. I wished I had a battalion of them.

"I hope," Burnside said, and not to me—his voice tight and not conversational—"that being dead has taught you something about soldiering."

His Japanese ghost stood beside him. It's amazing about kids, whether nurse Johnson or this kid; how the best of them can stand rosy with ideals and still firm as duty. This kid's smooth face was serious as combat, yet his lips did not conceal an excited little smile. I looked him over, thought of his record, and was not sure we wanted him.

"Step up to the edge of the grass," Burnside said. "I won't let nothing happen."

The kid stepped forward. Darkness tumbled, reached uphill, but did not manage to advance. On the other hand, it didn't retreat, either.

"You better stay out of this," Burnside said. "There's some real meanness down there." Burnside rolled forward, his chair side by side with the kid. Darkness did not flee, but it rolled backward at a faster rate. "Runs like a bunny," Burnside said, "but it don't run from ghosties. At the same time ghosties help." He looked up at the kid. "You bringing company?"

The kid pointed his index finger at his chest. Alone.

"It don't pay to be brave and stupid both," Burnside told the kid. "Think it over."

The kid smiled, then raised a fist without smiling, and then winked out.

I watched shadows creep across the terrain. Darkness lay beyond the city, but these shadows were natural darkness, which approached with normal things like t.v. news, and supper, and pills. Hurry sundown.

"I'm thinking about symbols," I told Burnside. "Flags and such."

"I'm thinking about recruiting posters . . ."

"Even given help, I don't see us winning."

"You're right about one thing," Burnside said, and no bull shone through. "I miss the Dust Bowl. Who would have ever thought?"

"The jarheads seem in pretty good shape."

"I talked to them. They actually turned out right smart. Their brains ain't never been used for nothing." As we left the terrace, darkness clustered within approaching night.

=

Among old men, night and day are interchangeable. Night is only dark, and not even that because subdued light illumes the hallways. We wake to think, or wake to pain. Most do not fear death. Our fears are fears of weakness, of peeing your pants, of becoming senile. The crotch and the brain are the engines of history.

When I woke I felt slugged. Silence lay between snatches of Burnside's gaspy breathing. Since he did not snore he was in some stage of waking. Beyond our room the dayroom would be swept, polished, silent as mice. The main desk down the hallway would shine like a halo of heaven above the history of this place, the history of a century . . . in Flanders Field where poppies . . . antique clustering of fear and fight.

I thought of saying something to Burnside, then thought silence best. As silence became restful, ghostland explained itself. Or, at least I understood how some things fit together.

The darkness in the dayroom had not been real. It was a message from ghostland about the darkness beyond these walls. The sight of coffins was a warning. The shenanigans of ghosts waving goodbye were also messages, desperate but colorful. The whole show was a hypothetical guidon, a flag, pointing toward foulness that stalked our perimeter. Our ghosts were helpless without us. It seemed that we old men were not only told to protect the future, but also to protect the past.

"I'm thinking of the disciplinary barracks at Leavenworth," Burnside muttered. "Right now it seems like a warm and happy place, real safe and friendly."

He understood most of what we faced. I had halfway hoped he did not, there being no sense in both of us feeling doomed. I decided not to explain about Harvey.

"I worry about my great grandkids," he whispered, and embarrassment almost choked him. "Keep that private. There's times I think we're guilty of a teeny bit of b.s."

Had Burnside undergone conversion and become a fledgling saint? When great grandchildren visited we pretended we were uninterested. We pretended all was well with them.

I lay in darkness, mute, without an ounce of tears or sweat, although I needed both. I lay in darkness admitting even I had managed to conceal truth beneath a pile of crap. For old men, Hell comes in two versions, lesser and greater.

The lesser version happens when history is rewritten, their records expunged, no credit given for ideals or aspirations, nothing bequeathed, all tales revised as the Present, turning, points to a false record and accuses the past for Present suffering.

That's a stern Hell, but the greater version is worse. Hell for old men arrives at that exact moment when we must admit we can no longer protect our kids, our families, our country, the shards and remnants of our love.

"I don't understand why it runs from us. It don't run from ghosties."

"We have the power of memory. We have the memory of order, and we still have voices. When memory dies civilization dies." From three or four rooms down the hall, a nurse stepped softly. No, two nurses, because two women murmured. Breeze sighed at the windows. I wondered how many of our people lay awake, listening, wondering about our worth, unable to show our loves, and, like Burnside, settling for feeling guilty. The soft padding of rubber soles moved away, the murmurs quieted.

"It's after a great deal more than us. We're in the way."

"I don't mind a scrap," Burnside said, "but not if it don't make sense."

"Flags are symbols. Words are symbols. Steeples are symbols. Red lights in front of cathouses are symbols. The world don't know it, but the world lives by symbols, some good, some as bad as flags."

"Dead guys don't drive wheelchairs. There's got to be advantages."

He had never talked about being crippled, except to make a joke. I thought of the tedium, of the many days and years in that chair, of the iron a man has to have in heart and soul in order to face each morning.

"I got to pee, and I was never one to favor bedpans," Burnside said, no longer muttering. "See you in the funny papers." He swung out of bed, a shadow in the darkened room; the last time I saw him alive, and all I really saw was a shadow.

Oh, nurse Johnson, you don't know how fast it can hit, and how hard.

=

I dozed, waked, fretted, dozed, then came fully awake with the rough knowledge that Burnside would not make roll call. Awol from the V.A.

Silent halls filled with echoes, voices of fear and hope. Somewhere in darkness Burnside made his move, and voices of the past sent whispers into that same darkness. Whispers sped like hushed and urgent messengers patrolling against a silent-walking enemy. Ghostland seemed poised for either success or disaster, and with nothing in between. Outside, in darkness, a storm rose on Shakespearian wings. Black feathers of storm rode gusts tumultuous as passion. Darkness surrounded, clasped; a coffin of wind and rain in which a man becomes breathless and shroud-wrapped.

I sat on the edge of my bed, cussing Burnside. This deal was supposed to include me. I sat with despair of a kind known only during times of total wreckage. Helpless to act, to change matters, helpless—but, I told myself—not doomed. Not without a fight. Meanwhile echoes sighed and whispers moved through hallways.

I stood, already heavy with grief, and made my way to a window; opened it and listened. Rain rode cold gusts blowing off salt water. Rain hammered on leaves of trees, and water gurgled in drains. Rain pelted its ancient song, and the lyrics of that song say "May God have pity on the Infantry."

Behind me sounded a rustle of clothing, and the pad of soft-soled shoes. An orderly stood, breathing hard. I had been unable to find tears earlier. I had them now. I did not turn.

"Where?" the guy said, and said it rough; a guy who already knew his tail was in a sling. No 'yes sir,' 'no sir,' 'please,' or 'go to hell.'

"Mind your manners." I still did not turn. My voice choked only a little.

"Him and them two candy-asses," the guy said. "I'll settle with you later." He hoofed it, almost running.

"You win the first round." I spoke into the rain and dark, speaking to Burnside wherever he was. "All hell is about to break. What you need, pal, is a miracle; you and your damn Marines."

I turned, headed for the dayroom toward people of my own kind. Grief is easier when tough-minded folk stand together and don't kid themselves about the odds.

Burnside needed a miracle, okay, but what he got was television. Search parties spread from the hospital, people—scared mostly for their jobs—bundled against rain. Headlights cruised the road, and police spotlights flicked through shrubbery as dawn rose gray and cold above the scene. No searchers imagined Burnside headed through the cemetery and downhill. It wasn't in them to imagine. They figured he went to town, or, like a senility case, wandered in a fog toward pretty lights and racket. As day broke, and in spite of attempts to keep a lid on the mess, somebody tipped the television. A traffic helicopter churned its course across the backside of the hill; one bumfoozled way to make the morning news.

The three lay on muddy ground pounded by northwest rain. A camera reported bodies like bundles of soaked rags, small, sprawled, distorted; and although news anchors knew nothing of combat, even they pretended to be impressed. The bodies lay fanned across the lower hill. Burnside made it to the bridge, actually had one hand touching the bridge, but did not get onto the bridge. Burnside lay as small and raggedy as any other dead soldier. No angels sang. A Marine sergeant lay just below the treeline, the body tangled in that awkward shape of corpses that have suffered breaks and fractures. Another Marine sergeant lay at the edge of the ravine. A torn Japanese battle flag tangled in brush within the treeline, hanging like a spot of blood and not a spot of sun; the kid a beautiful kid, but no samurai.

The man at the ravine still lived, but had become insane; his mind and hands clawed back up the hill, his body weak, powerless to save itself. When medics brought him in he still clawed at air, fingers hooked, his voice gone from screaming.

We patients looked at each other, muttered, shook our heads. TV showed bodies hauled out by chopper. The Marine lay lumped beneath a sheet, his knees tucked up; stiffened, probably broken. Burnside, with no legs to speak of, made a lump under the sheet like a muffin or a dumpling.

Patients did not have everything figured, but knew enough to wonder how Burnside got euchred, or how he screwed up.

Orderlies watched us as if we were kids on a playground, while we thought of basic infantry tactics.

Staff looked at each other to find who was guilty. Staff did not believe three old men—one a cripple—could go two hundred yards downhill without help. Staff blamed each other, dug political foxholes, dodged responsibility.

As this went on, doctors squared shoulders like little men and blamed everyone, patient and staff alike, for betraying some high purpose known only to docs. And, when nurse Johnson came on shift, she took the brunt. Staff blamed the day shift for not giving some warning imagined only by the night shift, and nurse Johnson was lead nurse on the day shift.

"At least," one little prick said to her, "we're rid of your main trouble maker." The punk had bad teeth, a manicure, and he smelled the way he looked; which is to say 'floral.'

Nurse Johnson did not answer. Nurse Johnson looked to her patients.

"Good riddance," another said. "Caused me nothing but trouble. Why do I always get the problem cases?" This guy looked like he spent most of his time trimming hair from other people's noses.

Nurse Johnson asked no question. Her form was stiff, her face controlled. Unless you knew her well, you could not spot her confusion.

No one but we geriatrics could understand why those guys went out like that. And we, by God, were not about to enlighten. The far side joined us, and every mother's son and daughter on that ward felt more in tune with the dead than with the live theater that quacked and moaned around us.

All through the morning hours spirits of men and women appeared with stony faces, and there were no antics. Burnside lost. It might well be that our last chance was lost. A sense of tiredness, a sense of doom, rode darkly through ghostland. The far side still had feelings, because it did what we were doing; which is to say it hid them. A few women wept, and one Japanese woman seemed shocked beyond all feeling except eternal sorrow. If her name was Yukiko perhaps she wept for Burnside. More likely she wept for the kid. I didn't want to know.

And if everybody felt guilty, or felt anger at being trumped, I had them beat. I had not told Burnside about Harvey. At the time I did not want to send Burnside deeper into his funk. Burnside walked into a mousetrap, an ambush, pressing back an enemy more dark and dangerous than even he believed. I screwed up. I should have told him. Should have.

On the other hand, he was the guy who jumped offsides. I had figured we'd use another day for organization, planning; and then Burnside goes in like a kamikaze, or the Lone Ranger. That one figured easy, and to each his own.

I would have slowed them up. Either that, or Burnside tried to keep me from walking into it. I think the first, because the man knew how to soldier. If he could have found more guys who could keep up he would have waited.

During the Hour of Charm I took inventory of our troops. Three wheelchairs, their people mighty frail, two Wacs, both tough little princesses, one fused spine, three mental blanks who drooled, two bedridden, one goldbrick, two mobile but getting over operations, a bosun mate with one arm and an appliance instead of a hand, and a blind quartermaster . . . the bosun mate looked pretty good, the blind guy didn't look too bad. I took myself to the terrace to think.

The terrain lay unchanged. The broken bridge still stood. The broken bandstand in the park remained. I wondered if Burnside had an objective, or if he just drove the enemy ahead of him until he dropped. The whole business lay ringed with mystery, with improbabilities, but also with certainty of total destruction if we failed. There might be total destruction if we succeeded, but that was someone else's problem. We could only set the standard, write our last will and testament through action, and hope someone could still read deeply enough to raise arms against the encroaching night.

Darkness glowered behind the city, reaching into the normal light of late afternoon; and it stretched toward the little park but did not enter. The bandstand stood empty in mixed sunlight. Some remnant of battle must remain, something halting an advance. The ghost of a ghost may be more than a memory. It may be a piece of history that refuses to be rewritten.

Maybe something was still left of those men. Maybe something was even still left of Harvey. Maybe Burnside had not completely failed. One thing was certain. I had very few hours to screw around.

After a battle there's a time that lies in between, a time of pause after bodies are collected, buried, or shipped. A vacuum exists between actions. The enemy does not yet arrive although the population may flee. It serves as respite, but it's not a good time for long range plans, or being born.

It might be possible to get as far as the park, to establish a position around that little place of order. Burnside and company had already absorbed the initial licking. The whole business was one of symbols, without which we cannot live. Symbols of evil abound. The world needed that symbol of order, a small Victorian park. Maybe the world would not avoid final darkness, anyway, but we could offer the world a chance.

We own the power of memory, and the memory of order . . . a door opened quietly behind me. Nurse Johnson, of course. A good kid in a bad world. Her footsteps sounded hushed across the terrace. She remained silent at first, standing beside me and looking at the terrain. The world went quiet. I could hear her breathing, practically hear her pulse.

"He was in a wheelchair," she whispered.

"He angled back and forth across the hill. When he got to the woods he dropped out of the chair and did body rolls. Where he couldn't roll he used an infantryman's crawl. You don't need much in the way of legs. You need shoulders."

Silence returned. She did not blame me. She is not like most other people. She doesn't see her patients, or her neighbors, as problems. She's old fashioned enough to grant room without a lot of explanations.

"They must have had reasons."

"If I explain," I told her, "it won't mean anything. It has to be discovered."

"I miss him badly. I miss all of them, but he was so ornery. Suppose I have to miss you too?"

From inside the ward, but faintly, some guy sang tuneless as a bluejay . . . "I'll be seeing you . . ." Sure, buddy, of course, right, you bet. Nurse Johnson's face came alert as a new mother hearing her baby squall. "You're too good for this place," I told her. "You shouldn't have to worry about a bunch of worn out carcass . . ." She raised her hand to shush me. The guy stopped singing.

"I don't want to lose any more of you." Her voice remained hushed. Slabs in the cemetery glowed beneath streaks of sun. A flag that, in other days, you didn't have be ashamed of, hung limp.

"I make no promises because I can't," I told her. "We may be playing out a script written half a century ago."—More than that, nurse Johnson, because it may go back to WWI. —I thought of all the courageous people I've known through the years. "I don't know why anyone would want to be a nurse," I told her. "I'm glad you are."

"Why would anybody want to be a soldier?" Her voice sounded husky. She controlled tears.

She doesn't know anything about Thermopylae. She is vague about the Battle of Britain. "There's blessed few who want to be soldiers," I told her. "Things happen." I felt a presence at my side, caught a glimmer of white in the corner of my eye. I didn't even need to turn in order to know that my Korean patriarchs were there, all five of them, three with staffs and two with those silly damn squirrel rifles.

"I have to do my job," she said, and it was obvious she didn't see my Koreans. "I figure you're going to try another heist." She showed more sadness than I've ever seen, even from her. "This place used to worry about what was good or bad. I can't be here every minute."

"Burnside was crazy about you," I told her, and that was the truth. Then I told a lie, but one that seemed fitting. "You're the only woman who ever made Burnside blush."

"I'm not above a little flirting." She tried to smile, "And it helps keep the guys alive. Plus, it don't cost a red cent." Then for a little while she wept.

I wanted to touch her hand, tell her it was okay, say how much her toughness and honesty meant. I wanted to say a whole lot of things; but of course there are things you shouldn't do, even if you could.

IV

Hours passed. I hobbled here and there, lining up the action—old folks at home—supper came and went. I talked to quartermaster Wilson, a good man and surprisingly sane. When a guy has been blind these fifty years you don't expect his brain to amount to much. Wilson figures he has precious little to lose, and it may feel good to be needed. TV bubbled around us, and evening news forgot Burnside in its pursuit of a new sensation; fornication between politicians and lady trust officers. I talked to Bosun Tilton who will lead us, because for this job we need legs, not hands. We press the enemy backward with memories, with the power of history, with scenes of sense and order.

Meanwhile, the ward remains tranquil on its face. The two Wacs hold court, and the b.s. level rises and shifts in their direction . . . a couple of real cute tale spinners, real purveyors, and who would've ever thought? The girls have set up a deal with the wheelchair guys, and the girls are conning staff out of its collective drawers. The Wacs are spellbinders, and our guys gather round them. Staff eases off, relaxes, sees things as normal, lets down its guard. Our people seem curiously free, some for the first time in their lives, and even the senility cases are more or less in touch. Light flickers against walls, red and black like cities burning, but the ward sits busy planning while pain comes to the evening Neilsens. Our troops set about using their last resource, their helplessness, to provide cover.

And ghostland surrounds. And ghostland remains voiceless. And ghostland reaches toward us, promissory of help or support; or maybe grateful for just being remembered. We have Japanese here, a few Germans. We have Africans from Kraut rubber planta-tions, and native coast watchers from the islands. We have mule skinners from the Burma Road, and resistance people, French and Greek and Eyetye, Dutch and Norwegians and Belgians; Russian and Polish horsemen.

And nobody brings a flag. We have Laps and Turks, Brits and Aussies; Waltzing Matilda. Music runs more faintly than echoes. We hear few marches, mostly ballads.

And soon it will be time to go. And if anyone hears this tape it may mean that you still have a little time. It may mean that one of us got through.

=

I come to the terrace, watch the night, and muse.

Across the terrain light swirls as faces of hell appear, the 20th century condensing in a way that would make jealous the good folk at Reader's Digest . . . this blood-saturated century.

As if on a movie screen the world's first operational tank appears, moving like a tilted triangle, squashing trenches and barbed wire. The first machine gun speaks, and the first airplane engine revs and purrs, spits and pops. In the background the first radio quacks about 1920s sex scandals while selling chewing gum and snake oil. Napalm flares from later wars and the Victory V hangs like a checkmark above blown bridges, shattered cathedrals, smoldering rings of fire where once stood huts of thatch.

And the message says that, unless it is stopped right now, it all begins again; the old hatreds, the egos rampant, the fists raised proclaiming that one or another god grants the right to yell instead of think. The message says that each time the world forgets how Evil exists, Evil gets a resurrection; and the word 'honor,' extinguishing, turns to smoke.

But there once lived men who knew that some things were worth dying for. There once were women who fought for their own, and fought for others as much as they were able.

In a geriatric ward a body is no big advantage, anyway, and so this is how it shapes: we can't form the future but we can show responsibility.

We'll not exactly perambulate singing, but we're going to go, a bunch of old men, some weak from operations; one blind with strong legs, one with eyes who can guide while leaning on the blind, another with a pincher for a hand; old men led or followed by ghosts of former allies and enemies fanning downhill against a void. It needs only one of us to get across that bridge in order to establish a presence, and we go with little hope of rescue; not of

Burnside, or Harvey, or of ourselves. Nobody here weighs much more than an angel. We suppose the bridge will hold.

And the comrades we leave behind, and the girls we leave behind will form our cover. The two Wacs plan a ruckus just before dawn. The wheelchair guys will feign seizures. Staff will be overworked, too occupied. We'll slip away, as silent as the far side, as silent as memory, with smallest hope of helping fallen comrades, but with no farewells and no apologies, as the far side weeps; as even ghostland waves goodbye.

Poetry Makes Nothing Happen

ONE MORE BOOK OF POETRY ARRIVES IN THE MAIL, AND THIS DULL DAY is made brighter. This particular book is titled *Reasons For Going It On Foot* by William Pitt Root [Atheneum $6.95]. Root is one of the most powerful young poets operating in this country today. We on the Peninsula are lucky. Root gets over our way every year or two.

When I say young, I mean approximately 40. Few poets become as good as Root, and only after 20 years of work. In the old days, back when poetry was tied to romance, some awfully good poets were successful while quite young: Keats, Shelley and Wordsworth are examples. Still, youth got in their way. Perhaps the worst line in English literature belongs to Wordsworth: "For nature never did betray the heart that loved her." That is straight schmaltz from a romantic who had never been bitten by a bee, frozen by a storm, or attacked by poison ivy.

The Peninsula, and especially Port Townsend, keeps missing the point when it comes to poetry and poets. Some of the finest poets in this nation regularly come to Port Townsend. Only a few people notice, although maybe the merchants notice when money descends on the town as Centrum holds a writers' conference. In addition, some fine poets live in and around Port Townsend and Chimacum. When we fail to listen to what these folks have to say it is our loss, not theirs.

Perhaps poets and poetry are not appreciated here because we believe that poetry is not practical. We think that poetry cannot be eaten, lived in, or worn. It cannot be spent, saved or invested. Poetry seems even more intangible than life insurance. This is a common opinion in many places. It only shows how common opinions can get.

Maybe we have simply never learned to read poetry.

Poetry cannot be read the way this newspaper is read. It is best read aloud, or at least slowly and word by word.

This newspaper tries to give concise information. Poetry tries to give information, but in a way that allows the reader to create something extra of his own. A newspaper allows us to form opinions. Poetry allows us to originate understanding for ourselves and others—even, sometimes, in spite of our opinions.

Here is Root drawing a picture, the same way that a painter uses paint to portray more than a simple landscape. The picture comes from the poem "Rain, You Say."

WHERE I AM

it is snow falling and columns
of shocked mercury falling
below zero, fixing all
the trees and houses,
all the hills and hollows
in a lunar nimbus
bright and frail yet capable
of shearing sheets of stone
from cliffs like stiff pages
turned in an old book.

This is perfect writing that is not in metre, but in cadence. The words step purposefully, exactly, and they are not unlike jazz. When we listen to jazz we hear the notes, but we also hear the spaces between the notes. In Root's poetry we hear the words, and hear the deep silences between the words.

"Poetry," said W.H. Auden, "makes nothing happen." He wrote that in a poem that wept over the death of William Butler Yeats. It was an angry poem, and the fury of his despair rose high and savage in his hunger to say exactly what poetry does make happen.

Poetry is the voice of love, of fury, of understanding. It does not preach. It does not pass laws, or throw anyone in jail. Poetry does not make anyone do anything.

Poetry allows. If we want to love well, to be tender instead of brutal, kind instead of cruel, then poetry allows us to do that. It helps us understand how to go about doing that.

Extended Copyright Info

"The Art of a Lady" originally appeared in the collection *The Burning and Other Stories*, published by the University of Iowa Press in 1973.

"Weird Row" and "Tattoo" originally appeared in *The Magazine of Fantasy & Science Fiction* in 2002 and 1996, respectively.

"Tinker" originally appeared in *Glimmer Train* magazine in 1992.

"Kilroy Was Here" originally appeared in *The Magazine of Fantasy & Science Fiction* in 1996.

"Poetry Makes Nothing Happen" was originally published as a broadsheet in a private edition and has not been previously collected.

Jack Cady (1932-2004) won the *Atlantic Monthly* "First" award in 1965 for his story, "The Burning." He continued writing and authored nearly a dozen novels, one book of critical analysis of American literature, and more than fifty short stories. Over the course of his literary career, he won the Iowa Prize for Short Fiction, the National Literary Anthology Award, the Washington State Governor's Award, the Nebula Award, the Bram Stoker Award, and the World Fantasy Award.

Prior to a lengthy career in education, Jack worked as a tree high climber, a Coast Guard seaman, an auctioneer, and a long-distance truck driver. He held teaching positions at the University of Washington, Clarion College, Knox College, the University of Alaska at Sitka, and Pacific Lutheran University. He spent many years living in Port Townsend, Washington.

Resurrection House, through its Underland Press imprint, is publishing a comprehensive retrospective of his work in a project called *The Cady Collection*.

Patrick Swenson was the editor and publisher of *Talebones* magazine from 1995 to 2009, and is the publisher of Fairwood Press. His first novel, *The Ultra Thin Man*, was released in 2014. When he isn't writing, he's teaching literature and composition in the Pacific Northwest. He runs the Rainforest Writers Village retreat, which is held every spring on the Olympic Peninsula.